ELUSIVE LOVER

"By the tides that bear me . . ." He was very close, so close that Rhea could feel the heat of him searching for her through the barrier of her robe. "I am a woman," she snapped. "As human as you!"

"I do not believe you." Zhao's eyes were boring into hers. "My eyes did not deceive me twelve harvests ago. And they do not deceive me now. You are evading my questions. Not only about who or what you are, but why you persist in haunting me this way. Why?"

A moment passed. Eyes locked together, they stood, bodies almost touching as their gazes probed and sought to map out the secrets of the other's face. Then Rhea reached out and took his hand. Zhao's palm was callused, as were his fingers, powerful and lean, the hand of a man accustomed to hard physical exertion. And it coiled tightly around hers.

Rhea swallowed, but did not let go. "My flesh is warm," she said softly. "Does it feel as though it belongs to the hand of a creature from the spirit world?"

He looked down at the slender, strong fingers entwined about his. "No." The deep voice was a near whisper. "Indeed it does not." Slowly, very slowly, his other hand took hers. "Woman . . ."

Dawn on a Jade Sea

JESSICA BRYAN

BANTAM BOOKS

NEW YORK • TORONTO • LONDON • SYDNEY • AUCKLAND

DAWN ON A JADE SEA
A Bantam Fanfare Book / September 1992

*FANFARE and the portrayal of a boxed "ff" are trademarks of Bantam Books,
a division of Bantam Doubleday Dell Publishing Group, Inc.*

All rights reserved.
Copyright © 1992 by Yaffa Chudnow.
Cover art copyright © 1992 by John Ennis.
Grateful acknowledgment is made to the following:

The Chinese Art of Healing, *by Stephen Palos. New York:
Crossroad/Continuum. Originally published in German, 1963.*

Divine Woman: Dragon Ladies and Rain Maidens in T'ang Literature, *by
Edward Schafer. Berkeley: The Regents of the University of California, 1973*

Ennin's Travels in T'ang China, *by Reischauer. New York: John
Wiley & Sons, Inc. 1955*

Great Ages of Man: Ancient China, *by Edward Schafer and the
editors of Time-Life Books. Copyright 1967 by Time-Life Books.*

Kung Fu: History, Philosophy and Technique, *by David Chow and Richard
Spangler. Burbank: Unique Publications. CFW Enterprises, Inc. 1980*

Pageant of Chinese History, *by E. Seeger. 4th ed. 1962*

The Tao of Love and Sex, *by Jolan Chang. Copyright 1977 by Jolan
Chang. Used by permission of the publisher, Dutton, an imprint
of New American Library, a division of Penguin Books USA, Inc.*

Taoist Tales, *by Raymond Van Over. Copyright 1973 by Raymond
Van Over. Used by permission of New American Library,
a division of Penguin Books USA, Inc.*
*No part of this book may be reproduced or transmitted in any
form or by any means, electronic or mechanical, including
photocopying, recording, or by any information storage and
retrieval system, without permission in writing from the publisher.
For information address: Bantam Books.*

ISBN 0-553-29837-2

Published simultaneously in the United States and Canada

*Bantam Books are published by Bantam Books, a division of Bantam
Doubleday Dell Publishing Group, Inc. Its trademark, consisting of the
words "Bantam Books" and the portrayal of a rooster, is Registered in
U.S. Patent and Trademark Office and in other countries. Marca Reg-
istrada. Bantam Books, 666 Fifth Avenue, New York, New York 10103.*

PRINTED IN THE UNITED STATES OF AMERICA

OPM   0 9 8 7 6 5 4 3 2 1

Author's Note

China, or the Middle Kingdom as its own people once called it, is a vast and ancient land possessing a civilization that dates from the beginning of time. Inhabited by a multitude of diverse peoples, its long and venerable history has often been poorly recorded. This is particularly true when one looks at the origins of *ch'uan shu*—fist art, or what is more commonly known as kung fu.

The early history of Chinese martial arts is cloaked in myth and legend, as mysterious and difficult to grasp as the ancient masters who could elude their opponents with the fluidity of the wind. Centuries ago numerous monasteries—also known as schools—dotted the landscape of China. It was here that priests, monks, and nuns developed the many styles of kung fu that are still practiced today.

Still more of those ancient martial-arts systems have vanished, though, lost in the passage of time, and the tumultuous and often violent history of China. The Temple of the Jade Waterfall described in this book, as well as the style practiced there, is fictional, although such a school and style could easily have existed at the time in which the novel is set.

The destruction of the monasteries depicted in the novel and the reasons leading up to that destruction are true, as is the madness of the man responsible for it: the Emperor Wu-tsung.

Wu-tsung's rule was short—less than two years—but during that time he dealt Buddhism an irrevocable blow from which it never truly recovered. In one year he ordered the destruction and looting of over forty-six thousand monasteries and temples and the forced defrocking of nearly three hundred thousand monks and nuns. And he was as obsessed with Taoism and the attainment of immortality as I have represented. In fact, it was that obsession which probably killed him, an ironic result of sampling one too many noxious potions in the search for an elixir that would grant eternal life.

With regard to the foreigners called Zhuhu, these people were actually Jews, said by the Chinese to practice the "sinew-plucking religion" because they removed the thigh nerve of animals slaughtered for food. Their presence in China dates back to biblical times, and they, as well as Muslims, once inhabited China in significant numbers.

It is an interesting footnote that except for being caught in a general backlash against foreigners during the T'ang dynasty, Jews encountered virtually no religious persecution in China. In other lands hatred and forced isolation caused them to band together, clinging to their traditions for protection and comfort in a hostile world. But in the more tolerant atmosphere of China, Jews assimilated, gradually adopting Chinese customs, taking Chinese surnames, and intermarrying, until eventually they vanished as a race and religion, blending forever into the myriad threads that form the rich tapestry of China.

Jessica Bryan

Dawn
on a
Jade Sea

Prologue

A.D. 829 in the Middle Kingdom during the late years of the T'ang dynasty—in the golden age of Buddhism ...

The storm struck at midnight.

It had been building since dawn, sending iron-gray clouds scudding and billowing over the horizon, their underbellies tinged an ominous yellow. With the sullen fury of a trapped animal, the approaching storm took over the sky until by late afternoon, not a shred of blue remained. When the sun finally disappeared behind the dark curtain, the wind rose, thickening the air and lashing the waters of the sea into a frenzy.

At last, freed from whatever constraints had held it back, the storm broke loose. In howling savagery it struck at the ragged coastline of the southern province of Fukien, enlisting the sea as its weapon to batter and slash at any building, boat, or person unfortunate enough to be within reach of the hungry waves.

Nothing was spared. Not the tiny villages nestled along

the coast, not the half-dozen fishing boats caught away from the land, and not the caravan of the merchant Ibn Gaos Tamudj, who at sunset had ordered his men to camp beyond the hills that bordered the beach in an effort to avoid the worst of the storm.

The merchant's foresight was futile. At the height of the storm crooked spears of lightning lanced down from the tortured sky, stampeding the camels and horses. Snapping their hobbles, the beasts fled into the rain-drenched night, and the caravan tumbled into pandemonium. Shouting and cursing and praying, the men ran in pursuit, to be swallowed up by the storm as completely as their animals had been.

As each man struggled through the frenzied night, one sound battered at his ears, making itself heard even over the mad tumult of wind and rain and thunder.

The sea.

Leading a sleepy-eyed horse through the early dawn, Zhao Tamudj toiled along the last of the hills that overlooked the sea. Their progress had been slow, for the path along the low cliffs was narrow and rocky. The horse, its packs half-full with firewood scavenged in the aftermath of the storm, had to pick its way with care. Summer heat had come early, despite the breezes from the sea, and both young man and animal were sweating.

By the time the path began to descend from the cliffs, the sun had fully risen above the horizon, staining the rocks, the sand, and the sea a glowing orange. "Just a little farther," the youth told his horse, "and we will return to the caravan, where you may drink and rest."

The horse flung up his head as though in answer, yet its gaze was not fixed on Zhao, but on the beach. The beast's ears swiveled nervously, his nostrils flared, then he shied and let out a resounding snort of alarm. Zhao froze. At the same moment that the horse had been frightened, something had called to him. Gripping the lead rope tightly in one hand, he used the other to soothe the animal as he stared across the sand.

The beach wound like a broad golden ribbon between the gray and green cliffs and the shimmering blue waters of the sea. Driftwood and debris from the storm lay scattered across it, as though thrown there by giant hands. Zhao saw nothing else, though the presence still called to him. He told himself it was only his imagination and was turning away when a soft sound, the merest whisper, came to him on the wind. The horse whinnied sharply, jerking his head so hard, the boy had to use both hands on the rope to prevent the beast from bolting.

Following the animal's gaze, he saw what he had missed before. Between a large boulder and a pile of driftwood lay a naked woman, her body almost hidden by the twin bulks of rock and wood. At the moment his gaze lit upon her, rays of the still-red sun struck the woman's entire body, bathing it in a scarlet mist, as deep and luminous as rubies.

Involuntarily he gasped aloud. Stumbling in his haste, he hurried down to the beach. By the time he reached her, the angle of the sun had changed, and the woman lay in shadow. Tethering the horse to a sturdy driftwood log, the boy knelt beside her.

She was so still, Zhao thought her dead. Then he caught the faintest flicker of an eyelid, and he let out a deep sigh. In the whole of his fifteen years he had never seen an unclothed woman. The sight of her transfixed him, so that for several moments all he could do was stare.

He had not realized—had never even considered—the

beauty of women. And this woman ... She was more magnificent than any living creature he had ever seen.

Strands of seaweed had threaded themselves through the glorious mantle of midnight-black hair that lay in wild profusion around her shoulders. More of the dark-green seaweed was draped across her throat and breasts. Though still shocked, Zhao noted that while the body belonged to a ripe woman, the face—with its clearly non-Han features—was that of a girl barely twenty. He also saw that the entire naked length of her had been darkened by the sun in a most unseemly manner, the smooth unblemished skin gleaming bronze-gold in the strong light.

Only the merest rise and fall of the woman's chest and an occasional fluttering of blue-veined eyelids indicated the presence of life. Although she was silent now, he knew the moan had come from her.

Slowly he reached out for one of the woman's arms. There were many pulse points in the human body, but his father—who had long been fascinated by the art of medicine and had passed this interest on to his son—taught that the most important was located in the wrist. A strange shiver went through Zhao as he tentatively laid his fingers upon her limp arm. The woman's flesh was unexpectedly warm, and, astonished at himself, he felt his heartbeat quicken.

He would not have believed the woman could become any more beautiful. But at the touch of his hand, her long black eyelashes quivered and her eyes opened. Gray eyes. As silvery deep and beyond fathoming as a sea in winter.

Stunned, Zhao stared into the depths of those misty, enigmatic eyes. Though the woman was a stranger to him, he could swear he saw a glimmer of recognition in her gaze. In the instant before she closed her eyes again, he knew his world had forever changed.

Trembling, he released the flaccid wrist he had been holding. Splashes of reddish-brown stained the sand beneath the woman's head. Looking closer, he saw that a deep gash, nearly hidden in the dark mass of her hair, was seeping blood. He drew in his breath. The woman needed help, but to move her without knowing the extent of her hurts could be even worse than not to help her at all.

He clambered to his feet. Ignoring the horse's plaintive whinny, he dashed off down the beach, running as though wings had attached themselves to his heels.

The caravan of Ibn Gaos—Zhao's grand-uncle and head of the Tamudj clan—was not far from where the injured woman lay. But by the time he saw the hide tents and kneeling camels in the distance, Zhao was gulping for air, his lungs burning as if he were breathing fire. To his horror neither his grand-uncle nor his father—the only two men in the caravan with any knowledge of healing—were in camp.

He would have to take his father's healing pouch and care for the woman himself, he thought as he raced toward the tent he shared with his father. Until his elder relatives returned, there was no one he could trust with the discovery of a dazed and naked woman on the beach. Moments later he emerged from the tent and tore out of camp.

When he finally caught sight of his tethered horse, Zhao heaved a gasping prayer that the woman would still be alive. Loaded down with the heavy pouch as well as a piece of satin to wrap her in, he stumbled toward the spot where she lay.

It was empty.

Only the bloodstained patch of sand showed that she had been there at all. He stared wildly around him, up at the cliffs, then toward the water. He saw her there, tall and proud-breasted, like some being not of this earth, wading deliberately into the sea.

"Lady!" he screamed as he ran toward her.

She glanced at him, a brief turning of that raven-maned head. In the bright sunlight he caught a glimpse of her eyes, silvery and strangely bright, like polished mirrors in the fierce glitter of sun and water. Then she dived.

"No, Lady, no!"

Frantically he threw himself forward. His arms grasped only air, and with a jarring thud he fell facedown in the wet sand. Leaping to his feet, he dashed into the sea, his gaze desperately searching the rolling waves. He saw her. She was swimming, but in a manner Zhao had never seen, nor even imagined possible.

Arms pressed close to her sides so that she resembled a pale-brown dolphin, the woman was undulating across the sapphire waves. Her body cut through the water with a speed and power that caused Zhao's next shout to strangle in his throat.

"La-lady," he croaked, then stood there in silence, watching her disappear. Unexpectedly a lump rose into his throat, and an inexplicable pain stabbed his breast. All around him he suddenly felt the presence of things unseen and not understood, but longed for nonetheless. Filled with grief and a strange yearning, he stood for a long time, ankle-deep in the shifting waves, gazing out to sea.

Chapter 1

A.D. 841 ... twelve harvests later ... in
the city of Ch'ang-an

Drums sounded throughout the city, signaling the end of
the nightly curfew, and the four massive outer gates that
led into Ch'ang-an swung open. Eager to start the day's
business, the city's inhabitants poured from their homes,
rapidly filling the wide thoroughfares and narrow alleys of
the capital city of the Middle Kingdom.

One inhabitant strolled along at an easy pace, not with
the frenetic energy of the scores of people around her. Tall
and slender, she was a foreigner, with thick dark hair and
oddly colored gray eyes. She was dressed fashionably in a
robe of peach-colored satin with winglike projections, a
deep neckline, and long looped sleeves. But whereas other
women might admire the lovely robe, Rhea considered it
a dreadful inconvenience. In the two moons she had lived
on the land, she had yet to accustom herself to the wearing
of clothes, particularly robes like these, with their long
skirts that inhibited natural, easy movement. Obviously,

she'd told her brother Matteo when she'd put on a woman's gown for the first time, such clothes were one more attempt by Terran men to repress Terran women. He had laughed, told her that some men wore robes even more elaborate and confining than hers, then had warned her never to walk around the city clothed in anything else.

At least, she thought now, looking around the already crowded streets with satisfaction, he hadn't warned her not to explore Ch'ang-an on her own. Of course, if he knew what she was seeking . . .

The muttering of an argument caught Rhea's attention, distracting her. Not far down the small lane stood four people: two women, a man, and a young girl. The man and the older woman were arguing as the other woman looked on, her eyes filled with anguish. The child stood with her trembling body pressed against the younger woman, and she was sobbing.

Matteo's injunctions to her not to get involved in the doings of Terrans—as her people, the merfolk, called these land inhabitants—reverberated through Rhea's mind even as she moved closer. She told herself she would only observe, as a Historian should. Yet she knew that if her suspicions about what was taking place were accurate, she would be hard-pressed not to try to rescue the child.

The older woman raised her voice, and her words immediately confirmed those suspicions. "I'll pay ten strings of cash for your daughter, but no more. After all, this is a matter of business, not kindness. Do I look like a Taoist or Buddhist nun here to perform good works? I deal in singing girls. It is *I* who must feed, clothe, and train this little slave until she is ready to entertain customers with her playing and singing, and then entertain them equally well with her body."

The child's mother flinched at the brutal words, and

Rhea felt her own insides twist with a rush of pity and anger.

Rhea knew the buying and selling of girl children was common. Indeed, slavery was practiced in all lands, not just the Middle Kingdom. But she had never actually seen someone sold as a slave before. And for it to be such a young child, sold by her own parents! The sight appalled her.

The father was shaking his head. "It is not enough," he said stubbornly. "The girl is beautiful. In a few harvests she will be even more so. The marriage broker in our village would have found many families interested in buying her as a wife for one of their sons. Yet I am a poor man, and the past harvest has been a bad one. I will sell her to you now so that I can buy seed for a new crop of millet, but only at a fair price. I have four sons and three other daughters to feed and shelter. Fifty-five strings of cash."

"Fifty-five!" The slave dealer's voice cracked with outrage, though her eyes gleamed shrewdly. "Fifteen."

"Fifty."

The child stared in ever-increasing terror as the two began haggling in earnest. The mother, one arm laid protectively around the small shoulders, swallowed a sob. She lifted her hand to dab at her eyes, and the girl bolted.

The adults stared in disbelief as she dashed wildly away. Then the father roared out, "Fourth Daughter, how dare you show such disobedience! Stop this instant!"

"Catch her," cried the dealer. "She is worth a great deal of cash. Catch her!"

Passersby turned their heads at the crone's words. A few sought to grab the girl, but with a fleetness borne of overwhelming fear, the child eluded them. Then Rhea moved, prompted by the instincts of her people, who could not allow any creature to suffer.

The child tried to dodge her, too, but Rhea was too fast and too sure. With gentle strength, her arms closed around the small body. The girl did not struggle. Instead, she seemed to sense Rhea's kindness and buried her head in her robe.

Out of breath and perspiring in the already torpid heat of the early summer morning, the parents and the slave dealer ran up to them. His face flushed with anger and humiliation, the father raised one hand, preparing to hit his errant child. But his eyes met Rhea's, and his hand faltered. Unthinkingly he stepped back.

The slave dealer felt no such qualms at confronting the foreign woman. "Thank you for catching this ill-behaved female," she said, still panting. Turning to the father, she snapped, "Now I see why you are selling her off. The child obviously has a rebellious nature and will never grow up to be a dutiful wife. Well, this little incident will lower the price. A singing girl is worth nothing if she is not obedient. I will have to work hard to teach her properly."

Before the man could speak, Rhea did. She spoke the Han language faultlessly, though with an unusual accent. "Why are you selling this child into slavery?" she asked, looking at both the father and mother.

The mother could not meet her eyes, but the father, regaining his composure, drew himself up.

"It is none of your business. The girl is mine. I am her father, and I will do with her as I wish. Now let go of her."

Rhea gently touched the girl's hair. If Matteo were there, he would agree with the father, that it was not her business. Having plunged in this far, though, Rhea could not leave the girl to her fate. "Why?" she asked again.

"Because we will starve if we do not!" The mother's voice, pleading and filled with agony, cracked the hubbub of the busy street. "We have no cash, and though it tears the very heart from my breast, we must sell her."

Rhea gazed at the woman, her instincts and her better sense warring. In the flash of an instant, she saw a way to help without involving herself too much. She would purchase the girl herself and then return her to her parents. "I will buy your daughter," she said swiftly, before her better sense convinced her to leave well enough alone.

"You'll what?" the slave dealer broke in. "How dare you, a lowly foreigner, try to mix in the affairs of Han folk! Take yourself on your way and stay out of what does not concern you!"

Rhea ignored her. "What was she to pay you?"

"We had not decided on a price . . . ," the father began.

"Fifty strings of cash," the dealer barked. "And I will be impoverishing myself to give such a sum, but I am a kind-hearted person, who has only pity for the plight of this poor family."

Rhea cast her a cynical glance, then reached for the pouch at her waist. "I will pay you sixty," she said to the parents. "If that is acceptable."

Eyes wide, the mother and father looked at each other. "Yes," the father finally said. "It—it is more than acceptable . . . Lady."

"You cannot do this!" The crone was practically dancing up and down in her rage. "You brought the girl to me. To me!"

"So I did," the father replied. "However, we did not agree on a price, and now I'm being offered more than I dared hope for."

The dealer let out a hiss. "Very well. Sixty-*five* strings of cash, and three bushels of rice to keep your family's bellies filled while you wait for your crop." She glared triumphantly at the foreigner, confident the bidding was won.

Rhea smiled. "Seventy," she said. "And the rice to go along with it." She opened her pouch and pulled out a great quantity of cash. "Here," she said to the father. "I have included extra so you can buy as much rice as you need."

After a slight hesitation, he took the cash. "What— what will you do with my daughter?"

"So now you are showing some fatherly concern?" Her voice turned cold. "I will return her to you, of course. A child's place is with her mother, even though you seem to have little concern for her well-being." Kneeling, she murmured to the girl, "Go to your mother, sweetling. She is waiting to take you home."

The child looked at her uncertainly, but only until her mother held out her arms. She rushed into that welcoming embrace, as the father stared at the cash clutched in his hands and the slave dealer scowled and muttered.

"Foreigners," she said, and spat loudly into the dust. "Who can understand them? They're all barbarians, with no notion of how to behave like civilized people."

She stomped off down the alley, then turned to shake her fist at the bemused father. "When your crops do poorly next harvest, you'll be back," she shouted. "Only don't expect to get such a good price for her the next time!"

As she disappeared toward her house, the father hastily tucked his new wealth inside his loose peasant's tunic. He headed off in the opposite direction with an alacrity that indicated he expected the foreign woman to change her mind about this transaction. The mother, arms still around her daughter, started after him, then paused. She bowed deeply to Rhea.

"Thank you, Lady," she whispered. "May Kuan Yin,

goddess of mercy, bless you for what you have done here today."

Rhea watched mother and child hurry after the peasant, then sighed. Kuan Yin may bless her, but Matteo certainly would not. Ever since she had joined him in the Middle Kingdom, he'd lectured her on her lack of objectivity.

"We Historians," he would say, "are here only to observe. We do not get involved, Rhea. We keep our emotions out of what we see."

Yes, she agreed silently as she walked up the alley to the main thoroughfare. That was how a Historian should act. She had been striving to emulate her brother's actions, his commendable lack of involvement with these Terrans. Yet all that she had learned about Terrans before she came to the land had not prepared her for the reality of them, the way they lived, their often brutal and cruel treatment of one another.

She knew how accepted slavery was among landfolk. She knew also that females were considered of little worth, and those born to poor families were held in the lowest esteem of all. Yet the eyes of the little girl haunted her. And the face of the mother. The anguish of that woman, forced to stand helplessly by as her husband sold her child, filled Rhea with a smoldering anger. It burned away the enjoyment she had taken thus far in being upon the land.

Pensively she passed from the alley into the street. As she did, the cacophony of the city, now fully awake, hit her full force.

Ch'ang-an, western capital of the T'ang dynasty, burst without warning upon one's senses. Rising up from the ancient hills that surrounded her, she was a vast and eye-blinding jewel, glowing like the Queen of Heaven.

Far from the lush and sensuous south, the city lay in

the north, a country of stark and austere beauty, with its endless arid plains covered with loess, the powder-fine yellow soil from which the capricious and swift-moving Ho River took its name.

Although the Pien Canal, the empire's main commercial artery between north and south, carried an uninterrupted flow of goods to Ch'ang-an day and night, the city's position by land was of equal importance. Situated at the end of the Great Silk Road, Ch'ang-an was the final destination for the caravans that wound along that famous route.

Being at the center of so much trade and boasting a population of well over one million souls, Ch'ang-an was the height of a cosmopolitan city. But for Rhea, the overwhelming impression was not of worldliness, but noise. The din of Ch'ang-an was incredible.

Shouting, laughing, eating, selling, buying, or begging, the people of the city washed through the main boulevards with the inexorability of the tides. They carried loads or were carried themselves in sedan chairs, carts, or carriages drawn by gaily caparisoned horses. They herded animals or even each other, for everywhere one looked there were soldiers shouting at groups of chained convicts who bent wearily to the endless task of washing debris off the streets.

From wharfs that teemed with laborers carrying boxes, sacks, and bales, narrow canals filled with muddy water and a solid line of freight barges ran through the capital. Lining the broad avenues and side streets were rows upon rows of concrete walls, brilliant in the harsh early sun, their whiteness set off by gates and doorposts of brightly painted wood. Despite their brilliance, they gave the city a closed, almost secretive feel. Unlike the cities in the warmer south, where a more outdoor way of life prevailed, the houses of Ch'ang-an were shut off behind high walls.

Taller than most of those who pushed and shoved their way along the street, Rhea struggled through this astonishing chaos. Movement was now frustratingly slow, for she could progress only as fast as those around her.

Even with the innate merfolk ability to always keep track of her bearings, she was amazed each time she left her house that she did not become lost. It was not only the city's size, but the wideness of the streets—broad tree-lined avenues with odorous ditches running alongside them—streets seething with more people and animals than she had ever seen together at one time.

She shook her head, her temples throbbing as they always did after a walk through these boulevards. Sighing with thanks, she saw she was nearing the house Matteo had taken on his arrival in the city seasons before. She left the jammed thoroughfare behind and walked down the narrow and far more peaceful lane that led to their house.

Though the eternal clamor of the Terrans irritated her to the point of longing to be back in her home, the endless and by comparison peaceful sea, she was happy to be on the land. The merfolk Elders had deliberated for twelve years on what to do with her, and their decision to allow her to return to the land had relieved her in more ways than one. Naturally she'd been pleased the Elders had at last made a decision, but more than that, she had her own reason for wanting to return to the land, a reason the Elders had no inkling of. Since that day on the beach, when a green-eyed youth had awakened her from her dream-walk and saved her life, she'd felt a powerful yearning deep inside her to seek him out. Though the Elders, of course, knew of the Terran youth, she had not told them of the strange bond that had formed between them during that moment when they'd gazed at each other. Just as she did not tell Matteo that her need to find the youth drove her out into the streets of Ch'ang-an from dawn to curfew.

Matteo must have been waiting for her, for as she neared the house, he swung open the gate. She lifted her hand in greeting and was about to speak when a *presence* suddenly entered her mind, jolting through her with such intensity, she felt it in every fiber of her soul. Her feet jerked to a halt, and she stared at her brother in bafflement.

"What is it?" he called, starting toward her.

"Something . . ." She was amazed to find that she was breathless. "Something just called to me."

"On the land?" Matteo looked skeptical. "That is not possible, unless the call came from one of our kind, in which case I would have felt it as well."

Rhea scarcely heard him. Swinging about, she broke into a swift, gliding run, heading back to the crowded street she had just left.

"Rhea!" Matteo shouted after her, but she paid him no heed.

The broad thoroughfare that had been so clamorous and jammed a minute earlier had mysteriously cleared itself. Gazing down the avenue, Rhea saw why.

Eight stone-faced men of the Imperial Guard, each bearing a gold standard and dressed in a long purple robe, with chest and shins encased in shining lacquered armor made of black leather, were marching toward her.

In the center of this escort, walking easily and deliberately, his face as impassive as the soldiers', was a man with hair the color of flame. Even the guards could not keep from casting surreptitious glances at this foreigner who strode quickly and smoothly, as though he were attached to the earth in some intangible way.

The man was truly impressive. More than six feet tall, he towered over the largest of the escort. He wore a dark gray monastic robe, at the neck of which was fastened a black satin collar as wide as a man's palm. His narrow waist was encircled by a silk ribbon of the palest yellow, its loose ends swinging back and forth as he walked. The white puttees which came to just above his knees were spotless, and upon his large foreigner's feet were yellow cloth shoes with thickly stitched soles, also of cloth.

Rhea shivered as she stood in the empty thoroughfare, staring as if spellbound at the red-haired man. Twelve seasons earlier, she had entered the dream-walk, as did all merfolk when they became adults. In that trancelike state, pictures had spread across her unconscious mind, vivid, burning, and lovely, of teeming cities and quiet temples, of a golden people with slanted black eyes, of violence and death, courage and love.

Permeating those visions with haunting clarity was the face of a man with bold green eyes. And the youth who had saved her life was a youth no longer. He had become the man from her dream-walk. The man striding toward her.

Chapter 2

. . . A ghostlike witch of Cheng, telling the
fortune of the Taoist Hu Tzu Lin, thought he
couldn't live long, and mentioned this fact to
his wife. She went weeping to tell Hu Tzu.
Hu Tzu replied, "I hold that our spiritual
nature comes from Heaven, and our physical
frame from the Earth. Honors and wealth are
not lasting, death comes on apace." Thus we
see that Hu Tzu looked on life and death as
being but the same thing. . . .

—*Taoist Tales*

Recognition surged over Zhao Tamudj in a wave of fire. It
was she! The woman from the beach! Shocked, he stumbled, and the guards glanced at him in surprise.

Angrily the leader of the escort picked up the pace,
waving his gold standard in a furious sweeping motion.
"Make way, foolish woman!" he shouted. "Make way for
the Imperial Guard or suffer the consequences!"

Slowly the woman stepped to the side of the boulevard. Zhao realized, with the force of a kick to the heart, that she was as unable to take her eyes from him as he was from her. The thought almost made him stumble again as he and his escort marched inexorably toward her. He stared fiercely over the guards' heads, his gaze fixed on her beautiful face, then he was past her.

Within seconds the human tumult that had parted to let the imperial procession through burst into the street once more. Though Zhao looked back, straining his gaze until his eyes hurt, her tall figure was quickly swallowed up by the pushing, shoving crowds.

Facing forward again, he maintained his impassive demeanor with great effort. Twelve full harvests had passed since the morning he had watched the mysterious gray-eyed creature swim away from him. They had been difficult years, filled with pain and hate and the festering of wounds still unhealed. Yet through all that had happened, he had never forgotten her. Even the twin horrors of massacre and homelessness had not erased the memory of those huge eyes fringed in black, their color the deep silvery gray of a sea in winter.

But if the woman who had watched him with such intensity was indeed she, how could she be so unchanged, so exactly the same as the last time he had seen her?

Perhaps she was a fox spirit, he thought grimly. An evil force who had returned to play havoc with his thoughts and disturb his harmony when it was crucial that he be strong and centered. Just ahead, down the broad street that continued to clear itself at the Imperial Guards' approach, he could see the massive gates that enclosed the mysterious Imperial City, where the Emperor and his court dwelled.

He *had* to recover his concentration and put the silver-eyed woman from his mind, for soon he would be standing before the Son of Heaven himself. Once admitted to that divine presence, he could not afford a poorly focused mind.

There was a disturbing murkiness about the events that had brought him to Ch'ang-an, a sense of things unseen and malevolent. Undercurrents of danger nagged at Zhao, and the nearer he drew to the Imperial City, the more they rippled. Amitabha, he had enough to think about without the inexplicable appearance of a spirit woman!

Abruptly one of the guards marching next to him spoke. It was the first time a member of his escort had addressed him since he had been fetched from the Temple of the Peaceful Mind.

"Your head is not shaved," the guard mumbled in an almost accusatory tone, "so you are not a monk, although you wear the robes of one. Are you truly a *jushi*?"

Zhao favored him with a brief glance. "Yes, I am a lay Buddhist who seeks to follow the Way."

"By the Thunder God flying across Heaven, a foreign *jushi*! Well, Youposai"—the guard used the name by which male *jushi* were called—"do you realize that you are likely going to your end? No one has yet been able to heal the Emperor's mother. The Son of Heaven will order you killed, just as he did the other healers."

"Silence," growled the head of the guard. "Do you not see that we are almost at the gates?"

They marched on.

The old woman shifted fretfully upon the thick cushions of her chaise. Despite the heat of the early-summer day, the chaise was draped with satin comforters, which she kept pushing away. Even as she did so, she shivered in the grip of fierce chills. A fur-lined satin jacket covered her bony shoulders, doing little to disguise the fact that this woman, one of several Dowager Empresses but the only one with the distinction of being the mother of Emperor Wu-tsung, was scarcely more than a gaunt apparition.

"Amitabha! Where is the Zhuhu healer, Only Son?" Despite the shivers that wracked her emaciated frame, the woman's voice was strong. The bloodshot gaze she turned on the magnificently attired man who stood watching her was narrowed and filled with ill temper.

"Peace, Honored Mother," the Emperor said placatingly. "The Imperial Guard is bringing him to the Peony Pavilion even as we speak. They will arrive in just a few moments. But in the meantime, why don't you take at least a sip of this ginger broth? It is quite good."

"Do not plague me with your broths!" The woman's clawlike hand shot out, knocking the fragile porcelain cup from the Emperor's fingers and spattering hot liquid over the cushions. "I want no mysterious potions from those who seek to poison me!"

From the crowd of eunuchs that surrounded them, one unobtrusively stepped forward to mop up the spill. The Emperor sighed, absently holding out his arm so that any drops that might have stained his sleeve could be dabbed away. "No one is trying to poison you, Honored Mother," he said in a weary voice. "Least of all ourself, your devoted son."

"Hmmph. Perhaps not. But Li Shan-po says there are many . . ."

The woman's words trailed away. Staring off into the distance, she mumbled unintelligibly to herself.

The Emperor met the gaze of the Chief Eunuch, who stood in an attitude of protective attention by the Dowager Empress's couch. He was a stately man, whose richly embroidered headdress and robes proclaimed his high position. He stepped forward in response to an imperious gesture from his lord, and the two men moved away from the chaise.

"Has she been like this since the day's beginning?" Wu-tsung asked in a low voice.

Ch'iu Shih-liang nodded sadly. "I'm afraid so, Divine One."

"Ah, well." The Son of Heaven sighed again. "We must pray this Zhuhu healer will be able to do something for her." His voice hardened. "But if he does not, then he will die, as those before him have. We grow angrier and angrier at these so-called doctors, who cannot heal a person of a simple fever."

"Majesty." Only the eunuch's age and length of service made it permissible for a note of exasperated disapproval to creep into his cultured voice. "I have said this to you before. You are blaming these unfortunate physicians, when it is the Empress who is at fault. She tosses away the medicines they prescribe and will allow none of them to perform acupuncture on her. She speaks of nothing but the noble Li Shan-po and her delusions that she is being poisoned. By the Queen of Heaven, Majesty, even the Buddha of the Western Paradise would have difficulty in helping such a patient!"

Wu-tsung's jaw set stubbornly. For a moment his expression resembled the petulant look upon the Empress's face when she had flung away the broth. "It is not the Buddha of the Western Paradise whom we have summoned, Ch'iu Shih-liang, but a healer from those who practice the sinew-plucking religion. Perhaps Li Shan-po is right, and a Zhuhu foreigner possesses medical secrets based on their strange religion. However, if he does not, then we will have no more patience with him than with our own Han doctors."

"Highness—" Ch'iu Shih-liang broke off as, eyes widening in surprise, he stared behind the Emperor.

Wu-tsung turned. "What is it? Ah, the guards are returning at last. But where is the Zhuhu? All we see accompanying them is a monk."

"I believe, Divine One," Ch'iu Shih-liang said slowly, "that *he* must be the Zhuhu."

"What? Impossible! A Zhuhu in the garb of a monk?"

"Perhaps, Majesty, he is a *jushi*. Such things are not unknown."

"But why were we not told this? My mother wanted a Zhuhu who practices the sinew-plucking religion. We said so, did we not?"

The Emperor's voice was rising into those high registers that presaged a tantrum. The consequences of those flare-ups could be dangerous, particularly after the strain of the last several moons. Hastily Ch'iu Shih-liang intervened.

"Surely it is of no matter, Highness. All that is important is that the man was born a Zhuhu and is a healer. My sources also assure me that he is most skilled."

"Son? Son?" the Dowager Empress cried. "Why do you call out? They are coming again to poison me, aren't they? I knew it. I knew it!"

Her gaze had fallen on the approaching guards, and with surprising strength, she was struggling to escape the gentle restraint of her eunuchs.

"You see, Majesty?" Ch'iu Shih-liang went on. "You have excited your royal mother. For her sake, you must remain calm. This man has come all the way from Yangzhou, also as the Empress wished. You are far too wise a ruler to deny him the opportunity to help her."

"Yes, yes." Wu-tsung drew a deep breath. "You are right, Ch'iu Shih-liang, as always. We are indeed too wise not to at least allow him to try."

The guards and Zhao halted and knelt to make their formal kowtow, known as the three kneelings and the three knockings. Palms flat on the floor, they touched their heads to the ground three times, then rose to repeat the procedure twice more. After the procedure was repeated the third time, they remained kneeling.

Not until granted permission could they lift their heads to look upon the divine Son of Heaven, and he did not seem disposed to grant that permission. Staring down at Zhao's bright auburn hair, he stood in grim silence while the Dowager Empress cried out dire threats against those who wished to poison her. Finally he glanced at Ch'iu Shih-liang and nodded.

"Arise," the Chief Eunuch called. "Guards, you may return to your duties. Zhuhu, what are you called?"

Zhao rose. He had recovered his composure and his attention was focused and complete. "My family name is Tamudj," he said as the guards left. "My given name is Zhao, and the courtesy name given me in the temple is Red Tiger."

The Emperor snorted. "Red Tiger, indeed. Tell us, what has a Zhuhu to do with Buddhism? Have you forsaken the sinew-plucking religion of your people?"

The Emperor's voice held a note of ill humor, and Zhao gazed with thoughtful surprise at this divine personage. "No, Majesty," he answered carefully, "I have not. One can never free himself from his origins, much as he might wish to. A . . . misfortune struck my family when I was fifteen, and the monks at the Temple of the Jade Waterfall offered me sanctuary, in accordance with Buddha's teachings that mercy must be given to all living things."

Of his mother's presence at the temple, Zhao said nothing. Nor did he intend to, not with the possibility that Li Shan-po was at court and somehow involved in bringing him to Ch'ang-an.

"Well-spoken," murmured Ch'iu Shih-liang.

The Emperor only snorted again. "Then why do you wear the robes of a *jushi*?" he demanded.

"Highness, I wear them out of respect for the teachings of those who saved me and instructed me in the ways of Shaolin. However, this does not mean I lack respect for my ancestral clan. There is much that is compatible between the wisdom of Buddha and the word of Shang Tian, the Supreme Being of my people."

"Well-spoken yet again," Ch'iu Shih-liang said, and added quickly, "Do you not think so, Divine One?"

"Perhaps." Wu-tsung's tone was grudging. "In any case, it is your skills as a healer that concern us. The Dowager Empress lies very ill, and you have been summoned here to cure her. Let us see you do so."

Zhao inclined his head. "Majesty, I shall do my best."

When Zhao approached the Dowager Empress, though, she struggled even more wildly in the grip of the eunuchs, screeching that this foreign monk meant to poison her. Zhao stopped, waiting patiently until the sick woman finally paused to draw breath.

"Royal Lady," he said, his tone calm and matter-of-fact. "Pay no heed to how I am dressed. I am the Zhuhu healer from the south whom you sent for. If you permit me, I would like to ease you of all the discomfort this long illness has caused you."

The Empress lay still, regarding him warily. "You won't try to give me medicine, will you?" she asked doubtfully. "Li Shan-po says it is sure to be poisoned."

With great effort Zhao kept any trace of emotion from

his face at the hearing of that name. Slowly he walked forward until he could kneel beside the couch. "Empress," he said, his deep voice as gentle as a song, "I will give you no medicine if you do not wish it. But will you allow me to examine you, to at least feel the pulse in your wrist?"

Clouded by fever and delusions, the rheumy eyes studied him for what seemed an eternity. Then, quite suddenly, they cleared. "Of course you may, young man," the Empress said in a changed voice. Requesting with firm politeness that the eunuchs release her, she held out her arm.

The Chief Eunuch swiftly stepped forward and bent down to Zhao's ear. "Please be quick," he whispered. "She has these lucid moments, but they rarely last for long."

Zhao gave him a brief, reassuring smile and laid long fingers upon the Empress's wrist. The old woman's bones were pathetically fragile, and he could believe he was feeling a twig or the leg of a bird rather than a human wrist. The Dowager Empress's pulse was as rapid as a bird's, too, thready and uneven—clear evidence of a person suffering from an excess of yang.

Her answers to his questions confirmed this. Yes, she was constantly thirsty, exhausted yet unable to lie still. Yes, she found herself gasping for breath and hot, so very hot, despite the fact that she shivered constantly. With careful thoroughness, Zhao completed his examination. He stared into the woman's eyes and noted the color of her skin and the perspiration covering it. He studied her tongue, which was reddened and coated with yellow, then he gently probed various points in her body.

The Dowager Empress tolerated all of this with a calm forbearance, even an interest in the proceedings. She was a different person now, and this glimpse of how she must have been made Zhao ache, both for her and for her royal son. He was tempted, while this new mood of cooperation lasted, to concoct a medicinal tea and see if he could persuade her to drink it. Even as this thought crossed his mind, the old woman's gaze blurred once again.

"Who is it that touches me so?" she demanded, and jerked back from Zhao. "An intruder has taken liberties with my person!" The cracked old voice rose to a screech. "Execute him, Only Son! Execute him!"

"Honored Mother," Wu-tsung said soothingly. "This is the Zhuhu healer you asked us to bring you. Do you not remember?"

"No!"

Zhao rose to his feet. "It is of no import, Your Highness. I am finished with my examination." He walked over to the Emperor, who was shifting impatiently from foot to foot.

"Well?" the Son of Heaven demanded.

"Divine One," Zhao began, "the Dowager Empress is in the grasp of an intermittent fever, a common enough illness for this time of year."

"Fool! That we know all too well. Tell us what we do not know. What can be done to cure her?"

Unruffled, Zhao said calmly, "I was coming to that, Majesty. A house with nine empty rooms must be found, and each room painted so that any cracks in the walls are covered. Thick curtains must be hung over all the doors and windows, and three charcoal fires built in each room. On top of each fire a large earthenware pot filled with water must be placed, to which I will add bags of specially prepared medicine.

"Your sacred mother must be taken into the house, with only a piece of silk gauze draped over her shoulders, and there she must sit quietly for three days and three nights. After this, she is to be taken out for one day to rest, then put back in the house for another three days. This regime must be done without fail a total of eleven days. If it is followed exactly as I have said, at the end of it, the Dowager Empress will be cured."

There was a long silence, broken only by the mumbling of the sick woman. Zhao folded his hands within the long sleeves of his robe and waited. Wu-tsung chewed his lip, plainly considering what Zhao had said. He took several steps across the pavilion, and beneath the glorious robes his shoulders seemed to sag, as though unable to bear the material's weight.

Zhao felt a stab of pity. The Son of Heaven was a disappointment, a weak-chinned and, from what he had heard, an erratic and dangerous ruler, who could order Zhao's death on a whim. But despite his faults, the Emperor was also a man who loved his mother.

Wu-tsung swung around. "It is clear to us," he said slowly, "that this treatment is different from any that have been tried before. If it were not for the fact that Honored Mother's condition worsens steadily, we would not pay heed to such a bizarre prescription. But nothing else has worked, and since she need do nothing but sit inside an empty house . . . it shall be as you suggest."

Chapter 3

... The seafarers tell of the Eastern Isle of
Bliss, It is lost in a wilderness of misty sea
waves ...

—Li Po

Zhao was amazed at how quickly the preparations were
made, though he should not have been. This was, after all,
the court of His Imperial Highness, the Divine Emperor,
whose rule extended over the mightiest empire in the
world, from the magnificent Great Wall in the north to the
southernmost city of Canton, from the limitless Eastern
Ocean to the Jade Gate in the west.

Within the hour, servants were conducting him to a
house on the palace grounds, where the occupants were
hurriedly packing even as painters swarmed through each
room, searching for cracks in the walls. Other servants had
already been dispatched to Ch'ang-an's two huge markets
with a list of things needed for the treatment, including an
order from the Emperor that the silk gauze for his moth-

er's shoulders must be from the finest silk merchant in the city.

When every window and door had been draped with curtains of heavy cloth and the twenty-seven fires lit, Zhao placed bags of herbs in the large water-filled pots that bubbled on each fire. Then, muttering and confused, the sick woman was borne tenderly to the house.

After that Zhao fully expected to be escorted someplace, too, to be kept under guard for the next eleven days. Instead, Chief Eunuch Ch'iu Shih-liang told him that he would be free to wander through the Imperial Park. He could spend that night again at the Temple of the Peaceful Mind, but then would be expected to stay at the Imperial City as a guest of the court for the remainder of the Empress's treatment.

Zhao took the older man at his word, and after he was certain of the Dowager Empress's comfort, he made his way to the Imperial Park. The park was so breathtakingly beautiful, it seemed impossible that human hands and minds could have designed it. Yet what appeared to be natural had in fact been fashioned entirely by men. Everything, from the artificial hills, lushly green against the sapphire water of the many streams, to the quiet ponds and the rare flowers, even the pine trees with their gnarled trunks and twisted branches, had been painstakingly placed to offer artistic enjoyment, peace, and, above all, serenity.

Here and there reposed rocks, worn by wind and water so that they resembled miniature mountains, some carefully situated to represent famous sites where Taoist Immortals were supposed to dwell. Planted with dwarf trees and pierced with tiny lakes and little grottoes, these curious spots sent out an almost irresistible invitation for one to lose himself in mental wanderings through the creation of tiny and unknown lands.

Also scattered about the grounds were small pavilions, their curved roofs supported by brightly painted columns worked in gold and the finest azures. Each had been built for a specific purpose: one from which moonlight could be admired, another for music making, another for intimate banquets, yet another, set in the shade of bamboos and pines and hung with paintings of snow scenes, for keeping cool in hot weather.

As he thoroughly explored the wondrous park, Zhao found several favorite pavilions built over the many pools within the park, some reached by curving wooden bridges, others only by boat. He was returning to one of these when a melodic, strangely accented voice broke the hush of rushing water and muted bird song.

"It is beautiful here," a woman said. "Is it not?"

Zhao whirled. A tall black-haired woman stepped out from behind some screening willow fronds. She walked slowly toward him and halted a few paces away.

Zhao stared. The sight of her sent the blood pounding through his veins in a rush of fire, yet at the same time he felt an odd lack of surprise. Here in such a dreamlike place it was fitting that this creature should appear, as if by magic.

Silence stretched between them until finally the woman spoke again. A tiny smile played about her lips as she murmured, "I can see by your face that perhaps you remember me."

Her words released him.

"Woman!"

In two strides he crossed the ground between them and caught her by the arms. Under the thin silk of her gown, her arms were unexpectedly muscular, the flesh warm and substantial, *alive*.

As that knowledge jolted through him, so did something else. Desire. The vision that had stayed with him for twelve harvests, of this woman lying naked on the sand, strands of seaweed trailing across one sun-browned breast, stabbed through Zhao's lower belly with a heat as sudden and fierce as summer lightning. Fighting the urge to slide his hands farther up her arms, he released her.

She did not move. She merely continued to gaze at him, her expression so calm, he felt the unexpected and startling desire replaced by a gust of anger as powerful as the desire had been.

"By the Sky-god T'ien, who *are* you?" Abruptly Zhao realized he was shouting and lowered his voice.

"For twelve harvests, you have haunted my dreams," he went on, more quietly but with no less intensity. "It is carved into my memory how I found you bleeding and senseless on the beach that day. Woman, I ran until the sweat poured off me in rivers to seek help for you! Only you disappeared into the sea, as though you were indeed nothing more than a dream. The other men of our caravan laughed at me when no sign of you could be found, and claimed you were a fox spirit. It drove me nearly mad to think that *I* was the only one to have seen you, that perhaps you had gone into the sea to drown!"

"I am sorry."

The woman's voice was low and musical, and it evoked strange images of warm winds and gentle waves. Zhao determinedly shook those images aside.

"But you had already helped me," she continued. "Far more than you knew. Please believe that I did not mean to distress you. However, I could not wait for you to return. There are too many things you do not—would not have understood. And besides," her dark brows rose. "It is not my fault that those of your caravan were foolish enough to make light of what is beyond their grasp."

Zhao glared down at her. "It is beyond my grasp as well. Here you are, looking not a whit older than that long-ago day, appearing to bedevil me once again! Woman or spirit, what drives you to seek me out in this way?"

She turned without answering, and his frustration surged anew. As it did, a part of him stepped back in surprise. It was not like him to give in to his emotions this way, much less act in such an undisciplined manner. But then he had never encountered anything like this creature before.

She aroused such a wild jumble of feelings within him—a roiling mix of anger and bafflement and desire, all of it overlaid with the nagging fear that she would vanish as inexplicably as she had appeared, leaving him even more bereft than he had been as a boy of fifteen.

His hands shot out. Seizing her none too gently by the shoulders, he swung her around. *"Tell me."*

The woman-creature's shoulders felt strong beneath his hands, and though his grip did not slacken, she twisted free from him with an ease that left him gaping at her.

Anger flared in her eyes. "Do not continue pawing at me. Perhaps the women here enjoy such treatment, but I do not. And I certainly did not seek you out to listen to you give me orders, which is what the men of your world seem most inclined to do with women."

"The men of *my* world," he repeated slowly. "And what world are *you* from, Lady, that you have such strength?"

"First of all, I am not a spirit!"

Striving to control the wrath that had flared up in response to his, Rhea took a step backward. This was not going at all as she'd planned. The man whose face had formed the crux of her entire dream-walk was so different from what she had expected! Her dreaming had not foreseen, had not given the least bit of warning, that the gentle youth of twelve tides ago would become a man so demanding and arrogant. A man, she reminded herself irritably, like all other Terran men.

And yet, not exactly the same. No Terran man could have the effect on her that this one did. Rhea knew this with a deep and unshakable conviction that was shattering in its intensity. She had been completely unprepared for the way her body had responded to the touch of his hands. The force of the man's presence in her dream-walk was nothing compared to the reality of him, the strength and warmth of his grip, the power and depth of his blazing green eyes, the deep voice that seemed to vibrate throughout her vitals.

He left her feeling shaken and confused, and though she could hide that from him, she could not hide it from herself. Relieved at being able to put some distance between them, she took another step away.

He followed her, though. "You have not answered me. And if you are not a spirit, what are you?"

"By the tides that bear me . . ." He was close again, so close that she could feel the heat of his body searching for her through the barrier of her Terran robe. "I am a woman," she snapped. "As human as you!"

"I do not believe you." His eyes were boring into hers. "No human woman with a gash in her head the size of the one you had that day could swim off into the ocean as though she were some sort of sea creature. Fish swim like that, not people."

"Ah. So you are familiar with every manner of being that lives in the world, are you?"

"Not every one. But enough to know that my eyes did not deceive me twelve harvests ago. And they do not deceive me now. You are evading my questions, not only about who or what you are, but why you persist in haunting me this way."

Long moments passed. Eyes locked together, bodies almost touching, their gazes probed and sought the secrets of the other's face. Then, in a move that surprised them both, Rhea reached out and took his hand. His palm was callused, as were his fingers, powerful and lean, the hand of a man accustomed to hard physical exertion. It coiled tightly around hers.

She swallowed, but did not let go. "My flesh is warm," she said softly. "Does it feel as though it belongs to a creature from the spirit world?"

He looked down at the slender, strong fingers entwined with his. "No." His voice was a near whisper. "It doesn't." He raised his eyes to hers and slowly reached for her other hand. "Woman . . ."

"Youposai Red Tiger! Where are you?"

With a muttered exclamation, Zhao drew his hands away and glanced behind him. "One of the Dowager Empress's eunuchs summons me," he muttered. "I must have missed the hour for checking upon her. Amitabha, Lady, you have made me lose all track of time."

He turned back to his companion. Where she had been standing, though, there was only a patch of empty grass dappled with sunlight.

A moment later the court eunuch came into sight, hurrying along the path toward Zhao, who stood in the same spot, bemused and silent.

"Youposai," the eunuch said in some annoyance. "Why did you not answer? Surely, you heard me calling. Have you forgotten that your presence is required?"

"No," Zhao replied in a distant voice. "I had not forgotten." He spun around so suddenly, the startled official took a step backward. "Tell me, is there a woman here at court? A foreign woman, tall and exceedingly beautiful, with long black hair and gray eyes. Who may have been walking in this park just now?"

Puzzled, the eunuch shook his head. "No, Youposai. I have served here a good many harvests, and I can truthfully say that no such woman belongs to *this* court."

Zhao turned and stared beyond the willow tree. "I see," he said quietly. "I see."

Chapter 4

... Knife sharpens on stone;
Man sharpens on Man.

—Ancient Martial Artists Axiom

Neck to neck, the roan stallion and the chestnut gelding
thundered around the dusty training ring. Perched in their
saddles, balanced by leg pressure alone, the man astride
each animal shouted savagely, slashing at his opponent
with a long wooden stave gripped in both hands. At length
one of the riders—a brilliant figure in his satin brocade
riding costume of purple pants and red embroidered
shirt—delivered an especially cunning blow, knocking the
other man from his horse. Pulling up his own mount, the
first man swiftly yanked a broadsword from the sash at his
waist and leapt to the ground. The fallen man had already
recovered his feet and, sword drawn, was awaiting him.

For several minutes the two men fought viciously in a
blurred circle of parrying blades and the whining song of
metal against metal. Then it was over. The defeated adver-

sary, a squat, powerfully built man with the long hair of a
soldier, bowed deeply to the brightly dressed victor and re-
trieved his sword with a bloodied hand.

"An excellent match, Master Li Shan-po," he said.
"The student surpasses the teacher yet again."

The other cast him a sardonic glance. "Perhaps. But
since I employ you to fight with me, it requires only the
basest of common sense to realize that it would affect your
comfortable position here if you defeated me. I am an interesting contradiction, am I not? A man wise enough to
hire only the best to spar with him, yet vain enough to insist that I must always win."

The brawny soldier smiled uncertainly. "As you say,
Master," he finally said. He bowed once more, then picked
up the reins of the gelding and led it from the ring.

Remounting the roan stallion, Li Shan-po rode slowly
through the open gate. Just outside the ring stood a youth-
ful eunuch, clad in the vermilion robe of the sixth grade.
He had been there for the entire match, waiting in ill-
concealed impatience for it to end.

"So." Li Shan-po halted his horse. "The Zhuhu has not
yet failed in his task."

The impatient expression on the eunuch's soft features
faded to one of awe and amazement. "How did you know,
Master Shan-po?" he whispered in a voice that was high,
almost girlish. "I said nothing."

"You did not have to." Swinging a muscular leg over
the stallion's withers, Li Shan-po vaulted easily to the
ground. "Thank you, my beauty," he crooned into a dainty,
pointed ear. "You carried me magnificently today as always." With tender hands he drew the reins over the animal's head and tossed them to a waiting groom. "Cool him
off thoroughly and rub him down well. If there is so much

as a hair on his coat that displeases me, it will not go well for you."

Li Shan-po's cultured voice was soft, even courteous, yet beads of sweat suddenly dimpled the slave's forehead. Cringing, he bowed so deeply, he seemed about to break in two. "Yes, my Master," he said. "Yes, of course."

As the horse was led off to the stables, the eunuch continued gaping at the man next to him. Although they were close to the same height, the burly Li Shan-po literally made two of the eunuch, possessing a build even more muscular and powerful than that of the soldier he had been sparring with.

"But if I said nothing," the eunuch asked again in an apprehensive whisper, "how did you know?"

Li Shan-po merely shrugged and strode off toward his house. After an uneasy moment, the eunuch hurried after him.

In the reception chamber, a large room graced by magnificent scrolls and a gleaming sandalwood floor inlaid with silver, Li Shan-po poured himself a goblet of chilled pomegranate juice. Favoring his visitor with a brief glance, he poured one for the eunuch as well. "Come," he said. "We will talk in one of the outer pavilions."

The burly noble led the way outside to a small pavilion screened off from prying eyes and shaded by the gnarled branches of half a dozen pine trees. Benches were set inside, along with two cushioned chaises. Stretching himself comfortably on one of these, Li Shan-po examined his companion out of half-closed eyes.

"You seem concerned, Chen Yü," he said in a sleepy voice.

The eunuch took several restless steps about the pavilion. "Indeed yes, I am concerned. You said the Dowager

Empress would die, yet she has not. If my part in this is discovered . . ."

Chen Yü's voice trailed off. His throat jerking in nervous spasms, he gulped down the liquid in his goblet.

"My friend, my friend." Li Shan-po's silken voice was filled with gentle reproof. "Do you doubt me? With all the powers you know I possess? How foolish of you, Chen Yü."

The eunuch blanched. "It is not you that I doubt, Master," he said hastily, "but the Zhuhu. This morning when he described his outlandish treatment for the Empress, the outcome seemed assured. Indeed, I had to struggle to contain myself, for I felt certain that by evening she would have joined the Ancestors and the first part of our plan have seen its success. Yet evening approaches with her still alive, perhaps even stronger, if the Zhuhu can be believed."

Li Shan-po ran a finger around the rim of his goblet. "Tonight," he murmured in a pensive tone, "I think I shall go to court. I am told there is to be an entertainment, a unique storyteller, which I may find diverting. However, after I have seen to my enjoyment, I will give this matter some more thought. Yet I think you concern yourself overmuch, Chen Yü. Sometimes the most effective manipulation is in allowing matters to follow their own course. The Dowager Empress is weak and old. I doubt very much that she will survive the bizarre treatment prescribed by this foreigner. And when she does not, the Son of Heaven will see to him. There is nothing we need do but watch."

Chen Yü sighed. "If that be your will, Master," he said reluctantly. "Only—"

He fell silent, and the other's eyes suddenly opened wide. He fixed the eunuch with a look darker and more malevolent than death itself. "Only *what*, Chen Yü? Do you still presume to question me?"

Chen Yü quaked. In the five harvests since he had come under the tutelage of this noble so notorious for his skill in the Dark Arts of Taoism, Chen Yü had had other occasions to see that look. Worse, he'd witnessed the consequences of it.

Still, Chen Yü did not completely lack backbone. He had, after all, possessed the courage to make the ultimate sacrifice: giving up his manhood in order to make a career at court. Now he was risking all that he had gained by seeking the secrets of ultimate power with this subtle and dangerous man, so skilled at controlling everything and everyone within his grasp that many, including Li Shan-po himself, referred to him as "the Spider."

"Only," Chen Yü made himself say, "do not underestimate the Zhuhu. I have seen many healers, Master. This foreign *jushi* possesses the manner of one who knows what he is about, for all that he is yet a young man."

"Hmmmm." Li Shan-po's eyes hooded themselves once more. "I shall keep your words in mind. Now you may leave me."

After the eunuch had bowed and left the pavilion, Li Shan-po's eyes opened again, and he glared into the pine-scented space about him.

So the whelp of the Tamudj clan had not only managed to hang on to life, but had prospered in his displacement. An intriguing development, though one which Li Shan-po would certainly have to deal with.

Eleven moons had passed since the night a rodent-faced Southerner had come to Li Shan-po's gates, proclaiming that he had knowledge to sell. Li Shan-po had paid the outrageous sum demanded for that knowledge, then had ordered one of his minions to follow the man and strangle him, more in payment for his audacious greed than for any other reason.

But the information had remained fresh in Li Shan-po's mind, forming a new strand in the web he had thought completed twelve harvests ago. The boy and his mother had been tracked to the Temple of the Jade Waterfall, but the head monk had told Li Shan-po's spies that both had died of a fever, brought on by the sudden privations they had suffered.

The sudden privations they had suffered. Those had been the head monk's exact words, faithfully repeated to Li Shan-po. A unique, albeit insulting, way of referring to the nights the beauteous Lady Tamudj had spent in his bed!

The fact that she had been there unwillingly, and that even after the twin masteries of kidnap and rape she had still possessed the audacity to slip out of his house and escape him, meant nothing compared to the pleasures he had enjoyed with her. Even now thoughts of those hot nights in his country estate outside Yangzhou, of that slender olive-skinned body graced with unexpectedly voluptuous breasts, its skin smooth and finely grained as silk, still caused his groin to tighten and swell with the most exquisite pain.

He had always enjoyed the bodies of foreign women. Indeed, though his young wife was of impeccable descent, from one of the noblest Han clans, all of his concubines—four or five at any given time—were foreigners, purchased especially for him by a private slave broker, who discreetly replaced them as soon as they lost their appeal.

It was truly a shame, Li Shan-po thought, sipping the sweet pomegranate juice. He contemplated, not for the first time, all the delights he would have experienced if he had been able to keep the Zhuhu woman and bend her proud neck to his will. He had intended on making her his concubine. He would have brought her back to Ch'ang-an with him, discovered the secrets of that resistance which so intrigued and aroused him, until, broken both in body and mind, she lost her defiance, and thus her interest for him.

Of course the woman was old now and no longer worth bothering with, at least sexually. Yet there was unfinished business here. A payment would have to be exacted for her thwarting the plans he had once had for her, and his manipulations regarding the son would do most admirably for that. Then there was the even more serious matter of the Buddhist monk's attempt to deceive an illustrious noble such as himself, an attempt that had actually succeeded for nearly twelve harvests.

Li Shan-po's smile faded. Revenge of the most subtle sort would have to be taken for that, a vengeance so exquisite and carefully plotted that it achieved the broadest effect possible. Yes, he decided as he rose from his chaise. These next moons should be most enjoyable. Most enjoyable, indeed.

"You are a fool, Rhea!" Matteo shouted at his sister.

Although Rhea hated to be in discord with her brother, she remained silent, saying nothing either to placate him or to further enrage him. It was early evening, and she had just finished telling him all she had done that day, and what she planned to do that night. She wasn't sure which angered him more, her warm-hearted yet doubtlessly useless gesture with the little girl—"Her father probably sold her to the next slave dealer he met," Matteo had said, "and considered himself blessed by the gods"—her actually seeking out and talking to the Terran from her dream-walk, or her plan to be the evening's entertainment at the Imperial City.

"I can understand why you bought the girl," Matteo went on, striding across the room and back. "You have not been here long enough to learn how to turn away from the more vile acts these Terrans commit. But to be foolish enough to speak to a Terran in a personal way . . ."

"You do," Rhea said calmly. "Why can't I?"

He swung on her, his gray eyes, darker than hers, narrowed in anger. "They are completely different situations, and you know it. You *cannot* get involved with Terrans, Rhea. It will only bring you agony."

He turned away from her, and she stared at his rigid back, knowing he was in pain yet unable to help him. Once Matteo had possessed a nature as cheerful and teasing as a dolphin. But that was long ago, during her early childhood, before he slipped away on his first and secret trip to the land.

She knew little about that notorious exploit, when Matteo and his heart-friends left the sea without the permission of the Elders. She knew only that they had joined in a war with Queen Thalassa's birth-people, and because of the foolish decision, one of them, Matteo's closest companion, Valya, had died. The details of Valya's death and why Matteo had come back alone to closet himself with the Elders was never spoken of in her hearing.

"Matteo, when you were younger—"

"That's not what we are talking about here!" He drew in a deep breath, almost visibly forcing aside his rage, then faced her. "I don't know everything about your dream-walk, Rhea, or what compels you to seek out this man. Nor can I tell you what to do. You are an adult, accountable only to yourself. I say that as your fellow Historian." He gave her a stern look. "But as your older brother I tell you to heed yourself. I have already warned you about interfering in the lives of Terrans and being too quick to use the powers of our kind. Remember, these folk of the land are not like us."

Rhea nodded and sighed, both in weariness at the familiar lecture and with a twinge of guilt. She had used the telepathy of the merfolk to convince an official at the Imperial City to allow her in as an entertainer. She hadn't told Matteo that, but assumed he had figured it out.

She crossed the room, heading for her bedchamber. "It is time for me to go," she said softly, then smiled. "Even if I can't explain my actions regarding this Terran, look upon my evening as research. You've probably never attended a banquet at the Imperial City, and I may learn much about the Han aristocracy this way."

Matteo smiled in return, albeit reluctantly. "Don't think you can soothe me with talk of how you're doing this as a completely objective Historian, Rhea. I know better."

She laughed and left the room, but her smile quickly faded. She wished she knew better herself. She wished she knew just where her compulsions about this red-haired man were leading her.

Lit by dozens of colored lanterns, the courtyard inside the Pavilion of the Moon Set within a Black Silk Night glimmered with muted elegance. One of the larger summerhouses within the Imperial Park, it was capable of seating up to forty people. On this night, all of its cushioned chaises and low heavy-backed "barbarian" chairs were occupied, as well as the extra seats crowded in wherever the servants could manage to put them.

Long legs crossed neatly beneath his robe, Zhao sat

upon one of the low chairs, gazing around the noisy pavilion. At the enclosure's far end, a group of beautifully garbed singing girls were demonstrating their skill upon the zither, flute, mouth organ, and stone cymbals. All around him, the brilliant company of nobles and officials chattered and laughed. Their silk robes, studded with gold and precious gems, glowed so brightly, they outshone the night sky.

Though he had received many curious glances, none of these elegantly attired court members had deigned to speak with him, and Zhao was grateful for that.

He had not wanted to be there that night. Earlier in the afternoon, though, after he had completed his second examination of the Dowager Empress, Ch'iu Shih-liang had sought him out.

"I know it is not customary for Buddhist monks to eat after midday," the elderly eunuch had said. "But then, you are not truly a monk, are you? In any case, His Celestial Majesty has instructed that you are to receive the same courtesies accorded any other imperial guest. It would displease him were he to find that a special entertainment had been held to which you were not invited." As an afterthought Ch'iu Shih-liang had added, "And it would displease him even more were he to find that you were invited and refused to attend."

Straightening his shoulders against the chair's wide back, Zhao sighed. Servants were hurrying into the pavilion now, bent under the weight of enormous lacquered trays containing the banquet food. Behind them, a late-arriving guest strolled up through the lantern-lit shadows. As he approached the pavilion's entrance, the servants nearest the doorway hastily stepped aside to allow him to enter.

At first Zhao gave the man only an uninterested

glance, but suddenly he drew in his breath and sat up, staring.

This newcomer was resplendent in a cap and robe of deep purple silk patterned with phoenixes and edged in crimson. Sideburns extended down his somewhat heavy cheeks, and a goatee adorned his chin, both clear signs that he wished to advertise his virility through a vigorous growth of facial hair. A magnificent peacock girdle fashioned from polished rhinoceros horn was clasped around his sturdy waist, its plaque made of solid gold and ornamented heavily with pale-green jade.

The man paused to speak with a plump and stately woman, who gestured in Zhao's direction with her fan. The nobleman's glance followed the pointing fan, then he casually walked toward Zhao.

Every muscle in Zhao's body tightened. There was something disturbing about this richly dressed man, something that made the hairs on the back of his neck rise. Instinctively he stood, as if preparing to face danger.

The man sauntered past the other guests, strutting with the inborn arrogance of one who has never known the denial of a single desire. He paused here and there to exchange pleasantries, and Zhao remained standing, staring fixedly at the glittering plaque on the man's girdle. Finally he stopped before Zhao.

The nobleman gazed at Zhao for a long moment. "How interesting," he murmured at last. "Your stubborn family was not utterly wiped out after all. And now, the last son of the Tamudj clan has deserted his people to become a *jushi*. Very interesting indeed."

Li Shan-po.

Zhao's gaze remained riveted on the twinkling gold and jade ornament. He had never seen the shadowy figure who stood behind his family's destruction. He had only heard of him.

A red haze descended, wrapping itself around his mind with long flaming fingers. Slowly, saying nothing, he lifted his gaze to meet that mocking face.

Even the worldly Li Shan-po faltered when he saw the hatred in those green eyes. But he quickly recovered. "May one inquire as to the health of your honored mother?" he asked in a silken tone.

Twelve years of training had taught Zhao a great deal, not the least of which was how to control his temper. Rather than clutching the gorgeously attired nobleman's neck between his fingers, he stared down at the shorter man and smiled. It was a smile that was as unexpected as it was chilling, for it in no way touched the icy hatred in his eyes.

"We will not speak of mothers," he said, and his voice was as silken as Li Shan-po's. "For on your lips the very mention of any harmonious ideal is an absolute abomination."

Zhao was satisfied to see Li Shan-po's dark eyes narrow in anger, although it was only a momentary flash. Li Shan-po, too, could control himself.

"A sharp tongue in the mouth of a lowborn Han is an insult," the noble said smoothly. "In the mouth of an upstart foreigner, it is intolerable, and begs to be cut off. Yet I am in a magnanimous mood this evening. I am aware that you have been summoned to court to care for the Dowager Empress. Therefore I will be charitable and not report this shameful lack of respect for your betters. But take care, Zhuhu, lest the next time I be tempted to remove that offensive tongue, along with another part of your anatomy that you may miss even more."

Turning on his heel, as if Zhao were beneath further

notice, Li Shan-po strode away. The banquet had already begun. All about the pavilion people were eating the dozens of exquisitely prepared dishes set out on the black and red lacquered tables that stood beside each chair or chaise.

Though he had never seen such a vast array of succulent dishes before, Zhao's appetite—at least for food—had deserted him. Instead, he sat amid the music and laughter in a pool of silence, his eyes feasting with a different sort of hunger upon Li Shan-po.

Apparently oblivious to that blazing scrutiny, the noble ate with obvious enjoyment from each of the steaming courses set before him. He laughed and chatted with those near him, drank goblet after goblet of chilled litchi juice, and smacked his lips in delight when the desserts were brought out, loudly proclaiming that his favorite, a cake made from corn flour and stuffed with peas, sugar-beans, and candied fruit, was among them.

It seemed to Zhao that this interminable meal would never end, that he had died and been transported to one of the Buddhist hells, where he was condemned to sit in this room for eternity, watching as the murderer of his father and the rapist of his mother enjoyed himself in the midst of luxury. But finally the rice wine was brought in to signal the end of the banquet. Clearing his throat, the Chief Eunuch of Palace Entertainments signaled to the musicians and rose from his chaise.

His gaze still focused with savage longing upon Li Shan-po, Zhao didn't hear a word of the eunuch's rambling introduction. He only glanced up as the rotund official sailed to the doorway and gestured to someone outside.

"You. Foreign woman." The eunuch's high voice was loud and filled with self-importance. "The guests are ready for you now. Come along."

The figure in the shadows waited just long enough to make the overbearing official uncomfortable, then she walked past him with slow and regal grace. A hush fell over the chattering company as the entertainer entered and stood between two gilded pillars. The perfume and incense burnt at banquets to freshen the atmosphere seemed suddenly stronger, hanging in the close air and drifting about her tall form, creating a soft mist that shrouded her in mystery.

Astounded, Zhao stared. It was she, appearing as if by sorcery yet again. Was *she* the exotic performer who was supposed to entertain that night?

Unable to tear his gaze from her, he stared entranced at the mysterious woman. Longing swept over him, a longing very different from that inspired by Li Shan-po. For an instant he was fifteen again, standing on a deserted beach as the most magnificent woman he had ever seen disappeared into a morning sea, diving through the waves with the wondrous grace of a magical being. Then Zhao came back to the present, and though his longing had not abated, the eyes he fixed on this woman were those of a man now.

Desire flared in his loins, sharp and startling, an unexpected and yet welcome sensation. He allowed it to wash over him without resistance or question. Enigmatic and puzzling though she was, he could not deny her fascination. She drew him, not only with the keen hunger of the physical, but with a peculiar allure that went far deeper than mere lust.

Seeing her, he suddenly realized, was the only thing that could have turned his thoughts away from Li Shan-po, that could still temporarily the blood-red hatred swelling so savagely in his breast.

The woman's slender feet were bare, and her hair hung to her waist, unadorned but for a heavy silver fillet that glittered against the black tresses and intensified the silver of her eyes. She was dressed all in black silk, in narrow trousers and a loose-fitting blouse that ended at the knee. The sleeves of the blouse were long and bordered with silver, and both blouse and pants were ornamented in an intricate design, also silver.

Black was a color reserved for common folk, but on this woman it assumed an entirely different mien, one of a deep majesty. How fitting that she should be within this pavilion named for the moon, Zhao thought. In her black and silver garb she was like the moon itself, gleaming with a queenly and luminescent grace amid the darkness of the night.

Her extraordinary eyes found his, and involuntarily his hand curled, as if it were her fingers and not her gaze that touched him. She looked away and spread her arms, the folds of her sleeves billowing out in long graceful wings of silver and black.

"I shall speak of things unknown and strange," she began, and her voice was like a river of gold bearing them all away.

The resonance of it hooked Zhao, drawing him even deeper into the waking dream she evoked. For an instant he pulled his gaze from her, and saw that every person in the room was sitting motionless, their eyes, including those of Li Shan-po, fastened with a strange yearning upon the black-haired storyteller.

The hours passed, and Rhea spun out her tales, each of them accompanied by fantastic leaps and dances, and by songs that not one person understood nor cared that he did not. She told stories of the sea, of magical and mysterious creatures and events that may or may not have been real. Some tales were tantalizingly brief—mere glimpses of existences beyond imagining—while others were long and convoluted, causing her listeners to feel as though they drifted aimlessly upon the tides of that compelling and melodic voice.

Only once was Zhao released from the spell she cast. It was during one of her dances, when she became a magical creature herself, whirling and leaping about the utterly silent pavilion in a soaring, flying dance that left him breathless. Her raven hair whipped around her face like waves lashing at the moon, and in between her amazing leaps, Zhao caught a glimpse of Li Shan-po.

Hands balled into meaty fists upon his knees, the noble stared at Rhea, eyes narrowed and glittering and his mouth open, the tip of his tongue continually stroking his lips.

Black rage surged through Zhao as he realized that Li Shan-po must have looked at his mother in just that way. Yet the rage ebbed abruptly, for the dance ended and her voice called him back from the darkness as she began a new tale.

It was late when Rhea finished her last tale. Bending to one knee, she swept her arms forward so that her long sleeves billowed around her, then she rose. An uneasy quiet filled the pavilion, as though the listeners could not bear to awaken from the dreams she'd created. Then the applause began, slowly at first, but building until it crackled all around the courtyard with cries of, "Delightful performance," "Well-done," and "Exceptional!"

The court's buzzing approval meant no more to Rhea than the cries of sea gulls squabbling over fish. She had eyes only for Zhao. He was the sole reason she had come there that night. He sat completely still, not applauding, only staring, his jeweled gaze seeming to reach into her very soul.

Man of my dream-walk, she said silently. *What is it that binds us together?*

Their gazes fixed upon each other, neither Rhea nor Zhao noticed Li Shan-po. He, too, was applauding, his large hands clapping in a slow, deliberate manner that managed to insult rather than acclaim. As he looked at Rhea, his eyes were filled with a sexual craving so savage, it resembled hatred more than lust. Then he looked at Zhao with a different emotion that went beyond hate and lust.

The speculation in his dark stare was as palpable as it was chilling in the warm summer night. He smiled.

Chapter 5

If a man dwells on the past, he robs the
present,
But if a man ignores the past
He may rob the future.
The seeds of our destiny are nourished
By the experiences of our past.

—*Kung Fu: History,
Philosophy and Technique*

By the time six soldiers of the Imperial Guard escorted
him back to the Temple of the Peaceful Mind, Zhao felt as
though several evenings had passed. His head was swimming from the overpowering odors of food and incense,
and his thoughts—filled with images of a silver-eyed
woman and the smug face of his sworn enemy—gave him
no peace.

At the temple gates, the monk in charge of looking after guests greeted him. "We have been expecting your arrival from the feast," he said. "The hour is late and no

doubt you are tired. But the Dyhana Master is still awake and wishes to speak with you. Will you come?"

In truth all Zhao wanted at that moment was to be alone, but he hid this desire in a polite bow and murmured his assent.

The moon had reached its zenith in the dark sky, gilding the graceful spires of the tall Buddhist pavilions with silver. The full weight of the long and eventful day hit Zhao as he and the monk walked in silence to the chamber where the Reverend Abbot Hui Jing awaited.

As they entered the chamber, the abbot, a small, well-fed man whose flowing robes made him look even more well fed, rose from his *k'ang*, a brick platform furnished with cushions. Zhao pushed the faces of the woman and Li Shan-po from his thoughts and willed the sleepiness from his mind.

Dancing forward, surprisingly light-footed despite his bulk, the abbot cried out exuberantly, "Welcome, welcome! I regret that I was not here to greet you when you arrived at our temple yesterday, but I had embarked upon a small meditation journey into the hills outside Ch'ang-an. However, I am delighted, *delighted* that you are to spend one more night with us, so we can get to know each other!"

The little man's smile was as broad and welcoming as the *k'ang*, and Zhao smiled in return as he bowed low, raising clasped hands to his forehead to show politeness and respect.

Accustomed as Zhao was to the Shaolin monks, whose discipline both in mind and body was clearly evident, the lively Hui Jing surprised him. For one thing, he did not fit what was often said about Northerners, that they were stolid, large, and rather slow-minded.

The abbot was quite short, and beside Zhao he seemed

even shorter, his head barely reaching the middle of the latter's chest. Rotund, his cheeks filled with high color that suggested an indulgence in meat, or even rice wine, he seemed a jovial person. His expression bespoke not only a joy in life but a sly sense of humor that made Zhao wonder if the cheerful abbot secretly subscribed to Taoism.

Settling himself comfortably on the *k'ang*, Hui Jing gestured impatiently for Zhao to do the same. "Sit, sit. Rest yourself, and we shall share a bowl of *t'e* before retiring."

As he spoke, he turned to the lacquered table beside the *k'ang*. In appreciation and admiration, Zhao watched him perform the ceremony of the tea with elegant grace. The steaming liquid he poured was so fragrant that, despite his tiredness and preoccupation, Zhao smiled in delight.

"This *t'e* is of poor quality," Hui Jing apologized, holding out a bowl to his guest. "I must beg your forgiveness for having nothing better to offer the honored student of my brother Master Wu."

Zhao bowed, accepting the drink. The porcelain bowl was so fine, he could almost see the liquid steaming through its pale green sides. "It is I who am honored," he said, "by the kindness and hospitality you and your brothers have shown me." Though it was part of the ritual for Zhao to say so, the quiet sincerity in his voice made the abbot nod in approval.

"Well," the latter said, sniffing his *t'e* with the love of a connoisseur. "Master Wu has written me several letters in which he speaks most highly of you. It seems that you not only study Shaolin at the Temple of the Jade Waterfall with great diligence, but despite the fact that you have only twenty-seven harvests, you possess a talent for healing as well."

Zhao tasted his *t'e*. "Master Wu does me great honor to speak so. I do not deserve such praise, for I am only a student."

Hui Jing grunted. "We are all students, Boy. And Master Wu sees things exactly as they are. If a singing girl farted peonies, your Master Wu would hasten to point out that while they looked like flowers, they still smelled like farts."

Zhao glanced up in surprise. For the monks of the Temple of the Jade Waterfall—indeed for any monk of his acquaintance—to speak in so irreverent a fashion was unheard of. A sting of disapproval pricked him, and he quickly took another sip of the delicious plum-flower *t'e* to hide it.

Watching him, Hui Jing laughed. "I know, I know. They don't say such earthy things in the Temple of the Jade Waterfall. But you're in Ch'ang-an now, and there are as many different sects of Buddhism here as flies buzzing along the river. Of course, the T'ien-t'ai school took care of some of the diversity when it began three hundred years ago, but everyone still has his own idea of how to best serve the Barbarian."

The further effect on Zhao of hearing Buddha called a barbarian seemed to please the little abbot. Slurping his *t'e* with evident appreciation, he waved an expansive arm. "The rich fall all over themselves building splendid temples like this one for us monks to live in. They think it will gain them salvation, but it's really just an opportunity to display their wealth.

"The poor seek to flee the harshness of their miserable reality—though life is only an illusion anyway—by joining our monasteries so they won't have to pay taxes. Then there are the scholars and the sects that spend their entire lives with noses buried in a so-called sacred text, insisting to all and sundry that *that* is the authoritative word of Buddha.

"Yes, this illusory world is a strange place, indeed. Filled with fools who believe eternal favor can be won simply by copying sacred texts, or by paying for images to be made or temples built."

Hui Jing fixed his twinkling gaze on Zhao. "Now boy, you needn't look as if you're about to choke on the *t'e*. Shaolin has its roots in the Ch'an sect, too, you know."

Zhao nodded. Of course. The abbot's cynical comments should have told him. How could he have forgotten that Master Wu had said the Temple of the Peaceful Mind belonged to the Ch'an sect, a faction openly critical of the pervasive and excessive concern for the external trappings of Buddhism? Those of the Ch'an school argued that the essential component of Buddhism was meditation. Their hostility to learning and to scriptural studies was well-known and had its roots in Taoist traditions.

"Forgive me, Dyhana Master," Zhao said, "for demonstrating my ignorance."

"Bah, there is nothing to forgive. Now, as to the business at hand. We received the message that you are to return to the Imperial City tomorrow, to stay as a 'guest' during the Empress's treatment. An escort will fetch you at the Hour of the Hare to conduct you to where you will be lodged, in the Official Monastery on the imperial grounds."

"Yes." Zhao's tone was dry. "The Chief Eunuch Ch'iu Shih-liang has already described my guest status to me. And how it will change if the Son of Heaven's mother does not improve."

Hui Jing's gaze roved thoughtfully over his visitor's robe and puttees. "It is most fortuitous that the Dowager Empress insisted only upon a Zhuhu healer from the south, with no other specifications as to age or ... appearance. From what I am told, she herself is a most disgusting woman."

"She is an ill one," Zhao said, "in body as well as mind." He thought a moment. "Perhaps you could enlighten me, respected one. Traveling the roads, I could have been here in a matter of days, yet Master Wu insisted that I come by boat. With the Son of Heaven's mother so sick, should I not have arrived as soon as possible?"

Hui Jing snorted. "Under any other circumstances, yes. But I myself sent a message to Master Wu that your arrival in the capital should be delayed. Too many have given up their lives as it is, and there was no reason for you to join them. Letting the Dowager Empress stew in her illness might cause her to be more receptive to your attempts to cure her."

"But, Dyhana Master." Zhao was unable to keep the dismay from his voice. "It was cruel and not of the Way to let her suffer."

"Now, now, don't misunderstand me, Boy. I know the woman is ill, but she is not about to enter the Terrace of Night. She is too stubborn, her feet set too firmly upon the path of refusing to allow herself to be healed to die just yet."

Sighing, Hui Jing leaned forward and refilled Zhao's bowl. "A most demanding and disharmonious creature," he grumbled sourly. "And where did she get the notion that only a healer of the Zhuhu people possesses the magical abilities to cure her?"

"I have wondered that myself," Zhao murmured. He looked away from the abbot, his thoughts tumbling over one another like the fierce currents of the Ho River as they raced back to the south and the start of his journey.

He had spent only hours in Yangzhou, ancestral home

of his family, before booking passage on a transport barge north. It had been long enough, though, for him to seek out Dasheng Tian, the one friend of his boyhood who still lived.

They had not seen each other in twelve years, and their time together had been too brief to ease his friend's consternation at seeing Zhao, born and raised a Jew, in the garb of a lay Buddhist.

Dasheng had not wanted him to go to Ch'ang-an, and had pleaded with him against it. "You are a Jew, Zhao," he had said in Hebrew. "Tell the monks to send someone else. Li Shan-po has grown in influence during these last years. He has become a powerful force at court and has befriended many of the highest-ranking eunuchs. If he learns that you still live, he will most certainly arrange for your death. In the name of your father, stay here and rejoin your people!"

"In the name of my father," Zhao had said quietly, "I must go to Ch'ang-an. Not only for the needs of others, but for my own, as well."

Li Shan-po, Zhao thought now. Could he in any way be responsible for the Empress's obsession to have a Zhuhu heal her? And did the silver-eyed woman play a part in all this? Why else should she reappear in his life now, of all times?

Hui Jing watched in concern as his guest's eyes clouded over, darkening with deep emotion. "Something is disturbing your harmony, Red Tiger." His tone was sharp. "This is not the time to be out of balance, in thought or in deed. One must have the forces of yin and yang balanced within himself in order to heal properly. You know that as well as I."

Hastily Zhao recovered himself. "Yes, Dyhana Master, I know that." Meeting the abbot's reproving gaze, he saw that for all his eccentricity, Hui Jing was a shrewd and keenly observant man. Clearly, though, Master Wu had not told the abbot of his visitor's past, and for that Zhao was grateful. "Please do not worry," he said as reassuringly as he could. "During these next days, all my energies will be strong and focused."

"Let us hope so," Hui Jing muttered, but the worried expression remained on his face.

"I must tell him, Matteo! How can I not?"

Dawn was poking around the edges of the shaded garden bordering the house Rhea and Matteo shared. She flung herself around to face her brother, glaring at him both in anger and appeal.

Jaw set, he glared back. "Because it flies in the face of all tradition, little sister. How can you even think of sharing dream-walk knowledge with a Terran? We do *not* share our secrets with Terrans."

"You are wrong, Matteo." She turned away, momentarily distracted as Zhao Tamudj's face, green eyes intent and blazing, took shape in her mind. "He is not like other Terrans," she said distantly. "Not to me."

Caught by the strangeness in her tone, Matteo stepped around her so that he could see her face. "What do you mean?"

She did not answer at once. "I mean," she said at last, "that he did not just appear in my dream-walk and then awaken me from it afterward. There is more to it than that. Far, far more. I think . . . I think we are bonded, this Terran and I. As a merwoman and a merman are bonded when love blooms between them. I know that such a thing cannot be—"

"Impossible!" Matteo broke in.

"So you see," she went on, as if she hadn't heard him, "that is why I must tell him of the dream-walk. It concerns him as much as it does me."

"Sea and Sky, Rhea!" Swinging away from her, Matteo strode up and down the garden. Coming to a halt, he flung out a hand in frustration and anger. "The stench and noise of this landfolk metropolis has surely robbed you of your wits. I can scarcely believe it is my own sister who speaks with such an astonishing lack of sense!"

His ire was contagious. "And I," Rhea snapped, "can scarcely believe it is my own brother who speaks like an Elder, sober and wise and with blood as cold as the northern seas. Your passion has gone, Matteo. Where is the bold brother who stole off to do what he thought was right when I was still a youngling?"

His eyes darkened until they were almost black. "Mind your tongue," he said in a low voice, enunciating every word. "You speak of what you do not understand, just as I once did. But I learned differently. I discovered that passion without wisdom is a dangerous and unpredictable force. It was a harsh lesson, and I am still paying the price for having learned it. I would not wish my suffering on anyone, least of all you, my only sister."

"You were younger than I when you went to the land," Rhea said gently. "There is much you have never told me, and I have been afraid to ask for fear of the pain I feel in you. But I am no longer a youngling, Matteo. My dreaming is done and I am an adult."

He shook his head. "Go back to the sea, Rhea." His voice was hoarse. "Take the river ways south and let them bring you back to our world. The Elders must advise you of what to do in this, not I."

"But Matteo—"

"Heed me, Rhea! This matter is beyond us. The Elders

must know about this so-called bonding. I cannot—I will not deceive them again because of landfolk doings. If I did, it would mean that I have learned nothing. Nothing!"

Rhea flinched at the raw note in her brother's voice. Tentatively she reached out to touch his clenched hand. "I know it is not easy for you to talk about what happened during that time. But if you did, it might—"

"No," he said curtly. Seeing the hurt look on her face, he softened his tone. "Someday, perhaps, we can speak of it. But not now. We have been arguing this for four days with nothing to show for it. I must ready myself to leave, for this evening I begin the journey to Mount Wu-t'ai in the northern mountains. The festival commemorating Buddha's birth starts soon, and I wish to make a scroll describing how it is celebrated in the monastery there."

Rhea sighed. "I was supposed to go with you. I have never seen mountains."

"Nor shall you see them now. I have told you what you must do. Wait until darkness falls so that no one sees you enter the river."

He stepped forward and embraced her, pressing a kiss to her temple. "Forgive me, Sister. I truly wish I could have been more help to you. But I know I am right in sending you to the Elders. Once you have spoken to them, I am sure you will be granted permission to rejoin me."

"No," she said quietly.

Matteo froze, his gaze fixed on hers.

"I will not leave, Brother. I cannot."

A long, tense silence passed between them. Finally Matteo cleared his throat with a harsh coughing sound. "Well, I will not try to force you," he said stiffly. "As I told you before, you are an adult now. I have no authority over you other than my own wisdom and experience, which are far greater than yours. If you are too clam-headed to see that, there is obviously nothing more I can say."

Turning on his heel, he strode from the garden.

Rhea gazed after him sadly. "I'm sorry," she whispered. "But I am right, Matteo. I know it."

In the most secluded of the several gardens belonging to the Official Monastery, Zhao moved through the rhythmic and powerful forms of tiger-crane. As he had done since his first days in the Temple of the Jade Waterfall, he had arisen early to practice his Gungfu. Then he had been at a disadvantage to the other students, because he had come to the monastery so much later than they. Each morning he had crawled from his sleeping mat earlier than any other novice and gone out alone to practice.

Because of that dedication, Master Wu had noticed him, and because of the bottled-up fury he saw in the boy, the old master had insisted Zhao learn "soft" Shaolin in addition to the "hard" style of tiger-crane.

"For just as yin and yang balance each other throughout the universe," he had explained, "so do the forces of soft and hard within Gungfu. You must learn the soft in order to balance the fire of the hard. Soft Gungfu will teach you restraint, my son. And restraint is something you have sore need of."

So on this morning, as on every other morning, Zhao completed his practice by turning to the elegant grace of the soft style. In truth, he now loved its slow, dancelike beauty, although it had not been that way in the beginning. He had studied then only out of dutifulness, far more interested in the obvious power and speed of tiger-crane than in any sort of gentle subtlety.

Gradually, though, he had learned to appreciate the

hypnotic peace that calmed his mind every time he performed the measured exercises. This morning in particular, he was grateful to them. Ever since he had seen Li Shan-po, his thoughts had been turbulent. There was no going back. He was committed, his feet set firmly upon a course of destruction, even if it meant his own as well.

In addition to Li Shan-po, Zhao had another problem to bedevil him: the black-haired woman. He was unable to clear his mind of her. Even the discipline of Gungfu could not keep her out, not completely. Smiling in her mysterious way, she slipped in and out of his consciousness, her eyes as luminous as the moon, touching him as no one and nothing ever had.

Zhao would not have believed that anything in the world could override his obsession with Li Shan-po's destruction of his family, but who knew if she was from this world? Clearly she was not like other women, if indeed she was human at all. Part of him still doubted that, although her appearance at court as an entertainer was a reassuring indication that she was.

Still, even that discovery lent Zhao little peace. The mesmerizing performance he had watched four nights earlier had remained so sharp in his mind, he felt even more haunted by the silver-eyed woman.

Strange as she was, though, he was convinced she was not evil. How he knew this was as mysterious as she herself, but he was sure of it. Therefore he did not fear her, and because he did not, he was angry with her instead. She was an annoyance, a distraction he was at a loss to deal with. She interfered with his concentration, got in the way of what should and had to be a single-minded path to revenge. She was baffling, maddening.

Flowing through the last steps of the soft style, Zhao

came to a halt. Rolling his taut shoulder muscles in a practiced stretch, he sighed. "Lady," he muttered irritably, "you are an even greater distraction in your absence than when you are standing before me. I wish you would leave my thoughts and give me some peace."

Half-hidden by the spreading branches of an oak tree, Rhea stood watching him. She had been there for some time, since the beginning of his practice, in fact.

She had been hurt and saddened by her fight with Matteo that morning, yet nothing, not even her brother's censure, could quell her need to see and speak with this Terran. The sight of him alone in the quiet garden, his long muscled limbs flowing in a dance of grace and power, had entranced her.

She had known what he was doing, though she had not realized he was familiar with the martial arts practiced by Terrans. In her time upon the land she had seen Terrans use these arts before. The kicks and punches of the men who put on demonstrations in Ch'ang-an's marketplaces, however, were a crude and awkward thing compared to Zhao's artistry.

His skills, she knew, were the result of endless practice, of years dedicated to the discipline and training of his body. His movements would have looked spontaneous, even simple, to another landperson, but to Rhea the tremendous control behind every step was obvious.

He had changed so much in twelve seasons, she thought, as she had when she'd first seen him again. Though she knew Terrans' lives were pitifully short and that they aged rapidly compared to merfolk, to witness this had been a terrible shock. The gawky, slightly built body of the boy who had saved her had become robust and powerful, corded with muscle, so that it was as sleek and effortlessly athletic as a shark's. He had grown in height as well, until he was as tall as any merman.

Most changed, though, were his eyes. Each time she saw him, she was keenly aware that the innocent wonder she'd glimpsed in his eyes twelve years earlier was gone. In its place was a piercing sadness, the shadows of an old pain not yet healed.

What had happened to him? And whatever it was, was it the reason for his becoming a *jushi*? From her studies before she'd come to the land and her observations since, she knew that three major religions were practiced in the Middle Kingdom: Buddhism, Confucianism, and Taoism. She knew also that as similar as the three religions seemed to her, to Terrans they were vitally different.

Confucianism was the official religion, and it venerated the Han people's most ancient gods. Buddhism taught that the world was an illusion, and if one could free oneself from all desires and attachments, Nirvana would be achieved. As for Taoism, which grew out of the folk beliefs of common people, its aim was to conform to the way of nature.

Matteo had told her that the followers of the different religions did not get along as well as in past times. Buddhism had grown increasingly popular in the last few hundred years, and so had its influence and wealth. There were many among the Taoists, Matteo said, who would like to see Buddhism's power wane.

The Terrans' arguments over religion, though, did not interest Rhea that morning.

She stood motionless throughout the red-haired man's entire routine, unable to take her eyes from him. She told herself she was fascinated because it was so unusual to see a Terran this accomplished, yet knew that was not the reason at all. What held her was the man himself, his muscled beauty, his grace, the way the spears of early-morning sunlight lanced through the tree branches to gild his bright hair. He was magnificent, and watching him set off an ache in Rhea's heart that seemed destined to remain there forever.

Her enchantment was shattered, though, when he spoke of her with such irritation. She felt as though a mischievous seal had kicked sand in her face, and she couldn't resist answering in kind.

"And I," she called out, "wish you would leave my thoughts and give *me* peace. But it is not that simple, for either of us."

At the sound of her voice, his head jerked up. He spotted her in an instant. He was clearly angry—*again*—and Rhea wondered if it was because she was there or because he had not known that she was. In a single smooth motion, he bent to retrieve his tunic, which he had discarded during his practice.

"How did you get into the Imperial City?" he asked, striding toward her. "And how long have you been spying upon me this time?"

"Spying?" She glared at him. "I did not wish to interrupt you. It seemed more respectful to wait until you had finished, though perhaps the concept of respect is difficult for you to understand."

His jaw tightened. Looking thunderous, he opened his mouth to retort, then, unexpectedly, his eyes softened. When he spoke, his voice was a murmur, his tone bemused and somehow caressing. "Your performance at court four nights ago was . . . most astonishing, Lady. I have never seen anything like it. I wanted to tell you so that night, but you disappeared. I had begun to think I would not see you again."

His sudden gentleness left Rhea far more discomforted

than she would have been by his continued anger. His gaze was devouring her face, as though it sought whatever secrets she might conceal. Schooling her features into careful impassivity, she said, "I am glad my stories gave you pleasure. But just a moment ago, it sounded as if your only wish was never to lay eyes upon me again."

He frowned. "No." His voice was still soft. "I said that I wished you would give me peace. It is not the same thing at all."

"Isn't it?" A terrible sadness welled up inside Rhea, and she looked away. He could not possibly understand, and how could she, who understood so little herself, explain it to him? The sureness of purpose that had stiffened her spine with Matteo deserted her in the presence of this Terran. For all the briefness of his tides he had the force and presence of a man much older, even one of her own world. Sea and Sky, he distracted her.

His gaze had not wavered from her face. "What did you mean before, when you said it is not that simple?"

She still did not look at him. Off in the distance, in another garden separated from this one by a row of pine trees, several monks were engaged in their morning ritual. Shaved heads gleaming under the steadily brightening sunlight, they moved in unison, practicing a soft style of Gungfu, although with not nearly so much skill as her Terran, Rhea noted critically.

Her gaze fixed on the distant monks, she finally spoke. "There is much I cannot tell you. But . . ."

Without warning a sensation welled up in the recesses of her mind, striking her with such force, it was as though a door had suddenly slammed open. She whirled to face him. "You are in danger. Great danger."

He stared at her, his eyes as bright and hard as jade.

His expression was grim, yet utterly without surprise. "Li Shan-po?" he asked in a clipped voice.

Bemused by the power of the warning that had blazed through her, she gave him a blank look. "Who?"

He repeated the name impatiently. When she still looked uncomprehending, he added, "He is also called the Spider. You've never heard of him?"

"No. Should I have?"

"Most assuredly. Especially after the way he watched you at your performance, as though you were the rarest delicacy at a banquet, and he the only diner."

As he said this, a vivid memory flickered across Zhao's vision: Li Shan-po, hunched forward, his eyes feasting hungrily upon this magical woman as if she already belonged to him.

A crazy mix of jealousy and hatred and grief broke over him, tearing through his belly with such intensity, it took every shred of his self-control not to throw his head back and howl his fury to the skies. The Spider had stolen so much from him, and now he threatened this beautiful woman whom Zhao was beginning to think of as his own. As his fiery rage trapped him, isolated him, he suddenly realized he was not alone. Two hands, long-fingered and cool against his fevered skin, were cupping his face. Dimly he heard the woman's melodic voice.

"Peace, my friend, peace," she murmured. "Come back from whatever torments you."

He drew a deep, shuddering breath. Lifting his own hands, he gently grasped her wrists and drew her hands from his face. But he did not let her go, nor did she seek release.

"I am more than able to take care of myself," she said after a moment. "I do not fear this person, and neither should you. He can work no harm upon me. But that is not the only reason the mere speaking of his name sends you to the point of madness. What has he done that you hate him so?"

Zhao looked down at her, his gaze grave and searching. "He raped my mother," he said at last. "And had my family killed."

"By the Mother . . ." Stiff with horror, Rhea stared at him.

"One year after the morning I found you on the beach. Only my mother and myself managed to survive."

"But how?"

He continued to look at her, only he seemed not to see her. His eyes dark with memories, he began to talk. "Li Shan-po saw my mother walking in the streets of Yangzhou one day. She was very beautiful then, and"—his mouth twisted bitterly—"the Spider's preference for foreign women is well-known. He conceived a lust toward my mother that could not be consummated in any way but by force. For as any virtuous woman would, she refused his advances, although in the end it did neither her nor our clan any good."

Rhea tightened her hands around his as his long fingers clenched in remembering. His muscles were taut with a pain so potent, it seemed to transfer itself from his flesh into hers.

Rape was a crime unheard of among merfolk. That so violent a deed should have been done to a loved one of *this* man filled Rhea with fury—and an ominous sense of doom. "Did no one try to prevent this violence?" she asked, hoping he did not notice her sudden apprehension.

"No." Zhao's voice was flat and hard. "He has many men in his service, men of low principles, who are willing to obey his every command. He ordered them to abduct my mother. Once he had her in his estate outside Yangzhou, he could do with her as he pleased.

"But my mother is a brave woman. She escaped. When she did, Li Shan-po, whose malevolence is matched only by the power of his influence, brought false charges against my father. They were utterly without basis, but when a foreigner runs afoul of a Han noble, the truth is no longer important. The goods and property of the entire Tamudj clan were confiscated and my father, his two brothers, and my grand-uncle were thrown into prison.

"My grand-uncle, who had seen the honor of many years, was unable to withstand the cruelties of imprisonment. He went to the Terrace of Night after only a few moons. My father and my uncles were executed along with their families in the winter of the following year."

He paused and drew a long breath. "My mother and I were spared," he finished heavily, "because of the friendship between my father and the master of a nearby monastery. Before the magistrate's runners could come to arrest us, we hid from them. Then we fled to the temple, where the monks gave us sanctuary."

He fell silent, but Rhea continued to stare at him. Her people's adage comparing the short lives of Terrans to that of minnows clawed into her brain, and involuntarily she shivered. How callous those casual words seemed now!

Shaken and speechless, she pondered his story of calamity and injustice. The barbarity of what had been done to his kin was terrible, though all too common among these savage landfolk. She had heard many such stories, but none had affected her like this. Deep within her, his words had awakened something.

Images from her dream-walk washed through her consciousness, images that had been disconnected and enigmatic at the time of her dreaming. Now, jarred loose by his pain, they assumed a stunning clarity. Trembling, she took a step away from him.

She had *seen* the destruction of the Tamudj clan, witnessed it in all its cruelty in her dream-walk. From its evil beginning to the tragic end, she had watched the events unfold, totally unable to protect or save anyone. Adding to this twisting maze of images and feelings, she understood that the premonition of danger she'd felt was linked to those terrible scenes. It was all connected somehow.

Standing there in the beautiful park, she ached for the Terran. She felt his emptiness and loss with such vivid slashing agony, for the first time in her life she wished for the landfolks' ability to shed tears.

"I am sorry," she whispered. "So very, very sorry."

Jolted from his own reverie by her pain-filled voice, Zhao gave her a startled look. "You have done nothing that requires forgiveness, Lady, except bedeviling me by appearing and disappearing so mysteriously. Indeed," he murmured, more to himself than to her, "I do not know why I talked so freely of my family to you. It isn't something I speak of often, or with ease."

Turning away, Rhea scarcely heard him. Could she have prevented the deaths of his kin? If she had paid more heed to what her visions had been trying to tell her, she might have been able to warn him. Would it have made a difference? She would never know. She had failed to save his family, but by the Great Mother Ocean Herself, she would see to it that she saved him!

"Lady? What is wrong?" Zhao's voice vibrated with concern as he grasped her shoulders. His touch was gentle, almost careful, as though she had suddenly become some fragile creature too delicate to bear his strength.

The poignancy of it made Rhea ache all the more. That he should treat her with such care in the midst of his own pain! Slowly she turned to face him and, without letting herself think about it or question the consequences, she kissed him.

He was so tall, she had to rise on her toes to do it, and as her mouth reached his, she felt him tense. Uncertainty and a stab of hurt rippled through her. He was going to reject her, push away her gesture of comfort, her need to ease in a small way his terrible grief. But then his lips opened on hers, his breath rushed warmly into her mouth. As he pulled her against his chest, the impulse to comfort was swallowed up by something far more potent.

His touch was no longer gentle. The powerful arms that enfolded her did so with sudden roughness, as if he gloried in the release of this need. He kissed her hard, his mouth moving on hers with fierceness and a sort of seeking, as though his lips would search out the secrets his eyes had been unable to. Twining her arms around his neck, she returned that forcefulness with a strength of her own, giving herself up to a sense of completeness she had never known.

For a trackless space of time there was nothing but the feel of him, his heart pounding hard against hers, the taste of his lips, salty and warm from his earlier exertions, and the power with which he held her. Then, inevitably, the closeness faded. In its place came reality—cold and inexorable. Slowly, reluctantly, they drew apart, and Rhea could not repress another tremor.

If she had held any doubt about what she had told Matteo, the kiss had removed it. She and this man were indeed bound together, linked as inextricably as any two merfolk who entered into a matebond together. How or why they were bonded was a mystery, but one thing was clear: it went far beyond his mere saving of her life. And the implications were overwhelming.

Only the ruler of the merfolk took a landperson as mate, and even that occurred only after the Elders performed the gravest and most powerful ceremonies. Bonding to a landman when she was not of the royal house . . . It was impossible. How could such an inconceivable pairing result in anything but anguish for both of them?

Seeing her reaction, Zhao hastily dropped his arms. His heart was still pounding, the blood rushing through him as violently as the night he had encountered Li Shan-po. The power that surged in him now was not driven by hatred, though, but by a physical need that was no less overpowering. He was stunned, both by the strength of his desire for this woman and by his unforgivable actions. He had offended her. The expression on her beautiful face made that obvious. She had reached out to him, but he was the man, and therefore the one responsible. The breach of manners was his.

"Forgive me." His quiet voice belied the passion still racing through his veins. "I should not have done that."

Unnerved as much by her thoughts as by the powerful yearning to be back in his arms, Rhea frowned at him. "Done what? It was I who kissed you."

He did not reply. His eyes were brilliant, like shafts of sunlight, and from the look on his face, she suspected—no, she knew—that another kiss would be only at his initiation, not hers.

At the moment she couldn't handle any more of the sensations he aroused in her. She had to get onto a different footing, find a firm place in the shifting maelstrom of feelings now swamping her. Glancing away, she said, "We have just kissed each other, and I do not even know your name."

She could still feel his penetrating gaze flaming at her. "I am Zhao," he said after a pause. "Son of An Tamudj—

honored be his memory—of the Tamudj clan. I also go by my temple name, Red Tiger."

"Red Tiger." Despite the wild racing of her thoughts, she could not keep from smiling. Since coming to Ch'ang-an, she had seen these magnificent animals called tigers, depicted both in scrolls and on porcelain. She had even gone with Matteo to a park where exotic animals, among them a tiger, were exhibited. There was no doubt why Zhao Tamudj, with his red hair and tawny skin, jeweled eyes and muscled grace and power, had received the name. "It suits you," she said. "And I am called Rhea."

"Rhea." His heated blood finally beginning to calm, Zhao sampled the unfamiliar name. "It is a strange name. Rhea. Unlike any I have ever heard."

She shrugged. "Well, it is my name, and I hope you will call me by it." Then she added deliberately, "And as for this Li Shan-po, I understand now why you feel as you do about him."

"Yes." His voice turned cold. The very mention of Li Shan-po was like a blast of winter wind. It turned every flickering ember of desire within him into dead ashes, and left him filled once more with anger—and a new emotion where this woman was concerned. Dread. "So you will also understand why you must leave Ch'ang-an at once," he said. "Have your father or brother or whoever protects you take you out of the city. Today, if possible."

Rhea sighed. First Matteo, now Zhao, were equally intent on getting her out of the city. "And why should I do that, Red Tiger? I have already told you this man cannot harm me."

"Listen to me, Lady Rhea. You have no idea what you're saying. Perhaps your male relatives taught you some simple techniques so that you could defend yourself against a common man of the streets, but Li Shan-po is more than that. Terribly more."

His warm hands gripped her shoulders. "The servants and eunuchs here gossip incessantly, and I have heard that Li Shan-po asked the eunuch of Palace Entertainments about you. He wants you, but he must not have you. He is the very embodiment of evil! I know what he did to my mother, and I will *not* allow it to be done to you."

Rhea stared wonderingly at him, his mouth drawn into a severe line, his eyes filled with worry. "Why do you care so much about what happens to me, Red Tiger?"

He dropped his hands, his expression suddenly bewildered. "I—that is not the point. I cannot stand by while yet another woman falls into his grasp."

She snorted. "I am not the sort to 'fall' into anyone's grasp, Red Tiger. Unless, of course, I am willing. In this case, I am not."

The sense of menace she had felt earlier returned. It had been banished temporarily by their passionate kiss, but now was even stronger than before. "You are the one who is in danger here," she said in a changed voice. "That is why I cannot leave."

Zhao saw the difference in her at once. He put out a hand to touch her, then quickly drew it back when she started. She gave him a dazed look, as though she had forgotten he was there.

"You spoke of this danger before," he said. "But when I asked you if it was Li Shan-po, you did not answer. Is it he?"

Rhea concentrated. Inside her head clouds swirled, dark and lowering, heavy with threat and an inescapable aura of foreboding—troubling emanations that grew larger the more she focused on them, stretching long evil fingers toward this man.

She shook herself. "I do not know," she said, and met Zhao's eyes. "Perhaps yes, perhaps no. But something or someone means you ill, and I will not leave you here in Ch'ang-an to face it alone."

"By the Sky-god—" Zhao felt like shaking this beguiling and incredibly maddening creature. Her nearness was a torment, tantalizing him with the still-fresh memory of how her body had felt in his arms—lithe and vibrant and so very real. What had driven him to kiss her? Was it merely her beauty, or was it something deeper, a compelling need for intimacy, for a oneness with her?

He wished it were the former, yet knew it was the latter. And he also knew that just that kiss had linked them together in a closeness he'd never felt with another person. In the space of a few days, a few moments, she had become vitally important to him—essential even—and his mouth went dry with fear at the thought of what Li Shan-po could do to her.

"I believe," he said, putting all the urgency and firmness he could into his voice, "that your powers, whatever they may be, are warning you against Li Shan-po. But he, too, has powers. Dark powers, Lady, that I will *not* have you challenge. For me it is different. . . ."

Her eyes hardened, instantly reminding him of twin pieces of flint. "Until I know you are safe, Red Tiger," she said in a voice that matched her eyes, "I am going to be your shadow. Do not make the mistake of believing me a helpless woman like other women of this land. I am not, and I intend to see that no harm comes to you. You have suffered enough."

Scowling, Zhao gave her a long, searching look, staring down at her as though to emphasize the difference in their heights. When he spoke, his voice was deliberately calm. "It is quite obvious that you are not like other women, if for no other reason than you are surely the most stubborn female in all of the Middle Kingdom. How can you protect me? And why should you wish to?"

This was the moment to tell him, Rhea thought. But in the face of these new revelations, she was suddenly reluctant. She took refuge in repeating his own response back to him. "As you said before—that is not the point."

His eyes seemed to catch fire. "Do not make light of me, woman. I am serious. Deadly serious!"

"So am I. And don't ask me to explain more to you, for I cannot. At least not now."

Their gazes locked in a silent test of wills. A minute dragged by, then two.

Zhao longed to grab her and shake some sense into her. He was unaccustomed to dealing with women who did not immediately defer to the better and wiser judgment of men. Indeed, he had never met a female so inflexible in all his life!

"Is there nothing I can say that will convince you to leave the city?" he finally asked.

She shook her head.

"You must have a male relative in Ch'ang-an with whom I can speak."

She shook her head again.

He sighed, admitting defeat. "So what are you going to do? Continue creeping up on me when I least expect you, only to disappear again the moment my back is turned?"

She smiled. "Something like that."

"Indeed? Such a strategy seems more calculated to drive me mad than to protect me."

"Ah, but a shadow is not always seen, is it, until you turn around. Turn around, Red Tiger, and if you have need of me, I will be there."

Stepping up to him, she brushed her lips across his, a brief touch, but one that burned through both of them with the heat of a flame. Then she was gone, slipping off through the trees, as Zhao stood motionless, watching her go.

Chapter 6

Hidden in the caverns of inaccessible mountains or coiled in the unfathomable depths of the sea, he awaits the time when he slowly rouses himself to activity. He unfolds himself in the storm clouds; he washes his mane in the blackness of the seething whirlpools. His claws are in the forks of the lightning, his scales begin to glisten in the bark of rain-swept pine trees. His voice is heard in the hurricane which, scattering the withered leaves of the forest, quickens the new spring. The dragon reveals himself only to vanish.

—*Kung Fu: History,
Philosophy and Technique*

Six days after Zhao and Rhea's meeting in the monastery garden, the slanting light of late afternoon found Li Shan-po stomping down one of the carefully manicured paths in the Imperial Park. He was in the foulest of moods.

Eleven days earlier Zhao Tamudj's treatment of the Dowager Empress had begun. That very same night Li Shan-po had sat in rapt silence, fascinated and lusting, as a foreign woman cast her spells in the Pavilion of the Moon Set within a Black Silk Night. Eleven days, and still he was unable to put that alluring creature with the peculiar silver eyes from his mind.

Following her performance, he had given discreet orders that she be sent directly from court to his mansion in the wealthy eastern suburbs. As the pavilion emptied itself of its audience, though, the Chief Eunuch of Palace Entertainments, bowing and uttering a thousand trembling pardons, told Li Shan-po that the woman had disappeared without the slightest sign of where she had gone. She had not even waited to receive her performer's fee.

Li Shan-po had sent the sweating eunuch a single freezing look before sweeping out of the pavilion. Undeterred, he had returned to his estate and immediately set his minions the task of finding her. They had combed the fashionable teahouses, and the Western Market, where most of the better entertainers plied their trade, but to no avail. Not a trace of the woman had been found.

It was frustrating, and to Li Shan-po, accustomed to attaining whatever he desired, infuriating. Neither his concubines, his horses, nor even his secret studies could dull the vivid picture of that arrestingly beautiful face and the lithe body clothed in clinging black silk. And Li Shan-po knew they never would. There was only one cure: to have the woman in his possession so he could use her as he wished, in all the various ways he desired, until his passions had been sated.

The more elusive she became, the sharper his appetite

grew. Not since the Zhuhu woman had a female affected him so keenly, and he was not pleased by this new infatuation. It was a poor time for indulging in the pleasures of physical obsession, when so many strands of the web he was weaving required his attention.

To make matters worse, it appeared Zhao Tamudj's unorthodox treatment of the Dowager Empress had succeeded—a development that greatly added to the Spider's ill temper. That particular strand had been poorly woven, he told himself sourly. However, he had done his best to rework it.

On this, the final day of the Dowager Empress's treatment, a crowd of nobles, officials, and palace servants had gathered outside the house in which she was ensconced. Many held branches of willow and peach in order to frighten away demons, and more branches had been piled in fragrant heaps along each wall of the house. In front of the bolted doors two watery-eyed servants stood guard over a smoking fire of artemisia, which they had been ordered to keep constantly burning to ward off evil influences.

As Li Shan-po neared the house, he wrinkled his nose at the smell. Chen Yü left a whispering huddle of eunuchs and came forward to meet him. Li Shan-po stopped walking, purposely distancing himself from the crowd about the house, waiting in aloof silence for the eunuch to reach him.

"Master." Chen Yü bowed low, then glanced nervously behind him. "Ch'iu Shih-liang is to arrive soon with the Zhuhu, and the Son of Heaven is also coming to see how the Dowager Empress has fared."

"Ch'iu Shih-liang." Li Shan-po spat out the name. "That old frog. His tenure upon the earth grows increasingly less needful."

Chen Yü looked horrified. "Please, Master." His girl-ish voice was a pleading whisper. "Others will hear you. Everyone knows that Ch'iu Shih-liang has the ear of the Emperor himself."

"Ah, but as a devout Taoist, so do I." For a moment Li Shan-po stared at the shut-up house, his face expression-less.

"Peace, Chen Yü," he said at length. "It is no secret that the Chief Eunuch and I hold each other in mutual dis-taste. Ch'iu Shih-liang has ever been kind to Buddhists, and as the Son of Heaven grows increasingly enamored of Taoism and its secrets of eternal life, so does he grow ever more hostile to the religions of foreigners.

"In time Ch'iu Shih-liang will regret his kindness to the purveyors of that bastard religion. In any case, the little errand I had you perform will ensure that neither the Zhuhu nor Buddhism gains credit for the Dowager Em-press's recovery."

Chen Yü shook his head, but before he could reply, drumbeats vibrated through the still air. The imperial pro-cession was approaching. All conversation ceased as those around the house fell forward on their faces, including Chen Yü and, a moment later, Li Shan-po.

Preceded by the bearers of the imperial kingfisher standards and flanked by the elite guards of the Imperial Army of the Left, Emperor Wu-tsung and his retinue strode rapidly down the path Li Shan-po had taken a few minutes earlier. As he neared the kowtowing assemblage, Wu-tsung's gaze darted impatiently over the throng of silk-clad backs.

"Where is the noble Li Shan-po?" he demanded. "We requested that he be here."

"I await your wish, Majesty," Li Shan-po said, his voice muffled.

"Arise then. All of you, rise!"

Surprisingly graceful for a man of his bulk, Li Shan-po stood. Wu-tsung nodded at him. "It pleases us that you are here, our trusted noble. Seeing your face after her confinement will no doubt give the Dowager Empress great joy." He cast a warning glance at the retinue behind him. "If she is indeed as well as we have been led to believe."

Li Shan-po followed the Emperor's gaze to where Zhao Tamudj stood beside Ch'iu Shih-liang, looming over the Chief Eunuch as well as the rest of the imperial escort. So the old bobtailed dog had found a puppy to nurse, he thought contemptuously. What a foolish decision.

The position of foreigners had been in decline ever since one of them, An Lu-shan, had nearly succeeded in toppling the T'ang dynasty less than a hundred years earlier. And now Wu-tsung, under the careful tutelage of Li Shan-po and other Han nobles and scholars long hostile to anything foreign, was questioning the pervasive hold of Buddhism, itself a foreign religion, on the Middle Kingdom.

Yet here was doughty old Ch'iu Shih-liang befriending a person who possessed the twin misfortunes of being both foreign and Buddhist. Yes, the Chief Eunuch must be growing tired of life.

"Majesty," Li Shan-po said loudly, "though it was I who suggested a Zhuhu healer come to your honored mother, I certainly could not foresee that the one who came would be a *jushi*, or that he would embark on such a strange and dangerous course of treatment. I have spent these last eleven days supplicating the Taoist Immortals to intervene on her behalf. If she is truly recovered, it is more than likely because they have given her their protection."

Zhao stiffened, but Ch'iu Shih-liang whispered to him,

"Say nothing. To respond will only make his position all the stronger."

Zhao caught himself, clamping an iron control over the hatred that had welled up in him at the sound of that cultured voice. He favored the eunuch with a small, serene smile. "There is no need for me to respond," he murmured. "The Dowager Empress has been healed. Isn't that all that matters?"

Ch'iu Shih-liang's face was grim. "Unfortunately, it is not."

"Zhuhu!" the Emperor called.

Zhao walked forward, and the imperial entourage quickly opened a path for him. Standing beside the Emperor, Li Shan-po watched him approach, a mocking smile twisting his lips. Zhao deliberately ignored him, although the noble's gaze burned upon his face, resting there with the livid heat of smoldering coals.

Behind Li Shan-po stood a young eunuch robed in bright crimson. Zhao had spoken with him several times during the Dowager Empress's confinement, finding him affable and friendly. Now, seeing the way the eunuch looked at Li Shan-po, Zhao threw him a hard stare. So this gregarious official was one of *his* creatures!

Frowning, the Emperor addressed Zhao. "It has been told to us that the fever has left Honored Mother. Is this so?"

Zhao inclined his head. "Yes, Divine One. The Dowager Empress has been fumigated three times now, and she is greatly improved. I believe she is ready to leave the house of her treatment."

"Bring her out then!" Wu-tsung ordered.

Zhao bowed and went into the house. The charcoal fires were still burning, creating a mist so thick that he and the servants who had followed him with clothing for the

Empress were immediately drenched. Within that cloud, the royal mother sat dozing upon an unheated *k'ang*, draped only in the piece of silk gauze.

Kneeling beside her, Zhao examined her pulse. The old woman stirred, lifting her head and glaring at him. "You again," she said testily.

He smiled. "Yes, Highness. This is the last day of your treatment, and I am pleased to say that it has been successful. The Son of Heaven is most anxious to see you. Would you like to finally leave this house?"

"Well, I certainly have no intention of leaving it naked as a peasant infant!" she snapped. "Where are my clothes?"

Zhao smiled again. He had grown used to the elderly matriarch's barbed tongue; indeed, he scarcely noticed it anymore. As the servants bustled forward to dress the Dowager Empress, he rose and began to move through the room, extinguishing the fires and removing the pots of herb-filled water from the braziers. Occupied as he was, he did not see the small piece of wood clutched in his patient's hand.

A short time later, leaning on the arms of her servants and followed closely by Zhao, the Dowager Empress hobbled out of the house. She was thin and pale, but her eyes were clear, and it was apparent to all that the fever that had ravaged her for so long was gone.

"There you are, Only Son," she railed weakly at the Emperor. "I have been shut up in that terrible house for days. Is this how a filial son treats his mother? And I am *hungry*! The only meal that silly Zhuhu would allow me to eat is rice gruel. You must execute him at once. Then order the cooks to prepare food for me immediately! I want shark fin boiled in chicken soup and roasted camel hump and pork with ginger and steamed crab and oh, yes, fish in plum sauce. With litchi nuts and honey fritters for dessert. Well? What do you stand there for?"

"Divine One," Zhao said in a low voice, "she must continue to eat carefully for the next several days. With your permission, I will speak to your cooks about her meals."

Beaming at the Dowager Empress, Wu-tsung nodded absently. "Oh, Honored Mother," he said happily. "How good it is to see you well. The Zhuhu's treatment succeeded!"

"The Zhuhu's treatment?"

"Yes, Honored Mother. It was your wise request that brought him here. Do you not remember?"

"Oh, that. Well, I suppose he was of some help, but what really healed me is this." She held up the small piece of carved wood, now dangling from the girdle about her skinny waist.

Ch'iu Shih-liang stepped closer. "A talisman," he muttered.

"Where did you get that, Honored Mother?" asked the Emperor.

For the first time since she had appeared, the Empress smiled. "From Li Shan-po," she said proudly.

"He gave you that?"

Li Shan-po shouldered past the Chief Eunuch. "Yes, Majesty." His tone was carefully modest. "Actually, it was a eunuch, acting on my orders, who brought it to her. But I made it especially for the Dowager Empress, since I had grave concerns about this treatment. There are specific designs inscribed on it for her health. And I have here"—he pulled from his sleeve a tiny container of white jade—"a worm gathered from the mountains of eternal snow. The creature is most difficult and expensive to obtain, thus I regret that I could not offer it sooner. It is reputed to be an excellent cure for the ravages of accumulated fever. I am told it is as cold as ice and has a flavor sweet as honey."

Bowing, he held out the small box. "With my deepest respects, Divine One."

Wu-tsung accepted the offering and studied it thoughtfully, then turned to Zhao. "This poses an interesting question. Was it the Buddha who healed Honored Mother, or the forces of Tao? Or could it have even been the Shang Tian of your people? How do you answer, Zhuhu in the robes of a *jushi*?"

Zhao looked from Li Shan-po, to the Dowager Empress, to Chen Yü, who would not meet his eyes. As he returned his gaze to the Emperor, Rhea's presence came to life deep inside him, tugging at him. He saw her as she had been six mornings ago, her lips swollen from his kiss, her eyes shimmering and filled with secrets. The vision had come to him repeatedly over the past several days, her spiritual presence and the warning she had given him as troubling as her absence. Was this the danger she had spoken of?

"Majesty," he said steadily, "to debate whether the Dowager Empress recovered because of the power of Buddha, Shang Tian, or the Tao is doing a disservice to all three. Your honored mother is well, and if any or all of those great forces had a hand in her healing, then I am most humbly grateful."

Wu-tsung's face turned brick red, and he glared at Zhao. Silence fell, a silence so profound it seemed as if everyone gathered there had ceased breathing. To speak as the Zhuhu had was risky, even foolish. The Emperor, as much as Li Shan-po, had encouraged the debate. Criticism, however mildly implied, was not something Wu-tsung reacted to favorably.

Ch'iu Shih-liang's voice shattered the tense stillness.

"Divine One," he said in a tone of quiet rebuke. "This man's skill has returned your mother to health. Amitabha, Majesty, he saved her life! And yet he claims no credit for it. He should be rewarded for his humility, not punished." Ch'iu Shih-liang paused. "But in his all-seeing wisdom," he added gently, "the Son of Heaven surely knows this."

Wu-tsung swung around to stare at Ch'iu Shih-liang. As abruptly as it had appeared, the fixed look in his eyes vanished, and his face relaxed. "Of course, of course," he cried expansively. "The entire court shall honor him for the service he has rendered us."

There was a collective sigh, and among the silent throng, men gave each other surreptitious glances of relief. Wu-tsung turned back to Zhao, and the latter saw that under the ornate jeweled headdress, a broad smile warmed the Emperor's face.

"An imperial plaque with your glorious deed inscribed upon it shall be hung from the doors of your monastery," Wu-tsung proclaimed. "Identical plaques shall be erected in the foreign district of Yangzhou and the merchants' ward of Ch'ang-an, so that all your people may know of your skill. As for yourself, we shall cause an imperial edict to be produced bestowing the title of"—he thought a moment—"Most Grand and Magnificent Physician of the Court under Heaven.

"Under this edict you are free to travel anywhere in the Middle Kingdom, and in all villages and cities you will be accorded the honor and respect due only the highest officials of the realm. However, you may continue to stay within the Imperial City and attend to the illnesses of any members of the court who might seek you. Thus have we spoken, and thus shall it be done." With a pleased expression Wu-tsung gazed at his audience. "Are we not great?"

Instantly a chorus of assent answered him. "Your wisdom outshines the sun!" "Compassionate as one of the Immortals is the Son of Heaven!"

The accolades continued for several minutes. Accepting them, Wu-tsung stood in a pose of studied nonchalance, his head regally high. Finally he held up a hand for silence. "Return to your duties now. It is time for Honored Mother to be conducted to her apartments." With the imperial drums beating out a measured rhythm, the Emperor led his entourage away.

Promptly the crowd began to disperse. Zhao was surprised and a little amused when he became the center of a throng of well-wishers. In the space of a few moments he had been elevated to a person of importance. Powerful officials, who for the last eleven days had behaved as though he did not exist, bowed and smiled and offered their congratulations. Others praised his skill, then asked if he could heal them of this ailment or that. Eventually the group thinned, and Zhao found himself face-to-face with Li Shan-po.

Zhao was greatly satisfied to note that Li Shan-po was no longer smiling. "You think yourself very clever, don't you?" The noble's voice was a soft hiss. "Enjoy your favored position while you can, *foreigner*. For it will be brief indeed."

"Will it?" His passion for revenge coursed through every vein in Zhao's body with such fierce intensity, he felt physical pain. The familiar pounding was back in his head, as though the imperial drums were being struck inside his skull.

"Those who do good," he said, "bring upon themselves happiness a hundredfold, along with the blessing of the gods. Those who do evil receive retribution a thousandfold, and the devils are bent on their destruction."

"Do not quote your monastic platitudes to me, you absurd pretender to the priesthood—"

"I have fulfilled the first of my obligations," Zhao said, his voice overriding Li Shan-po's. "Now I can turn my attention to why I am really here." He was silent, and the antagonism reverberating between the two men left them alone in the entire world. "To repay evil," Zhao went on. "To destroy *you*, Li Shan-po, as you destroyed my family. It is merely a question of deciding how."

The noble was livid. "You—" he began, then his gaze fell on Ch'iu Shih-liang. The eunuch was standing nearby, watching them with obvious curiosity. Li Shan-po caught himself. "We shall see, Zhuhu," he said through gritted teeth. "We shall see."

He stalked away, and Ch'iu Shih-liang walked up to Zhao. "It appears you were having a most interesting conversation. You are not without courage, Zhao Tamudj. To speak to the Son of Heaven as you did was most astonishing. Now you seem willing to take on Li Shan-po himself. He is most influential here at court, you know."

"I know," Zhao said in a forbidding tone. "Why does the Dowager Empress set such store by him?"

Ch'iu Shih-liang sighed. "No one truly knows. There are many who say he has used his knowledge of the Dark Arts to bewitch her. But in my opinion, he has simply taken advantage of a lonely old woman whose mind wanders. I think he makes the Empress feel young again. But allow me to ask you a question: what lies between you and Li Shan-po?"

Zhao studied the older man, wondering if it would be wise to confide in him. It was said by many that the court eunuchs were the real power behind the Dragon Throne. Having met Ch'iu Shih-liang, he could well believe those stories.

Both in bearing and demeanor, the Chief Eunuch exhibited far more power than the petulant yet divinely descended Son of Heaven. His age alone made him worthy of respect, though but for the whiteness of his hair and beard, it was difficult to guess how old he was. Intelligence and humor stamped his lean features, and he had a quiet strength that reminded Zhao of his own Master Wu. Still, his battle with Li Shan-po was his alone. He would not involve an innocent person.

"There is much between Li Shan-po and me," he said at last, watching as the nobleman disappeared into the lush gardens of the Imperial Park. "Much."

Li Shan-po rode back to his mansion at a gallop, pushing his horse uncharacteristically hard. Once there, he shouted for his concubines to be assembled. Breathing hard from the swift ride and his mounting rage, he strode up and down the line of trembling women, his glittering gaze fixed upon them.

He stopped in front of his newest one, a slave of fifteen whose ridiculous foreign name he had changed to Submissive Pearl. She was adorned with long black hair as thick and soft as satin, but her eyes were a normal shade of brown rather than the bewitching silver-gray he hungered for. Still, she would have to do. The fury in him needed a quick release, and this female who bore a faint resemblance to the elusive storyteller would be the receptacle of that rage.

He fingered the crop around his wrist, then drew it down the path between Submissive Pearl's breasts. "Await me in my bedchamber," he commanded, and smiled at the fright in the concubine's eyes. "If you do not live up to the promise of your name, this"—he slapped the crop across her backside, just hard enough to make her jump—"will instruct you. Now go."

The night was well advanced when Li Shan-po left his bedchamber and summoned all of his minions and disciples, including those who had been searching for the foreign woman.

These latter ones returned to the great estate quivering with dread. Servants who displeased Li Shan-po generally died in mysterious and horrible ways, either of illnesses that could only be the result of some malevolent curse, or by gruesomely violent means.

"Master," the leader of the quest began in a quavering voice. "We are—"

"Never mind about the woman," Li Shan-po interrupted. "At least for now. I have a different task to set you. Listen and pay heed. This must be done with great care."

Chapter 7

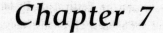

To rejoice in the conquest is to rejoice in murder.

—*Kung Fu: History,
Philosophy and Technique*

The next day it began, simply, with such delicate subtlety one might have thought the terrible rumor had been borne by the wind itself into the teahouses, restaurants, and markets of Ch'ang-an. A whisper here, a softly uttered phrase there, and the tale began to spread, gathering its own momentum. As one of the major events celebrated in Ch'ang-an approached, the Festival of Buddha's Birthday, the tale flowed out into the capital's one hundred and ten wards, its two huge market places, and finally into the outlying suburbs, growing louder with each telling.

Outside the capital stood an old Buddhist monastery. Inside its hallowed walls lay one of the most sacred relics in all the world: the finger-bone of Buddha. Only the four teeth of the Great Lord, each housed in a different monastery within the capital itself, were worshiped with equal reverence.

Three days before the Festival of Buddha's Birthday was to begin, the finger-bone disappeared.

Upon discovering the theft, the temple monks did their best to keep the disaster a secret. For it truly was a disaster. With their carnival atmosphere of storytellers, magicians, and other entertainments, religious festivals were popular and heavily attended. They greatly relieved the monotony that was the lot of life for common people.

At the same time, there was an element of religious hysteria at the festivals that easily reached fever pitch, especially when relics of the Buddha were reverenced. This reverence, attended by processions and offerings where the populace stormed the relics, tossing cash donations at them like rain, was a feverish and wild affair that often turned violent. Self-mutilations, even to the point of worshipers severing arms and legs in an ecstasy of religious fervor, were common.

Who knew, the appalled monks said to each other, what horrific forces would be unleashed if news of the sacred finger-bone's disappearance reached the masses? At all costs, the catastrophe had to be kept quiet until the holy relic could be found. But the monks did not know of the wind that was already blowing through the city. . . .

The day before the festival, the Reverend Abbot Hui Jing slipped through the gates of the Temple of the Peaceful Mind and hurried off down the quiet lane. The jovial good humor that characterized the little monk had completely vanished. His rotund face was set in lines of worry, and all color had drained from his ruddy cheeks, leaving them pasty and unhealthily pale.

It was not yet dawn and still dark, and the abbot carried a small lantern to see his way through the unlighted streets. All about him Ch'ang-an slept, but it was an un-easy sleep, as though the city were a slumbering monster that would awaken with a roar of rage. There were guards about, posted in front of the walled and locked wards, but beyond giving the abbot an occasional incurious glance, none seemed concerned to see a monk stirring so early.

Hui Jing was unsure whether he should be relieved or concerned about that. Obviously the guards did not know of the calamity looming over them all, and staring at the wards' high walls, he shivered. Such walls were meant to keep the populace under control, but in his memory they had never been tested, particularly in circumstances as serious as this.

He had nearly reached the Imperial City when the bells of the Buddhist and Taoist monasteries within and without the city began to ring, tolling the Hour of the Tiger. In the east, the hills were lightening in the gray of a cloudy dawn.

Within the Imperial City, in the same garden where he had last encountered Rhea, Zhao was already completing his early-morning practice. He had come to this spot every morning since that day, hoping with mingled worry, irritation, and longing that she would meet him there, reassuring him that she was still unharmed.

She had not come, though, and every day Zhao grew more worried. Where was she? What if, despite all her brave talk about shadowing him and being able to take care of herself, Li Shan-po already had her in his grasp?

Zhao had put off the long journey home indefinitely. Welcomed at court, he intended to stay on for a time, mulling over the best way to seek his revenge, and in the meanwhile make himself a perpetual reminder to his mortal enemy that it was only a matter of time before the Tamudj family was avenged.

Yet he found himself held in Ch'ang-an by another reason as well: the mysterious Rhea. He had to know that she was all right. But more than that, he wanted to see her again, experience again the wild, exhilarating emotions she roused in him. He wanted to touch her, kiss her, feel once more that unfamiliar yet wondrous sense of oneness he'd felt before. Her absence and the gnawing fear that he might not see her again ate at his inner harmony, unbalancing and disturbing him as nothing ever had.

But if the days were bad, filled with concern and the yearning to catch even a glimpse of her, the nights were much worse. He slept fitfully, haunted by dreams filled with more sensuality and erotic delight than he'd ever known with the few women he'd bedded. Though he had not taken a Buddhist monk's vow of celibacy, his sexual appetites were often submerged beneath his keen desire for vengeance. Yet after only one kiss from Rhea, his body was sending out incessant cravings for more. Much more. For a physical joining that would bind her to him forever.

But where was she?

This dawn had passed like the others, with no trace of her. Disappointed and brooding, he had just begun to walk back to the monastery, when Hui Jing appeared between the pine trees. Puffing and gasping, robes flapping about his ankles, the abbot waved an arm at Zhao. He jogged awkwardly toward the younger man, clearly unused to such exertion.

In three long strides Zhao was beside the winded monk. "Dyhana Master." He bowed hurriedly. "What is wrong? Has something happened in your temple?"

"Wait—must catch—breath." Panting heavily, Hui Jing bent over, hands on his knees, and drew gulps of air into his lungs. "They told me you would be out here." His voice slowly returned to normal. "It is just as well. I must speak with you, Red Tiger, privately."

"Why, Dyhana Master?" Zhao gazed down at the abbot, utterly mystified.

Hui Jing straightened. "Do you mean to tell me you have not heard?"

"Of the sacred finger-bone? Yes, of course. We have been told not to speak of it to anyone outside the monastery."

"Which is as it should be. Yet I have learned something, and I must tell you before it is too late."

Zhao waited, Rhea's warning suddenly echoing in his ears. He knew what the little monk was going to tell him.

"It is being said . . ." Although the garden was deserted, Hui Jing glanced behind him and took a step closer, lowering his voice. " . . . that Buddha's sacred finger-bone was taken by a foreigner." He paused, his gaze fixed upon Zhao. "A green-eyed foreigner with red hair, dressed in the robes of a *jushi*."

"Reverend Abbot, I assure I did not—"

"Don't be foolish, boy. I don't believe one of Master Wu's students could commit such sacrilege, or even that the story is true. But that is not what matters. What matters is that you are in grave danger, for there are those who will believe it. And in all of Ch'ang-an, there is no other man who matches that description."

"Who?" Zhao's voice was soft and amazingly contained, despite the certainty pounding through his veins. "Who is behind such nonsense?"

"I do not know, and it is not important. You must leave Ch'ang-an, Red Tiger, before the dawn grows too old. We monks have been trying to keep the theft quiet, but the fates seem to have allied themselves against us. This is the largest city in the world, yet a rumor can spread more swiftly through these streets than in the smallest village. It is common knowledge that a green-eyed *jushi* foreigner with red hair healed the Son of Heaven's mother. If people think you are in any way responsible for the theft of a holy relic, mobs of uncounted thousands will rage, even to the Imperial City itself, hunting for your blood."

Hui Jing shook himself, as if to dispel the images his words had created. "Now," he said in a brisk tone. "I will help you with arrangements to leave. You must begin your journey immediately."

"No."

Hui Jing continued as though the single word had not registered. "After all, with the Dowager Empress healed, there is no reason for you to stay, and when this blows over—" Abruptly he caught himself. "*What* did you say?"

"Revered Abbot, I will not leave. Why should I? I have done nothing to merit my fleeing the capital like some sort of criminal."

"Foolish boy!" the abbot exploded. "That is not the point! Don't you see the peril you are in?"

"Oh, I see it." Zhao's voice was ominous. "And I see a great deal more, as well."

"What in the name of the Western Heaven does *that* mean?"

Zhao gazed off through the trees without answering. It had stormed the night before, and in the weak light of the gloomy dawn, the trees stood like wet black sentinels, drooping under the beginnings of a warm drizzle. The brightly painted porticoes of the Official Monastery gleamed through their gnarled branches, and Zhao caught flashes of yellow as the monks made their way to the Meditation Hall for morning prayers.

Unconsciously his fists clenched. He was tempted to share his suspicions with Hui Jing, for the abbot was shrewd and clearly knowledgeable about what went on in the city. Yet if Zhao involved him and Li Shan-po learned of it, Hui Jing would surely be exposed to the greatest risk.

To see another innocent person suffer from Li Shan-po's malevolence, especially in payment for helping him, would be unbearable. It was bad enough that Rhea had adamantly refused to flee Ch'ang-an. And now he did not know where she was. . . .

"Well?" Hui Jing demanded. "Why are you so quiet, boy?"

Zhao drew himself up to is full height and stared down at the abbot. "Dyhana Master," he said slowly, "you are concerned about me. For that I am grateful and deeply honored. But please do not ask me to explain. You are right. There is danger here, and not just from the people of Ch'ang-an. I will not expose you to that danger. The responsibility for dealing with this problem is mine and mine alone."

Hui Jing opened his mouth to protest such complete insanity, but the look on Zhao's face was so savage, and yet so contained, the words died in his throat. With far less anger than he had intended, he asked, "And just how do you intend to deal with it, my son?"

"The only way I can. By finding the sacred finger-bone and returning it to its rightful place."

After the previous night's rain, the Ho River was flowing swift and strong. Rhea negotiated it with an absentminded ease, though her thoughts were as turbulent as the rough waters.

For too long she had been away from the natural world of her people. The river, with its waters hemmed in by the land, was a poor substitute for the unfettered and ever-changing freedom of the sea. Unexciting though it was, the Ho would have to satisfy her desire to be immersed, if only for a short while, in water, the one element where she truly belonged. Her fears for Red Tiger had held her in Ch'ang-an these past many days, as she watched and waited for she knew not what.

Fearing that if she visited him too openly she might somehow worsen the peril that hovered over him, or even prevent it from appearing so that it could be dealt with, she had deliberately stayed out of his sight. A practical decision but a difficult one, she had soon found out. Watching him as he performed his morning rituals, as he meditated, as he strolled through the city, often stopping in the marketplace to browse though never buy, she had been assailed constantly by the longing to be with him openly, to learn his thoughts and to share her own. Such compulsion was foreign to her, and as frightening as it was powerful.

Even more frightening were the fantasies that assailed her whenever her gaze lingered too long on his strong, handsome face, or his broad shoulders, or his narrow hips, or his muscular legs. Then memories of their kiss would flood her like a wave of fire, arousing startling images of the two of them, their bodies naked and pressed together as they rode the salty waves of the sea, his face fierce and loving as he gazed down at her. Rhea was no innocent, but the potent sensuality of those images, so real they could have been actual memories rather than mere fantasies, both embarrassed and excited her. Often she had to leave him for a short while, returning after she'd regained her composure to stare at him again.

Her only solace from all her baffling emotions had been these rare swims in the river, and long before dawn broke on this gloomy morning, she had slipped out of Ch'ang-an and come down to the Ho to swim once more.

Driven by a physical restlessness and the relentless thoughts swirling through her brain, she'd swum eagerly and hard, moving through the currents without cease, stopping neither to rest nor forage for her breakfast among the many fish that inhabited the river world.

By midmorning she had entered one of the turbulent Ho's few calm stretches. Remembering to be cautious—for the landfolk would surely be stirring by now—she kicked her way to the surface and carefully popped her head through the water.

Her caution was warranted. Only yards away, a large ferry boat was crossing the river. Its flat deck was crowded with passengers, and over the quiet water their agitated voices carried clearly to Rhea's ears.

"It's gone, I tell you!" a man was sputtering. "The most holy relic of all!" He started to say something else, but he was drowned out by an uproar of shouts and questions from the other passengers.

Despite the tumult of voices Rhea was able to discern that all these people were travelers, on their way to the capital for the Festival of Buddha's Birthday. As she realized this, an inexplicable chill raced through her entire body, and she swam closer. The Terrans were so aroused they did not notice, not even the two ferrymen working the poles.

"I will tell you this," one raggedly dressed man was yelling. "I can guess who was responsible!"

He shouted this several times, until finally those nearest him turned. "Well? Who was it, then?" a young man called out impatiently. His question was taken up by others. Within moments, the entire boat was screaming, "Who? Who?"

The atmosphere was oddly contagious. Gripped by the same sense of foreboding that had swept over her in the monastery garden with Red Tiger, even Rhea held her breath awaiting the answer. Preening at the attention, the ragged man glanced about him with a self-satisfied air. "The foreigners took it," he said smugly. "Or rather, one foreigner took it, with the intention of selling it to others. I heard this from one who knows."

Pandemonium greeted his words. Among the frantically gesturing people, though, Rhea saw an elderly woman sitting in silence, shaking her gray head in disgust. Beside her a man—probably her husband—had jumped to his feet and was shouting along with the others despite the woman's irritable tugging at his sleeve to make him sit down. When the crowd finally paused for breath, she spoke out in a surprisingly strong and educated voice.

"Why are all of you paying such heed to this man?" The matriarch cast a disapproving glance at the ragged passenger, who returned her look with a glare of his own. "To me he appears nothing more than a beggar, yet you wail after him blindly, as though he were descended from Heaven itself. 'I heard this from one who knows,' he says." The woman snorted mockingly. "What knowledge could such a low personage possibly have that is important? We do not even know if the finger-bone has been stolen. Reason and wisdom are what should prevail here, not madness."

For a moment it seemed her words would overcome the hostile mood of the group. Many passengers shifted their feet and looked away in embarrassment, while others who had been jumping about in fury sat down again rather quickly. But the ragged man, seeing how rapidly his position was evaporating, waved his arms wildly in the air.

"By what right does a woman tell men how to behave?" he shouted. "How dare she speak of reason and wisdom, when all know that Confucius said such qualities are totally lacking in the female race? Why, for her to talk of such things is as unnatural as tits on a stallion!" Glaring at the old woman, he snarled, "I may not be an important person, but *I* am a man. And I know what I know!"

"And what is it that you know?" one of the boatmen shouted.

The ragged man stared at the passengers triumphantly, then lowered his voice in what seemed to Rhea a true flair for the dramatic. "I know that a foreigner with red hair was seen fleeing the monastery three nights ago. The very next morning the monks discovered the loss of the sacred relic. But that is not all."

The complete attention of every single person on board the packed boat, even that of the elderly woman, was focused on the ragged man. Clearly savoring it, he paused. "The foreigner I speak of," he finally continued, "was clothed in the garb of a *youposai*. A *jushi*."

"What!" burst out one of the more prosperous-looking passengers. "I live in the capital, and everyone there is talking of the *jushi* who miraculously healed the Dowager Empress. A red-haired foreign *jushi*. Are you saying—"

"I only pass on what was told to me," the ragged man interrupted, his eyes modestly lowered. "But how many red-haired foreigners in *jushi* robes can there be in Ch'ang-an at one time?"

Red Tiger!

Mesmerized, Rhea had been drawing ever closer to the ferry. At the moment the ragged man asked his question, a student sitting near the railing glanced out at the river, to see an astonishing and terrifying sight—an impossibly beautiful woman, her thick black hair streaming over her naked shoulders and her round breasts bobbing gently upon the river's surface.

The instant the Terran's gaze touched hers, Rhea realized her mistake. Like a flash of sunlight, she disappeared beneath the surface. But it was too late.

His eyes threatening to pop from his head, the scholar pointed a trembling finger at the spot where she had been. "Aaah," he croaked. When this produced no effect upon the other passengers, he gulped several times and finally managed enough control to shriek, "Nü Kua! I have seen Nü Kua, Water Goddess of the Subcelestial Realm Herself!"

New pandemonium broke out, this time so wild that the ferrymen, as terrified of the boat capsizing as they were of the goddess, pleaded desperately for calm. Far beneath the river, Rhea did not hear any of this. She swam swiftly ahead of the ferry toward shore and surfaced in a clump of reeds where, unseen, she could watch it approach.

Even before it neared the land, the sound of wailing prayers and imprecations reached her, and she ruefully understood that she was the cause. The boat nosed its way into shore, the ferrymen already letting out the plank by which the passengers would disembark. From her hidden spot, Rhea listened with more than a little surprise to the excited voices.

"It was an omen, a sign that what that man said was true."

"Yes, but it could also be a harbinger of evil. Nü Kua could only have appeared to protest the taking of the Lord Buddha's finger-bone."

"Aiiie, it is ill-omened. What is to become of us? One day before the Festival and such evil descends upon us!"

"We must go quickly to the capital."

"Yes, yes. The Ch'ang-an monks must explain this!"

The voices died away as the travelers straggled toward the road that led to Ch'ang-an. Muttering to themselves and casting apprehensive glances at the quiet water, the two ferrymen pushed off again. Rhea peered through the reeds and saw that another group of pilgrims had already assembled on the opposite shore, waiting to be ferried across. She also saw that the raggedly dressed man had not followed the other passengers up the road to Ch'ang-an.

He was standing instead behind the clump of reeds, almost as if he did not wish the boatmen to see him. She wondered about this, then her sensitive ears picked up the sound of footsteps. Two people were approaching, and from the way the muscles in the man's legs tightened, she suspected he'd been waiting for them. Moments later this was confirmed.

"Something unforeseen has happened to aid us." Rhea recognized the voice of the ragged man, though there was a quavering note in it now. "I have been spreading the rumor as instructed," he hurried on. "But on this ferry, after I told my tale, one of the passengers claimed he saw Nü Kua. Now all of the passengers are rushing to Ch'ang-an, crying that Her appearance is an omen proving the truth of my words."

"Excellent!" a raspy voice exclaimed.

"But the Water Goddess!" the third man said fearfully. "Do you think he truly saw Her?"

"Had you seen his face you would not ask," the first man said. Now Rhea understood that his unsteady tone was because he, too, was afraid.

"It does not matter if he did or not," the second man said. "All that matters is that we can turn this to our advantage, which means the Master will be pleased."

"Yes, but Nü Kua may have come as a warning," the

third man said still more apprehensively. "Because of what we and the others have done. The goddess knows, even if mortal men do not, that we stole the sacred finger-bone. Sacrilege has been committed, terrible sacrilege. And I cannot put it from my mind!"

"Nor I," the ragged man agreed.

There was a loud snort, and a raspy voice said, "Both of you are fools. Sacrilege or not, I would happily face Nü Kua a dozen times rather than Li Shan-po once when he is angry. Return to your tasks. There are other ferries, and the roads are filling with travelers coming into the city. Word of the finger-bone must continue to be spread. After I have seen how the rest of our men are faring, I will report this sighting of Nü Kua to the Master."

Their voices faded, mingling with the sound of footsteps as the men trudged away.

Hastily Rhea rose out of the water. Belted around her waist was a small waterproof traveling pouch containing Terran clothing. She threw on the loose blouse and pants of gray satin, then ran after the men. Just before a bend where the road sloped up from the river, she caught up with them. They were standing beside the road, and one of them was untying a small animal she recognized as a pony, which stood tethered to a tree.

"Men," she called. "I would speak with you for a moment."

The three Terrans whirled. Seeing her, their eyes bulged and their jaws dropped in unison. Their reaction was almost comical, but knowing full well the reason for it, Rhea gritted her teeth in annoyance. Landfolk women did not accost strange men in deserted places, not if they were well-bred and therefore deserving of respect.

By the Mother, she thought irritably, she was tired of these men's eternal preoccupation with females and their control! What were males so afraid of that they had to constantly keep women bound by a myriad of ridiculous rules and codes of behavior?

One man stepped forward, his gaze sweeping over her with a leering appreciation that was mirrored in the faces of his companions. "Indeed?" he said in his raspy voice. "A woman shameless enough to linger out here alone, calling to any man who passes is surely interested in other things besides talking. You must be quite eager for customers."

Rhea ignored this. "Why are you blaming the *jushi* called Red Tiger for a deed he did not commit?" She genuinely did not understand, and within her was a burning need to fathom these actions. "What harm has he done you," she continued, "that you should go about spreading lies that anger people? And what is the significance of this thing you call the sacred finger-bone?"

The men were no longer leering. "The bitch heard us," the raggedly dressed man said. "She heard everything!"

"Yes." The raspy-voiced man was staring at her with an odd combination of speculation, fury, and lust. "We will have to remedy that. But she may as well spread her legs for us before we do. Let's enjoy ourselves on her. Then a knife blade across that pretty throat, a toss into the river, and no one will be the wiser. After all, she's obviously nothing more than a low-grade foreign prostitute."

Rhea held back her growing aggravation. "Are you going to answer me or not?"

Raspy-voice gestured at the others. "We'll take turns. I'll go first. You two can hold her for me."

Leering once more, the three men walked forward. Rhea glared at them. Her annoyance was rapidly turning to anger. Laughing in anticipation, two of them reached out to grab her arms.

Effortlessly she avoided them. She tried to remind herself of the physical weakness of Terrans, yet in her concern for Red Tiger and her anger at these men, she drove the heels of her hands against their chests harder than she had intended.

They were powerful blows, though not lethal ones. At least, they would not have been to merfolk. With amazement she watched both men fly up into the air. They crashed down some distance away, let out gurgling cries, and collapsed in obvious lifelessness upon the dusty ground.

Rhea stared in consternation. She had meant only to reprimand, to push the men away with enough force to warn that she would not be trifled with. Babbling filled her ears, and she turned to see the raggedly dressed man backing away, his eyes huge and his hands held out as if to ward her off.

"Wet, wet," he mumbled in nearly incoherent gibber. "I see it now. Wet, as though she has just emerged from the river. It is She. Come to punish us."

"Wait." She started after him.

At her first step the man let out a shriek. Stumbling and falling, he fled to where the untied pony grazed, its reins dragging along the ground. He flung himself upon the animal's back, his heels battering wildly at its round sides. The startled pony broke into a sluggish canter. Craning his neck to keep Rhea within sight, the man shouted at it to go faster, although after that first step she had stopped and now stood still, staring at him.

Perched awkwardly on the pony's back, nearly falling in his attempt to ride and watch her, the man presented such a ludicrous sight, Rhea would have laughed under other circumstances. She could have caught up to him easily, for even at a gallop the fat little pony was far slower than a merperson was capable of running.

She didn't move, though. She watched the pony lumber out of sight, then walked slowly over to the bodies of the two men. Distressed and unhappy, she gazed down at their death-twisted shapes. She had killed Terrans, she who had never taken the life of any warm-blooded creature, much less a human one.

Worse, it had been so easy—so terribly, terribly easy. Even the shark whose skin had gone to make her waterproof bag had been far more difficult and dangerous to fight than these men. But they had been humans, albeit evil ones, and without meaning to, she had ended their lives with a carelessness that shamed her. Guilt swept through her, and grief.

"I am sorry," she whispered. "You meant me harm, but I certainly did not mean to kill you."

She turned away. There was only one thing to do now. Return to Ch'ang-an and find Red Tiger, before it was too late.

Chapter 8

Man may remove all obstacles through quiet
perseverance. Unseen power can move heavy
loads.

—*The I Ching (The Book of Changes)*

Despite the attempts of Ch'ang-an's monks to keep its
loss quiet, word of the missing finger-bone had spread.
Now, with the Festival only a night away, the capital had
erupted. The rumor was no longer a breath of wind. It was
a roaring fire, sweeping through the vast populace with
horrific fury.

Entering Ch'ang-an through the Wu-T'ai Gate, Rhea
stared about her with unbelieving eyes. She had rushed to
get there before sundown, when the giant gates would be
closed and the individual wards locked for the night. But
she need not have hurried. There was such chaos in the
streets, the harried and vastly outnumbered guards were
not even attempting to enforce the curfew. Those few
whom Rhea saw were standing ineffectually at their posts,

watching in seeming helplessness as one yelling mob after another ran past.

Her fear for Red Tiger increased a thousandfold, and she headed for a maze of tiny lanes that branched off from one of the main thoroughfares. As she sprinted down an alley, she heard a burst of screaming, sudden and ear shattering. Then, with horrible abruptness, it was cut off. Driven by instinct, she darted into the shadows of a closed shop. Seconds later a yelling mob poured through the narrow lane.

There were so many people, it took several minutes for them all to pass. A great number were armed with pieces of wood or large jagged rocks, and, squeezed far back into the shadows, Rhea took care to remain motionless. Never had she seen such uncontrolled rage. Merfolk would not act in such a manner for any reason. The sight of this mob violence was as unsettling as it was alien, leaving her aghast and filled with a cold, clutching dread. What if these wild-eyed creatures had found Red Tiger?

When the last of the furious voices had faded, she stepped cautiously from the shadows and continued down the lane. At the spot where it intersected with several other alleys, a bundle of rags lay on the rough cobblestones. Another would have passed it by, but Rhea, accustomed to detecting the slightest flicker of motion in dark ocean depths, saw the bundle move.

It was a man. His clothes were in tatters, and his body was so battered and beaten, it was almost impossible to recognize him as human. As she ran toward him, he struggled to lift his blood-soaked head, whispering, "Help me."

She knelt. "Who has done this to you?"

"Rioters." The man's voice was so weak, she had difficulty hearing him. "Thought I was Zhuhu that took finger-bone. I am Zhuhu, yes, but . . . not the one they want. They wouldn't listen. . . ."

"Hush," she said gently. "We must get you somewhere safe. Where do you live?"

Unhearing, the man struggled on. "Said my hair was same color as his, said I must die. Wasn't me, wasn't . . ."

The bruised eyes rolled back into his head, and the feeble voice rasped into silence. Gazing down at the dead man, Rhea shook her head incredulously. In no way did this unfortunate man resemble Red Tiger. His hair was not even red. It was brown, and a dark brown at that. Sea and Sky, what sort of madness had gripped these landfolk? Out of all this she understood only one thing: her premonition of danger was true. Red Tiger was in the greatest peril.

Rising to her feet, she walked rapidly away from the lifeless man. He was beyond her aid, and the stench of death would interfere with what she needed to do. Randomly choosing one of the winding lanes, she strode down it for several minutes before stopping. In the distance she could hear the hollow roar of the angry city, but here—at least for now—it was quiet.

Closing her eyes, she brought all the powers of her inner mind to bear, focusing them on a single image. Painstakingly she let herself sink into the deliberate blankness of *vision-seek*. As she did, Red Tiger's face began to form, feature by feature, on the black canvas before her closed eyes. Slowly the rest of him appeared. He was lying on a plain wooden bench, and clasped around his wrists and ankles were metal chains that sent off a dull gleam in the uncertain light.

Red Tiger was in prison.

Rhea's eyes jerked open. Incarceration was unknown in her world. However, she had studied this Terran concept before coming to the land, and she and Matteo had spoken about it.

Any person accused of a crime was immediately thrown into prison. Even if innocent, he was still guilty of having disturbed not only the tranquillity of the community, but that of the magistrates who oversaw the courts. Innocent bystanders, too, who were unlucky enough to have witnessed the committing of some crime could be imprisoned until their testimony was needed. Her brother had gone on to tell her of the starvation, torture, and mistreatment common in Middle Kingdom prisons.

And now Red Tiger was in one of those places. Pressing her palms against her eyes, Rhea forced the fogginess that was the usual consequence of vision-seek from her mind. The image of Red Tiger had faded, but a clear sense of where to find him remained. She shivered. From all that she had seen and heard this day, she had little time to do so.

"In death avoid hell, in life avoid prison."

It was a common proverb, and lying in chains upon the rough bench, Zhao repeated it to himself with an ironic twist of his mouth. He was the lone occupant of the tiny cell, a departure from the usual practice of crowding prisoners together and chaining them head to head and foot to foot, so that they lived and even died without any means of turning away from each other.

Zhao's isolation, though, had not been granted out of any sense of kindness. Rather, the runners at the imperial prison feared that the charges levied against him were so great, the other prisoners might, despite their chains, find a way to kill him before the proper punishment could be carried out.

That pleasure, the runners assured him, belonged to them. The senior runner had cheerfully clarified this after the guards of the Imperial Army of the Left, who had been waiting for Zhao in the monastery courtyard, arrested him, despite the outraged protests of Hui Jing.

"Now, if your family or your monastery pays us well enough," the senior runner had explained as he supervised the manacling of Zhao's ankles and wrists, "we will see to it that the torture used to extract your confession is relatively painless. And since you will likely receive the highest penalty of all, death by slow slicing, we will stab you in the heart right away so you won't suffer. For a price, of course."

"It is most kind of you to educate me," Zhao had said quietly. "But I am already familiar with how these matters are conducted."

Hours had passed since then, and Zhao was still completely alone. He frowned, then realizing that the tension in his face was communicating itself to all his muscles, deliberately relaxed. The dank cell was windowless, though a faint orange glow filtered through the bars on the door, coming from oil lamps set in niches along the walls outside. The prison had been locked for the night, and the stench of urine and excrement was stifling.

Breathing deeply and regularly, Zhao closed his eyes and lay still. Had any of the runners seen him, they would have been struck by the utter serenity on his face. And they would have been dumbfounded at what happened next. After several minutes, he drew a particularly long breath, exhaled deeply—and pulled his wrists from the manacles.

Quickly he sat up, reaching for the iron circlets around his ankles. With a steady, powerful pressure he pried each of them apart and slipped his legs loose.

Well-fed rats skittered across the filthy floor as Zhao crept to the barred door. In either direction the corridor outside was deserted. With the prisoners chained and helpless, there was little for the runners to do at night, and thus they were rarely about. Instead, they spent the long hours from dusk to dawn eating, drinking, gambling, and availing themselves of the bodies of those female prisoners who were attractive but lacked cash or influence.

Zhao concentrated once more on calling up the inner force known as *chi*. Bending his knees, he assumed the low "horse-riding" stance, the position from which one summoned power. Extending his arms and then drawing them in to match the rhythm of his breathing, he inhaled and exhaled until the veins in his arms stood out in ridges. Finally he reached out, grasped one of the iron bars in both hands, and pulled.

At first nothing happened. Then with a grinding rattle of iron against stone, the bar started to bend. The muscles and tendons in his whole upper body straining, Zhao pulled as the bar bent even more, then with a loud snap and a groan it popped out of the door.

He set it on the floor and listened to be sure the noises had not been heard. No runners came pounding toward his cell. Only coughing moans, weeping, and curses from the other prisoners greeted his ears. After a moment, he gripped a second bar and steadily levered it loose, then a third. Now there was an opening large enough for him to slip through. Soundlessly he eased out of the cell.

His footfalls noiseless as those of a cat, he padded off down the corridor. Earlier, when the guards had brought him to this huge dank jail, he had wasted neither time nor energy in struggle and protest. Instead he had paid close attention to the route his captors followed, and now that alertness stood him in good stead. He found his way quickly to the main doors of the prison.

Escape was going to be surprisingly easy, he realized, perhaps because the potential for it was so slim. The great doors that led into the imperial jail were locked and barred, but the outer walls contained windows, although they were tightly shuttered. Zhao swiftly paced along one wall, his strong fingers prying at each of the closed portals. He found a pair of shutters that had come loose, and smiling grimly, pulled them open.

"Red Tiger."

It was the merest wisp of sound, but he wheeled toward the shadows behind him. Honed by years of rigorous training, his reaction was instantaneous. Unthinkingly, he leapt at the figure that had stepped forth. The form seemed to melt aside at the very moment he recognized it. Hastily he brought himself up short, his feet finding the filthy floor with something less than his usual grace.

"Rhea!" His shock was so intense that for an instant he simply stared. Then a burst of anger, flavored by relief so profound it only made him angrier, overwhelmed him. "What in the name of all that is sacred are you *doing* here? I almost killed you!"

Her eyes aglow in the dimness with a light of their own, she stared back at him. She seemed as astonished to see him as he was her. "That is not very likely," she said, and before he could respond, added, "What are you doing out of your cell? I came to rescue you."

"Rescue me!" His anger gave way to exasperation. "It is you who are in need of rescuing. Shang Tian bear me witness, but you are the most troublesome female I have ever had the misfortune to be plagued with! I have been out of my mind with worry for you, yet here you are, turning up out of nowhere again. And at the most inconvenient time of all!"

Rhea let that pass. "How did you get out?"

"I might ask how *you* got in." Zhao drew a deep breath, schooling himself into a calmer state. As astounding and infuriating as Rhea's appearance was, this was no time for an argument. Too much was at stake. In control once more, he said tersely, "We'll save such questions for later, or else I may find myself back in a cell, and you along with me. Now come. Can you get through this window by yourself?"

She looked at him with what he could have sworn was condescension, then nodded, an abrupt and soldierly gesture. "Of course. It is how I entered this place."

Silently, one after the other, they maneuvered themselves through the narrow window. Outside, the night was humid and windy, the stars hidden behind the veil of clouds scudding across a pale moon. Surprisingly, no one had been set to guard the huge prison.

Just as Zhao turned to close the shutters behind them, a small door to their right banged open. They froze.

Illuminated by the lamplight from the room inside, a disheveled runner staggered out. He was clearly drunk. He stumbled twice, the second time falling full on his face.

"Hey, dog prick!" someone called impatiently from the room. "Lift your leg and get back in here. It's your turn at the dice."

"Ah, keep your balls on," the drunken one growled. "You don't want me to piss on the doorway like a stinky-stinky eunuch, do you?" Giggling a little, he struggled to his feet and lurched toward Rhea and Zhao.

Absolutely still, they watched him come. The shadows would offer concealment from his drink-befuddled gaze, so long as he did not stagger too near. But one step more,

Zhao told himself, and the man would have to be dealt with.

The runner stopped. Swaying unsteadily, he fumbled at his crotch. A moment later they heard the splatter of urine against the wall. Groaning with relief, the man emptied his bladder for what seemed like hours. Finally he tottered back into the room.

Zhao let out his breath, unaware until then that he had been holding it. "A close call," he muttered. "Let's get away from here before more runners come stumbling out to relieve themselves."

He led the way across the unlit grounds, and Rhea followed him. He, as well as this entire situation, had taken her by surprise—and not at all pleasantly. Not only did her help appear unnecessary, but Red Tiger seemed actually to resent her presence, as though she had done something wrong in coming to free him from that terrible place! Pensive and a little annoyed, she quickened her strides to catch up with him.

They had entered a grove of trees and were well screened from anyone who might come out of the prison. Zhao showed no inclination to slow his pace, though. Preoccupied, his expression grim, he strode ahead, apparently unaware that Rhea was even there. She spoke his name in a soft voice. When there was no response, she leapt lightly into the air, sprang past him, and landed facing him.

"We must talk," she said firmly.

Startled, Zhao halted in his tracks. "How did you— Never mind. You should not have come here. It is not safe for a lone woman to be abroad at night, especially on this night."

Rhea had heard enough. "It is not my safety that is at risk, Red Tiger," she said angrily. "It is yours."

His eyebrows drew together. "Now listen to me, Rhea.

I have no time to match wits with you or fall into the beguilement of your pretty stories. All I ask is that you tell me where you live so I can get you safely home."

"No. *You* listen to me, Red Tiger! This has nothing to do with pretty stories. I have traveled a long way to bring you this news, and whether you wish to or not, you're going to hear it. Your fate is of great concern to me, although by the Mother, I am beginning to wish it weren't!"

There was a brief silence as they glowered at each other. Then Zhao said in a gruff voice, "Very well, I am listening. But be quick."

Rhea obliged. Speaking concisely, she related all that she had seen and heard during this bewildering day. She did not say that two men had died by her hand, but she did describe the death of the unfortunate man the mob had mistaken for Red Tiger.

"So you see," she concluded, "the danger I saw surrounding you has become real. The people of this city have gone mad. If you are seen walking about, they will kill you, and all because of a finger-bone." She shook her head. "I must confess I don't understand any of it. What or who does this finger-bone belong to?"

"It belongs to the great Buddha." Zhao's tone was distracted, his gaze fixed upon the ground.

"Ah. One of your deities."

"Yes." He lifted his head, and she was stunned by the hatred and grief distorting his handsome face. "I suspected it right away, of course." His deep voice was hoarse. "But I did not know for certain. To do such a thing, to plunge this entire city into chaos, causing innocent people to suffer violent death, simply to get at me— It is an act of the utmost evil, even for him. And who knows how many more will die before it is over?"

Rhea gripped his arms. His muscles were iron hard

with tension. "Red Tiger, why does this Li Shan-po wish you harm? Hasn't he done enough to you already? I asked the men by the river, but . . ." She hesitated, then finished stiffly, "They would not tell me."

Zhao was not listening. "So his creatures were the ones who took the sacred relic." He turned to look at her, and even in the darkness his eyes blazed with emerald light. "Did they say where it was taken, Rhea? Did they give any hint at all where it might be?"

"No," she said with regret. "I heard nothing about that."

A thought roared into her mind, and suddenly uncomfortable, she looked away from him. What she was thinking was unheard of, so far beyond the bounds of propriety, she could scarcely believe it had even occurred to her.

Yet strange forces were alive this night, forces that had been set in motion from the first moment of her dreamwalk. They were taking on a strength of their own, and with a sense of inevitability, Rhea felt herself drawn toward a precipice, her fate unknown and inescapable.

Red Tiger's powers of observation were greater than she would have expected in a Terran. His keen eyes still fixed on her, he said quietly, "There is something else, isn't there?"

She did not answer. Instead, she squared her shoulders and took several steps away from him. Closing her eyes, she once again sent herself into the darkness of visionseek.

Zhao started after her, but as the uncertain moonlight shone upon her face, he stopped. Never in his life had he seen such an intense look of concentration, not even when Master Wu entered his daily meditations. It puzzled, even awed him, and he stood very still, watching but not interfering.

Despite the urgency driving him, he was gripped anew by the beauty of this woman who had come so inexplicably into his life. The loose-fitting gray tunic and pants she wore emphasized the winter-sea color of her eyes, closed now in mysterious deliberation. Even with her long hair tied carelessly back, she still reminded him of a piece of moonlight come to earth.

Without warning the yearning he felt for her returned full force. He wanted to touch her, to reach out and test the silkiness of that ebony hair, to take her in his arms and feel the pressure of her warm mouth once again. . . .

Rhea was unaware of his presence. The seeking took longer this time. She had no bond with this peculiar object, and so the task of finding it was considerably more difficult. Finally, though, she opened her eyes.

Accustomed to performing the process alone, she was disconcerted to find Red Tiger standing so close. She could feel the rhythm of his breathing, the strain and eagerness in him, as if he sensed something important had occurred. A sudden longing touched her, and she was uncertain whether it had come from him or her.

"It is done," she told him, feeling tired and drained. "I have seen where the finger-bone is being kept."

Perhaps the exhaustion she felt showed in her face. Zhao was studying her with such concern, he seemed ready to put his arms around her to keep her from falling down. The thought sent a sensual wave of anticipation through her, so sensual that she swayed toward him. Ill at ease, she quickly took a step back.

"This is impossible." His face still revealed concern, but mingled with it now was disbelief. "You told me you were a human woman. Only a supernatural being or an ascended master could accomplish such a feat."

Rhea tried to hold back her irritation, but short-tempered from the rigors of the vision-seek, she answered more sharply than she had intended. "My people are different from yours, Red Tiger. And they would not be pleased if they knew what I had done, for it goes against all our customs. Yet when I lay helpless upon that beach, you helped me. I have not forgotten that. Now I will help you in return. Shall we go?"

His gaze was steady upon her face as he plainly weighed the situation, and her. "No." His voice was decisive. "It is far too dangerous, and you have already risked yourself enough. If you indeed have knowledge of the relic's whereabouts, share it with me. Then I will get you home."

"I'll do no such thing," she said in a tone as decisive as his. "We will go together or not at all."

"In the name of all that is holy—" He clamped his lips shut and glared at her. "Very well, then! I won't stand here arguing with you about it. Take me to the finger-bone, Lady, if you truly know where it is. And hurry."

They loped through the trees in silence, Rhea leading the way toward the city and its eastern suburbs. Running along beside her, Zhao kept glancing at this enigmatic woman who seemed bent on haunting his life.

He was astonished at the pace she was setting, particularly because after the trance she had put herself into, she had seemed ready to fall down from weariness. The trance. What had she done to find the relic? Did she actually possess the power of a seer?

They were well away from the Imperial City now, following the high walls that enclosed the huge area where the majority of Ch'ang-an's populace lived and worked. This section of the city was quiet, eerily so. It worried Zhao, and unconsciously he lengthened his strides.

"Rhea," he said as they jogged across a patch of open

land. "How do you know where the sacred relic is? What powers are these—"

"Do not ask. It is enough that I have found it for you. More than that you do not need to know."

Her answer left Zhao far from satisfied. "Why do your people's customs forbid—" he began, then fell abruptly silent.

The ominous quiet of the plebeian city had ended. From over the walls a steady swell of roaring voices raced toward them, mingled with the pounding of thousands of feet as a massive mob ran through the windy night. Halting, Zhao and Rhea listened as the throng drew near. They could hear words. The crowd was shouting something over and over. Zhao stiffened as he made out what it was.

"To the Temple of the Peaceful Mind!" men were roaring. "Join us, join us! A corrupt abbot has hidden the sacred relic there. Join us, join us!"

Their cries meant nothing to Rhea. She knew the finger-bone was not where these crazed Terrans thought it was. But looking at Red Tiger's face, she realized he did not know that. "They are wrong," she said quickly. "The finger-bone is not where they think it is."

Still intent upon the screaming mob, he did not answer. She gripped his arm. "Red Tiger, what is it?"

Zhao's face was pale and set. "The abbot Hui Jing," he whispered. "They will kill him."

Chapter 9

Sun Tzu, the brilliant strategist, said: "To win a hundred victories is not the zenith of skill. To subdue the enemy without fighting is the zenith of skill."

—Kung Fu: History, Philosophy and Technique

"Who is Hui Jing?" Rhea asked Zhao.

Without answering, Zhao began trotting along the rampart. "I must get over this wall," he muttered, more to himself than to her.

Fearing for his safety, Rhea darted after him. "But who is Hui Jing?"

He halted, staring up at the wall. "Rhea—" Whirling around, he grabbed her hands, his grip warm and strong. "Wait for me here. I will try to return as quickly as possible. Take care to hide yourself from any crowds that might come this way, and if I do not return by sunup . . ."

He gazed into her face, releasing one hand so he could

stroke her cheek. For a moment she thought he would kiss her, despite the urgency she sensed within him. But he only brushed his thumb across her lips and murmured, "Just wait for me. And do not do anything foolish."

She started to protest, but he released her other hand and stepped away. Pressing his back against the rough stone wall, he drew a deep breath, then started moving up the steep rampart, propelled by the incredible strength of his heels and elbows alone.

Wall climbing, Rhea thought in amazement.

She had read about it in one of Matteo's scrolls, but she had never seen it done. In fact, neither had Matteo. He speculated that wall climbing, as well as the other secret Kung arts he had heard about, were no more than fanciful legends.

Yet here was Red Tiger proving Matteo wrong. Rhea watched in fascination as he slithered up the wall, traveling almost as effortlessly as an agile lizard and with surprising speed. Far more quickly than she would have expected, he reached the top of the wall and slipped over to the other side. If she intended following him, she suddenly realized, she had better act.

She gathered herself, took several steps backward, and leapt. The force of her spring carried her up to the wall's narrow lip, where she balanced for an instant as her eyes sought Red Tiger. He was already more than halfway down the wall, and as she watched, he leapt to the ground, nearly as gracefully as any merman.

So intent was he on following the mob, he did not at first notice her above him. As she readied herself to vault to the ground, some inner sense warned him. He looked up just in time to see her soar lightly off the wall.

She landed with noiseless feline grace, then walked toward him. The expression on his face was so incredulous, she wasn't sure whether to laugh or apologize. But the astounded look was swiftly replaced by one of severity.

"I will not ask how you learned Leaping Kung," he began.

She shook her head. "It is not—"

"At least for the moment," he went on. "But now I will have to pray that I am able to protect both you and the Reverend Abbot. Come with me if you must, but only if you can keep up. I must reach Hui Jing before that maddened mob does."

Keeping to the narrow side streets, they ran through a city teeming with shrieks and the flickering light of torches. All around them was chaos, but the raging voice of the throng bound for the Temple of the Peaceful Mind rose above it all, growing ever louder as more men flocked in response to its wild call.

Hampered by its very bulk, the mob's progress was slow, enabling Rhea and Zhao to reach the temple before it did. But stragglers had split off from the main force, and a group of about a dozen men had taken a shortcut through the winding lanes. As Zhao started to call out to the trembling monk in charge of the gates, a cry went up from the advance party.

"It's he!" a voice screeched. "The foreign *jushi* himself!"

Zhao and Rhea whipped around, and he gave her a firm push.

"Run, Rhea."

She ignored both the nudge and the terse command. "No."

"I said run!"

The rioters were surging toward them, their faces ghastly and distorted masks in the tossing light of their torches. In a single stride Zhao put himself in front of Rhea.

"Hold," he shouted in a ringing voice. "I have no wish to harm you. Please do not seek this violence."

He may as well have spoken to the wind. With incoherent yells the group plunged forward, and there was no time for anything but meeting its savage rush.

The confrontation lasted only minutes. Some of the rioters were armed with stones or clubs, but even so, they were no match for one trained in the art of Shaolin. Zhao dropped to the ground in the posture of "iron broom," and his legs shot out in powerful sweep kicks that knocked attackers from their feet as if they were blades of grass. Regaining his feet with a flying back flip, he sent several more opponents spinning with well-aimed kicks and punches. Yet even as he did so, he realized this clash was being resolved too easily. A quick glance behind him told him why.

Not only had Rhea disobeyed his order to leave, she was fighting, too, disposing of the rioters with an ease so flowing and effortless, it was almost insulting. He watched for only an astonished moment, before two men ran at him with upraised truncheons. Eluding their attack, which contained more fury than skill, he struck simultaneous backfisted blows that knocked both men unconscious.

He whirled, ready to confront whatever rioters remained. No one was left standing, though, save for himself and Rhea. She was not even out of breath, but was smiling with delight, her eyes glittering with excitement.

Rhea was exhilarated. This time she had conducted herself with far more care, and thus the Terrans had only been knocked senseless rather than killed. A thrill ran through her veins.

"Hah!" she exulted. "By the tides that carry me, these

men will regret starting this fight. When they finally awaken, that is."

The look Zhao gave her was long and measured. "Rejoicing in violence has never brought good to anyone," he said. "I wish it had not been necessary for either of us to use our skills here. And speaking of which, who taught you—"

"Youposai Red Tiger!" The monk at the gate was beckoning wildly. "Come inside, you and the woman. Hurry, hurry! The rest of this rabble approaches!"

Instantly Zhao's thoughts flew back to Hui Jing. He and Rhea ran to the entrance, past the fiercely grimacing door-gods painted on either side of the gates to protect the temple from evil.

"Where is the Dyhana Master?" Zhao demanded.

"Here in the temple, of course." The monk slammed and barred the gate with shaking hands. "He is leading prayers, asking Buddha to intercede in this madness that has infected the city. Now we must find you a safe hiding place—"

"No," Zhao said. "It is the Reverend Abbot who is in danger. The mob is screaming for him. You must take me to him before it is too late."

Compelled by the note of authority in Zhao's voice, the frightened monk did not argue. Even as he led them down the hallway, they heard the shouts of the first rioters as they reached the gates.

The three ran through an open courtyard toward the large Meditation Hall. The fifty odd monks of the temple were assembled in the hall, and when they entered, Hui Jing jumped off the dais reserved for the temple head. A joyful smile creased his round face as he hurried forward.

"Red Tiger! Buddha be thanked, you are free! How

was it managed? Did they listen to my protestations of your innocence at last?"

A splintering crash cracked the air. Though it was muted by the distance from the main gate, both Zhao and Rhea knew instantly what it was.

They looked at each other, and Zhao muttered, "So much for the protection of door-gods. They must have found a battering ram. Quick, Dyhana Master, there is no time to explain. We must get you out of here—"

A roaring sound boomed through the temple. Hearing it, Rhea was reminded of storm-whipped waves beating upon the sand. Around her, the apprehension of the monks was a palpable force. Yet there was a strange peace mingled with it, a calm that verged on complete acceptance of whatever was to come. A number of them surrounded the little abbot, who had stepped back up onto the dais, while others stood quietly, waiting.

"No!" Zhao shouted at them. "We must not let ourselves be trapped in this hall. If this crowd sets eyes upon the Dyhana Master, they will kill him!"

"Do not fear for me, boy," Hui Jing said. "The eyes of Buddha will protect us from the eyes of those who wish us harm. It is you who must flee from here. Quickly, my son, go!"

The thundering grew louder, punctuated with crashes and the splintering sound of breaking objects. The mob was storming through the temple. Now a chant could be heard, a single word bellowed with chilling regularity. "Kill! Kill! Kill!"

Rhea yanked on Zhao's sleeve. "Do these priests know how to fight?" she asked above the increasing clamor. "For despite your feelings about violence, they and you will have to, if we stay here a moment longer."

"They do not," he said in a voice thick with frustration. "Their sect does not teach the study of Shaolin."

"Sea and Sky!" she burst out. "Leave them to their fates then, if they are too foolish to see the danger hurtling down on their heads. You have done all you can!"

She gave his sleeve another tug. Bracing his feet, Zhao started to answer her, but the words never came.

The first wave of rioters rolled into the hall. Perhaps the retinue of assembled monks intimidated them, for their steps faltered and slowed, their shrieks died away in a confused babble. It was a fleeting lapse only. Propelled by its own momentum, the rest of the mob flooded in, and the time for escape was lost.

"Stop!" The deep voice thundered out over the heads of the throng with such wrath, such intensity, that the frenzied men were momentarily stilled.

Zhao was no longer beside Rhea, but had hurled himself up onto the dais. Towering over Hui Jing, he glared down at the rioters.

"How dare you!" he raged. "How dare you enter this temple and profane it with your hatred and destruction! You stand in the holiness of a Meditation Hall, frothing and snapping like a pack of rabid cur-dogs, screaming your thirst for the blood of those ordained in the service of the Great Buddha. And you have the effrontery to call *me* a barbarian!"

An uneasy muttering rumbled through the packed hall. To be confronted with such fearless outrage was not what these men had expected, and it left them confused—but still very dangerous. All around the hall they cast embarrassed glances at one another, yet they still brandished their crude weapons, menacing the tall man upon the dais.

Zhao was so caught up in his tirade, he did not seem to notice. Eyes blazing, he roared on.

"Is this how tomorrow's Festival is celebrated? By death and blasphemy? What madness has infected the citizens of Ch'ang-an? Murder is not a part of Buddhism, and neither is violence!"

"Then who beat those men outside the gates?" someone called out.

"I did!" Zhao's voice lost none of its power. "To fight in self-defense is very different from slaying innocent unarmed men. And any true follower of Buddhism knows that!"

"We know it, Barbarian!" another man shouted. "But the sacred finger-bone still remains stolen. What do *you* know of that?"

Rhea stiffened, her gaze sweeping the hall. That voice sounded familiar. Others were swiftly taking up his cry, threatening the tenuous control exerted by Zhao's sheer force of will. Rhea searched the packed room until she found the source of the familiar voice. He was standing near the doorway, the ragged man from the ferry.

Even before Zhao answered, she moved. With the fluid speed of the merfolk, she slipped through the crowd toward the ragged man.

"I know," Zhao called in a tone so strong and cold, it temporarily drowned out the hostile shouts, "that it was not I who took it. Nor is the Reverend Abbot of this temple hiding it."

His attention fixed on the dais, the ragged man was unaware of Rhea's approach until she grabbed his arm and jerked him around. When he saw her, his jaw dropped nearly to his chest.

"So." She fixed a cold gaze upon the man's terrified face. "Here you are spreading your cobwebs and moontalk once more. I think it is time you shared the truth of this matter."

Speechless, the man gaped at her. She smiled, a smile that was not intended to offer comfort and surely did not. Tightening her hold upon the Terran's skinny arm until his knees threatened to buckle, she raised her voice to its full strength.

"People of Ch'ang-an! If you are truly interested in knowing who took your sacred object, here is the one who can tell you."

A sea of astonished faces turned toward them. With inexorable strength, Rhea hauled her captive through a swell of questions, gestures, and exclamations until they reached the dais. Looking as surprised as anyone else, Hui Jing stared down at her. Next to him, Zhao frowned and started to speak.

She made a quick motion for him to be silent. "Tell them," she whispered to the ragged man, "or you will pray for the quick and painless death of your two companions by the river. Only you will not receive it."

It appeared that the threat would work. Trembling violently, the man tried to mumble something.

"Louder!" countless voices bellowed.

"The *jushi* did not—"

His courage failed him, and the man gulped. Abruptly his gaze was drawn back to Rhea's. There was a power in her silver-ice eyes, and compelled beyond his terror, words tumbled from his whitened lips.

"—did not take the sacred relic," he finished. "Neither he nor the abbot are responsible for its theft."

There was a stunned silence, then the hall erupted. It seemed that half the mob was screaming, "Who did take it?" while the other half shouted, "Why should we believe you?"

Looking at the mass of maddened men, Rhea reined in her disgust with an effort. The unaccustomed noise was painful to her sensitive ears, and her patience was growing short. She knew this sort of unbridled frenzy flared up among the landfolk often, but that did not make the witnessing of it any easier. Small wonder the Elders held them in such low regard, she thought. So far, Zhao Tamudj was the sole Terran she had encountered who demonstrated admirable qualities.

"Explain to these people why they should believe you," she said. Twisting the man's arm behind his back, she pushed him in front of her while Zhao called for silence.

"I know," the ragged man squeaked when the uproar had subsided, "because I am in the service of the one who arranged for the relic's theft, and it was not this *jushi* . . ."

Desperately he looked at Rhea, then at the ominously listening mob, and finally, off into the distance, as though something terrible awaited him there. But the implacable will burning in Rhea's eyes left him no choice.

"The noble Li Shan-po is behind everything that has happened," he said in a barely audible voice.

Rhea tightened her fingers. "Louder."

The man drew a gasping breath. "It was Li Shan-po!" he shrieked. "He planned it all. The finger-bone is hidden somewhere on his estate, and now that I have said so, my life is forfeit! I would rather die by my own hand than face him after this!"

He pulled a dagger from the waistband of his pants and slashed it across his throat.

Blood sprayed out in a scarlet fountain, splattering all who were within range. Men screamed, and those in front cried out in panic, lurching wildly back.

Because Rhea had been standing behind the man, the bulk of his blood missed her, although several thick droplets stained her sleeve. Shocked, filled with a strange mingling of revulsion and pity, she released the dying man's arm. A hideous noise bubbled out of his destroyed throat as he pitched forward. He shuddered once, half lifted an arm, and lay still.

A vast murmur of horror rippled through the hall. In a single flickering motion, scores of hands lifted in the sign of protection against the evil eye. Someone called out Buddha's name in supplication. Immediately the appeal was taken up, and within seconds the entire room was bathed in a wailing invocation of superstitious dread.

Zhao was quick to take advantage of the changed mood. "So now you call out to Buddha," he said, and though he was no longer shouting, the condemnation in his voice carried to the ears of every person in the great hall.

"After disgracing yourselves and everything that is sacred about the Way, you call out to Buddha. Yet you have invaded this temple and threatened to kill its abbot and me. Now you must bear the stains of this man's blood. He told the truth, else he would not have taken his life. But if your appetite for killing is still not satisfied, come ahead and slay me."

No eyes met his fierce gaze. Indeed, no one moved at all. Finally Hui Jing spoke.

"Go home, my children," he said gently. "Surely the madness of these last hours has been purged by the blood of this poor soul. Now we must all prepare to purify ourselves. As for the sacred relic, there is surely a reason that Li Shan-po has it. It will be returned to its proper place, my children. Have faith in that. But for now, go home."

His soft voice spread a balm over the room. Shamefaced, the mob shuffled from the hall. Rhea's keen ears, though, overheard the murmurs of many who said that Li Shan-po's estate should be converged upon and the noble made to give the relic back.

Zhao stepped down from the dais and lightly touched her shoulder. "Are you all right?"

She turned to him. The concern in his eyes warmed her. She was tired, burdened by the blood and madness of these strange people, and filled with a deep desire for the clean and limitless expanses of the sea. "Yes," she said quietly. "I am all right."

As if he sensed her need for greater comfort, he drew her into his arms. Not caring about the abbot and the monks around them, not even caring about the dead man at her feet, she allowed herself to lean against him, to share his warmth and strength. And amazingly some of her pain and weariness eased away, healed by his touch.

After a silent moment he moved back enough to see her face. His gaze was troubled and questioning. "How did you know he would confess?" He lowered his voice. "Rhea, what did you do to him?"

"It doesn't matter." She stepped away from Zhao, glancing at the dead man and the crimson pool that had spread out to surround him. A group of monks had gathered around the body. As she watched, some of them lifted up the limp form and carried it from the hall, while others began to clean up the gory mess. She looked at the bloodstains on her sleeve. "Red Tiger, the danger I saw—I do not think it is over yet."

"I know," he said somberly. "I know."

Chapter 10

"(Buddha) was of Barbarian origin. His language differed from Chinese speech; his clothes were of a different cut. . . . Let us suppose him to be living today, and that he came to court at the capital as an emissary of his country. Your Majesty would receive him courteously. But only one interview in the audience chamber . . . and he would be escorted under guard to the border that he might not mislead the masses. How much the less, now that he has long been dead, is it fitting that his decayed and rotten bone, his ill-omened and filthy remains should be allowed to enter in the forbidden precincts of the Palace?"

Memorial to the throne attacking Buddhism, written in 819 by Han Yu, a famous man of letters.

—*Ennin's Travels in T'ang China*

The finger-bone was returned in the darkest hours of the night.

Through his vast spy network, word had quickly reached Li Shan-po of the disastrous events at the Temple of the Peaceful Mind. Livid though he was, he had no choice but to replace the relic. He was black with rage, and not only because of the fiasco, the failure of the mob to kill both Zhao Tamadj and the fat abbot who had dared to intefere with Li Shan-po's careful machinations. He was furious, too, with the incompetent who had confessed the entire plot and then slit his own throat. A wise act on his part, but one which denied his master the small pleasure of personally dealing with the man's ineptness.

As carefully as he had plotted its removal, Li Shan-po engineered the relic's return. With the Festival set to begin in just hours, the monks at the Asoka Monastery were so relieved by the finger-bone's miraculous reappearance, they wasted little time in questions.

The sacred finger-bone was in its appointed place and the world was in harmony again. The mood of the city on the first day of the Festival was radically different from what it had been the night before, yet it was no less violent. Ironically, the danger was not to foreigners, but to the populace itself. The frenzy of the previous three days reached such a pitch, people began disfiguring themselves in a fever of joyful ecstasy, slashing at their faces or hacking off fingers—or even entire limbs—at temples all throughout the city, including the Temple of the Peaceful Mind.

These self-mutilations horrified Rhea, who along with Zhao had stayed on at the temple at the insistence of a grateful Hui Jing. Telling herself that such barbarity was to be expected, that it was the role of a Historian to observe these events calmly and without emotion, did little to ease her disgust. She had lost all objectivity, and for one simple reason.

In acknowledging, and deliberately strengthening, the bond between herself and Red Tiger, she had done more than just forge a link between the two of them. She had become part of his confusing and bloody world as well. To distance herself from his world was impossible. But she did need to understand through his eyes the things she saw around her.

"How can these people do such things to themselves?" she asked on the first day of the Festival. "Shedding their own blood, ripping away pieces of themselves. There is no sense to it."

Before a throng of screaming devotees, they had just watched two men sever their arms in front of the temple gates. Even Zhao seemed distressed as he tried to explain. "It is the way in which they show their religious devotion. In their fervor, they are driven to symbolize their love of the holy relic by creating it on their own persons as a sort of offering."

As he spoke, an uncharacteristic flush of embarrassment stained his cheeks. "Yet," he added, "many of the Buddhist faith, including myself, heartily disapprove of such extremes."

Rhea shot him a skeptical glance, then eyed the mass of chanting worshipers that lingered in front of the temple. The two injured men had been carried off, she noticed, probably to bleed to death. "If this is the measure of religion among the folk of land," she muttered, "then I have witnessed more than enough to satisfy my curiosity."

Zhao was contemplating her, his gaze probing and attentive. "But all religions have their excesses," he said, "unfortunate as that may be. Surely it is that way among your people."

"No," she said firmly. "It most certainly is not, and never will be."

He regarded her in silence. "There is much I still do not understand about you," he said at length. "But I do know that I have not, and probably never will, meet anyone like you again. One could sooner call a Ferghana steed from the imperial stables a cart horse than believe you are as other women."

For the first time that day, she smiled. "I assume that was meant as a compliment. At any rate, I shall take it as one."

He did not smile back. "If you are truly human, Rhea, then you must have a god or gods whom you pray to. *All* people worship in one way or another."

"Not all people." Her smile faded as she contemplated the events of the last few days. "My folk are as human as yours, but we have no need to prove it through bloody displays of violence and brutality. You are so preoccupied with my humanity, or lack of it, Red Tiger, yet the things I have seen in your land are far from what *I* consider human."

She fully expected him to take offense at her outburst, but he surprised her by looking ashamed. "Your criticisms have merit," he said, and sighed. "I'm not proud of the things that have taken place these last days. Obviously, you are new to the Middle Kingdom. I'm sorry your first impressions have not been better ones."

She stared at the pools of blood where the two worshipers' severed arms still lay. "I am too." She turned to face him. "But my low opinion does not extend to you. You have behaved as a brave and honorable person from the first moment I met you. Indeed, in many ways, you seem like a man of my own people."

He smiled. "Since you clearly mean to favor me by comparing me to your kin, I thank you."

"You should." The look she gave him was deep and serious. "It was not a thing lightly said."

He did not reply. Outside the temple gates, the crowds continued to scream out devotions, but inside the man and woman stood in silence, contemplating each other. Several moments passed until Zhao broke the strange quiet. His voice was soft, reflective.

"Are all the women of your people as beautiful as you?"

"I don't know." The odd question took her by surprise. "We do not examine ourselves to see if one of us is more beautiful than another. Why should we? What difference does it make, for men or for women?"

He seemed mystified by her answer, then amused. "My lovely Rhea," he said with a little chuckle. "It makes a great deal of difference. The attraction between men and women is as old as time."

"There is more to the bond created between a woman and a man than mere physical appearance, Red Tiger." She paused. "A great deal more."

He was watching her so closely, she wondered if this might be the moment to talk about her dream-walk and the meaning it held for both of them. But was he ready to hear of it? Even more important, was she ready to speak of it? She was relieved when he spoke instead.

"I understand there is more.

"The love shared by my mother and my father— blessed be his memory—went far beyond the fact that my mother was beautiful. My father admired her in other ways. He thought her wise and always encouraged her to speak her mind. Indeed, he sought her advice on just about everything, even matters of business—a habit which used to annoy the men of our family to no end." A bitter smile crossed his face. "They thought he was mad to seek the opinion of a woman."

The smile died, and his features turned hard as stone. "I often think it would have been better for us all if my mother had not been so beautiful. Then she would not have attracted the notice of Li Shan-po."

"Red Tiger!" Rhea was appalled. "A woman's beauty gives no man the right to violate her body. Do you blame your mother rather than the wicked man who raped her?"

Zhao's expression was equally appalled. "I would never blame her," he said indignantly. "That is not what I meant at all!"

"Good." Disturbed by her constant nearness to Red Tiger and her inability to decide what to do, Rhea plunged recklessly on. "My people may not devote themselves to strange manners of worship, but we do believe that there are certain constants in this world. Ancient Harmonies, we call them. One of the most sacred of those is the physical joining between a man and woman. It must be done with joy and willingness by *both*, or it is a crime against the great Mother force who gave birth to all life. The fact that your man-ruled societies no longer acknowledge Her presence makes it no less true!"

"Peace, Rhea." Zhao's indignation dissolved into thoughtful wonder. "Man-ruled societies? Mother force? What are you talking about?"

Rhea caught herself. "Nothing."

He stared at her, unconvinced. "I've never heard of these Ancient Harmonies, yet neither Buddhists nor Zhuhu would quarrel with you over the wrong of a woman being forced against her will. But what were these other—"

"I said they were nothing."

Zhao lapsed into surprised silence. Rhea could almost

feel the weight of his curiosity, but she refused to say anything more.

Myriad emotions roiled inside her. The more she witnessed of life upon the land, the more it depressed her. After what she had seen during these last days, she would have been happy to go back to the sea, were it not for Zhao. He compelled her to stay, this Terran man with eyes like the great cat he was named for, his hold on her as strong as the sea's. What in the name of Mother Ocean was she going to do?

She looked up as his long fingers, warm and callused, curled around hers. "Rhea." He spoke softly as he gazed at her with the searching look she had come to recognize. Despite the questions he so obviously wanted to ask, he said only, "The first processions of the Festival are approaching. Watch them, Lady, for they are truly glorious."

He was attempting to calm her, she realized, to let her know he would not press her any further, and she appreciated his gesture. Though her soul still felt bruised by all she had witnessed, and she craved solitude, she accompanied Zhao wherever he went throughout the Festival. Not only did she wish to see his world through his eyes, she could not be apart from him. Her very flesh ached whenever he was not near, and countless times she longed for him to hold her again. The slightest, most casual touch from him would send her blood racing through her, hot and urgent. Even though she knew a physical bonding between them would only worsen their already vexing plight, both her body and soul yearned for that intimacy. And if the piercing looks he gave her when he thought she wouldn't notice were any indication, he felt the same. As painful as it was to be with him and have him treat her as a sister, and as disturbed as she was by the sense that the danger to him had not yet passed, she was glad her promise to protect him allowed her to stay with him. She was not yet ready to leave him.

As the Festival drew to a close, Zhao lost all interest in the celebrations. He was outraged, instead. With the finger-bone's timely return, Li Shan-po's role in its loss seemed to have been forgotten, not only by the people of Ch'ang-an, but by the very monks from whom it had been taken.

"So they plan to ignore what has happened?" he exclaimed in Hui Jing's reception chamber the day after the Festival had ended. "Li Shan-po's role in this has been made only too clear!"

"Yes," Hui Jing said glumly. Seated upon a large *k'ang*, he lifted a bowl of *t'e*. "But the one who implicated him is dead, and believe me, no one else will dare to accuse him anew. The finger-bone is safely back, and there is no proof that Li Shan-po was ever involved."

"No proof?" Rhea stared at him, incredulous. "That man killed himself, so great was his fear of what Li Shan-po would do to him."

The abbot sipped from his bowl. "I know that, my child," he said. "But you and Red Tiger are young and therefore impatient. You do not understand these matters. Least of all, you do not understand how things work for one who is favored at court."

"Perhaps I don't." Rhea looked hard at the abbot. "But there is a natural order of life in the world. If you are saying that a person can offend against that natural order with impunity, then what you describe is corruption of the worst sort."

"It is indeed." Zhao's voice was tightly controlled. "The accuser may be dead, but *we* heard his words, and so did uncounted numbers of people. Do you mean to tell me the streets of Ch'ang-an are not buzzing with what those people heard? And saw?"

Hui Jing's expression was as weary as his voice. "The people of this city are exhausted. They are drained from days of rioting and the fervor of the Festival of Buddha's Birthday. It is over for this year. The people want only to get back to their shops, their market stalls, and their fields and forget any unpleasantness. After all, things did turn out well in the end."

"That may be so," Zhao said, "but what of the abbot at the Asoka Monastery? He surely will not let this pass. And what about you, Dyhana Master?" Although his tone was respectful, the look Zhao fixed on Hui Jing was piercing. "What do you intend to do?"

The abbot calmly returned Zhao's gaze. "Li Shan-po is a person of very high rank, my son. And persons of high rank, who are also in favor at court, have many special privileges, especially with regard to the law. Now I realize you are probably not familiar—"

"I am only too familiar." Zhao's voice was so harsh, the abbot blinked at him in surprise. "I have had occasion to see the law at work, Reverend Abbot, and while I know that someone of Li Shan-po's status is immune from *minor* offenses"—his lip curled in bitter derision—"I would have thought that a deed of this magnitude would override even his prestigious station."

"Well, it does not, at least not in this world. But you must take heart, Red Tiger, and remember your teachings. The world is an illusion. What happened these last days is an unfortunate part of that illusion, yet illusion nonetheless. Retribution awaits Li Shan-po for what he has done, although you will not see it. When his time upon this world is ended and his soul joins the wheel of life in order to be reborn again, then will he be called to account for the things he has done."

"I do not think," Zhao said, "that I care to wait that long."

Rhea moved restlessly on her soft cushion. *Keep silent,* she warned herself. This was neither the time nor the place to express her opinions. Losing her composure with Zhao because of the religious mutilations had been awkward enough. Angry as the abbot's passive view of the world made her, she would not repeat her mistake.

Hui Jing studied Zhao with both worry and speculation. "I think," he finally said, "that you should tell me what lies between you and Li Shan-po. Whatever it is, it is drawing you away from the Eightfold Path that prescribes the proper way of living for us all."

Zhao threw a quick glance at Rhea. "Dyhana Master, it would be dangerous to draw you into this any further."

"Nonsense." Hui Jing shifted his portly form with unconcealed annoyance. "How much further into this coil can I be drawn? Now I insist, my son. You must tell me what this is about."

Still Zhao hesitated, and Rhea murmured, "Perhaps you should, Red Tiger."

He glanced at her again. "Yes, perhaps I should. For even without knowing what is behind these events, Revered One, your life and the very existence of this temple has already been threatened."

And so, speaking in the same quiet, reserved voice he had used when telling Rhea, Zhao told Hui Jing of the Tamudj family tragedy.

The abbot seemed to have suspected something of this magnitude, as if nothing less could have created such outrage in Zhao. He listened intently, shaking his head now and then, an expression of compassion and grief on his face.

When the story was done, he sat for several moments, his head lowered. "Ah, this world is indeed a cruel dream," he said at last. "How apt are the Four Noble Truths in this case. You must hold them in your mind, Red Tiger. Life is suffering; the cause of suffering is desire; the end of suffering is freedom from desire; and only the Eightfold Path leads to the end of suffering." He sighed. "So that is why Master Wu took you under his wing. He knows all of this?"

Zhao nodded. "He does. I also believe that Li Shan-po ordered his spies to incite the attack on this temple as a punishment, because you came to the imperial monastery that morning and tried to warn me. Somehow he must have found out."

Hui Jing let out a disgusted grunt. "That is more than likely. What Li Shan-po does not know of at court is not worth knowing.

"However." He bent a stern gaze on Zhao. "Be that as it may, you must leave Ch'ang-an at once. And you must take Lady Rhea with you, for she, too, may be in danger. I will give you a letter asking Master Wu to give her sanctuary."

Rhea smiled and shook her head. "My thanks, Abbot, but you do not need to do that."

"What is the matter with you, girl?" Hui Jing asked testily. "Are you mad? As surely as the great Kumarajiva was able to swallow needles, so will Li Shan-po discover your part in making his man confess. Do you think one who wields a power so great you could warm your hands against it will ignore that? Even your family will not be able to protect you if you stay in Ch'ang-an. And speaking of your family, where are they? You have not said."

Before Rhea could answer, Zhao broke in. "As fortune would have it, Dyhana Master, she is from the south."

Dumbfounded, Rhea stared at him, and he met her gaze. His own was determined, but beneath that determination lay an apprehension so painful, her denial went unsaid.

"And I think you are right about our leaving as well," he went on. Though his words were directed at the abbot, he continued to look at Rhea. "That foul excuse of a man knows my mother is alive. At first I thought it did not matter, that he would seek to strike only at me. But he has tried twice, and both times he has failed. Now he may turn his evil toward my mother." His eyes were haunted. "She is all of my family that remains to me. Nothing must happen to her. Nothing."

"Of course," Hui Jing said understandingly. He thought a moment. "It will be most unorthodox for the Lady Rhea to travel without the chaperonage of a male relative, yet it cannot be helped. However, I can send along one of the temple brothers."

"No, Dyhana Master." Zhao was emphatic. "I will not allow anyone else to be drawn into this. It is enough that you and the Lady Rhea are at risk. Indeed, I fear Li Shan-po may not be done with you."

"Bah." Hui Jing dismissed the idea with a contemptuous wave. "When you leave Ch'ang-an, he will lose all interest in me. No, his threat is of a deeper sort."

"But not to me," Rhea said. She had absolutely no intention of allowing Zhao to leave without her, but Sea and Sky, she was tired of these two men arrogantly discussing her as though she possessed no will of her own!

"The decision of where I go and with whom," she said coolly, "is mine and mine alone." She let her gaze travel from the abbot's face to Zhao's. "Have I not proved by now that I am able to protect myself?"

Zhao met her eyes, and Hui Jing seemed to fade into insignificance. The memories of what they had gone through together quivered in the air between them. Looking at her with wonder and puzzlement and even an uneasiness at the strength he had witnessed, Zhao answered her question as though they were alone. "Yes, you have more than proved it."

"My dear Lady." Hui Jing's impatient voice sharply recalled them both to his presence. "You do not understand. I was not going to tell either of you this, but I see that I must. I have heard that since the Lady Rhea's performance at court the other night, Li Shan-po has been obsessed with her."

"We know about it," Zhao said shortly.

"Do you?" Hui Jing was taken aback by his curt tone. Uneasily he turned to Rhea. "You are a striking young woman, Lady Rhea. For a foreigner, that is. It is doubtless that word has already been carried to Li Shan-po that you are at this temple along with Red Tiger. I do not wish to see you fall into his hands. Li Shan-po's obsession with acquiring foreign concubines is known throughout the capital. His cruelty to them is equally notorious."

Staring at Zhao, his cheeks blushing with discomfort, Hui Jing plunged on. "Please forgive my speaking so plainly, but as the son of a woman who suffered those cruelties herself, you should know that better than anyone, Red Tiger."

Zhao's lips tightened, and his eyes were like shards of ice. Yet his voice was perfectly, almost too perfectly, calm. "Oh, I know it, Dyhana Master. You have said nothing about that one which I have not already had cause to learn."

His tone and expression shook Rhea. How dangerous he was! But how equally dangerous were the malevolent forces she still felt hovering around him.

Hui Jing rose from the *k'ang* with a rustle of saffron robes. Apparently he felt matters had been settled, for he said, "I will go and arrange provisions for your journey. Both of you should get some rest. Night will arrive quickly, and that is when you must leave. Li Shan-po's spies will be less likely to notice you then."

He acknowledged Zhao's respectful bow with one of his own, smiled at Rhea, and hurried from the chamber.

Left alone, Rhea and Zhao traded glances; then as if by some unspoken signal, they both rose. Zhao slowly walked toward her, and Rhea stood still, watching him.

"I would like to go with you," she said softly, when he had reached her. "But it may complicate things for you."

He shrugged and gently grasped her hands. His touch was warm and strong, quickening her blood and evoking in her the familiar longing to be alone with him. "Everything is complicated already. A little more at this point cannot matter."

"I see." She cocked her head, smiling suddenly. "Why did you lie to your abbot and tell him I am from the south?"

A rare grin lightened his own somber features. "But I did not lie, Lady. I found you on the beach beside the sea, and the sea is in the south."

Caught off guard, she stared at him. "It is," she said at last. "It is indeed."

As the drums announced the Hour of the Dragon, Emperor Wu-tsung paced restlessly through the Reception Hall of the Illustrious Celestials. The folds of his yellow satin robe whispered over the gold-tiled floor as he walked, and with each stride he impatiently kicked the robe out of the way.

Although the hall was agreeably cool, shaded from the heat of the morning sun by a large artificial hill covered with old pine trees and bamboo, the glorious fabric of his robe was too heavy for early summer. Wu-tsung had awakened that morning in a contrary mood. He had insisted on being dressed in the heavy court costume, despite his servants bringing out several more appropriate outfits in an attempt to persuade him otherwise. Now as he sweated under the thick robes, his mood grew increasingly sour. But he was too perverse to summon attendants with a change of clothes. Instead he paced, muttering and staring down at the scroll gripped in his damp hands.

When the carved doors opened to admit Ch'iu Shih-liang, Wu-tsung swung around and glowered. Grave and serene, the Chief Eunuch walked into the chamber and performed his kowtow.

"Oh, get up, get up," Wu-tsung ordered him. "Look here. Do you see what we have been reading?"

Getting to his feet, Ch'iu Shih-liang peered at the scroll. "Han Yu's memorial to the throne," he said. "The one which resulted in his banishment to the Shore of Pearls because it contained so vicious an attack upon Buddhism."

"Yes! And every word as true today as when he wrote it over thirty harvests ago. We tell you, Ch'iu Shih-liang, if *we* had been the Son of Heaven then, Han Yu would have been promoted, not banished. The truth is contained in this scroll."

Wu-tsung eyed the Chief Eunuch closely as he spoke. Along with a vast majority of eunuchs, Ch'iu Shih-liang was a devout Buddhist. Despite this, Ch'iu Shih-liang met his ruler's gaze without guile, and his voice was calm and unperturbed. "There are many in this world who claim to know the truth, Majesty. The trick lies in separating the gold from the dross."

"Ah, so now you speak of alchemy, which makes you sound more Taoist than Buddhist. Well, never mind. What is important is the reason this scroll was written. These— these outrages against filial sentiment!"

"You mean the self-mutilations."

"That is exactly what we mean. A person is to treat his body as a gift from the parents who gave it, and therefore him, life. But our people are bewitched by these foreign teachings. They have forgotten the word of Confucius and they deface their bodies, thus dishonoring their parents. As this eminently wise man said . . ."

His voice rising, Wu-tsung unrolled the scroll and read aloud. " 'They make the rounds of temples and cut off their arms and slice their flesh in the way of offerings.' " He closed the scroll with a snap and glared at Ch'iu Shih-liang. "It is utter and complete abomination!"

"Divine One," Ch'iu Shih-liang said gently, "you just participated in the Festival of Buddha's Birthday by welcoming the processions at the Imperial Gates. Indeed, you did so most graciously. I do not understand this royal change of heart."

"Come now, Old Eunuch, you know full well that we have had our reservations about foreign influences such as this one for a long time. But it was Li Shan-po's informing us of certain matters that set us to thinking. Last night that good noble and I drank wine and played our flutes beside the Pool of the Jeweled Maidens. We are very wise to have made Li Shan-po one of our most trusted advisers."

Wu-tsung paused, measuring the Chief Eunuch with unusual shrewdness. "Although we are well aware, old friend, that you do not share our opinion."

Early on in his long years of imperial service, Ch'iu Shih-liang had learned the value of limited honesty. He returned the Emperor's stare with great directness. "Let us say, Majesty, that it is not your wisdom I question, but his."

Wu-tsung digested this, then let out a bark of laughter. "Ah, Ch'iu Shih-liang, you are indeed a master of tact. However, we did not summon you here to bestow compliments upon you."

He resumed his pacing. "It has reached our ears that the rioting and mutilations in the name of Buddha this year were the worst since Han Yu wrote this ill-appreciated memorial. And the chaos that ravaged the plebeian Ch'ang-an, we are told, was caused by a foreigner, the Zhuhu *jushi* who healed Honored Mother, to be exact."

Ch'iu Shih-liang listened as the Emperor raged on, his expression carefully blank. Isolated within the Imperial City, Wu-tsung was no different from all the Sons of Heaven before him. Despite the absolute power an Emperor supposedly possessed, total despotism was an impractical concept.

Any ruler of the Middle Kingdom was totally dependent on the advice that came to him from those who acted as his eyes and ears outside the palace. Even if Wu-tsung were a stronger and less impressionable Son of Heaven, he still would be bound by the pressures of relatives and by the need to rely on well-informed ministers.

Of which Ch'iu Shih-liang was one.

"Divine One," the Chief Eunuch began. "You have heard only one version of these last days' events. Do not forget that I, too, have my sources. First of all, the *jushi* did not—"

The Emperor motioned angrily for silence. He had warmed to his subject and was determined to ignore anything that might interfere with the flames Li Shan-po had ignited within him the night before.

"Buddhism is an idolatrous religion," he declared. "Its ways are strange and contrary to both Confucianism and Taoism. Within recent times it has grown so powerful that now it corrupts the morals of the people, seducing their hearts and leading them astray.

"Our treasury cries out for copper in the making of cash coins, yet these Buddhists roll in wealth, adorning their temples with statues and bells of that valuable metal. The number of monks and nuns increases daily, robbing us of citizens who would otherwise be producing babies, crops, goods, and most of all, taxes to enrich the imperial coffers. Once they enter those religious communities, they give their allegiance not to the Son of Heaven, but to Buddha!"

Ch'iu Shih-liang smothered a sigh. The aroma of flowering jasmine in a large vase beside him teased his nostrils. Seeking to gather his thoughts, he absently contemplated their beauty.

Rare flowers demanding special attention were greatly sought after, and jasmine had become much the fashion. An extremely fragile plant, it was brought in pots from the provinces of Fukien and Kuang-tung. The most highly skilled and complicated treatment was required to produce its large flowers and make the plant last over the summer. Ch'iu Shih-liang knew he would have to be equally skilled if he wished to diffuse the Emperor's dangerous mood.

Adopting his most placating tone, he said, "Your Majesty has shown his wisdom once again. There are many venerable scholars who have voiced these very concerns."

"There has been too much talk. It is time now for measures to be taken."

The harshness in Wu-tsung's voice sent a wave of apprehension through the Chief Eunuch. "And what," he asked warily, "does the Divine One intend?"

Wu-tsung folded his arms. "This matter must be handled carefully, lest we arouse the masses. And Li Shan-po in his cleverness has shown us precisely how to do it."

Chapter 11

The Way is an abyss:
however you may use it, it needs no filling.
A gulf, Oh! Seemingly the ancestor of the
Myriad Creatures!
Fathomless, Oh! Seemingly it will endure.

—*Taoist Tales*

"What do you mean they have left?"

Li Shan-po jumped to his feet, unceremoniously dumping his yellow and white "lion cat"—a gift from the Emperor himself—out of his lap and onto the floor. He stared at the man who stood before him, his expression malevolent, alive with menace.

In surprising contrast to others who worked for the Spider, this man was not cowed, but steadfastly returned his master's gaze. He was an older man, although powerfully built, with the luxuriant side-whiskers, beard, and shoulder-length hair that was proudly sported by soldiers who had the distinction of being boxing champions. His wide-set eyes carried a look of grim cynicism, as if he had seen too much of life to let anyone, even Li Shan-po, intimidate him.

"I mean exactly what I have told you," he said in a gruff voice. "The two foreigners departed the capital last night. How they managed it is a mystery, since the wards were locked, the city gates closed, and the curfew in force. But they are gone."

Li Shan-po glowered. "Perhaps you are mistaken," he suggested in a tone of ominous threat. "Mistakes enough have been made during these last days to make that possibility more than likely."

"The mistakes have not been made by me," the other replied bluntly. "Last night they were in the temple, this morning they are not. It is as simple as that."

"Nothing in this world is ever simple, Strong Man. I should think that even an uneducated soldier like you, good for nothing save feats of strength in the West Market, would realize that."

Strong Man shrugged. "Insult me if you wish, the situation remains the same. The only question is what you want to do about it."

"To start"—there was a hiss in Li Shan-po's voice, like a poisonous snake coiled to strike—"I could lay a spell that would cause the flesh to peel from your body in tiny bleeding strips."

A rasping chuckle rumbled from Strong Man's barrel chest. "You could, indeed. But you will not and we both know it. I am too valuable to you, Master Li Shan-po. I am the only one in your service who does not turn to a trembling milk-faced girl at the very sight of you. And as for those flutter-flutter eunuchs who run at your heels stinking of their own piss because it drips out of a metal tube rather than a jade hammer." Strong Man spat with excellent aim and obvious contempt into a potted shrub. "They are utterly worthless."

"You are ignorant, Strong Man," Li Shan-po said coldly. "Brave but ignorant. All men have their uses, whether they possess their manhood or not."

He bent to caress the lion cat, who was rubbing herself against his legs. When he straightened, his face was blank, and that somehow made him appear far more dangerous than when he was angered.

"Now tell me," he continued, "since you consider yourself so valuable, where did they go?"

Another shrug of the broad shoulders. "I don't know," Strong Man said. "But give me a little time and I'll find out. One of the temple monks goes out every day to purchase fresh fish and vegetables. Persuading him to talk should not be difficult. Monks are feeble creatures at best."

"Not all monks. Those trained in Shaolin might give you a surprise or two. But that is beside the point." Li Shan-po studied the other man. "Once this monk has been persuaded, as you put it, he cannot be allowed to return to the temple to tell that fat bowl of congee they call an abbot what has happened. You realize that, don't you?"

"Of course I do." Strong Man looked disgusted. "After he spills his guts, I'll wring his neck." He smiled, showing a few gaps where teeth were missing. "I'll do it just the way the butchers ready a fat chicken or duck for the pot. He won't feel a thing, Master, believe me."

"It is of no concern to me what he feels. But you, Strong Man, what will you feel? Many would consider having the blood of a Buddhist priest on their hands a sin of no small consequence. If there is any chance you might turn faint-hearted, you had better say so. Now."

"Me? Faint-hearted?" Strong Man was outraged. "I

would kill a lesser man than you for even daring to suggest it! Look at me, Master. Is *this* the motto of a man who is faint-hearted about anything?"

He thrust his arms up in the air, allowing the loose sleeves of his tunic to fall back. Tattooed on the flesh of both burly arms a complicated device twisted: *Alive, I fear not the governor of the capital; dead, I fear not the king of the infernal regions.*

"There," Strong Man said proudly. "Thirty harvests have I challenged the power of Emperors, both in this world and in the Terrace of Night. Yet I continue to stand here unafraid. Of them or of you, Master Li Shan-po. I quail not at the doing of any deed, nor will I, as long as you continue to pay me as well as you have up until now."

"That," Li Shan-po said in a cool tone of dismissal, "will continue only so long as you continue to please me. And after this fiasco, I am not pleased, although I admit you are not as much at fault as others. For your sake, let it remain so."

Strong Man bowed perfunctorily and strode out of the villa's summer chamber, an underground room extravagantly cooled by ice rushed in from the western mountains. Li Shan-po watched as the brawny figure passed up the stone steps and into the cloudy light of morning. After a long moment, he seated himself once again on the black-lacquered chaise. His face, now that he was alone, was no longer impassive. It fairly smoked with rage.

The previous night's drinking bout with the Emperor had been largely successful, but for one thing. Wu-tsung had not rescinded his imperial edict concerning Zhao Tamudj. It was as frustrating as it was unexpected that this ruler, malleable in so many ways, had remained firm on this one subject.

Still, Li Shan-po had been able to steer the conversation in the direction of Buddhism and its excesses, and the fruits of the evening could be the downfall of that foreign religion.

Like many nobles and officials of a scholarly bent, he had long been offended by Buddhism, by its wealth and by the threat it represented to all things traditionally Han. And he was not alone in those feelings.

Since the harvest of 800, many of the Middle Kingdom's most famous scholars had advocated that the *tao*—the wisdom and truth of the ancients—had been corrupted by foreign intrusion. Only by returning to the purity of Han moral standards could it be regained.

For many seasons distrust of non-Han people had been growing steadily. Added to that was an increasing disapproval among educated classes of the insolent wealth of the Buddhist church, the power of the monks, and the close and secret ties those monks maintained with the imperial ladies and the court eunuchs.

This hostility toward Buddhism drew Li Shan-po more than anything else. The Buddhists had amassed entirely too much power. It interfered with Li Shan-po's own; therefore it must be destroyed. About the foreigners themselves, he cared little. Unless the foreigner in question was a beautiful silver-eyed woman. Or Zhao Tamudj.

The lion cat had returned to Li Shan-po's lap, and under his caressing hand, she lifted her head, purring loudly. He gazed down into the animal's eyes. They were a deep, brilliant green, exactly the shade of emeralds. Exactly the shade of Zhao Tamudj's eyes.

Zhao Tamudj, who, under the terms of that accursed imperial edict, would be able to travel freely, treated with honor and respect everywhere he went. And with him would be that foreign woman—whom his men had been unable to locate and who continued to obsess him.

Why was she with the Zhuhu? And how had they come to be together?

Li Shan-po had heard this woman was responsible for the forced confession of his spy in the Temple of the Peaceful Mind. He had also heard an exceedingly strange story of a sighting and then an actual confrontation with the Goddess Nü Kua. And the description of the goddess precisely matched the baffling black-haired creature with gray eyes.

Heat flooded Li Shan-po as he thought of her—heat and a devouring wave of hatred, as the image of her and Zhao Tamudj together rose in his mind. How dare the Zhuhu take this woman he had marked for himself?

That tall, lithe body belonged to *him*, yet the Zhuhu would surely take any opportunity to possess it. Any man would. And as a lay Buddhist, Tamudj had taken no priestly vows. He was not bound by a restriction of sexual abstinence.

By T'ien the Sky-god, oldest and greatest of all deities, he would crush Zhao Tamudj and this woman who mocked his attempts to find her.

Sharp pain slashed along his wrist as a spitting yowl pierced his ears. Lost in furious thoughts, he had tightened his hand with increasing viciousness on the lion cat's neck. The animal had finally twisted onto her back and was clawing furiously at him.

In surprise and pain, he jerked his hand away, allowing the cat to spring free. With a loud hiss, she streaked out of the room and disappeared into the garden.

Li Shan-po had already forgotten about her. Absently he nursed the bleeding scratches and stared out the high windows at an iron-gray sky.

He wished it had been Zhao Tamudj's neck he gripped so tightly.

"In the south go by boat, in the north take a horse."

"What did you say?" Rhea shook a strand of wet hair from her eyes and glanced over at Zhao in the quickening darkness.

"Nothing of importance. I was merely reminding myself of an ancient proverb about the best way to travel through the Middle Kingdom." He ran his hand along the sweaty neck of his horse. "We have done well today, but our animals need rest, and so do we. Anyway, it is ill-advised to travel these roads at night."

"Why?" Rhea frowned into the dusk. "It looks safe enough, and we will attract less attention at night."

"Yes, but there are gangs of bandits all through this countryside. They are particularly dangerous after dark. The lights of that inn beyond the trees look to be less than one li away. We will take shelter there."

Rhea nodded, turning the head of her mare to follow Zhao's horse. They had left the Temple of the Peaceful Mind the night before, slipping over the city walls and loping off through the darkness until they could stop and purchase horses at first light, the mare for Rhea and a strong gelding for Zhao. Attended by a light but penetrating and constant rain, they had ridden for hours, all through the day and into evening, stopping only for brief intervals to rest the horses.

The road they followed was impressive, paved with large even stones and lined with trees. It was so wide, Zhao had told Rhea during one of their rests, that three chariots could travel abreast. He called it the great Imperial Road, and explained that it led all the way to the seaport of Canton, the farthest southern point of the empire.

Now, as they walked their tired horses through the swiftly gathering shadows, Rhea caught Zhao studying her. "I think you have lied to me," he said. "I do not see how anyone who has never ridden a horse before could have traveled this day as you have."

She smiled. "I have only kept up with you."

"Yes, but I learned to ride almost before I could walk. My father—may his rest be ever peaceful—loved horses. He passed that love on to me and he taught me well."

It was the first time Rhea had heard Zhao speak of his father in such a reminiscent fashion. But she also caught the pain behind the remembering. "I love animals, too, as do all my people. There is a special kinship between my folk and them."

He was still watching her, and even in the rainy dusk she could see the questions in his eyes. Before he could speak, she asked one of her own. "Why was the abbot so upset when we left his temple?"

Zhao looked surprised. "So you noticed? He tried to keep it from you. It is only that he wanted us to take the water route south. While it is longer, it is also safer. But I would not do it. To find boat passage at this time of year would have been difficult, if not impossible, and Li Shan-po would have certainly learned of any inquiries we made."

The warm rain was falling with more force. Rhea parted her lips, letting the taste of it slip onto her tongue. As much as she was enjoying the novel sensation of riding a horse, she still missed the sea with a longing that was subtle but unceasing. Even the rivers would have been welcome, although boat travel was one thing she had no desire to experience. She sighed. There were so many differences between her people and Zhao's, and their means of travel was only the least of them.

By the time they reached the courtyard of the inn, the wind had risen, driving the rain into their faces. The lamps in the windows of the two-story building cast a glow that even Rhea, accustomed to all types of weather, found welcoming. As she and Zhao dismounted, the front door opened, spilling out a long square of yellow light. Framed in the flickering light of a small lantern, the innkeeper hurried out. He held the lantern up and peered at them.

"Who waits until darkness to seek shelter for the night?" His voice was heavy with suspicion. "Do you have cash to pay for lodging?"

Looking down at the innkeeper, Zhao drew himself up, emphasizing the difference in their heights. That difference was considerable, and from the look on his face, the innkeeper realized that.

Wrapped carefully in oiled cloth within his robes, the imperial edict lay against Zhao's chest. He was reluctant to use its awesome power, though. These were poor people. To force them to provide the best of their food and lodging without recompense was wrong. However, this innkeeper could certainly use a lesson in manners.

"If I were not able to pay," he said in a tone that brooked no dissent, "we would not have stopped here. Now, we have had a long day and are tired. I wish you to see to the horses first. Rub them down well and give them a good feed. Then ready lodgings for us. I assume this amount will be sufficient."

He drew a string of cash, one of the many pressed on him by a worried Hui Jing, from the belt at his waist and tossed it to the man.

At the sight of the money, the innkeeper's attitude underwent a startling change. "Of course, of course," he exclaimed, bowing deeply. "You and the lady are most welcome at my humble establishment. Please do me the honor of going inside. My wife will prepare a meal for you while I stable the horses. I will care for these fine animals as if they were my own!"

He bowed again, beckoning them toward the open door with one hand as he gathered the reins of the horses with the other.

Bobbing up and down in welcome, a short woman whose pleasant face was prematurely lined from hard work and harsh weather came forward as Rhea and Zhao entered the inn's smoky lower room. Having never been to an inn before, Rhea glanced around with interest. A charcoal cooking fire smoldered in one corner, and most of the room was taken up by a long table and wooden benches. The floor was packed dirt, and off to one side she saw a rickety staircase that led to the second floor. Undoubtably that was where the guests stayed.

"A very good evening to you," the woman said. Unlike her husband's, her cheerful smile was genuine. "How weary you both must be, especially the poor lady. Having to travel on such a night! Sit, sit, my dears, and I will bring you soup, then some nice hot millet with salt fish."

Rhea smiled her thanks, and Zhao said, "I have already given cash to your husband. If the food is extra—"

"Chut!" The woman gave him a shocked look. "To take money from a holy man? What can my husband be thinking of? I will make sure he returns it to you immediately!"

"That will not be necessary," Zhao told her. "We would like to pay you for your trouble. And I am not a holy man."

"You're a *jushi*," the woman replied stoutly. "It is the same thing. To have you in our poor inn is honor enough. Accepting cash would be a sin. Particularly after what has happened."

Zhao and Rhea exchanged glances. "And what has happened?" Zhao asked. A cold feeling rose up from the pit of his stomach, a chill that was mirrored in Rhea's suddenly dark eyes.

The woman shook her head as she carried two steaming bowls of soup to the rough table. "Tragedy and misfortune, that is what. Ill omens are about to fall upon the Divine Land. Mark my words. Where have you been that you have not heard of it?"

"We have been traveling since before dawn," Rhea explained. "We have spoken with no one."

"Ah, that explains it then. Actually, we would not know of it either had not a purveyor of concubines arrived early this evening from the capital." The woman glanced at Rhea. "He is on his way to Suchow to purchase a new crop of slave girls, so you should keep your . . ."

Without a moment's hesitation, Zhao said, "This is my cousin. I am taking her to relatives in Yangzhou. Now, what is this misfortune you speak of?"

Satisfied, the woman nodded. "Of course. As for this misfortune . . ." She pulled at her thin hair in unconscious distress. "The Emperor, holy be his name, dismissed forty of his court priests just this morning. And that is only the beginning. It is said that he plans to dismiss more."

"Forty Buddhist monks of the imperial court?" Zhao stared at the woman in disbelief. "Why would he do such a thing?"

Shaking her head, the innkeeper's wife turned to the cooking fire, where a large pot of millet bubbled. "I am only a woman," she said apologetically, "but it seems to me that this Son of Heaven does not revere Buddhism as his predecessors did. Since he ascended to the Dragon Throne a year ago, my husband and I have heard much talk from those who pass through our inn on their way from the capital."

She stirred the grain as she poured a dark brown sauce and a small amount of oil into a scarred heavy wok that was heating over the fire. "This Emperor is a Taoist, and all know that Taoists are jealous of the glory of Buddha. Well, it has long been whispered in the capital that the Divine One is becoming more enamored of the Taoists in his court. And as his love for them grows, so does his contempt for our holy priests."

Kneeling beside the wok, the woman added pieces of fish to the spitting oil. "Now things are growing worse. Even a stupid woman can see that this may be just the beginning."

Still on her knees, she turned around to face them. "The dealer in concubines has it on good authority, he says. From one of the eunuchs in the Great Luminous Palace itself. Right before the Emperor dismissed the priests, one of his most favored and highly ranked noblemen petitioned the throne to have all monks and nuns in the land regulated."

"Regulated?" Rhea gave her a puzzled look. "What is that?"

Zhao answered. "It means they will be examined, and their sacred vows possibly revoked, which could lead to them being forced to leave their monasteries or nunneries." He stared down at his soup, then lifted his gaze to the innkeeper's wife. "The nobleman who petitioned for this regulation. Did the concubine dealer mention his name?"

The woman had gotten to her feet and was bustling around, fetching wooden chopsticks and filling two ceramic bowls with heaping portions of millet and fish. "Why, yes he did," she said nervously. She paused, and Zhao and Rhea saw her shudder. "There is no one who does not know of him," she whispered. "For his powers in the Dark Arts are supposed to be very great. It was the noble Li Shan-po."

Chapter 12

These are divine persons dwelling there,
whose flesh and skin resembles ice and
snow, soft and delicate like sequestered girl-
children; they do not eat the five cereals;
they suck the wind and drink the dew; they
mount on clouds and vapors and drive the
flying dragons—thus they rove beyond the
four seas.

—*Book of Chuang Tzu:*
Immortal Sisters

The scent of sandalwood hung heavy in the air, mingling
with the fragrance of the million or more alpine flowers
that had recently burst into bloom, covering the slopes and
summits of the holy Five Terraces of Mount Wu-t'ai like
a far-flung tapestry.

The smell was as overpowering as incense, and clung
to Matteo's clothes with the persistence of perfume. His
footsteps slow and thoughtful, he walked along the pilgrim

trail that wound around the terraces and past dozens of small stone pagodas. Other pilgrims walked ahead or behind him. Occasionally one of them smiled and nodded at Matteo, but gripped by a deep sense of reverential awe for this holy place, few of them spoke.

At the broad level summit of the Central Terrace, Matteo stopped to gaze out below him. As with the view from the other four terraces, the panorama was magnificent. The mountains of the Wu-t'ai region stretched out in unending miles, with birds circling far below and the sound of flowing waters rising from the unseen floors of deep ravines and profound valleys.

In the middle of the Central Terrace stood a pool of crystal-clear water, shallow but about forty feet wide. A perfectly round island reposed in the center of the pool, and on it stood a small but ornate edifice called the Dragon Hall. Matteo gazed at the building for a few moments, then stepped into the icy water and waded out to it.

As he reached the island, a thin voice floated out to him from inside the hall. "Good morning, and may Buddha's blessings be upon you. I am pleased that you have come back."

"Thank you," Matteo called in return. "May you be similarly blessed. I wished to see you again," he added as he entered the quiet sanctuary.

As with many of the more intimate buildings constructed by Terrans, he had to duck his head as he went inside. The Dragon Hall consisted of one large room filled with sacred images. The central one was a magnificent jeweled statue of the ancient Dragon King of Mount Wut'ai. On either side of him, mounted upon white jade lions, stood equally glorious representations of Monju, the legendary Bodhisattva who had conquered the Dragon King.

"But you are planning to leave the Five Terraces," said the reedy voice as Matteo walked toward the shadowy figure at the back of the hall.

"Yes."

"I shall miss your visits, although having companionship and being without it are two sides of the same circle. Thus they are essentially the same."

Matteo smiled. "Are they?"

The emaciated monk who sat in the corner smiled back. "I have found our discussions most illuminating. It is unusual to encounter a foreigner and a nonbeliever who is so learned."

"I have enjoyed our talks as well." There was sadness in Matteo's voice and eyes as he gazed at the monk, who was rapidly becoming a living skeleton. "However, I have come not only to bid you farewell, but to ask one last time if you will cease this strange course you have embarked upon."

"I cannot. As I told you before, I have taken a vow."

"Vows can be broken, Brother I-yüan." Matteo's mouth twisted cynically. "It happens constantly. In the Middle Kingdom, and everywhere else upon the land."

"Yes, but not here. These terraces are the holiest places in all the world. How will I be reborn if I fail in my task to achieve oneness?"

Matteo strove to keep the irritation from his voice. "You will not achieve oneness by limiting yourself to eating dirt and mud once a day, Brother." He sighed and tried again. "You are an intelligent and perceptive man, one of the few I have met in my travels here. It will be a loss to your world if you starve yourself to death over some peculiar notion of faith."

"My world, Matteo? Is it not your world as well? And who is to say what is peculiar and what is not?"

"This is not a question of esoterics. Refusing rice and millet or any other food for three harvests, insisting that you will be able to subsist on dirt instead, is peculiar. And there are worlds within worlds, Brother I-yüan, far beyond what our eyes may perceive."

"Ah," the monk said in serene triumph. "Then you have made my point for me. For it is the world which is not of the body that I seek. Earthly concerns such as food will only interfere with my seeking."

"And what else," Matteo snapped, "is mud and dirt but earth?"

I-yüan merely smiled, and Matteo shook his head. It was hopeless, he thought. These Terrans were the most illogical beings, even those like I-yüan who showed signs of being more evolved.

Memories of all the Terran lives he had taken during his time with the Amazons suddenly welled up in the merman, bringing with them the sight and the smell of their blood upon his hands. Of course that was the very reason the Elders had sent him back to the land. Being among Terrans was not only a form of penance, it was also a way to ease those memories by relearning the compassion for life which the love of killing had robbed him of.

Matteo had reluctantly come to see that the Elders were right. There was much about the Terran Buddhists that even he could admire. The sincere ones were gentle souls, filled with kindness and concern for all life. I-yüan was such a one, which made his deliberate journey toward death all the more tragic.

"As long as you are forcing me to stay on the subject of worldly matters," the gaunt monk said, "I will tell you that I have had disturbing news this morning from my successor at the Monastery of the Golden Balcony."

"Oh?" Matteo seated himself on a carved stone bench and waited for I-yüan to go on.

"The new abbot tells me he has received word that the imperial emissary is not going to make his annual trip to the Wu-t'ai monasteries. This has never happened before."

"These visits are very important then?"

I-yüan nodded. "They are a sign of imperial favor. Every harvest, shortly after the Festival of Buddha's Birthday, an emissary is sent to the twelve great monasteries of the mountain. With him he brings the same gifts."

The monk closed his eyes and recited from memory. "Five hundred fine robes, five hundred packages of silk floss, one thousand lengths of cloth dyed blue-green for Buddhist scarves, one thousand ounces of incense, one thousand ounces of tea, and one thousand hand cloths. He also brings one thousand bushels of rice and millet and other provisions for the monasteries. Finally, he hosts a great maigre feast for all the monks and nuns before returning to the capital."

"And this year he is not going to come," Matteo said thoughtfully. "Does anyone among you know why?"

I-yüan's eyes opened. The look in them was haunted and far away. "Evil times are coming to the faithful, evil times, indeed. But these are not your concern, my son. There are other matters that cry out for your attention."

"Truly?" Matteo's tone was sharp. "And how would you know that?"

"You are planning to return to Ch'ang-an." The monk's voice became strangely disembodied, as if it were coming from somewhere outside his body. "Do not go. Travel south instead, to seek your sister."

There was a long silence in the chilly stone hall.

"I never mentioned that I have a sister," Matteo said at last.

I-yüan seemed not to have heard him. "You say that your world is distant from the Middle Kingdom. But it is even more distant than you would have me believe. My meditations have shown me this. The planes of enlightenment I seek so desperately, you in many ways have already attained. How easily you walk upon paths of wisdom I can only yearn for.

"And yet we all seek something in this life. What you seek is a healing, and you will not find it here. You must go south . . ."

The weak voice trailed away, and staring at the monk in amazement, Matteo finished for him. "To find my sister."

I-yüan's eyes, huge in that wasted face, fixed themselves upon him. "Yes. For she is one of the keys to your healing, although it is beyond my understanding how. Go find that healing, my son. Without it, you will never be whole."

The eyes closed. "I am through speaking for today," he whispered. "Farewell. May Buddha watch over you."

Deep in thought, Matteo emerged from the little hall. Outside, the temperature had lowered drastically. The weather had changed once again, turning cold with the threat of one of the oncoming storms that commonly tore through the region.

Clouds were massing in the valleys to the east. Now purple, now white, they swirled upward as thunder rumbled so loudly, the very mountain shook. The rain had already started elsewhere on the terraces. Matteo caught glimpses of several dozen pilgrim monks walking down a path, their straw hats smashed by hail, their saffron robes soaked, but their serene composure unruffled.

Still lost in ruminations over what I-yüan had said, Matteo ignored the courteous nods the monks gave as they passed. He had often heard that the gift of seeing was vouchsafed to a few Terrans, but until that day, he had never encountered one with the true gift. Generally, when closely examined, their abilities were found to be sham, and often poorly done sham at that.

Not this emaciated monk, though. Despite his bizarre determination to starve himself to death, he possessed an authentic ability, the true gift. Had he been born with it, or was it a result of his physically deprived state? Either way, Matteo thought, when I-yüan died the gift would die with him. How sad, and how utterly wasteful.

With a thundering roar, as if dragons actually did inhabit the mountain, the storm struck, drenching Matteo almost instantly. But while the other pilgrims ran for the dubious shelter of trees or the ubiquitous stone pagodas, he walked on unheeding.

Since leaving Ch'ang-an, he had tried to put Rhea from his mind, for he was still angry with her. She was stubborn, intransigent, set upon a course that was as unnatural as it was disastrous. And she was his only sister. Every time he thought of her, new fury overwhelmed him, a fury borne of fear and love, and of utter frustration at his helplessness to save her from what had befallen him. Why couldn't she see that only evil would ever come of getting involved with landfolk?

And there was something else. I-yüan had told him to look for his sister in the south. The day before, acting on impulse, he had used telepathy to see if Rhea was still in Ch'ang-an. To his surprise and wary relief, he had found no trace of her in the city. But had she returned to the sea? He could use his powers to search for her further, but what if the Elders, who were highly attuned to such things, picked up on the fact that he was seeking her? A great many questions would be asked.

He thought of his sister's dream-walk and her preoccupation with the red-haired Terran. She had told him the Terran's home lay in the south. So did the sea.

The path wound down from the summit, and he strode past the Sacred Platform, past the magnificent and wealthy Monastery of the Golden Balcony. Near its gates the imperial highway beckoned. Taken one way, it would lead him back to Ch'ang-an. Taken the other, it would bring him to the southern lands of the Middle Kingdom, lands which those in the north considered uncivilized and savage, more like a frontier than part of the empire.

Matteo stood for a long time considering. The rain had stopped and the sun was struggling to part the clouds, warming him with its brief, pale light. It quickly lost the battle and was once more blanketed by massive cloud banks as another storm started to form.

By then Matteo had begun walking again.

To the south.

Sleepless, Rhea lay on the flat, hard bed of rush matting, her mind filled with thoughts of Red Tiger. Four days had passed since they had left the inn with its avaricious owner and his talkative wife. That inn had been replaced by others, for there were a great many inns, as well as the smaller post stations, along the route of their journey.

The country was changing, turning from the arid yellow of the north to the lush green of the south, and much to their surprise, it seemed that Li Shan-po had not sent men to follow them. At least not yet.

The long days of travel were strengthening the ties that

had sprung between them in Ch'ang-an, cementing those tenuous strands into something immutable and beyond tearing. But it was still a disturbing intimacy, as unsettling as it was intense. Neither of them knew what to make of the other and their strong attraction, yet they could not keep apart.

A dozen times each day Zhao found some excuse to touch Rhea, a quick brush of his hand across hers, a light press of her arm, a gentle stroking of her windblown hair, all of it done in an offhand manner, as if keeping any physical contact casual would diffuse its intensity. It did not. For him or for her.

A storm of feeling smoldered behind those nonchalant touches, simmering just underneath the surface of the long conversations they held as they rode, thigh often grazing thigh. In many ways, this closeness was tentative, often awkward, marked by the enormous differences that lay between their worlds. And because of those differences, their talks often turned to arguments, particularly about women.

"Why are you men so afraid," Rhea burst out on the third day, "that you must constantly strive to convince females that they are incapable of doing any of the things a male can?"

Zhao was taken aback by her vehemence, but his beliefs were too powerful to allow such a radical statement to go unchallenged. "It is not a question of fear," he retorted with equal vehemence. "You yourself spoke of a natural order in life to the Abbot Hui Jing. It exists in nature, as it does among mankind. Surely you cannot argue that even among the animals, males are always the superior creature, larger and stronger than the females of their kind."

"Pah." Rhea did not try to hide her contempt. "The

natural order I described has nothing to do with treating women as though they have no minds. And as for nature, I could show you many examples of the female being superior to the male. What about your own philosophy of yin and yang? Yin represents the female force and yang the male, and for the world to remain in harmony, both those forces must be in balance."

Zhao half turned in the saddle, gazing at her in surprise. "Yes," he said after a moment. "They do."

"And," she continued, pressing her point, "one force is regarded as being no better than the other, isn't it?"

He nodded. "That also is true." A slow smile lit his eyes. "Do you know"—he sounded thoughtful and oddly pleased—"you are a most interesting person, Rhea. You give me a great deal to think about. I find it . . . stimulating."

She laughed. "I can say the same of you, Red Tiger. And you are most unusual yourself. At least you listen and try to understand, whereas I suspect other men would fly into a wild rage at the barest mention of what I've said."

Her mare suddenly jostled against his horse, and she felt a leap of heat, all out of proportion to the quick brush of her leg on his. Her laughter died away. He continued looking at her, but he was no longer smiling either. As she stared back at him, his gaze dropped to her mouth before he quickly glanced away.

They had not kissed again since the morning in the garden of the Official Monastery. The memory danced between them constantly, an unrelenting reminder of how easy it would be to repeat that kiss. And of how much they both wanted to.

Yet they did not. Without it being said, each knew that another kiss would rush them to the edge of a cliff neither of them, for very different reasons, was ready to tumble over.

In the inns they stopped at each evening, Zhao always arranged for separate rooms. And in those rooms, no matter how tiring the day had been, their sleep was restless, haunted by dreams that brought them awake all through the long night. In the morning, neither spoke of it. They rode steadily south, tangled in a web of anticipation and unvoiced desires that enfolded them more tightly with each passing day.

Rhea's situation was made no easier by the fact that, curious as she was about Zhao, he was even more curious about her. He asked a great many questions. She soon tired of her evasive answers, but each time she readied herself to tell him the truth, something held her back. Was it fear of his reaction? she wondered. Or fear of the irrevocable nature of such a step? Whatever the reason, she did not tell him. Eventually she realized that the only reason he did not press her harder was because he was as preoccupied as she.

They talked of other things instead, searching for topics that would ease the magnetic tension pulling them so determinedly toward each other.

That day she had asked him about his red hair and green eyes, saying that she had seen no one else in this land who possessed similar coloring.

He had touched his head in an unconscious gesture. "Yes, that is true. It is why the monks gave me the name Red Tiger. However, my mother says that such coloring has appeared among my people from time to time, as far back as when they lived in our homeland of Yisroel."

Rhea then asked him about the desert land from which his ancestors had come. In Zhao's eyes the migration of the Zhuhu to the Middle Kingdom was an event of great antiquity, and he knew little about the former home of his people. Clearly he considered himself more Han than Zhuhu, and when she mentioned that, he nodded in agreement.

"Much to my mother's displeasure, I'm afraid. Now that I am a man, she wishes me to leave the monastery and join the Zhuhu in Yangzhou, become a merchant and marry a Zhuhu maiden."

He paused, and Rhea was surprised that he looked almost ashamed. "I know that as a filial son I should honor my mother's wishes, but—"

"Why?"

"Why?" His shamed look vanished, and he stared at her with amazement. "A son must always respect his parents' desires. The same is true for a daughter. How can you ask such a question?"

"People should follow whatever life paths bring them happiness and contentment," she said quietly. "If you wish to stay in the monastery and your mother wishes you to become a merchant, why don't you do both?"

His expression became even more incredulous. "That would be impossible. One cannot dedicate his life to the Way and in the same breath become a merchant. He must do one or the other!"

Troubled, Rhea turned away. *Spoken like a true man of the land,* she thought resignedly. And no matter how much she might wish it were different, that was precisely what he was.

To her, the idea of a person being restricted to doing only one thing throughout his whole life was outrageous. But Terran life spans were so short, there was little time for them to perfect more than one skill.

Frowning, she pushed that thought away. She refused to consider that even if he survived Li Shan-po and whatever other dangers facing him, Red Tiger's life would still be as regrettably brief as any other Terran's.

"Among my . . . family," she finally said, "one may do many things if he or she chooses."

"Is that so?" Zhao eyed her closely. "Well, I think your family must be strange indeed, to allow such things."

"I suppose to you they would be." Pain stabbed through her as the huge gulf that lay between them loomed up anew. "But no more than yours are to me," she muttered.

Recalling those conversations now, Rhea moved her head restlessly upon the narrow pillow of plaited rush. Her room was the best this particular inn had to offer, another result of the plentiful strings of cash Hui Jing had given them. Zhao had been adamant that she occupy it, saying he would be content with the one next door. The chief attraction of the chamber was its large wooden bed, enclosed on three sides by partitions hung with paintings.

The bed's luxury was lost upon Rhea though. The partitions and the silk floss curtains that hung inside them to give the sleeper privacy, only made her feel stifled. She had pushed the curtains apart, but the partitions still confined her. The vast sea with its limitless, rocking swells, was where she was accustomed to sleeping, not in these cramped little cubicles.

At last she threw the light coverlet aside and climbed from the bed. Despite it being so late, the air was warm and humid, an unmistakable sign that they had entered the southern regions.

At least it was a clear night, the first Rhea had seen since they'd left Ch'ang-an. She rested her elbows on the sill of the room's one window and gazed out at the moon. Three-quarters full, it hung in the soft black sky, lighting the paved courtyard and the trees beyond with a deep orange brilliance. Beside the inn the Imperial Road meandered off like a dark ribbon, and in the distance she could hear the rushing murmur of one of the many tributaries that would eventually flow into the mighty Long River. The water's music echoed the familiar yearning inside her to be in her own world, filling her with a compulsion impossible to ignore.

Pacing to the door, she laid her hand on the knob before remembering she was naked. Muttering under her breath, she returned to the rumpled bed. Carelessly she threw the coverlet around her shoulders, then slipped out of the chamber. There was no sound in the adjoining room as she crept down the stairs. Tired from the long day, Zhao must surely be asleep.

Outside, the night air carried the odor of water, and she breathed it in gratefully. In the shadow of the attached stable, the two tailless dogs kept to warn off intruders lifted their heads. They lowered them again as she spoke several murmurous words to them, then walked past them toward the river. One of them whined deep in his throat as he watched her go.

Lit with silver, the tributary ran beneath the moon and stars, heading for the majestic Long River like a child racing to her mother. Standing on the shore, Rhea smiled to see it. Deep joy filled her. This small flow of water was a poor substitute for the ocean, but it would do. Oh, it would do.

She swam for a long time, then floated on the river's surface, letting the currents carry her where they would while she gazed at the moon. Heaving a sigh of regret, she finally rolled off her back and slipped beneath the water, undulating with slow reluctance back along the river's course to where she had left the coverlet. As her head broke through the surface, her eyes widened.

A man was standing by the tangle of cloth thrown carelessly on the grass.

Zhao.

Chapter 13

Let us now lock the double door with its
golden lock,
And light the lamp to fill our room with
brilliance,
I shed my robes and remove my paint and
powder,
And roll out the picture scroll by the side
of the pillow,
No joy shall equal the delights of this first
night,
These shall never be forgotten, however old
we may grow.

—Chang Heng, A.D. 100

He stood motionless as Rhea emerged from the river. He
was clad only in his loose-fitting trousers, and the powerful muscles of his naked chest and shoulders were moon
dappled and glowing in the silver-orange night. Even from

a distance she could feel the intensity of his gaze. He did not speak, and neither did she.

She glided toward him. The still air coated her wet body, thick and hot after the rushing coolness of the river, its heaviness making her wish she had never left the water.

He suddenly moved forward, his steps swift and noiseless on the grass. In three strides he was in front of her. Reaching out, he placed his hands upon her shoulders.

She halted, paralyzed by his touch, by the warmth of his broad hands on her bare skin. She stared up at him, into eyes that were black in the shadowy moonlight.

"Red Tiger—" she began.

"Hush." He laid a gentle finger across her lips. Then he lowered his head and kissed her.

Rhea stood motionless. It had come at last, the moment she had shied away from and yet wanted so desperately. Zhao's following her was inevitable. She knew that now. As inevitable as the promise held within his lips. His kiss was filled with such a sense of release, a fire storm ignited along her nerve ends in response, sending her reeling with pleasure.

His mouth swiftly grew demanding, and his arms rose to curve around her, pulling her to him with gentle but unmistakable determination. His body was iron hard against hers. His chest, bristling with hair, pressed into her breasts with a rough tickle that felt strange to her, for merfolk had little body hair.

Sheer sensation overwhelmed her, loosing a deep and sudden need that went oceans beyond caution, reason, or even physical desire. Scarcely before she realized it, her mouth had parted under his and she was kissing him back, fiercely, her hands running over the smooth, hard planes of his back.

Melded together, they slipped to the grass. His long

fingers teased her breasts, circling and stroking, then sliding down over her ribs to her firm, flat belly.

Zhao felt as though hours had passed since the watchdog's low whine had awakened him. Ever a light sleeper, and especially so during this journey, he had come out of his fitful slumber instantly, every sense wary and alert. But not until he had patrolled the outside of the inn several times, had he finally gone down to the river.

And there had been Rhea, emerging from its depths, as naked as that morning twelve harvests ago. The moon had shone down on her sleek, wet form, turning the water droplets cloaking her into a thousand glittering jewels.

In that moment, the world beyond this small patch of river and shore had ceased to exist. Hatred, retribution, the need for discipline and control, all vanished in the overwhelming desire that roared over him with the force of a hurricane.

She was magic, this glimmering woman, sent either to enchant him or drive him to madness. But goddess or ghost, it no longer mattered. Nothing mattered but seeking the mysteries that lay behind her beautiful and enigmatic eyes.

The feel of her in his arms dizzied him. He had never thought a woman's body could contain the muscled strength of a man's. The female adept who had first instructed him in the Tao of Loving, and who had later claimed in delight that the student had surpassed the teacher, had been a soft, perfumed creature. Rhea, too, was soft, but only in the satin of her skin. The muscles beneath that skin were as hard as his own. And her perfume was uniquely hers, an intoxicating blend of sun-swept breezes, shaded grottoes, and the clean scent of running water.

He rolled that strong, taut body beneath him, gripping

her tightly, and the festering wound he had carried since the death of his family was eased.

Rhea welcomed the pressure of his lean, powerful frame with a low cry. She opened her eyes, and without warning the ethereal boundaries that separate dreams from reality blurred and lost their sharpness. His face looking down at her, his expression, his eyes blazing with passion, all were an exact replica of the vision of Zhao's face that had haunted her dream-walk.

Waves of doubt swamped Rhea, as intense as her desire. Anguish raged through her, borne of the unavoidable, unanswerable questions raised by an impossible future. The wonder of their loving was marred with futility, and instinctively she drew back, already aching with the loss of this bonding that could never truly be.

Misunderstanding her reaction, Zhao paused. Driven by the fire of his need, he could not bear the thought of pulling back from her. But she must be willing. If not, the yin of woman and the yang of man could never achieve harmony.

Lowering his head to hers, he caressed her with lips that were light as air, his tongue voyaging into her mouth with tender skill. At the same time his fingers embarked on their own erotic journey along the soft crevices of her jade gate.

Her hips surged against his hand, a low moan vibrating from her mouth to his. As her Tide of Yin dampened his fingers, Zhao struggled to maintain control, so that they would both attain the highest pinnacles of delight. He entered her with one slow deep thrust, and she cried out again, murmuring words in that strange language that carried the sound of running water in it.

They were in harmony. Deeply satisfied and wildly aroused, Zhao began the ancient rhythm of A Thousand

Loving Thrusts, tantalizing Rhea with the method of nine shallow and one deep. She accepted his thrusts and greedily asked for more until they moved as one being, fused by passion and the eroticism of their growing excitement and thirst for each other. But beneath those extraneous sensations was a deeper yearning, a hunger that touched them with a tenderness so exquisite, it was almost like pain.

The moment of climax came. Engulfed by pleasure, Rhea crossed her legs over Zhao's back, lifting her body so powerfully that a weaker man might actually have been dislodged. She cried out again, this time without words, and his voice joined hers. Clutching her to him, he met her upward thrusts with a driving force that toppled both of them over the edge.

The surges of blissful satisfaction and release seemed to go on forever, but at last they lay satiated and at peace.

Drifting back from the pool of contentment that lapped her body, Rhea became aware once more of the sounds of the night—the rushing song of the river, the wind's whisper as it rustled through the trees, the small sounds of night creatures as they crept through the shadows. The rhythm of Zhao's heart beneath her cheek was deep and steady, and when she lifted her head to look at him, she saw that his eyes were open and he was watching her.

"You are a great surprise," she said softly.

"Oh?" The corners of his mouth lifted in a faint smile. "And why is that?"

"Your experience in pleasure making. It was quite . . . unexpected. I had heard that in the monasteries such physical joining is forbidden."

"It is." He caressed the curve of her throat with light fingers, but in his voice she heard a touch of sadness. "The Buddhists, however, are not truly my people, a fact

my mother never fails to remind me of. Zhuhu do not pro-
hibit sexual congress. Indeed, they consider it a blessed
act, for it leads to children, which are very important
among them—us."

"Yes, children are important to my people as well.
But . . ." She drew a finger through the mat of hair on his
broad chest and smiled. "You were still a surprise. Who
taught you so well?"

Teeth glinting in the darkness, he smiled back. "My
mother."

"Truly? Is that a custom?"

Shock rippled across his face, then was quickly followed by a laugh, the first true laugh she had ever heard
from him. "No, no, not in *that* way. When I was nineteen
she grew very concerned, for most Zhuhu men have mar-
ried and even fathered children by then. But in devoting
myself to my studies in the monastery, I had little interest
in such things."

Despite the shifting night shadows, Rhea could see
how serious his face had become. "My poor mother," he
went on quietly. "It's been very difficult for her. She holds
the highest respect and gratitude for the temple monks, yet
she's greatly troubled. She thinks she has failed in bringing me up within the traditions of her people. So she requested that I go to a Taoist adept who would teach me the
joys of love. It was an attempt on her part to draw me
away from the monastery and into the outer world. She
hoped that once I discovered physical pleasure, I would be
willing to meet marriageable girls from among the Zhuhu
community in Yangzhou."

Rhea was fascinated. "And were you?"

He gave her a strange, piercing look. "No, else I would
not be here with you. Faithfulness to one's spouse is a ba-
sic tenet of the sinew-plucking religion." Abruptly he

switched the conversation to her. "Is it not that way with you?"

Rhea did not reply.

The enchantment of moon and water was fading, leaving her to face once again the significance of what had occurred between her and Zhao.

It was not uncommon for merfolk to make love to Terrans, but the coupling was always superficial. For the landman or -woman involved, it was a fantasy encounter with a glorious and anonymous lover, who then disappeared, never to be seen again. For Rhea the pairing with Zhao had been matebonding of the purest and most ancient sort.

He was not the first man she had known in pleasure. There was Tinat, her closest heart-friend, and later her lover. They had shared many adventures as youths, and as they'd grown to man- and womanhood, they had taught each other pleasure, learning how to give and take love while drifting on the undulating waves or lying together far beneath the surface in caves only the merfolk knew of.

The anguish of Tinat's death—taken unawares by white sharks during the trance of his dream-walk, one of the rare moments when a merperson was vulnerable—had left a gaping wound in her that had not and might never completely heal.

As close as she and Tinat had been, though, they'd known they were not destined to be mates. Although she had never entered into that sacred pact, Rhea possessed an inherited knowledge of the compelling force that came to life when two who had chosen each other made love for the first time. She had not experienced that with Tinat, but with Zhao. . . . Ah, how different it had been. And how she had gloried in the power of it!

Now, as the impact of what had passed between them

struck her with all its force, she was sure of only one thing: she would have to tell him the truth. She could avoid it no longer.

"We do not have a marriage custom as you do," she said carefully. "But we do choose one person to join with. It is called matebonding, and once done, it lasts for life." She did not mention that a matebonding had just occurred, for she didn't have the least idea what would come of it.

Zhao scowled at her words. "And what about you, Rhea? Have you been chosen by someone in this—this mating?"

"Me?" His tone, more than his question, startled her. "No. But when the time arrives, Red Tiger, it will be my choice as much as the man's. Among my folk, *both* people do the choosing."

The expression on his face was one she'd grown quite used to, a blending of disapproval and astonishment, with relief mingled in this time. He moved her off his chest and rolled onto his side.

"Women are allowed to participate in such an important matter as that?" His tone was openly skeptical. "My beautiful Rhea, you continually astound me with your unusual customs. I can scarcely believe such a thing, even among your peculiar clan. No female is capable of making those types of decisions. That is the province of her male kin; only they can judge what is best, both for her and the family."

Rhea drew in a deep, calming breath. "The ways of my people were ancient long before the Middle Kingdom ever came into being. Our beliefs have always worked well for us, and one of the reasons is because we realize that a woman's reasoning power is just as great as a man's."

She fixed him with a stern look. "There was even a time in the very, very ancient past when women ruled instead of men. And not just in rare exceptions, as in the case of the Empress Wu several hundred of your harvests ago, but all the time!"

With Rhea lying on her stomach and Zhao resting on his side, their faces were on the same level. They stared at each other for a moment, then a deep chuckle rumbled out of Zhao.

"Nonsense," he said, grinning. "That is the most utter and complete foolishness I have ever heard. Women ruling instead of men." The chuckle turned into a full-blown laugh. "What madness!"

She shook her head. "It is the truth. My people are extremely old, Red Tiger."

A somber note in her voice stopped his laughter. He looked at her with fresh speculation. "And what of you, Rhea? Are you also very old?"

She did not answer. The gulf that separated their worlds seemed to have widened, becoming as vast and unfathomable as the ocean itself. It left her with a pain so profound, she wished she could wail her anguish and frustration to the skies.

"There is so much I haven't told you," she said softly.

"About yourself?"

"Yes."

"Tell me then." Laying a gentle hand on her cheek, he turned her face to his. "There shouldn't be any secrets between us, Rhea. Not now."

Putting her hand over his, she drew a breath. "My people do not live upon the land as yours do. We never have."

His gaze remained intent upon her face. "If your people do not live upon the land, then ... where do they live?"

Only silence answered him as Rhea looked away. The words she had hoped would spring easily to her tongue seemed destined to remain stuck in her throat. There was no precedent, nothing to guide her in this step she was taking. She would have to muddle through it as best she could, trusting Zhao and the bond that pulsed so strongly between them.

"In the sea," she finally said. "After you saw me enter the water that morning, I went to my home, a place that lies far beneath the waves. My people live in the sea, just as yours live on the land."

There it was, out at last. She heaved a deep sigh of relief and waited for Zhao's reaction.

He said nothing. His hand tightened around hers, but he remained silent. Indeed, from the expression on his face, it seemed he might never speak again. Then he abruptly found his voice. "In the sea? I—That makes no sense Rhea. Surely you mean your people live near the sea, or on it, in boats perhaps?"

She turned to him. "No, Red Tiger, that is not what I mean. I swam away that morning, and I know you stood on the beach watching me go. Where do you think I could have gone? I headed straight out to sea, and there were no boats about anywhere, were there?"

He stared at her without answering.

"You said there should be no secrets between us, and you are right." The need to make him believe her surged through her, and a hint of desperation crept into her voice. "Think of all the things you find so odd about me: my ideas, my strength, the way I have come and gone so mysteriously, the—the fact that I seem no older than the day you came upon me on the beach. You have often said that

I am unlike any woman you have ever known. Well, you could not guess how close you were to the truth. There are similarities between you of the land and us, especially with regard to physical appearance. But there are great differences as well."

He slowly pulled his hand from hers and sat up. In the pale moonlight his stunned expression was painfully obvious to Rhea. "So." His voice was hoarse. "You are a supernatural being, after all. A creature of magic, as I first thought."

"No!" She sat up too. "I have certain abilities, yes, but I am human, Red Tiger, and so are my people. Although—" She paused, suddenly seeing this through *his* eyes. Through the link that bound them together, she felt what he felt—uncertainty, shock, the superstitions he had been raised with, and most surprising of all, anger.

This last emotion caught her unprepared. Better that than fear, she told herself resignedly, and finished in a quiet tone, "I suppose we would seem supernatural to you."

"Why didn't you tell me this before?" His anger broke loose, throbbing fiercely in his voice. "*Why* did you deceive me and keep the truth from me? Why?"

Rhea kept her own voice calm. "Because I feared you might react exactly as you have, with anger and fear and superstition. Believe me, Red Tiger, my people would not approve of my speaking to you of these things. It has long been our custom to keep our existence a secret from Terrans. Your race is too violent and too fearful of what it does not understand."

Rather than placating him, her words seemed to further infuriate him. "Then why violate your customs and reveal yourself to me? After all, I belong to this race you speak so ill of!"

"Yes." She suddenly felt very weary. "You do, indeed. But too much has happened between us for me to keep the truth from you any longer. You are no ordinary man, Red Tiger. If you were, I would not have told you any of this, much less shared love with you as we did."

At the reminder of their lovemaking his face changed. Wordlessly he rose to his feet and walked to the edge of the river, staring out over the star-shadowed waters, his back to her.

She watched him, but said nothing more. It was up to him now, either to accept her or flee from her. Yet it was right to have shared this knowledge. Despite the heavy pounding of her heart, she took comfort from that. Though Zhao didn't know it, he was the compelling force that had imbued her dream-walk and shaped her present life. Who more than he had a right to hear of her true origins?

Long minutes passed, and still the tall naked man who had given her such pleasure remained motionless. The moon was beginning to set, its light fading into the blackness that portended the night's darkest hour. Suddenly Rhea could not bear it any longer. She had to look at his face, to see if he felt hatred, fear, or something else entirely.

She rose, lithe and noiseless, but at her first step, he swung around. She froze at the expression on his face. Then he was in front of her, his hands—disconcertingly cool in contrast to the heat burning in his eyes—running up and down her bare arms.

"I do not care what you are." His voice vibrated with an emotion she could not name. "Do you hear? *I do not care.* No one knows the face of evil better than I, and I feel in my very soul that you are not evil. As for the rest, be what you will. You have set a fire in my blood that I cannot be rid of. No spirit . . ." His hands went to her breasts, and involuntarily she gasped, her breasts jutting forward as if in eagerness to fill his palms. "No spirit could feel like this. You have stood beside me, taken on my battles as your own, risked your life to save mine, and yet you give me no peace. No peace . . ."

His voice trailed off as his lips found hers in a kiss that was bruising and tender and searching. A cry of joy trembled deep inside Rhea. Giving herself up to this happiness so rare and so unexpected, and so yearned for, she threw her arms around him. They both fell to the grass.

Later, hand in hand, they walked back to the inn. The sky was a deep purplish black, though the first tinges of gray were already appearing in the east.

Zhao studied Rhea's silhouette in the faint light. "What do you call yourselves?" he asked.

Still lost in the music of the river and the haze of pleasure, Rhea started at his question. "Merfolk," she answered. "Or the sea people. But merfolk is probably the most common."

"And—there truly are more of you?"

"Of course." She smiled at him. "Not as many as you who live upon the land perhaps, but enough. And we have mothers and fathers and sisters and brothers, just as your people do."

His eyes clouded as he tried to imagine this. "Do you all live in the sea, then?"

"Most of us."

"I see." His tone was one of awe mixed with fascination. "It seems scarcely possible." He pondered this a moment. "So you, Rhea, have parents and sisters and brothers as well?"

"Only an older brother named Matteo." She smiled wryly. "Who would not be at all pleased to see us together."

Zhao was shocked. "You mean your brother Ma-Matteo"—he stumbled over the unfamiliar name—"is also here in the Middle Kingdom?"

Envisioning Matteo listening to this conversation, Rhea sighed. "Yes. Actually, he has spent a great deal of time here, and elsewhere upon the world of land as well."

"He has?" Zhao looked thunderstruck. "In the name of Heaven, why?"

"Sending merfolk to the land has always been our custom. We like to keep track of Terran doings, a wise precaution given your bloodthirsty nature."

Zhao seemed about to argue, then thought better of it. "This brother of yours," he said tentatively. "He sounds harsh. And with a low opinion of us."

"How right you are. And his low opinion extends to me also."

The sadness in her voice struck a painful chord deep within Zhao. "Why do you say that? Is there trouble between you?" Before she could answer, he went on. "You mustn't allow it to continue, Rhea. I don't know how things are with these people of yours, but nothing is more important in life than loyalty to one's family. I have lost all of mine, save for my beloved mother, and know that better than any. What did you do to estrange your brother from you?"

"You don't understand." She tightened her hand around his. "There is great love between Matteo and me. We are my parents' only children, and as younglings, we were very close."

She looked past the river, its waters dull now that the moon and stars were gone, out over this wide sealess world of Zhao's. To a Terran much of it would still be lying in darkness, but to her sensitive eyes the outlines of trees and fields were already plain.

"Merfolk children, especially girls, do not grow up as they do here, Red Tiger. All of the Mother's oceans are our home, and we roam Her waters freely, learning Her secrets from mothers and fathers and older friends and kin. For me, Matteo was many things: teacher, playmate, brother, and friend. If he is displeased with me now, it arises out of the deep love and concern he holds for me."

They walked on for several minutes in silence. Zhao was obviously deep in thought. "You still have not answered my question," he finally said.

She nodded. "Purposely, I'm afraid. You see, I came to the land only recently, and I have allowed myself to become drawn into the lives of Terrans, yours in particular. The Elders of my people will not be pleased. We're not supposed to do such things, much less reveal our origins."

Despite the wilting heat, she shivered, her mind taken over once more by the dream-walk and its unrelenting message of the link between her and this man, a link that seemed doomed to lead them to misery and loss. For how could Zhao follow her to the sea, or how could she stay upon the land, watching him rapidly age while she remained virtually unchanged?

However, she had done this of her own will, Rhea reminded herself, with her eyes wide open. She could have listened to Matteo and fled back to the sea, but she hadn't. Now she must bear the consequences instead of mewling like a newborn seal.

Zhao was watching her. "Do you know, Rhea," he said, his tone both thoughtful and angry, "since we met, you have had a great deal to say about the inferior and shameful conduct of us ... Terrans. Yet listening to you speak of your own kin, it seems merfolk are a critical and unforgiving people, a people who lack tolerance and love for their fellow creatures."

"That is not so!" Rhea caught herself. In some ways it *was* so, though not without good cause. "I realize it must seem that way to you," she admitted. "But only because you know so little about my ancient folk, and so very little about your own. We of the sea were an ancient and highly learned race long before the Zhuhu *were* the Zhuhu, or the Han the Han. It is because of our great age that we seem intolerant. After watching countless civilizations arise upon the land only to fall in death and destruction, many of my people—and my brother is among them—have a very jaded view of yours."

"Why don't you share that view?" he asked. "Especially since it would make things easier between yourself, your brother, and your Elders if you did?"

"There are reasons." Rhea hated the evasiveness in her voice. Yet all her instincts warned against talking about the dream-walk now. Zhao had accepted so much already. How much more could he hear before his Terran sensibilities took over in earnest, driving him away from her, perhaps for good?

Carefully she tried to explain. "We have spoken of so much tonight that I don't think this is the time to go into my reasons. Let's just say that I've done what I've done because you are more important to me than the approval of my kin." His gaze was hot upon her face as she said this, but she steadfastly refused to look at him.

"That is no answer. By the Sky-god, woman, I thought the secrets were over. Why do you put me off now?"

She sighed. "I do not mean to, Red Tiger. But aren't things difficult enough as it is?"

He let go of her hand and stared hard at her. He looked stern, as if he intended to push for a response. But then he lifted his arm and encircled her shoulders, pulling her gently to him.

"Yes," he said, and let out a small sigh of his own. "Things are indeed difficult enough as it is. I shall not press you, Rhea. For now."

If the innkeeper noticed that his two guests had apparently spent more of the night together than they had apart, he made no mention of it. He was a dour sort, strongly of the opinion that with rooms already paid for, whatever his guests did afterward was none of his business.

In yawning silence, he led out the mare and gelding and watched as Rhea and Zhao climbed into their saddles and walked the horses out of the courtyard and toward the Imperial Road.

The morning had broken, the clear, bright sky presaging a sunny day, an unusual and welcome departure from the rain that had dampened most of their journey. There were few travelers out as yet. Most preferred to wait until full daylight before braving roads that might still be menaced by bandits.

Rhea and Zhao let the horses pick their way onto the broad paved road that followed the river. They did not look at each other. They did not have to.

Gone was the tension of the last few days, that unsettling intimacy neither had dared to acknowledge. In its place was something far more powerful, an awareness, a physical remembering of each other so keen, it gave them even less peace than before.

They rode close together as the animals settled into the steady rhythm of travel. Rhea could feel Zhao's nearness in every nerve, every pore. So this was what matebonding was like, she thought. A recognition of the other so sharp, she could not concentrate on anything else.

She knew he was looking at her and glanced up to meet his eyes. His face wore its usual mask of grave serenity, but there was such warmth and concern in his eyes that she smiled.

He smiled back. "Are you tired?"

"No more than you."

His smile faded. "You gave me a great gift last night," he said seriously. "One I fear I will never be able to repay."

Her voice was as gentle as the hand she ran along her mare's neck. "Gifts do not require payment, Red Tiger, but I don't recall giving you any last night."

"Ah, but you are wrong." He shooed a fly from his gelding's head and fixed his gaze on her once more. "You gave me yourself. You gave me a joy and delight I have never known. You have used your wondrous powers on my behalf and taken on my causes as your own. Yet I have done nothing to deserve it. Indeed, I may end up only causing you pain."

She gave him a puzzled look. "Why would you do that?"

He shook his head. "I would not wish to, but the gods do not always give us a choice in these matters. The customs of your people are strange to me and apparently very different from my own. Yet I can tell you this about myself: I am not the kind of man who makes love with a woman lightly. To visit singing girls is one thing, but to share embraces with someone like yourself is quite another."

She reached over and touched his arm. "There is naught to explain, Red Tiger. I wanted what happened as much as you, or it wouldn't have happened. And you are wrong about not deserving my help, although you don't really seem to need it. We have helped each other from the moment we met. Do not forget that."

Several peasants pushing heavily laden wheelbarrows came trundling along the road, and they pulled up their horses to let them pass.

"There are many reasons behind my concern for you," Rhea went on, when the farmers were beyond earshot. "Reasons you would not understand because I hardly understand them myself." She nudged her mare back into a walk, glancing at Zhao as he heeled the gelding after her.

His face had come alight with fierce curiosity. "What reasons? You must tell me, Rhea. You must trust me! I may understand more than you think."

"If I did ..." She tensed as the sound of numerous hoofbeats drifted to her on the breeze. "Horses are approaching. Many of them."

Zhao froze, listening intently. A moment later he, too, heard it. "Off the road and into the trees," he said. "Swiftly!"

He drove his heels into the gelding's flanks as he spoke, urging the startled animal into the grove that lined the road. Rhea followed. Within the copse, Zhao leapt from the saddle and motioned for her to do the same.

"We must hold our hands over the horses' muzzles," he instructed, "or they may call out to the approaching animals. And if those astride them work for Li Shan-po, that would not be a good thing."

"You have a talent for understatement," Rhea muttered, sliding off the mare's back and grasping the animal's nose.

Peering out through the branches, they waited. The sound of shuffling hooves grew louder, attended by a low, trilling cry that obviously issued from a human throat.

Zhao relaxed a little. "It may not be men of Li Shan-po, after all," he whispered. "But we will wait to make certain."

Walking single file, the animals came into view. They were small, shaggy creatures with long flopping ears, heavily laden with sacks. Zhao grunted in relief.

"A caravan of rabbit-horses," he said with satisfaction. "They must be heading to Yangzhou. Look, there are the drivers bringing up the rear." He pointed to two poorly dressed men who were trotting along behind the last of the ponies. The odd "wooh, wooh" call was being made by them.

Rhea studied the procession with interest. "Why are they called rabbit-horses, and why do the men sing?"

"They sing to soothe their beasts and keep them moving." Zhao took his hand from the gelding's muzzle and smiled. "And as for why they're called rabbit-horses— look at their ears. Isn't it obvious? We may continue now. There is no danger here."

They led their horses out from the trees. Sighting the newcomers, the lead pony threw up its head, long ears swiveling, and nickered loudly. Others in the train took up the neigh, causing one of the drivers to hurry to the front to see what the commotion was. His dark face filled with consternation when he saw Zhao and Rhea.

"Good day to you, driver." Zhao made his voice reassuring as he stepped onto the road. "Please do not be concerned. We are merely travelers like yourselves going south. We mean no harm."

The driver grasped the halter of the lead pony and brought it to a halt. "Greetings, Jushi," he said hoarsely. "But it is not myself I am concerned for. It is you."

By now the second driver had joined the first. Both men stood rigid, their worried gazes fastened upon Zhao.

"What has happened that you should have such concern?" Zhao asked.

"We are devout in the ways of Buddha," the first man said. "Therefore it is our duty to warn you. Take great care, for imperial emissaries are coming like a plague of grasshoppers upon the land. With them they have soldiers. They are going to temples and monasteries, large and small, even to the nunneries, and are forcing all those within to abandon their holy vows. It is horrible, Jushi, horrible—"

"Yes," the second driver broke in. "We're from a village fifty li from the capital, and on the morning we began this journey they came there to read the proclamation." He spat contemptuously. "A fat, bejeweled emissary, with one hundred soldiers to back him up."

The first driver took up the tale, his voice grating with indignation. "Then they went to our local temple and forced, Jushi, *forced*, our good-hearted priests to take off their robes and renounce their vocation. They made sport of those holy men, treated them shamelessly, without the slightest respect. May Amitabha forgive me for speaking of it. They even rubbed excrement on the shaven heads of those who resisted and then killed them."

"And now," the second man said, "there are soldiers here in this country. We saw them not two hours ago, as we left the post station we camped at last night."

Zhao's jaw was taut. "What direction were they headed in?"

"Yangzhou," the second driver replied.

"But," his companion added, "I'm sure they will stop at any Buddhist places of worship they see along the way. And you, Jushi, if they see you, they will certainly strip you of your lay robes, or even worse. Hide. In the name of Buddha, hide."

Chapter 14

The eleventh day of the sixth moon in 841
A.D. was the Emperor Wu-tsung's birthday,
and the monarch celebrated it by inviting
two Buddhist and two Taoist priests to the
Palace to engage in a four-cornered debate
on their respective scriptures. Significantly,
the two Taoists were rewarded by being
"granted the purple" to wear, an honor
restricted to courtiers of the fifth rank, while
the Buddhists received no reward.

—*Ennin's Travels in T'ang China*

Grand General Wang of the Chin-wu Guards shifted his
rump on the hard saddle and bit back a groan. Never in his
life had he experienced such pain as during these last ten
days, the bulk of which he had spent on the back of this
accursed nag.

Wang did not share the overwhelming love of T'ang
society for the horse. To him it was not a noble creature

descended from Heaven, but a cantankerous and ill-tempered beast, just as happy to kick or bite him as look at him.

Indeed, that very morning the disgusting animal—given to him as a gift to celebrate his new status—had decided to rear up when he climbed into the saddle, throwing Wang squarely and ignominiously on his posterior, right in front of his assembled men!

Raising one buttock off the saddle, Wang discreetly broke wind—an inevitable result of the horrid and far too spicy food Southerners insisted on serving him. How he wished he was back in Ch'ang-an, thrusting his jade hammer through the exquisitely tight jade gate of his fourteen-year-old concubine. He had only just purchased the delightful little thing, but had barely had time to enjoy her, he reflected morosely.

Even on his last night in the capital, before he was to leave on this hideous mission, Wang had spent those precious hours not in the arms of his beautiful slave, but listening to the tirades and instructions of his equally hideous wife. By all Under Heaven, he despised that woman. It was hard to know whom he disliked more, her or his horse.

"Now you listen to me, Husband, and listen well," the old harridan had screeched at him. "This mission could establish you as a man of influence and power at court, *if* you act decisively. Do not forget, brainless one, that only one harvest ago we were destitute, because you could find no better way of making a living than to peddle chrysanthemums and violets. Now look at us. Elevated beyond our wildest dreams, and all because of *my* honored uncle!"

Wang's plump hands clenched around the reins. He had wanted to strike that ugly face and silence her for daring to address him with such disrespect. But to do so would have been unwise, and the old water buffalo was correct about at least one thing. It was indeed her uncle who had arranged for his appointment to grand general of the Chin-wu Guard.

"But that is all she is correct about," Wang mumbled. "I am more man than *she* will ever know. And I didn't just sell chrysanthemums and violets, I sold turnips, the largest and best in all of Ch'ang-an."

"Did you say something, General?"

Wang jerked, nearly causing the annoyed horse to unseat him again. Cursing, he barely managed to keep his position in the saddle. "No, no," he quickly said to the officer riding beside him. "I was merely reflecting on my great responsibilities as leader of this delegation."

The officer coughed, a noise that sounded suspiciously like a laugh. Wang threw him a furious look.

"The dust on this road is atrocious," the man explained, hiding his mouth behind one hand.

Wang relaxed. "Well, a man like myself does not notice such minor discomforts. It is rather warm, however."

With an effort he refrained from letting loose a diatribe on the tropical heat of these southern lands. Even though he was always accorded the best of quarters in whatever village the company commandeered at night, nothing could make up for the sticky, uncivilized climate of this savage country.

"How many li are we from the next monastery or temple?" he asked in a surly tone.

"No more than four at the very most. I believe there is a nunnery nearby, as well."

Wang looked up with interest. So today's business would entail stripping women of their nuns' robes. He sighed. It probably didn't matter. With his ill luck, he could count on them all being as ugly as his wife.

"Both the temple and nunnery are rather large," the officer went on, "and are near a small farming village. It is probable that the priests and nuns perform many acts of charity, such as caring for the sick or aiding the farmers in times of drought or pestilence."

Hearing a note of approval in the man's voice, Wang glanced at him sharply. "Do you presume to defend these evil ones, when the Son of Heaven has declared their ways unnatural and corrupt? Perhaps I should report that your morals have been seduced, along with so many of the common folk."

The officer blanched. "I was not defending Buddhism, General," he said hastily, "but merely describing the situation, so that you would be prepared. The farther away we get from the capital, the greater the likelihood that we'll encounter resistance from villages near Buddhist places of worship. The people are Southerners, after all, and do not possess the high morality of us Northerners. And they love their priests. It would be wise to remember that."

Wang's stomach lurched. The man's words were convincing, and more than likely, he was a Buddhist himself. Wang himself had once been Buddhist. But when his sharp-eyed wife had noted the Emperor's increasing interest in Taoism, she had insisted they both adhere to that religion instead.

For Wang it had presented no great hardship. He was not the devout sort, regardless of the religion involved. His greatest concern was ever with himself, and the officer's words had awakened in him a great fear for that precious self.

"We have certainly experienced no resistance as yet," he said nervously. "Just a lot of moaning and whining. And the T'ang Code forbids the common folk to carry arms. What possible problem could there be?"

"You are quite right, General. The law does forbid the people arms." The officer's tone was grave. "But it says nothing about the implements necessary for farming. Have you ever seen what a scythe or pitchfork can do to a man when swung by strong arms? It is an unpleasant sight."

Wang's stomach lurched a second time, gurgling so loudly that his horse's ears twitched. By the Sacred Dragon, he thought, the accursed food of this savage country would kill him yet. If the villagers didn't do it first. His stomach plunged again.

"And as for those Buddhists monks who have been trained in Shaolin," the officer continued, "we have not yet encountered any of them, and to be truthful, I am not eager to. They are well-known for their boxing skills. They probably will not be as meek as you might wish, Excellency."

A city dweller all his life, Wang had no experience whatever with farming implements. However, it took little imagination to picture what a scythe would look like as it tore through a man's belly. His belly. And as for Shaolin monks: everyone knew of them and the mysterious powers they possessed. Queen of Heaven, what was he doing there?

Awkwardly, his bowels churning, Wang yanked his horse to a stop. "I—I will return presently," he muttered as he struggled to dismount.

The rest of the detachment pulled up in some confusion. With an amused look on his face, which Wang did not see, the officer shouted, "Company will halt. Our esteemed general has need of the bushes!"

During the summer months, the people of K'un Yang village were at work long before sunrise. That day, though, as Zhao and Rhea entered the village, the entire populace stood crowded upon its one muddy street. Rhea found the sight disconcerting.

"I warned you coming here was not wise," she told Zhao in a fierce undertone. "In those robes you can hardly be called inconspicuous. And even without them your height and coloring is enough to alert any spies of Li Shan-po that you are here."

Zhao's mouth was set in a grim line, yet his tone was gentle. "You are right, of course. But I must do this, Rhea. I have to see what they're doing to the monasteries, so I can bring word of it back to my own temple."

"Very well." She threw him an exasperated look. "If you are foolish enough to do this thing, then we will do it."

"Look there," a woman's voice rang out. "A *jushi* comes!"

Her cry was instantly taken up by others until the murmur of *"jushi, jushi"* ran through the crowd. An elderly man whose bearing and demeanor proclaimed him the village Elder walked toward them, followed by a cordon of what were probably the town's most important men.

Halting in front of Zhao's horse, the old man kowtowed reverently, glancing behind him to see that the others were doing the same. They were. The entire village was kowtowing, in fact.

"Arise, all of you," Zhao called in obvious embarrassment. "I am not worthy of such a reception from good people like yourselves." He slid gracefully from the saddle, then reached up to the mare, swinging Rhea to the ground.

The village Elder clambered stiffly to his feet, assisted by two of his companions. "You wear the robes of a *jushi*," he said stoutly, "and that is enough for us. In these

evil days, a place in the Western Heaven will surely be reserved for those who continue to show respect for the
priests of Buddha."

Zhao nodded. "Where is your magistrate, Honored Elder?"

"Gone, Youposai. He and his retinue are on their way
to meet a contingent of imperial soldiers, which even now
is approaching our village."

The old man pulled at the wisps of his white beard and
exchanged looks with the men around him. "He is a good
man, our magistrate, and so is our prefect, but like most
scholars, they hold to what they say is the logic of Confucianism. Myself, I'm not educated. I know nothing of
philosophy or fancy talk. All I know is that I follow
Buddhism, as did my father, my grandfather, and their
fathers before them. What was good enough for the ancestors of my clan is most certainly good enough for
me."

A rumble of assent rose from the villagers. Looking
around with a satisfied air, the Elder spat into the dust.
"And as for imperial edicts—well, the Emperor has never
shared his own catties of rice and millet with me when
famine sat upon my fields. But the priests of our monastery have. And it was not the Emperor who healed my
firstborn son and brought him back to life. It was the
priests. Now to whom should I give my loyalty?"

The rumble became a chorus of loud approval. "Chang
the Elder describes what lies in the hearts of us all," one
man shouted. Elbowing his way to the front of the crowd,
he bowed to the old man and Zhao.

"With all respect, Grandfather Chang," he said, "there
is little time. The soldiers will be here any moment, and
while there may be little we can do to save our own

priests, we can at least see to it that this *jushi* does not have *his* robes stripped from him."

"Yes, yes." Chang looked at Zhao with worry in his eyes. "It would do me great honor if you stayed in my poor house until these visitors from the capital are gone." His gaze slid to Rhea, and he added, "The woman, too, of course."

Zhao shook his head. "Your hospitality does all within this village great credit. But I did not come here to hide away while wrong is being committed."

"You should hide," Rhea muttered in an undertone, but he ignored it.

"I must hear the words of the edict carried by these soldiers," he went on, "so that I may warn those of my own temple of what is coming. All I ask is to blend in among you as the order is being read."

"You are very tall, Youposai," the Elder said doubtfully, "and you are a foreigner. I do not know how easily that may be accomplished. And what of the woman? She is also tall. Do you wish her—"

"The woman," Rhea cut in, "is well able to take care of herself. Thank you for the offer of your house, old one, but I will stay here."

Though her words were addressed to Chang, they were clearly meant for Zhao. He turned to her, but his response went unspoken, for she suddenly cocked her head. "There is no more time to argue," she said flatly. "I hear the sound of many horses, and they are coming down the road to this village."

Dozens of heads whipped around to stare at the road. "The foreign woman's wits are addled," a man muttered, after they had all listened for a moment. "I hear nothing."

Zhao put up a hand. "If she says they are coming, then they are indeed coming. Now quickly, you must gather around us so we are not the first people these soldiers see when they enter your village."

Even as he spoke, the sound of hoofbeats and shouted orders drifted to the waiting crowd, causing a near pandemonium. It was one thing to talk about the stupidity of imperial edicts; quite another to voice those criticisms to soldiers and officials.

Yet the people of K'un Yang possessed a courage as simple and stubborn as the hard lives they led. By the time the first horseman—an overweight, nervous-looking man perched awkwardly upon a fine chestnut stallion—rode down the village street, Zhao and Rhea were well concealed, their height mitigated by Chang's house and the tallest of the villagers, who had positioned themselves in front of them.

In silence the people of K'un Yang watched as the official contingent invaded their village. It was an impressive and intimidating sight. Aside from the various bureaucrats in the train, there were at least one hundred and fifty soldiers riding in close, orderly ranks. They were in full uniform, garbed in heavy padded armor and carrying spears and crossbows.

Glancing from villagers to soldiers to officials, Rhea was struck by the utter lack of expression on the faces of all of them. The only emotion was on the sweating features of the plump man in the lead. She whispered, "Red Tiger, why does the pudgy one look so uneasy?"

His gaze fixed on the horsemen, Zhao shrugged. "He is the leader. Perhaps he is troubled by his task."

"That one their leader?" She stared in surprise at the fat man. Even Terrans, she thought, must see what a ridiculous figure this corpulent person presented in his sweat-stained tunic and pants of garish orange and green silk.

As she watched, the man tugged at his mount's reins.

He tugged too hard. The horse stopped with such abruptness, its rider tumbled from the saddle, landing on his well-padded rump with a resounding thud.

A laugh bubbled into Rhea's throat. Noticing that no one—not even Zhao, though the corners of his mouth quirked for an instant—followed suit, she stifled it.

With surprising speed the plump man got back on his feet, brusquely waving off the two officers who had hastily dismounted to help him. His paunchy cheeks were flushed a deep crimson as he began to give orders, shouting harshly at the men in an obvious attempt to cover his embarrassment.

The soldiers sprang into action, lifting several objects from the backs of packhorses. Two richly patterned carpets were carefully spread on the flattened space that comprised the village square. A gold stand was set upon one carpet and on top of it a purple cloth was laid out. Upon this was placed the imperial edict, a scroll made of the finest yellow paper, wrapped and tied with purple silk.

These preparations were carried out with a swiftness and efficiency that suggested they had been done before, and often. When they had been completed, the portly leader stalked over to the golden stand.

"I am General Wang of the Chin-wu Guard of the imperial court," he bellowed much more loudly than was necessary. "Magistrate of this village, what is your response?"

A dignified man stepped forward from the crowd of soldiers and bureaucrats. "I, the magistrate of K'un Yang, await with reverence the exalted wisdom of the Son of Heaven," he said in a clear, calm voice.

The preliminaries of the ceremony seemed to go on forever. At last Zhao whispered to a restless Rhea, "Do you see those two men in green robes who are approaching? They are assistant judges. They will now read the edict."

The two men took the scroll and untied it. Alternating with each other, they began to read. The imperial order was long, but no one among the listeners sat down or even fidgeted. Even the children remained unnaturally still, as though they realized the gravity of this occasion.

As Rhea listened to the ornately phrased order, she glanced at Zhao's set face with growing concern.

". . . In recent times its strange ways have become so customary and all-pervasive as to have slowly and unconsciously corrupted the morals of our land. The hearts of our people have been seduced by it and the masses led astray. . . .

"In exhausting men's strength in construction work, in robbing men for their own golden and jeweled adornments, in forsaking ruler and kin to support their teachers, in abandoning their mates for monastic rules, in flouting the laws, nothing is worse than this religion. . . .

"The monasteries and temples are beyond count, but they are all lofty and beautifully decorated, daring to rival palaces in their grandeur. . . ."

The voice droned on and Rhea looked around at the villagers. They continued to stand in respectful silence, but outrage flickered in the eyes of many. It was strange to see so much anger contained within such passivity.

The reading of the edict drew to a close, and in unison both judges chimed out the last line, their solemn voices rising to a shout. "This evil must be reformed!"

Under the complete stillness of everyone present, they carefully rolled the scroll shut and secured it with the purple ribbons. After placing it upon the gold stand, they stepped back to make way for General Wang.

"People of K'un Yang," the general boomed. "We will now go to the monastery and nunnery of your village wherein the evil described in this edict is housed. The immoral monks and nuns there will be dealt with in accordance with imperial command. As for all of you, return to your business and make yourselves useful to the empire!"

Still, not one person spoke. Resentment was building in that mute crowd, circulating through the villagers with a palpable force. It seemed even General Wang felt it, for as he waddled back to his waiting horse, he glanced behind him with ill-disguised wariness, as though he expected these quiet peasants to roar suddenly with rage and fling themselves upon him.

Of course no one did. They only watched as the imperial symbols were gathered up and reloaded upon the pack animals. That done, the officials, the soldiers, and finally, their ungainly leader mounted and prepared to ride out of the village.

As the column of horses started to trot, Chang the Elder began singing, his cracked voice rising in a villagers' song so ancient, it went back to the mythical days of Emperor Yao.

> "We rise at dawn
> And rest at sunset,
> We dig wells and drink,
> We till our fields and eat:
> What is the power of the Emperor to us?"

His old voice was joined by others. In moments the entire village of K'un Yang was singing in an eerie musical protest.

It was a stunning act of defiance, and General Wang

could easily order his men to ride back and slaughter the unarmed peasants. Indeed, it seemed he would do just that. His face flushed brick red as he twisted around in the saddle to stare at the singing village.

His expression was disbelieving, filled with an astounded fury that was reflected on the faces of some of the officials. The village's magistrate looked horrified. Rigid, he gaped at the villagers, his eyes sending a mute appeal for them to stop.

General Wang raised one hand and started to shout something. But an officer rode close to him and spoke in an urgent undertone.

Zhao frowned. "They are too far away to hear. I wonder what he is saying."

"He is pleading with the fat one not to do anything that would cause further chaos," Rhea said. "Too many valuable farmers have been lost to Buddhism as it is, and your Emperor will be displeased if there are more."

Zhao threw her a surprised glance, followed by a brief smile of relief. "He is a wise and good-hearted man, that officer. People of K'un Yang," he called out in a low voice, "you have proved your point. Cease your singing, lest this unstable general order his soldiers to bring death down on the heads of your children."

Slowly his request circulated through the villagers. With some reluctance they allowed the song to die away. The officer continued speaking to the general, gesturing toward the crowd. Whether because of his words or the fact that the villagers were now silent, General Wang dropped his hand and nodded brusquely for the company to continue.

As the hoofbeats of the horses faded, Chang the Elder turned to Zhao.

"Well, Youposai," he said sadly, "now you have seen. One does not use good iron for nails, and a good person never becomes a soldier. Faugh." He spat to one side. "Where will you go now, Youposai?"

"Home," Zhao said. "As quickly as possible."

Chapter 15

Wounded times! wounded affairs! even
more—wounded hearts!

—Wei Chuang

Strong Man had been riding for some days, and though he
was not nearly as tired as his horse, he was tired. The sight
of a small well-kept inn nestled beside a briskly flowing
stream was enough to make him decide a rest stop was in
order.

The innkeeper who came out in response to his call
was as sour looking as the inn was pleasant. "You're
too late for the morning meal," he said bluntly, "and too
early for the midday one. I suppose the wife can find
something to fill your belly, if you have the cash to pay
for it."

Strong Man stared down at his unwelcoming host,
wondering whether he should break the man's neck or
laugh. "Is this what passes for hospitality in the south?" he

finally growled. "Or is there something about me you don't like?"

The innkeeper shrugged as he took the horse's reins. "I don't know you. But guests come and guests go. I treat all of them the same. Do you want the horse fed or watered?"

"Both, unfriendly one! And do not stint, for I do have cash, though I'll not stand for being robbed by the likes of you."

The man seemed unaffected by Strong Man's threatening tone. "Oh, I'll treat the horse well," he said laconically. "I like horses. They don't try to make conversation."

An hour later Strong Man strolled out of the inn toward the river. He had been given a surprisingly good meal by the innkeeper's wife, but she was a silent creature who could not be prevailed upon to say more than one or two words to him.

Scowling, he poked a fist against the trunk of one of the trees that bordered the river. He had hoped to put this stop to good use not only by resting himself and his horse, but also by seeing whether those he followed had come this way. Thus far, such inquiries at the various inns and post stations he passed had proved fruitful. In this case, it would be easier to squeeze rice wine from a stone than to get this iron-jawed innkeeper to talk.

Strong Man walked back to the stable, where he found the innkeeper busily cleaning his horse's hooves. At least the man had not lied about liking horses. The gelding's coat gleamed, and the animal's long tail was swishing contentedly as he munched on a liberal measure of grain.

"You have certainly taken good care of him," Strong Man said, putting as much hearty approval as he could into his voice. "And the food and *t'e* your wife served was good as well. Despite the personality of its owner"—he tried to lighten this into a joke by smiling—"you have a very fine place."

There was a noncommittal grunt from the region of the horse's rear left leg. Letting the hoof he held drop to the ground, the innkeeper moved around to the gelding's other side.

"And with its location so close to the Imperial Road," Strong Man continued with determination, "you must receive a great many guests."

This time there was no grunt, but Strong Man was not going to give up. "That is true, is it not?" he persisted, trying to maintain his cheery tone.

The innkeeper finally answered. "I do well enough," he muttered, and clamped his mouth shut.

Strong Man gritted his teeth. Bending iron bars and knocking people about was one thing. This type of polite diplomacy was something quite different. Perhaps it would be more effective if he planted a foot squarely on the rump of this taciturn fool, he thought, eyeing the potential target. Li Shan-po, however, had given him a great deal of cash to see that he did otherwise.

"Purchase your information," the Spider had ordered. "Do not beat it out of people. Save that crude strength of yours for the Zhuhu, underling."

Underling. Strong Man's lip twisted. In many ways he loathed his highborn employer, but there was no denying that his life was now more comfortable, thanks to Li Shan-po. And he had been promised taels of silver if he succeeded in his task.

Strong Man sighed and reached into his tunic for four strings of each. "Here," he said, shaking them to catch the innkeeper's eye. "In payment for your services."

The innkeeper glanced up. His closed expression altered with surprise when he saw the money, but he quickly recovered himself. "That is too much," he said. "Unless you plan on staying here several days."

"I do not. But I am looking for some . . . acquaintances of mine. Perhaps you could be of some help in finding them."

"Ahh, so that's how it is." The man gave him a look of such cynical disdain, Strong Man itched again to kick him.

The innkeeper turned back to his hoof cleaning. "I pay little attention to who stays at my inn. All I ask is that they pay what they owe and cause no trouble. Beyond that, what they do or look like is their affair and not mine. Their faces mean no more to me than last year's fleas."

"I think you would remember these guests if they stopped here," Strong Man said, striving to hold on to his temper. "They are very distinctive looking."

He waited for the usual, "Oh, and how are they distinctive?" The innkeeper remained mute. Strong Man drew another cash string from the belt inside his tunic. "*Very* distinctive looking," he added.

For the first time avarice glimmered in the other man's eyes, although he tried to conceal it. "In my business it is important for a man to be discreet," he warned. "But I *suppose* I could be persuaded to search my memory."

"Hmmm. I suppose you could." Strong Man mumbled a curse and pulled out a sixth string of cash. "There are two, both foreigners. A man and a woman, traveling together. The man you could not possibly forget. He is very tall, with the coloring of the *se mu ren*—red hair and eyes like dark jade. Strangest of all, he wears the robes of a *jushi*. The woman is extremely beautiful, if your taste runs to barbarians, with long black hair and gray eyes. Now, have you seen them?"

The innkeeper's gaze was on the dangling strings of cash. "Two such foreigners did stay here," he said warily.

Strong Man's eyes lighted. "When?"

"Last night. They left early this morning, before first light."

"I see. And in what direction did they head when they left your fine establishment?"

The man shrugged. "South, I think. Yangzhou is only two days ride and—"

"Did they say that was where they were going?" Strong Man interrupted.

"No, but that would be my guess. A great many foreigners live there."

"I see," Strong Man repeated. Slowly he pulled out a seventh cash string. The next question he had to ask filled him with distaste, but Li Shan-po had been explicit in his instructions. What was more, he expected regular reports on the answer. "There is one more thing I would know. Did—did the two of them share a chamber, or did they sleep separately?"

The innkeeper did not answer. Strong Man was debating adding another string when the man finally spoke.

"Yes. And no."

"Yes and no? I am not playing riddle games here, man! Did they or didn't they?"

"I am trying," the innkeeper said coolly, "to tell you. They took two rooms for the night, and when it came time to retire, he entered one and she the other. But in the morning, they both came out of her chamber. I said nothing about it. They paid me well for the rooms, and what they chose to do in them was their business." He held out his hand for the money. "That is all I have to say."

Strong Man dropped the strings of cash into the waiting hand. "I wish to write a sealed letter and leave it for the next post rider passing by on his way to the capital."

"You can write?" The innkeeper looked impressed. "I would not have expected it."

"Is that so?" Strong Man eyed the man with ever-increasing dislike and imagined the pleasure in squashing him headfirst into a pile of horse droppings.

With so much cash in hand, though, the innkeeper had become almost genial. "Oh, I meant no offense," he explained. "It is just that your looks and manner tell me that you must have once been a soldier, and how many soldiers possess even the smallest skill with a brush and ink stone?"

"This one does," Strong Man snapped, pointing to himself with a blunt finger.

Actually, his proficiency in drawing characters was marginal at best. He had been taught many harvests ago by a Taoist monk whose command of calligraphy was far more impressive than his ability to hold his wine. Despite the drunken nature of the lessons, Strong Man had, to his enormous pride, learned the rudiments of writing. It made him highly valuable to Li Shan-po, for of all those at this level of the Spider's service, Strong Man alone could write.

Some time later, his laborious efforts over the brief missive completed, Strong Man was on his way once more. As he rode south, he ruminated on this strange coil in which he found himself.

He was not a great thinker; no one knew that better than he. Even he, though, was finding this whole situation strange. First, there was the complicated business with Buddha's finger-bone, which Strong Man still had not figured out. Now there was his own assignment: to follow the two foreigners, kill the man, and return the woman to Li Shan-po.

Strong Man sighed. He had taken a great many lives in his time, but he did not enjoy killing a man who could not fight. He hoped the Zhuhu was indeed trained in Shaolin, as Li Shan-po had said he was. At least then the two of them could engage in a decent manly combat, which would be won by him who was the best fighter.

Coming out of his reverie, Strong Man realized his hands lay loose on the reins. The gelding, taking advantage of it, had fallen into a slow amble as he nibbled at the grass alongside the road. He gathered up the reins.

"Come on, horse," he said, nudging its flanks with his heels. "Let us go to Yangzhou and get this over with."

The gelding picked up its pace. As they moved down the road at a brisk walk, Strong Man saw a lone figure in the distance, a man walking south.

He paid little attention at first. Many people traveled the Imperial Road, on foot as well as on horseback. There was nothing unusual about one more. But as the minutes passed, he noticed something odd about this lone traveler.

Although the man was only walking, Strong Man's horse did not overtake him. Frowning, he urged the gelding faster, then faster still. The man continued to remain ahead, his strides long and even and utterly without effort.

By now Strong Man was intrigued. He put his horse into a trot, but barely gained on the man. Feeling a touch of aggravation, he kicked the gelding into a canter and finally began to close the distance between them. As the gelding drew even with him, the man halted, staring up at

Strong Man with mild curiosity. His features and height marked him as belonging to the *se mu ren*.

Strong Man reined in his horse. "For a person on foot," he said, "you keep up a very swift pace."

"And what," the stranger asked politely, his voice deep and cultured, "is that to you?"

Strong Man shrugged. "Nothing I suppose. It is just a little strange to see a well-dressed foreigner traveling alone and on foot. Most travel in droves, well mounted, and with hired guards to protect them from bandits. Aren't you afraid?"

"Should I be?" the man asked with a slight smile.

"That depends on whether you are carrying anything of value. Are you?"

"Why? Could you be one of those bandits that you just spoke of?"

The foreigner's voice contained an amused and almost mocking note that set Strong Man's teeth on edge. Perhaps it was the man's puzzling speed, or perhaps it was that Strong Man's temper, never particularly tolerant, was shorter than usual. After all, he had been traveling for over seven days without any opportunity to engage in his favorite activity: showing off his enormous strength. Suddenly he realized how keenly he felt that lack. It would feel good to fight, he thought. Very good indeed.

"I am not a bandit," he said. "And I am in a hurry to reach Yangzhou. But I suppose I have enough time to teach an ill-mannered barbarian some notions of proper behavior."

The man's eyebrows arched in surprise. "You think I was not behaving properly? I believe I was. But then, like most of your kind, you seem an argumentative sort."

"Hah." Spoiling for a fight, Strong Man now had all the reason he needed. "So you presume to insult not only me, but my ancestors and every Han person in this great Middle Kingdom. I should probably kill you for such disrespect, but because I am a merciful man, I will only thrash you."

So saying, Strong Man kicked his feet out of the stirrups and, with a savage yell, flung himself at the tall stranger.

He fully expected to tackle his opponent, bringing him down, then pummel the luckless man into moaning submission.

Things did not go as planned. The foreigner did not stay where he was, and instead of wrapping his arms around a body, Strong Man found himself clutching only air, and then the unforgiving surface of the road.

He landed hard. Before he could grasp what had happened, a hand seized the scruff of his neck, carelessly lifted him as though he were a newborn kitten, and flung him once more into the air.

This time Strong Man landed even harder, the breath knocked completely out of him. Wheezing, he lay on his stomach, then managed to get to his knees. He stayed there for some minutes, doubled over in pain, gagging and gasping as he struggled to draw air into his lungs. When he had recovered enough to stand up, he saw that the foreigner was beside his horse, absently stroking its neck as he watched his erstwhile attacker.

"Why—" Strong Man gagged again and spat into the grass. "Why did you not flog me as I lay helpless? That is what I would have done to you."

The foreigner gave him a look that combined pity with contempt. "I do not fight when there is no reason for it," he said with dignity. "Especially with those who are weaker than myself."

Normally such a remark would have sent Strong Man into a paroxysm of rage, but all he did was grunt. "Since you just tossed me through the air like a girl infant," he said, rubbing the back of his neck, "I cannot take offense at that.

"But tell me." He drew himself up and met the stranger's dark gaze. "Are you a foreign ghost who is now going to send me to the Terrace of Night? If you are, I am not afraid. And if I must die, at least it will be at the hand of a strong male ghost."

To his astonishment, the foreign ghost laughed. "Killing you is the furthest thing from my mind. And I have not come from the realm of the supernatural. I am only a traveler on his way to the city of Yangzhou. Despite the belligerence you showed toward me, I still have no quarrel with you. Here." He held out the gelding's reins. "Mount your horse and continue on your way."

Still somewhat dazed, Strong Man walked forward. He was mightily confused. Above all, he did not believe this soft-spoken stranger was mortal and that he truly intended to let him live. But mortal or not, the foreigner's strength deserved respect. Of course Strong Man was also grateful for his life, though in his personal view, such generosity bordered on weakness.

However he felt about it, though, the ritual courtesies had to be observed. Cautiously he grasped the gelding's reins. "You defeated me in fair combat," he forced himself to say, "and then spared me." Awkwardly, for it had been a long time since he had had to concede this kind of defeat, he made his obeisance. "I am in your debt. Ask of me what you will."

The stranger gazed down at him. "I have nothing to ask of you," he said, then was silent a moment. "But who knows? Life has a way of surprising even the wisest of us.

For now, I would be content if we traveled together for a while. I have come a long way alone and would enjoy some conversation. Tell me, man who is not a bandit, what is your name?"

More confused than ever, Strong Man told him. The stranger smiled. "A fitting name," he said. "I am called Matteo."

They were near the sea, so near that Rhea's blood called out to it. The rush of waves pulsed through her ears, throbbing in her head and all the way down into her belly, setting up such a roar of white-foamed sound that at first she did not realize Zhao was speaking to her.

With an effort she brought herself back. His fingers were warm and firm around her wrist. He was staring at her, and his eyes, though shadowed with fatigue and worry, still held that new and deep awareness of her in their depths.

"What ails you, dear heart?" The endearment slipped out so naturally, he did not seem to notice it. Rhea did, and its touch was like a wound in her heart.

"Your face suddenly became so strange," he said, "and you started to ride off from me, as though I were not even here. Where were you going?"

She glanced away. "To the sea," she whispered. "Can't you hear it?"

There was a long silence.

"No," he said at last, his voice quiet. "I cannot."

She looked at him again. "No, of course you can't." She realized his hand still imprisoned her wrist. "Do you wish you could, Red Tiger? Do you wish you could hear Her as I do?"

An expression of pain crossed his face. "There are many things I could wish for, but this is not the time to speak of them. Not with this madness Li Shan-po has let loose in the land. The sea calls to you, Lady, and my obligations call to me."

"I understand." Slowly she drew her wrist away. "But, Red Tiger, obligations can become burdens that one is never able to set down, even when one finally wants to."

The gaze he turned on her was grim. "Until I have avenged myself on the destroyer of my family," he said in a low, savage tone, "I will carry my burdens gladly." As he stared at her, his face slowly changed. "But those burdens are not yours, Rhea." His voice was gentle again, and she could feel the ache within him. "If your world calls to you so strongly, then perhaps you should go to it. There are no bonds upon you to stay with me."

She hesitated, gazing off into the distance from where the call was coming. She had been away from the sea for so long, and now Mother Ocean was singing to her, sending Her song out with an ancient and irresistible force. *Come home.*

A tremor rippled through her. "But there are bonds upon me, Red Tiger," she said. As she turned back to meet his eyes, the depth of relief she saw in them stunned her. The ties between them seemed to grow even stronger in that moment, and Rhea knew she'd made the right choice. But what would she do when her need for the sea overpowered her need for Zhao?

Late that afternoon Zhao pointed out the first fields that belonged to the Temple of the Jade Waterfall. Now that they were within the holdings of his temple, and perhaps because he wished to keep the sea from her thoughts, he showed her the groves of mulberry trees, fruit orchards, and rich farmlands with a tired pride.

His monastery was actually an estate, with the temple and its grounds surrounded by a large village. The peasants of that village farmed the lands owned by the temple. Within the walls of the monastery itself still more people lived. Many were employed by the monks as craftsmen and artisans, though the largest number were slaves.

The temple gates teemed with activity, and as Zhao and Rhea clattered through the press of people and animals, they could hear voices calling out: Red Tiger! Red Tiger has returned!

As they entered the inner courtyard a row of monks already stood there, as grave as statues. Before this silent assembly stood the most ancient Terran Rhea had ever seen. Though small and slight, he emanated a sense of calm power and strength that reminded her of the merfolk Elders. To her surprise, the old man's eyes, dark and burning with wisdom and insight, were fixed upon her, not Zhao.

She wondered about this as her weary mare gratefully halted and she and Zhao dismounted.

Zhao bowed reverently. When he rose, his expression was as grave as the others'. "Master Wu." His tone, too, was troubled. "Why do you stand in the sun waiting for me as though you deserve no respect? Is it my mother?" His gaze swept the courtyard. "Has something happened to her?"

"Your mother is well, my son. She comes even now to greet you." The old master's voice was deep and strong, as though it belonged to a man half his age.

Reassured, Zhao nodded. "Then it must be because you have already heard the news I bring, of the imperial edicts that are sweeping the land."

Master Wu's gaze turned from Rhea to Zhao. "We have heard this grave news, yes. And we have heard something else as well. This morning a messenger brought me urgent word from my brother, the Abbot Hui Jing. Seven days ago, the Dowager Empress passed into the Terrace of Night. They are saying in the imperial court that she was poisoned."

Chapter 16

Lao-tzu, the Supreme (founder of Taoism),
concocted an elixir and, taking it, attained
immortality and became one of the realm of
spirits and produced great benefit without
limit. We ask that a terrace of the immortals
be erected in the Palace where we may purify
our bodies and mount to the heavenly mists
and roam about the nine heavens and, with
blessings for the masses and long life for the
Emperor, long preserve the pleasures of
immortality.

—Memorial presented to
Wu-tsung by Taoist priests,
Ennin's Travels in T'ang China

The quality of the paper on which the letter was written
was atrocious, the rendering of the characters even worse.
For all that, it was still readable, and Li Shan-po's jaw
clenched as he made out the message.

This final confirmation of his suspicions did not arouse sweeping fury, as it once would have. Over the last several days, he had regained enough composure at least to present an icy calm whenever he considered Zhao Tamudj and the woman who had slithered from his grasp.

Their escape, though frustrating, was only temporary. In any case, other matters now occupied his mind, matters that loomed far greater than a troublesome Zhuhu and a desirable but insignificant foreign whore.

The circumstances he'd so cleverly set in motion were gathering force, rolling with a momentum that had taken even him by surprise. Intrigued by the idea of manipulating the downfall of Buddhism, he still had not expected his plans to bear fruit to such an astonishing degree. All unwitting, he had tapped into a groundswell of hostility, an antagonism that he had underestimated.

As the vast majority of the imperial court cheered the imperial edicts against Buddhism, Li Shan-po discovered a change within himself. This was no longer a simple reprisal against a barbarian clan that had displeased him and the foolish monks who had sheltered its two survivors. It was a grand and sacred enterprise with ramifications that would influence the future of the Middle Kingdom.

The scholars who recorded the history of the T'ang dynasty would write long and well of him.

This thought crossed Li Shan-po's mind with increasing frequency, and each time it did, he found himself smiling. Li Shan-po: the noble who had rid the empire of foreign influences and brought it back to the correctness of ancient and traditional values . . .

"Master."

Rudely jolted from his reverie, Li Shan-po turned in annoyance. Chen Yü stood in the doorway of the library, looking apprehensive.

"Your house slave told me you were expecting me," he said, bowing hastily.

Li Shan-po nodded. "And so I am. Come in. What news do you bring me?"

The young eunuch stepped into the chamber. Fixing his gaze on the tile floor inlaid with jewels, he spoke in a hushed voice.

"The Chief Eunuch is quite ill. Today he rode out along the Imperial Road to where the Dowager Empress's mausoleum is being built, and he could barely stay upon his horse. He remains convinced that you—we—are behind the Empress's death. As yet, though, he has found no way to prove it."

"He won't." Contempt rippled through Li Shan-po's words. "And he is not ill. He is dying. I have used my arts, and they have foreseen it. His demise approaches too rapidly to allow him time to prove anything. Even if he went to the Emperor this very instant and accused me openly, it would make no difference. It is I who bask in the Son of Heaven's favor, not he."

Chen Yü lifted his eyes. "Do not discount him too easily, Master. Ill or not, Ch'iu Shih-liang is still a wise man, and a powerful one."

Li Shan-po only shrugged. "It's a shame the Dowager Empress proved herself such a problem, but then one can never completely count on people—particularly women—to act intelligently. The old woman slipped too easily from my control back to that of the Chief Eunuch. Even then, I might have spared her had she not protested to the Son of Heaven about his edicts against the Buddhists."

"She did not know you were behind those edicts," Chen Yü said. "If she had known, perhaps—"

Li Shan-po silenced him with a wave of his hand. "It does not matter. The deed is done, and there are benefits to be reaped from it, aside from the silencing of an old woman's flapping tongue."

As he spoke, Li Shan-po gazed down at the letter he still held in his hand. An icy smile twisted his lips, and he seemed to forget that Chen Yü was there.

Watching him, the eunuch shivered. Clearly, with his devastatingly facile mind, his master was plotting further against those who already struggled in the meshes of his web, a web that included the Son of Heaven himself!

Chen Yü shivered again. His blood felt chilled, flowing thick and sluggish through his veins, as though a curse had been placed upon it.

Despite giving himself into the service of the Spider in exchange for promises of secret power—promises that Li Shan-po had yet to keep—Chen Yü was in his heart a Buddhist. Li Shan-po's ire, once directed at a red-haired Zhuhu whose fate did not concern Chen Yü in the least, now threatened beliefs the eunuch would never have dreamed vulnerable to attack.

Distressed as he was, Chen Yü dared not protest. To utter so much as a word would surely send him the way the Dowager Empress had gone, down the same dark path that awaited Ch'iu Shih-liang, the Zhuhu, and anyone else who displeased Li Shan-po. Of that Chen Yü was as certain as he was of anything in this life.

"May Amitabha forgive me," he whispered soundlessly, his lips barely moving. "I am trapped as much as any of the others. Perhaps even more so."

Li Shan-po glanced up sharply. "What are you mumbling?"

"Nothing, Master." Chen Yü lowered his eyes. "Nothing of any consequence."

Late in the evening, the Emperor sent word that the company of his trusted friend Li Shan-po was requested. The Spider prepared himself hurriedly, ordering his body-slaves to dress him in one of his finest robes. It was the first time he had been summoned into Wu-tsung's presence since the Dowager Empress had died. The lack of audience had not worried him. With the exception of some Taoist priests and the Commissioner of the Imperial Mausoleum, the Son of Heaven had secluded himself from everyone.

When the Imperial Guards admitted Li Shan-po into the Pavilion of Restful Breezes, though, he felt a stab of concern.

Lying on a cushion-strewn *k'ang*, the Emperor of the Middle Kingdom huddled in a rich froth of disheveled silk and satin brocade, mumbling to himself. He seemed unaware of Li Shan-po's arrival, and not until the noble finally rose from his kowtow and cleared his throat, did the Son of Heaven lift his head.

Sunken deep in his gaunt face, Wu-tsung's eyes glittered with a wild light. "So you're here at last," he said. "It is about time. We have made a decision. And you, our most trusted adviser, must be the first to hear it."

The Emperor stumbled off the *k'ang* and started to pace the pavilion. His movements were jerky and uneven, and he spoke in a rapid mutter, the flow of words so disjointed that Li Shan-po had difficulty understanding him.

". . . going to have a terrace built. Taoist priests have asked it, and Honored Mother and we have agreed . . . shall be called the Terrace of the Immortals, and it will be a full one hundred and fifty ells high ... tribute to her, as well as to Lao-Tzu, the Supreme. Honored Mother—revered be her name—came to us last night and specified the height exactly—"

Wu-tsung spun around, fixing Li Shan-po with those strange eyes. "She specified it exactly! Exactly!"

"Yes, Divine One," Li Shan-po said quickly. "And who is to construct this glorious tribute? Palace slaves, or conscripted laborers from the city and the countryside, perhaps?"

"None of them." The Emperor tugged irritably at the hanging tassels on his headdress. "Such creatures are not fit to work upon something so important as this. No, the legionaries of the Left and Right Guard Armies of Inspired Strategy shall do it. I will command that they be set to work immediately. Immediately!"

Li Shan-po took care to keep his face neutral. "The Left and Right Guard Armies of the Inspired Strategy are commanded by Chief Eunuch Ch'iu Shih-liang. I assume that in your great wisdom, you have told him—"

"The Chief Eunuch is a fool and an unbeliever!" Wu-tsung's voice rose to a shriek, and globs of spittle sprayed from his lips. Under Li Shan-po's startled and speculative gaze, he drew several deep shuddering breaths, visibly fighting to compose himself.

"Ch'iu Shih-liang does not yet know of our plans," he continued in a slightly calmer tone. "We *told* you that you would be the first of all our court to hear them. And anyway, that old eunuch has displeased us greatly. He has tried to tell us things, things about the foreign demon Buddhists, about Honored Mother, even about you, our good friend!

"We do not credit his lies, and here is his punishment for having displeased us." The Emperor leaned forward, eyes distended and blazing. "Ch'iu Shih-liang will *not* be granted immortality! For that is the secret of the terrace, you see. Once it has been built according to our plans, whoever mounts it shall live forever. Forever, Li Shan-po. Think of it! And we have not even told you the best part yet."

He let out a high-pitched giggle. "When the terrace has been finished, we shall bring Honored Mother to it. When she is upon the platform at the top, she shall arise as one of the Immortals, just like the Queen of the Western Heaven Herself!"

So it was true, Li Shan-po thought. The death of the Empress had driven him mad. Chen Yü and others had told him of the rumor. Concerned with other matters, he had not paid a great deal of attention, attributing it to mere gossip, which always ran rampant through the court. Now, with more than a little consternation, he wondered how he could best use this new development to his advantage.

Mental instability could make the Emperor easier to manage, but extreme madness could also make Wu-tsung unpredictable, and therefore highly dangerous. To see others in precarious situations pleased Li Shan-po, but he didn't wish to be in such a position himself.

He frowned uneasily, then, with the force of a thunderbolt, a new thought struck him. Many believed that the Mandate of Heaven—the doctrine that legitimized an Emperor's claim to the throne—could expire. Heaven was quite capable of withdrawing its mandate from a ruler who had become unworthy, handing it instead to any virtuous hero. Such a one would be infused with a spiritual power so potent that none could stand against him. What if he, Li Shan-po, were that man? More to the point, why should he not be?

"Ah, our faithful adviser frowns." Wu-tsung gave Li Shan-po a reassuring smile. "You need not worry, dear noble friend. We have already decided that in reward for your wise advice about the demon Buddhists, you shall ascend the terrace, along with Honored Mother and whomever else we so honor, to achieve immortality. Is it not a wondrous gift we offer you? Are we not a great and peerless ruler?"

Li Shan-po called up a smile in return. "Your magnificence is unrivaled, Exalted One," he murmured, and bowed deeply. "Your humble servant is honored by such gracious generosity. I am not worthy of it."

"That is quite true." Wu-tsung waved a magnanimous hand. "But we are in a kind mood today, and Honored Mother is pleased at the thought of you joining us in immortality. She has told us so."

"Has she." Concerned with his own twisting and weaving thoughts, Li Shan-po did not realize his sardonic tone until it was too late.

The Emperor's serene smile vanished with horrific speed. The madness in his sunken eyes intensified, causing them to blaze like hot coals. "Do you *doubt us?*" he shrieked. "*Do you, do you?* We, who are all-knowing, divinely appointed by Heaven Itself, are to stand here allowing ourself and Honored Mother to be *insulted?*"

Spittle and froth flew from that raging mouth, and Li Shan-po saw his own death in those black and bulging eyes. Sweat dampened the back of his robe, but he commanded himself not to look away.

"Your Majesty misunderstands," he said in the same tone he would use to calm an ill-tempered horse. "Never would this faithful servant presume such sacrilege. I was merely wondering if Honored Mother had also discussed

with her Divine Son the precise architecture of this terrace."

"Oh." As swiftly as it had come, Wu-tsung's fit of
rage vanished. "Well, no, she hasn't. But—but it will be
splendid beyond anything ever built by the hand of man.
Gold, silver, precious gems, all shall be used without
limit."

"I see." Li Shan-po waited a moment before asking
carefully, "And how will an undertaking which requires
such great wealth be accomplished? The imperial treasury
is vastly depleted, and the shortage of copper grows worse
with each passing day."

Wu-tsung's gaze grew confused. "Yes," he said in a
faltering voice. "That is true, isn't it? We . . . we suppose
we shall have to discuss this with Honored Mother."

"If Your Highness would permit, might I make a suggestion?"

"Yes." The Emperor nodded vaguely. "What is it?"

Li Shan-po smiled. "The Buddhist monasteries and
temples possess riches beyond counting. Let *them* provide
the means to construct the Terrace of the Immortals, and
solve the problems of the imperial treasury as well."

Work began the next day on the Terrace of the Immortals.
Summer lay full upon the land, and streaming with sweat
in the unrelenting heat, three thousand legionaries labored
like slaves in a copper mine.

Their task was as unpopular to the soldiers as it was
incomprehensible. And nowhere was this discontent more
evident than in the outraged face of their commander,
Ch'iu Shih-liang.

The Chief Eunuch, despite his debilitating illness, was
furious. Commander of the Left and Right Armies of In-

spired Strategy was one of his most important posts, the other being Commissioner of Good Works for the Streets of the Left. This combination of administrative power with control over two of the principal military forces in the area was enough to place him in a virtually invulnerable position. Or so Ch'iu Shih-liang had thought.

Yet here he was, helpless to contravene orders he disapproved of with every fiber of his being. To see proud soldiers from his command being used like beasts of burden was bad enough, but to have them set to such work without his knowledge or consent was even worse. And it boded still more ominous things to come.

The day after the massive task of moving earth to the construction site had begun, Ch'iu Shih-liang entered one of the palace buildings on routine business. Immediately he saw something was wrong.

The Buddhist images, and the sacred scriptures that had reposed there since earliest times were gone. In their places stood magnificent sculptures of Lao-Tzu, the reputed founder of Taoism, and statues of various other heavenly deities.

Ch'iu Shih-liang called over a passing clerk. "What is the meaning of this?" he demanded, gesturing at the Taoist images.

The clerk looked embarrassed. "Honored Superior, you—you do not know?"

"If I did," Ch'iu Shih-liang snapped, "would I now be asking?"

The clerk lowered his gaze. "It has just been ordered. All Buddhist images and scriptures must be removed from any building within the Imperial City and destroyed."

"Ordered!" Outrage swept Ch'iu Shi-liang, banishing for a moment the pain that had ripped continually through his body since the Empress's death. "Save for the Imperial

Palace itself, these halls of government are *my* domain! Who dares to give such orders?"

The clerk continued to stare at the floor. His voice was almost inaudible. "The noble Li Shan-po."

"What?"

"But acting on the command of the Son of Heaven, or so it is said."

The clerk's voice was carefully neutral, but Ch'iu Shih-liang heard the fear in it. A fear that probably had as much to do with the reputation of Li Shan-po and his growing favor with the Emperor, as it did with the actual power of the throne.

Waving the clerk on his way, the Chief Eunuch held himself straight as he proceeded through the busy corridors. Other subordinates bowed and greeted him, but lost in bitter reflection, he barely responded.

Why was he so taken aback at these events? He had watched many others climb the stairs of advancement, then tumble back down them. Surely it should come as no surprise that it was now his turn.

After all, he was an old man, ill and with little time left on this earth. If Buddhism was destroyed, and Taoism—worthy of the utmost reverence in its own right—was distorted beyond recognition by the mad acts of an unbalanced ruler, what difference did it make to him?

The old eunuch sighed. Despite all that had happened, he grieved for the fate of his Emperor. He grieved, too, for the murdered Dowager Empress, whom he had known when she was young and right in her mind. He even grieved for the evil destiny that was visiting itself upon thousands of devout Buddhists, who would suffer punishments they had done nothing to deserve.

"How venal and wicked are the acts of the unprincipled," he muttered as, bent over by the unrelenting pain in his joints, he opened the carved door to his office. "And how the innocent must suffer for those acts."

"Come now," a silky voice from inside the office said. "Surely it is not as bad as all that."

The Chief Eunuch's head jerked up. Seated comfortably behind the ornate desk, Li Shan-po jiggled an elegantly slippered foot upon one knee and smiled at him.

Her blood racing with the desire to join them, Rhea watched as the monks of the Temple of the Jade Waterfall went through their Shaolin drills. Each day it was the same. In the huge monastery courtyard set aside for that purpose alone, student and master alike gathered to practice.

The less skilled, most of them very young, stood in orderly rows under the tutelage of several monks, repeating a single feint or maneuver without pause until ordered to change to a new one. Those who had passed beyond the initial stages sparred together, while still others practiced complex series of movements, alone or in pairs.

The flat stones of the courtyard rang with the slap of two hundred pairs of feet, punctuated by shouts meant to summon up the maximum amount of inner strength. The air itself seemed alive, vibrating with these rhythmic cries and the dull thwack of practice swords.

Studying the deftly swirling figures, Rhea fidgeted with pent-up energy, aching to take part in the intense workout. The movements of Shaolin reminded her of the physical art forms her own people used to keep themselves fit, to train their minds in concentration, and to gain proficiency in self-defense.

Restlessly her gaze sought out Zhao. He was in a

far corner, engaged in a furious sparring contest with a
shorter but very muscular monk. Both men were bare-
chested, and each was armed with a six-foot wooden staff.
They circled and countered, the long staves clashing
against each other.

How well the name Red Tiger fit him, she thought.
Lithe and powerful, he stalked his opponent, moving with
flowing ease, leaping in to parry and block, then leaping
out to hunt and circle for new opportunities.

The sight of him, naked to the waist, muscles swelling
with grace and strength, increased her restlessness and
aroused her. It made her think of being held against that
chest, of feeling him plunge and shudder inside her with
the force of their shared passion.

So vivid where those memories, she throbbed with
yearning at the mere thought of them. They had not made
love again since that night by the river. With the rush to
reach the monastery they had barely stopped to rest the
horses, much less themselves. Now that they were there,
the improprieties were all too obvious.

Ah, but she missed him and that compelling closeness
they had shared. And yet, an insidious voice whispered inside her head, it would only worsen matters to make love
again, for it would further strengthen the bonds between
them—and the conflict.

"He is most skilled, isn't he?"

Rhea turned to the woman who had stepped up beside
her. "Yes, Lady Tamudj. Most skilled."

The elderly woman nodded. Glowing with a troubled
pride, her gaze rested upon her son.

Thoughtfully Rhea studied Zhao's mother. In the three
moons she had been upon the land, she'd had few opportunities to converse with Terran women, especially in private. Still, she could see that Zipporah Tamudj was a

unique woman, and an imposing one. Although generously built, she was far from plump, the full curves of her body indicating strength and sturdiness rather than softness. Her hair had once been black but now was shot through with great swatches of white. She wore it piled high upon her head, perhaps to give herself greater height.

It was an unnecessary affectation. Lady Tamudj was not an overly tall woman, but she possessed the dignity and stately grace that comes to those who have gone through great suffering.

Zhao had some of that same quality, Rhea mused. In his case, though, it was often forced, cloaking fires that were fanned constantly by his unrelenting hatred for Li Shan-po.

His mother was different. She was a calm and quiet woman, and the deep lines grooved into her face detracted little from her beauty. Rhea wondered how old she was. She strongly suspected that grief and hardship were responsible for the many wrinkles on that lovely face, rather than the passage of seasons.

Zipporah finally turned to her, gazing at Rhea with eyes so similar to Zhao's. "My son is apparently not the only one who is skilled," she said. "He tells me that you also possess . . . certain abilities. He says you are unlike any woman he has ever met."

"Yes." Rhea smiled slightly. "That is true."

Zipporah did not return the smile. "Why have you come here?" she asked suddenly.

A note of tension had entered the calm voice, and Rhea saw worry fill the woman's eyes, along with a barely concealed fear. "Lady Tamudj," she said quickly, "I mean no harm to either you or your son."

Unconvinced, the other woman eyed her. "About myself I care nothing. But about my son, I care a great deal.

Now as a mother, I am asking you: what do you want with Zhao?"

Rhea hesitated, wondering how much Zhao had told her. "It is not a question of what I want," she said at last. "There are other considerations here, matters that are difficult to explain."

She glanced out over the crowded courtyard. Zhao and the sturdy monk were still sparring, but without weapons now. Gleaming in the hot sunlight, the powerful muscles of Zhao's chest rippled as he danced in and out, exchanging kicks and punches with his opponent.

Zipporah followed her gaze. "May Shang Tian forgive me," she murmured, "but there are times when I wish we had never been given refuge here. Our teachings say, *And therefore choose life*. This I did, for myself and my child. But who could have foreseen that he would grow up a stranger to the ways of his people, more faithful to the traditions of this monastery than the ones he was born to?"

"You do wrong to fault yourself, Lady," Rhea said, her voice gentle with sympathy for this sad and dignified woman. "You had little choice and you did what was necessary. Red Tig— Zhao has grown up healthy and strong, in heart as well as in mind. What more could you wish?"

Zipporah looked at her. "I could wish that he would put off the robes of a lay Buddhist and never pick them up again. I could wish that he would leave this place and go to Yangzhou, where his boyhood friend would take him into the merchant trade."

Her green eyes grew hard. "I could wish that he would consent to my hiring a go-between, so a match could be arranged with a Zhuhu maiden from a good family. And most of all, I could wish that he would forget all the skills these monks have taught him. He will only use them to seek revenge."

Rhea decided to respond just to the last. "Li Shan-po did great harm to your family, Lady Tamudj. Doesn't he deserve a just punishment?"

Zipporah shook her head. "Punishment, no matter how well deserved, will not bring back my husband or any of my other beloved kin—blessed be their names. I have accepted what happened. It is in the past now. All that is left to me is my son, and I will not allow *him* to take Zhao too. And if Zhao persists in seeking vengeance, that is what will happen."

"Zhao must do what he believes to be right," Rhea said, "even as you did when you first sought refuge here."

The gaze Zipporah fixed on her was shrewd and wary. "My son is most taken with you, and I cannot decide how to feel about that. In truth, I have prayed for something like this, though it has always been a maiden of our people who has answered my prayers, not a stranger about whom I know nothing." She hesitated. "Please understand, I mean no offense. Indeed, you look as though you could be of the Zhuhu yourself. But Zhao has been very mysterious about your origins, and I am concerned. Especially because you still have not answered my question. Why are you here?"

Rhea was silent, gazing again at the wheeling, darting figures of Zhao and his opponent. Zhao threw her a quick glance and narrowly avoided a windmilling attack of fists by the burly monk. He returned his full attention to sparring, and still watching him, Rhea made up her mind.

"I cannot tell you everything," she said. "I can only say that twelve harvests ago, a vision brought me to the shores of this land. It holds me here still, and your son is part of that vision, perhaps the most important part. We are bound together, he and I, in ways I do not fully understand."

She turned back to Zipporah. "I have not even spoken to Zhao of this, but Lady Tamudj, I also carry a burden concerning your kin.".

"You?" The older woman looked puzzled. "Do not be foolish. Why, you are younger than my son. You could scarcely have been more than a child when these . . . these things happened. What could you possibly feel responsible for?"

"A great deal." Rhea's steady voice masked her anxiety. If she shared this knowledge with Zipporah, then she would have to share it with Zhao as well. Unconsciously she squared her shoulders.

"My vision contained a warning of what would befall your family, Lady Tamudj, only I was too dull-witted to see it. Had I been able to decipher it in time, your loved ones might still be alive. That is my burden, Lady, and it is one that grieves me deeply. Your son saved my life those twelve harvests ago, and I have repaid him poorly."

"Saved your life?" Zipporah seemed confused by what she had heard. "Zhao has never spoken of it. All I know is what my husband—blessed be his name—told me on returning from their last caravan: that my son had found a woman unconscious on the beach. But when he went back to help her, she was gone."

"Yes," Rhea said quietly. "I know."

Zipporah stared at her, understanding dawning slowly in her eyes. "Are you saying," she asked, her voice still calm but her hands twisting convulsively within the folds of her gown, "that you know something about this woman he found?"

Before she could answer, a deep voice spoke. "Beloved Mother, the Lady Rhea was that woman."

Zhao stepped up to stand beside her. A fine sheen of moisture glittered across his chest, and his gaze was searching as he looked at Zipporah and then at Rhea.

"Tell me the rest of what you have said to my mother," he ordered quietly.

"You must understand," Li Shan-po said to Ch'iu Shih-liang. "There is nothing personal in all this. I harbor no ill will toward you, Old Eunuch. It is merely that—for lack of a better way to put it—you are an obstacle to my desires, just as the Dowager Empress was. And obstacles must be removed. You have amassed enough harvests to accept these things."

Ch'iu Shih-liang stood very still. His body pained him greatly, but he would not let this usurper of his private office see that.

"Is that why you have come skulking about in my domain?" he asked in contempt. "To tell me you are my friend?"

"Oh, not at all." Li Shan-po was smiling again. "We are not friends, Old Eunuch, nor have we ever been. Friends are an impediment to desire. Once a man becomes your friend, you begin to care about his well-being, sometimes at the expense of your own. A bad bargain, if one wishes to advance in this world."

"Perhaps," Ch'iu Shih-liang said. "But after a man's days are ended, there is always a reckoning for the deeds he committed while in this world. Always."

Li Shan-po laughed delightedly. "How self-righteous you are now that mortality stares you in the face. Why, I could almost believe that in your secret heart you subscribe to the foreign demon faith our Son of Heaven has so wisely denounced."

"Accountability for a man's acts is Confucian as well as Taoist." Ch'iu Shih-liang gazed at Li Shan-po a moment, his lips curved in a frigid smile. "An educated man," he added, "would know that. But then, I am not in the company of an educated man."

He was immensely satisfied to see anger flash across Li Shan-po's face before the noble looked away. Sliding from behind the desk, he began to wander around the Chief Eunuch's office, his hands lingering on various objects. From a lacquered table, he picked up one of Ch'iu Shih-liang's favorite possessions, a flawless statue of two rearing stallions.

"A most beautiful sculpture," he said casually. "Perhaps you might let me have it, after you have gone."

"Gone?" Ch'iu Shih-liang's voice was ice. "I have no intention of going anywhere, *Spider*. It is you who will be going. And now."

"Ah, my brave old bobtailed dog." Li Shan-po smiled benevolently. "How flattering that you refer to me as others who know my power do. But you are wrong about my going. Which brings me to the purpose of my visit. You will soon receive official word, but I wanted to tell you about it myself, to see your face when you heard."

He waited, obviously savoring the moment, even more obviously hoping Ch'iu Shih-liang would snap at him to blurt out his news. With grim fatality, the Chief Eunuch schooled himself to silence. It was too late to change what was. In any case, he would not give this smirking noble the satisfaction.

The silence wore on for several minutes, weighing heavily in the hot chamber, disturbed only by the voices of passing clerks in the corridor outside and the distant shouts of the legionaries slaving on the terrace. Finally Li Shan-po broke.

"Since I have pressing business elsewhere," he said, "I suppose I must get to the point. The Emperor wishes you to resign two of your posts. It has reached his ears that you are unwell, and he is concerned. There is great work to be done in the days ahead, important work, requiring men who are strong and unafraid."

He gazed down at the horse sculpture, caressing it with a proprietary air. "You, Chief Eunuch," he went on carelessly, "will not be counted among their number. But the decision to relieve you of the greatest of your responsibilities was made with your best interests in mind."

"Of course." With an effort Ch'iu Shih-liang kept his voice calm. The dry sarcasm in it was another matter. That required no effort at all. "And might I ask what posts the Son of Heaven wishes me to resign?"

"Oh. Did I not mention it?" Li Shan-po carefully replaced the statue upon the small table. "You are to relinquish your positions as Commander of the Armies of the Right and Left and as Commissioner of Good Works for the Streets of the Left. Your replacement has already been selected."

Ch'iu Shih-liang's heart pounded with his effort to control his rage. Pain slashed at him, centering in his belly, seeming to set it on fire. "Who," he asked through clenched teeth, "selected my replacement?"

"Come now, Eunuch. You are not that stupid. Alone in this room with no one else to hear, we can both speak the truth. Wu-tsung is as mad as a cave-dwelling hermit. You know that as well as I. The one who is to replace you was selected by me. And it is only the beginning. But with this illness eating at your vitals, I fear you will not be around to see the conclusion of these very interesting events."

"I might surprise you." Ch'iu Shih-liang forced himself to stand erect. Yet as he stared at the other man, a horrible suspicion leapt into his mind. "How did you know that this pain now affects my vitals? No one else knows of it yet, not even my physician."

"I wondered when you might ask that," Li Shan-po said. "I know, of course, because I put it there."

Chapter 17

In ancient China there was a certain worm used for bewitching people. It was called Ku and it was employed in conjunction with magic rites and incantations. A handful of worms was put into a receptacle, and the magic ingredients added. The receptacle was then covered up and allowed to remain untouched for a year. The worms inside were soon starving and ate one another up, the last survivor being the Ku. This worm was especially suitable for casting a spell since, according to superstition, it now concentrated all the "poison" contained in those it had eaten up. The Ku was used to destroy unpopular people whom one wanted to get rid of . . .

—*The Chinese Art of Healing*

Ch'iu Shih-liang did not die at once.

Death from the Ku worm, although certain, was never

easy. In resorting to this dark magic, Li Shan-po had committed his one grave error. Ensconced in his magnificent house on the palace grounds, lying on what he knew would be his deathbed, Ch'iu Shih-liang considered this. As he did so, his twisted features moved in a ghastly grimace meant to be a smile.

"Master." The aged body-slave who crouched beside his couch leaned forward. "The pains are worse? I shall send a servant to fetch the physician—"

Ch'iu Shih-liang managed a feeble motion with one hand. "No, no, old friend, do not bother. Summon my assistant, Ah Shu, to me instead. Please do so at once. He is what I need now, more than anything else."

His mouth set in a thin line of disapproval, the slave rose. "Very well," he grumbled. "But this is hardly a time for visitors. You should be telling me to summon the physician, rather than worrying about affairs of state."

Still muttering, he shuffled out of the bedchamber. Watching him, the Chief Eunuch prayed Ah Shu would come quickly.

That prayer was granted. The eunuch Ah Shuh—Ch'iu Shih-liang's personal assistant and, until recently, his second in command—arrived so swiftly, it seemed he had been awaiting such a summons.

In contrast to many young men who took on a plump or feminine appearance when castrated, Ah Shu had retained much of his masculinity. He was a strong and competent-looking man, with the rolling walk of a born horseman, and his large eyes were always calm and direct. He greatly reminded Ch'iu Shih-liang of himself at that age, which was the main reason he had taken the younger man under his wing several harvests ago.

Ah Shu hurriedly bowed and raised clasped hands to his forehead before kneeling by the bedside. Ch'iu Shih-liang was surprised to see his eyes blurred by a film of tears.

"My faithful assistant," he whispered. "Why so distraught? I have not left for the Terrace of Night yet."

Ah Shu blinked hard. "But it will not be long, will it?" His rising grief led him to speak with more bluntness than usual. "Your personal slave tells me you have refused any further attempts by physicians to heal you, and now you have summoned me here with great urgency. Plainly your time is approaching."

Ch'iu Shih-liang chuckled, an act which brought immediate punishment in the form of spasms that raced through his body. "Ah Shu, my trusted one," he gasped when the pain had eased enough to allow him to speak. "I can always rely upon your candor." He shifted in the bed and forced himself to continue. "And as usual, you are right. Time does indeed grow short. That is why we must talk. But first, help me to sit up."

Frowning but obedient, Ah Shu complied. Propped up on cushions, the Chief Eunuch fixed his eyes, bright with fever and approaching death, on Ah Shu. "Three days ago Li Shan-po paid me a visit, not only to gloat over the events of these last moons, but to tell me that he is responsible for this illness that is robbing me of my life."

Ah Shu's eyes widened. *"Li Shan-po?"* His voice was thick with incredulity and building fury. "I have never liked that man, but I would never consider that he would dare to meddle with you, the favorite Chief Eunuch of the Son of Heaven!"

"Yes," Ch'iu Shih-liang said wearily. "But I am neither favorite nor Chief Eunuch any longer. As you well know, all my posts and titles have been stripped from me."

Ah Shu could barely restrain himself. "In my mind you retain each and every one of those offices, especially that of Chief Eunuch!" In his indignation, he was almost shouting. "And as for Commander of the Left and Right Armies and Commissioner of Good Works for the Streets of the Left, it is you who the soldiers and clerks give their loyalty to, not that fool, Chen Yü, who has supposedly replaced you!"

"Chen Yü is only a puppet, a frightened slave carrying out the commands of his master. And that master is Li Shan-po."

The pallor in his mentor's face brought back a semblance of Ah Shu's customary control. "Chief Eunuch," he asked slowly, "do you really believe he is responsible for your sickness?"

The effort of the conversation was taking its toll. The Chief Eunuch's voice was becoming slurred and weak. Knowing there was little time, he hurried on.

"Li Shan-po possesses the secret of the Ku. He has used it against me, and everyone knows there is no cure for its evil. He is also responsible for the Dowager Empress's death."

"The Ku," Ah Shu breathed, and involuntarily made the sign against evil.

"He thinks he has won," Ch'iu Shih-liang said. "He boasted to me of the Ku, and of how he poisoned the Empress. I cannot let him win. I cannot—"

His words dissolved into a groan, and Ah Shu leaned forward. "Please, Chief Eunuch, no more. You must rest."

"No. There is no time." Ch'iu Shih-liang struggled to clear his mind. "What has happened to me is only the beginning. Li Shan-po must be stopped, and that is why I have summoned you, my faithful Brother Eunuch. You must do what I would have done had I lived."

Ah Shu stared at his mentor, and despite the pain that

clouded his vision, Ch'iu Shih-liang could see doubt growing in the younger man's eyes.

"But if Li Shan-po truly committed these terrible deeds," he said cautiously, "why would he speak to you so openly of them? He is an arrogant and ruthless man, Chief Eunuch, but not a stupid one."

"True enough." Ch'iu Shih-liang shifted again. His head was swimming, and fiercely he fought the temptation to lie down. It was essential that Ah Shu believe him. "Bear this in mind, Ah Shu." Even to his own ears, his voice sounded appallingly weak. Straining, he sought to make it louder.

"All men, no matter how clever, have a weakness. Li Shan-po has revealed his to me. He has surrounded himself with creatures who are thoroughly obedient and therefore thoroughly boring to a man of his intelligence. He needs to boast of his accomplishments to those he thinks he has vanquished, particularly if he considers them capable of appreciating his skills. He has paid me that dubious honor.

"In his own subtle fashion, Li Shan-po is as mad as our poor Emperor. Even madder perhaps."

Ah Shu's expression changed from puzzlement to horror. The Chief Eunuch had been expecting such a reaction. Grimly he went on. "Yes, Ah Shu, the Son of Heaven's mind has been undone by the loss of his mother. I do not think even Li Shan-po foresaw this happening, but he has taken full advantage of the tragedy nonetheless.

"News of the Emperor's decline has not yet spread through court, perhaps because the Emperor has stayed in near seclusion since his mother's death, or perhaps because Li Shan-po has found some means of keeping it quiet. It will not last, though. The lunacy of this 'Terrace of the Immortals' will see to that."

"I cannot believe it." With a jerky movement, Ah Shu stood and began pacing the bedchamber. "The Son of Heaven mad? What will become of the Middle Kingdom? What will become of us?"

"The downfall of the T'ang dynasty itself, if Li Shan-po is not stopped," Ch'iu Shih-liang answered. "But if you are quick and clever, and if the gods are with you, the only man who may be able to prevent that from happening can be reached before events go too far."

Startled, Ah Shu spun around. Even as the questions sprang to his lips, the Chief Eunuch raised a hand to forestall them.

"I have written and sealed a letter." From some unknown source, strength trickled into his voice and limbs, and Ch'iu Shih-liang took hold of it. He feared this might be the last surge of strength he ever felt.

"I have done a great deal of thinking during these last days." He smiled thinly. "After all, when a man lies waiting for death, there is little else he can do. Li Shan-po told me much as he gloated over my downfall, and therein lies his madness. He possesses a truly powerful need to boast of what he has accomplished, as well as what he plans to do. I listened that day, Ah Shu, and I remembered. Now, it is all here."

From beneath the cushions, Ch'iu Shih-liang withdrew a leather bundle. "He thought me finished, useless and of no threat to him. But he underestimated me, and with your help, my friend, I will prove it to him."

His eyes were ablaze, glittering with pain and determination and the effort of fighting off death. "Li Shan-po will encourage the Emperor in his campaign to destroy Buddhism, and in so doing, cement his own position as the real power behind the Dragon Throne. When that position is secure, he will dispose of the Son of Heaven and begin a new dynasty—his own."

A long moment passed, then Ah Shu spoke, his voice low and tense. "What must I do?"

Ch'iu Shih-liang smiled, a smile that seemed more a death's grin. His brief spurt of strength was already fading, and with shaking hands he held out the leather bundle.

"I am placing this letter in your charge. It must be delivered to a certain man as soon as possible. You are the only one I can trust to do it."

Ah Shu stepped forward and took the packet. "I will do so. But what can this man do?"

"Much, if my faith in him proves true. Though he is young, he possesses a power and strength that impressed me from the first moment I met him. I believe he also has arts that may rival Li Shan-po's.

"What is more, the ashes of an old hatred lie between him and Li Shan-po. I do not know what caused that hatred, but Li Shan-po spoke about this person at some length. He is strangely obsessed with him, and though he would never admit it even to himself—afraid."

He pointed a wavering finger at the bundle in Ah Shu's hand. "All of it is there, in that letter. The man to whom you will deliver it will need to know everything he can about his enemy's weaknesses if he is to bring him down. For bring him down he must. Li Shan-po will not stop with destroying Buddhism. He will destroy the T'ang dynasty, and through his lust for power, perhaps the Middle Kingdom itself."

A shudder went through Ah Shu. "I pledge my life that this letter will be delivered, Chief Eunuch. No force, whether it be of man, of nature, or even the spirit world, shall stop me. This I pledge."

Ch'iu Shih-liang nodded. "Good." His voice was

weary now, the waning of life ever more pronounced in his ravaged face. "Then I will tell you his name and where I believe you will find him. You must take great care, Ah Shu. Above all else, do not underestimate the danger of this task. It has to be done in the greatest secrecy. If Li Shan-po has the merest inkling of this letter, you will never leave Ch'ang-an alive, much less reach your destination."

Ah Shu bowed. "I will remember."

"The man's name is Red Tiger."

The Chief Eunuch died as imperial drums signaled the Hour of the Hare. At peace now, his suffering ended, he would have been appalled to see what took place in the hours following his passage into the Terrace of Night. Even he, with all his cynical experience, could not have foreseen it.

Whether the orders came from the Son of Heaven himself or from some other, more sinister presence whispering in his ear was never to be known by those at court. What was known, and terribly so, was that on the day of Ch'iu Shih-liang's death, the destruction of his household began.

It was carried out with a speed and ruthless efficiency that stunned every member of the imperial court. There was no secrecy about it, and somehow that was the most horrible part—the utter arrogance with which it was done.

All the members of Ch'iu Shih-liang's household were shackled, taken to the execution ground of the imperial prison, and put to death. No one was exempt. Hired servants, house entertainers, gardeners, grooms, cooks, and slaves, all were summarily beheaded, their families along with them.

Later that day, the palace officers were ordered to take

over the wealth of the Chief Eunuch. Though Ch'iu Shih-liang's time in the world had been cut short by the Ku worm, he had lived a long life. During that life, he had accumulated riches with a love for beauty and a wise and discerning eye, amassing a magnificent fortune indeed. Jewels, gold, and silver completely filled the estate storehouses, and the cash, silk, and other assorted goods were beyond count. The treasures in the house itself were no less breathtaking: exquisite painted scrolls and standing screens, rare sculptures of fine ceramic and bronze, wall hangings and even furniture of flawless beauty.

It would take several weeks for all of it to be transported to the palace storehouses. During the course of that day filled with screams and the cloying stink of blood, thirty carts were loaded with plunder, and still the sweating officer in charge of the teamsters saw no end in sight.

When this was told to the Emperor, he went in person to see the treasures that had been brought to his repository thus far. Walking among the neatly piled possessions of his former Chief Eunuch, the Son of Heaven clapped his hands in delight.

"Our storehouses have never contained such things!" he exclaimed, and proceeded to giggle and caper about in glee until his elaborate headdress threatened to topple from his royal head.

It was the first time since the death of his mother that Wu-tsung had come out of seclusion. He had commanded a number of high functionaries to accompany him, and all of them—even Li Shan-po—were subdued. Despite the speculation running rampant through the court, Li Shan-po was the one man who knew the truth: Wu-tsung was acting entirely on his own.

The news of the executions had reached him early that morning, catching him utterly by surprise. He did not like surprises, and he especially did not like this one. To wipe out the old eunuch's household had never occurred to him for the simple reason that there was nothing to be gained by it. Ch'iu Shih-liang had been the obstacle, not a bevy of doddering old slaves, crying women, and suckling babies. This was a wanton act—the act of an unbalanced mind.

Wu-tsung had behaved unpredictably, and with frightening independence. Complete control over the Emperor was the foundation upon which the success of all of Li Shan-po's machinations rested. If that was lost, who knew where things might lead?

As for looting the old eunuch's estate, that made a little more sense. It had long been rumored that Ch'iu Shih-liang possessed great riches. Since his wealth had to go somewhere, it may as well go into the imperial stores, which Li Shan-po fully expected to call his one day. Yet here also, Wu-tsung had acted without his prompting.

Now Li Shan-po cast about in his mind, searching for some means to reestablish his influence. Only he had been permitted into the Emperor's presence during the last several days, and as he glanced around at the gathered officials, he felt considerably more cheerful.

Their shock and dismay at the Emperor's erratic behavior was hardly surprising, and their fear at witnessing the excesses of this day was all too evident. Perhaps these events, Li Shan-po mused, could be manipulated to his advantage after all. As worthless as the slaughter had first appeared, there was merit to the idea of removing the Chief Eunuch's associates, forces that could organize against him in the future. Smiling, he stepped forward.

"Divine One," he said, interrupting the Emperor's dance. "These treasures which the old bobtailed Buddhist lover accumulated behind your back are indeed wondrous. But perhaps you might wish your other orders to be carried out before the day grows too advanced."

"Orders?" Wu-tsung turned and regarded him vaguely. "Oh, yes, orders." His eyes, bloodshot and sunken, grew crafty. "You take care of it, Li Shan-po," he said. "But repeat for us what is to be done, so that we can be assured our wishes in the matter are clear."

"Of course, Majesty." Li Shan-po's smile widened, hidden by the flourish of his respectful bow. "You have taken the exceedingly wise precaution of commanding that the principal associates of Ch'iu Shih-liang be summarily executed and their households, even to their slaves, exterminated."

Wu-tsung beamed at him, then began twirling in a circle. Lifting his arms, he twirled faster and faster until the long sleeves of his robe billowed around his thin body like brilliantly colored wings. After several moments, he awkwardly stopped. Stumbling and dizzy, he fixed his gaze on the assembled officials behind Li Shan-po.

"Yes, yes." His voice was happy, eerily childlike. "How wise I am. Mother suggested it, but only *we* can give the commands! Are we not a great ruler?"

Gathered in the storeroom filled with stolen wealth, the screams of the dying still ringing in their ears, the high functionaries bowed their heads and did not speak.

Chapter 18

The dragon woman—from whence does she come?
But when she comes—she rides the wind and rain!
At the hall of her fane, below the blue woods,
She coils sinuously, as if about to speak to you.
Men of Shu vie there, with worshipful thoughts,
To offer her wine to the beating of drums.

—Ts'en Shen, a poet of T'ang,
The Divine Woman

Zhao stared out at the flat vista below him. The familiar view of rich green fields crisscrossed by streams and irrigation canals had always cast a spell of peace and contentment upon his soul. This evening the spell failed. The worries gnawing at him continued to churn, unabated by the tranquil scene.

Shimmering in the relentless heat, the sun—a perfectly round platter of fire in the hard blue sky—sank toward the distant line of purple that was the sea, dripping blood-red flames across the horizon. Heedless of the day's ending, the scores of peasants who dotted the fields and orchards worked on. This was the growing season; they would stay at their labors until long after dark.

Turning away from the busy scene, Zhao wandered over to the waterfall from which the Temple of the Jade Waterfall took its name. Sheltered in a grove of trees, the cascading water sounded its music, constant and soothing, untroubled and unmoved by man. Spray from the waterfall cooled his face as he paused beside the large pool into which it emptied.

Beside just such a pool in the magnificent gardens of the Imperial City, Rhea had come to him for the second time, to enchant his life and in that stubborn, bewildering, and generous way of hers, to take the weight of some of his burdens onto her own shoulders. Now she was gone. Seven days had passed and still there was no sign of her. Had she left him, returned to the sea that was supposedly her true home?

If she had, he could hardly blame her. There had been little welcome for her in the Temple of the Jade Waterfall once her true nature had been revealed. Only he had wanted her to stay, and apparently that had not been enough.

"But it should have been," he said to the gurgling waters. "It should have been."

On that terrible day in the practice courtyard, his mother, normally a composed and rational woman, had dissolved into hysteria. Zipporah had gestured repeatedly at Rhea, covering her eyes and invoking the Zhuhu sign for protection against the evil eye, and babbling such a multitude of Hebrew prayers, even Zhao had difficulty understanding her.

Efforts to calm her had been useless until Rhea left the courtyard. She did so without being asked, and every time Zhao remembered the stricken look in her eyes as she went, pain lanced through his heart.

He had been determined to go after her, but Zipporah, trembling and shaken, needed to be put to bed first. As soon as she was, Master Wu, who had a way of knowing everything that went on within his domain, sent for him. They talked for some time, and the master asked many questions. Finally he said,

"My son, this woman could be many things. She could be a human female known as a *shamanka*—a woman who communes with gods and spirits. Or she could be a goddess herself. Either one of these is not to be feared. However, she could also be a fox spirit, sent to tempt you into evil ways, or even worse, a crake, thirsting after your blood and your soul. These are to be greatly feared."

A vision of a night in Ch'ang-an rose in Zhao's mind, of Rhea refusing to flee to safety while he faced the angry mob in front of the Temple of the Peaceful Mind. Protectiveness surged through him, and he said, "Master, I would trust the Lady Rhea with my life. Of that I am as certain as a man can be."

Master Wu studied him. "We shall see," he murmured at last. "There is much to meditate on here."

Zhao had left him to search for Rhea, but she had vanished. No one in the monastery had seen her go, and though he walked the grounds all that night and every night thereafter, he found not a trace of her.

Zhao seated himself on one of the large boulders that ringed the pool. Many in the temple shared Zipporah's reaction to Rhea, but his own doubts about whether she was spirit or human had disappeared the night they made love. He knew, even if Master Wu and the others did not, that Rhea was not some malevolent spirit come to destroy him. She was a comrade who had fought and endured beside him, a lover who had shared her marvelous body with him in a gift beyond price. She was in a way he did not fully understand the mate of his soul.

He loved her.

It was an amazing realization, completely unlooked for, for vengeance had dominated his life for so long. And to find himself in love with a woman who claimed the sea was her home ... It was beyond any of his imaginings.

His emotions where Rhea was concerned were as shattering and complicated as they were undeniable. He was certain she was human, but if she truly lived beneath the waves, how could she be? And worse, if she did live in the sea, what could come of his love?

The questions went round and round in Zhao's mind, and no answers appeared to offer him the least bit of comfort. He knew only one thing. He missed Rhea with a hunger as fierce as that which drove him to seek Li Shan-po's blood.

Restless, his thoughts chafing at him, Zhao got up. Locking his fingers together, he raised his arms to the sky in a long, arching stretch that loosened every muscle. An hour earlier, he had attended the evening meditations in the Great Hall. Surrounded by his brothers, immersed in the familiar aura of quiet discipline, he had cleared his mind and found tranquillity. It was a fleeting peace, though, giving way as soon as he left the hall to the strength of his relentless yearning for Rhea.

Long indigo fingers spread across the grass as the sun sank lower. Even in this shaded grove the thick, hot air of day lingered, refusing to be defeated by the coming night.

Zhao stretched again, then abruptly pulled off his clothes and waded into the pool of the Jade Waterfall.

The water's icy touch soothed his body, though not his mind. For here in this pool, all he could think of was Rhea, of the night by the river, when he had stood on the bank and watched her leave its moonlit waters. To come to him.

The summer dusk melted toward full darkness, and Zhao stayed in the shallowest part of the pool, leaning against a boulder, letting the spray from the falls cascade over him. There was still light left, when he abruptly sensed that he was no longer alone. He jolted upright in the water.

Rhea glided through the trees and stopped at the edge of the pool.

"Rhea!"

She did not speak. Staring at him, she loosened the closures of her tunic, one by one, and pulled the garment over her head. The loose pants slid down over her hips. Then she was in the water, and in his arms.

Questions, recriminations, even expressions of joy, all fled from Zhao's thoughts. There was only Rhea, warm, alive, and *here*, in his embrace once again.

They came together fiercely, bodies straining as the pool's waters splashed and rippled wildly around them. The waterfall was a shield, its rushing noise muffling the sudden cry Rhea gave when Zhao entered her. His hands were under her buttocks, and her legs, smooth and strong, rose to lock themselves around his narrow waist. They found their rhythm, moving like creatures spawned of the waterfall itself, as Zhao supported her weight and the soft, cool water supported his.

Their movements grew more erratic, more urgent, then a low, exultant cry came from Zhao as he found his release. The sound of his pleasure joined with Rhea's. She gasped, shuddered, murmured something in her own tongue, then said his name, so softly he wondered if he had heard it at all.

Panting, they leaned against each other. Rhea's legs unlocked themselves from Zhao's waist. Unwilling to let her go, fearing she might disappear again if he did, he kept his arms tightly around her as her feet found the shallow bottom.

"I am furious with you," he began in an angry growl, then softened his tone. "But you are back, and that is all that matters."

There was no trace of a smile on her beautiful face. "I did not mean for us to make love," she murmured in the musical voice that had so haunted him these last seven days. "But when I saw you in the water, in *my* element— You were so beautiful. . . ."

"Why did you go, Rhea? Didn't you think I would look for you? What were you trying to do, drive me mad?"

"Of course not!" Indignation sparked in her eyes, then the somberness returned. "It seemed the best thing to do, Red Tiger. I did harm enough to your poor mother."

He shook his head. "It was her fear that harmed her, not you. There was no need to slip away like a person of no honor. Especially after all we've been through together. How could you do it, Rhea, leave me without a word? I was beginning to think you had gone back to the sea and I would never see you again."

In the faint light her expression was enigmatic. "And your mother?" she asked after a moment, "How is she?"

He grinned. "She's a tough woman, my mother. She got over her fright, although it took a while. Master Wu has insisted she stay in bed and rest. It is not a suggestion she's happy with."

Rhea did not return his smile. "After all the suffering she has known, I had no right to inflict anything further on her." She glared at him, as if frustrated. "All the traditions of my people, everything I have ever been taught, says that I should not have come back to the land. But I was drawn here so strongly. You walk within my mind, Red Tiger. I cannot make you leave."

She started to pull away from him, but he refused to release her. "Have you ever heard the myth of the dragon ancestor?" he asked. She shook her head.

"The tale is a very old one. A hunter roving the wild steppe lands to the north one day comes upon a mysterious and beautiful woman who announces that she has been divinely ordained as his mate. They lie together. But after this wondrous lovemaking, the woman disappears like the wind and rain. The following year, she meets the hunter again in the same place and presents him with an infant son, the destined founder of his family's fortunes."

He fell silent, gazing into her sea-gray eyes. "Tell me, Rhea. Have you been divinely appointed as my mate?"

She said nothing. His voice sliding to a whisper, he asked again. "Have you?"

She spoke at last, her voice as soft as his. "There was a time when I would have said such a pairing could not be possible."

He was still holding her, his gaze fixed upon her. "Will you go away from me again, then? Disappearing like the wind and rain, leaving me nothing?"

She shook her head. "I tried." Her voice strengthened with anger. "For both our sakes, I tried. But you drew me back."

"I am glad." His own voice was gentle. "Very glad, indeed."

"Are you? By the Mother, I don't know why. I have

caused such confusion in your life, I would think you'd be pleased if you never saw me again."

He touched his lips to hers. It was a delicate kiss, yet was filled with an intensity all the more powerful for its subtlety. "Does that," he asked when he lifted his head, "make you think I would be pleased?"

"No," she said, and her smile was touched with sadness. "No, it doesn't." Reaching up, she pulled his head back down to hers.

"Don't you see?" he said when their lips had parted. "Both of us are torn between two worlds. You, caught between sea and land. And I, caught between the ways of my people and those of the monastery."

"Oh, Red Tiger." She flung her arms around him. "What are we going to do?"

He held her tightly. "I don't know."

They stood in silence, pressed against each other, the song of the waterfall loud in their ears. Finally Zhao said, "I feel a distance between us that was not there before, Rhea. Why is that?"

"The distance has always been there, only I was able to conceal it before. Now . . ."

"Now?"

She opened her eyes, and they seemed as fathomless as the reaches of the sea. "Now I cannot."

He tightened his arms, pressing his chest against her breasts. "Tell me what you are thinking. I must know."

It was fully dark now, but Rhea could make out every nuance of expression on the face of the man above her. He was frowning with puzzled determination, his eyes catlike in the darkness, glinting with emerald flames.

Slowly she began to talk. It was difficult to speak of the dream-walk with him, even more difficult than it had been during the ill-fated attempt with his mother. But there was relief in it, too, the release of a burden long carried. Once she started, the words came with increasing ease.

"There is a ritual among us," she said, gazing past his bare shoulder, "a portal very old and very sacred, that leads each one of us, woman or man, into adulthood. We call it the dream-walk, and it is a journey of the mind. Until we embark upon it, we are youths, possessing all the seas as our playground, but given none of the status and responsibility of grown men and women. Only after the dream-walk can we start the next stage of our lives: matebonding and entering into the Eight Strata—the various callings of Teacher, Historian, Healer, and so on. And only then, are we free to visit the land whenever we wish."

She paused, waiting for him to speak. His attention utterly focused on her, Zhao remained silent, so she continued. "My people's greatest powers are those of the mind, and the dream-walk calls upon those powers. There are secret places in Mother Ocean, known only to us, deep within Her depths and filled with strange forces that have bided there since the dawn of the world. When a young merperson is deemed ready, he or she seeks out one of these places and goes to sleep there. It is then that the dream-walk begins. The threads of thought that lie buried when we are awake come to life. They blend with the power of these deep places and create doorways into the merfolk's past, doorways to help us learn and grow in wisdom."

Zhao was mystified. "And is it the same dream for each of you?"

"No. Each experience is different, for what is an important lesson to one is not so to another. We go on a dream-walk only once. It is a journey into our inner selves, a way of discovering lessons that will be important to us. People's destinies can be changed forever by their dreaming." She paused, gazing up at the sky. "The morning you found me on the beach was the time of my dreamwalk."

Zhao was silent. He was so still, in fact, Rhea grew concerned. Half-afraid of the fear and loathing she might see, she returned her gaze to him. He was watching her, his face stamped with a look of wonder so profound, tenderness swelled through her heart.

"So it is a meditation," he said, his tone filled with marvel. "A journey to seek the Way, and thus the path to Nirvana."

She smiled, joy as well as relief warming her at his acceptance. "Yes. In some manner, that is true."

"We, too, have our holy places." His deep voice was overlaid with a sense of delight she had never heard before. He had discovered a common thread between them, she realized, one that with his own sense of spirituality, gave him great joy.

Eagerly he went on. "Buddhists and Taoists have always sought out beautiful grottoes and mountains and waterfalls in which to meditate. My own monastery is named for this very spot. But—you spoke of secret places deep in the sea, Rhea. How did you leave yours and come to be on the beach that day?"

"I will probably never know," she said, somber once more. "The Elders believe the storm that raged over sea and land that night tore me from my place of dreaming and washed me up on that shore. But I think it was something more. I think a force and purpose beyond the wind and waves brought me to this land. My dream-walk was not of the sea and my people's past, as all the others' are. Mine was of the land, of the Middle Kingdom. And," she finished in a whisper, "of you."

"Of me?" Zhao went rigid. Not noticing, Rhea kept talking.

"We never dream about Terran events or about people of the land. Our lives are wrapped up in the sea. To have a dream-walk such as I had is unheard of. It was so extraordinary, even the wisest of the Elders could not interpret its meaning. They debated and argued for tide after tide about it, and still they could not agree. I have seen now at least a part of what they did not."

"And what is that?"

"When I met you that morning in the imperial gardens and you told me of your family's destruction, I ached for you, but it was more than sympathizing with your tragedy. I hurt because *you* hurt, because we are bound together in a way that happens only between a man and woman of the merfolk . . . a man and woman who are matebonded."

They stared at each other for a long moment. "How do you know?" Zhao finally asked, his voice hushed with both disbelief and hope.

She sighed. "The dream-walk showed me. It is difficult to explain, but there is no mistake. We are bound together as irrevocably as though you were born of Mother Ocean. The Elders were not pleased with my dream-walk, and they would be even less pleased if they knew I was speaking to you about it. They are the upholders of all our ancient customs, including a long-standing tradition that encourages the separation of your people and mine. For obvious reasons."

Zhao continued to gaze at her. "You mean that you cannot stay upon the land, and I cannot dwell in the sea."

She looked away. "Yes."

"So." The hope left him. "What will become of us?"

"As you said to me before, I don't know."

She levered herself out of the pool and sat down on a

large boulder. Zhao joined her. She waited for him to speak, and when he did not, she reached out and touched a single finger, feather light, to his forearm.

"I carry a pain deep inside me, Red Tiger, knowing that *your* pain need not have occurred. I could have stopped what happened to your clan. As I told your mother, you saved my life twelve years ago, and I have repaid you poorly."

Closing her eyes, she raised her face to the sky. A wind was building, and the heavy air smelled of approaching rain. She wished Zhao would say something.

"You must not chastise yourself." His voice was as soft as the night. "What happened was not your fault. It was Li Shan-po's. He must be called to account for what happened to my family. Why do you insist on holding yourself responsible for something you didn't do?"

She opened her eyes, gazing at the scattered clouds blowing across the stars. "Because I foresaw it," she whispered. "And foreseeing it should have been enough to stop it."

"But it wasn't," Zhao said evenly. "And who knows? Even if you had understood the message in these visions sooner, it would likely have made no difference. Li Shan-po's fate is to be evil. My fate is to see that he is punished for that evil—and my family's fate was to die."

She shook her head. "You do not really believe that. I know the teachings of Buddhism urge acceptance of such things, but I feel the rage in you, Red Tiger, the desire for revenge. Why do you try to hide it?"

He stared toward the waterfall, only a rush of sound and spray in the breezy night. "I seek to live by the teachings of those I respect. It is difficult for me, sometimes very difficult. Still, one cannot change what is, one can only accept. In that way lies peace."

"But you have not found your peace."

He didn't answer. Then, "No, but I will. In time."

"And does destroying Li Shan-po have anything to do with finding this peace?"

He slanted a glance at her, but did not reply. "If the teachings you respect urge acceptance of all that happens," she asked, "why do you pursue vengeance?"

His mouth hardened. "You ask a great many questions, my love. I seek and will have a just retribution. Even Master Wu would not gainsay me that. It is why he taught me the secret arts of Shaolin. But now, I will ask you a question. What other events did you foresee in these visions?"

"I saw enough." She closed her eyes. "The meanings are only now coming clear. What is happening to your temples and monasteries was also in my dream-walk. And it will get worse, Red Tiger. Much worse."

"How?"

"A madness is set to sweep over this land. It will not hold sway for long, but while it does, a great many will suffer."

"The madness," Zhao said grimly, "is already here."

"No." She opened her eyes and fixed them upon his shadowed face. "It has barely begun. Death is coming, and destruction. Those who live in the temples and monasteries are in danger."

He reached out and clasped her hand. "And the Temple of the Jade Waterfall. Is it in danger?"

"None will escape what is coming. None."

They stared at each other. Then in a single lithe move, Zhao stood, drawing her up with him. "Get dressed," he said quickly. "We must warn Master Wu of this."

He threw his clothes on in moments, and when Rhea was dressed, he grasped her hand and took a long stride toward the path that led from the grove. Rhea did not move. With smooth strength, she resisted the pull on her arm and stood still as a rock.

"It would not be a good idea for me to go with you, Red Tiger. Your Master Wu distrusts me, and your mother is terrified of me. It would be better if I stayed away."

"It would not be better for me!" He forced himself back under control. "I do not want you to disappear again," he said roughly.

He faced her, and the words came rushing out. "You say your visions tell you that we are bound to each other, that we are 'matebonded.' Well, I am glad of it. My heart cries out to you, Rhea, as much as yours does to me. I have never loved a woman before. But you—peculiar and exasperating though you are—live in my heart, my thoughts, my very soul. I will *not* let you leave me again. And I have enough concerns without worrying that you may try!"

"But both of us know that such a day will eventually arrive."

"I know nothing of the sort." He took her other hand and bent his fierce gaze on her. "However, this is not the time to speak of these things. Let us deal with the present for now. I will smooth the way with my mother. As for Master Wu, he will understand. Now, will you come?"

Hand in hand, they stood, eyeing each other. Far to the east, a first dire rumble signaled the approaching rain. Mingled with it came the faint sound of the sea.

Rhea gave Zhao's hands a swift squeeze. "I will come, Red Tiger. And I will not give you cause to worry about where I am. At least for now."

He continued to stare down at her. It was not an answer he liked, but there was no time to persuade her into a more satisfactory one. "I suppose I must be content with that," he growled. "At least for now."

As they left the grove, finding their way by feel alone down the rough path, Zhao glanced at her. "Where have you been all this time? You still haven't told me."

"With my brother," Rhea said.

Ah Shu stumbled to a halt. Exhausted, sweating, and gasping for breath, he rubbed his eyes. They had not deceived him after all. The pale orange lights flickering in the distance did indeed belong to a village.

"Amitabha, let it be the one that belongs to the Temple of the Jade Waterfall," he muttered fervently, and forced himself on.

Ten and a half li back, the valiant stallion that had carried him out of Ch'ang-an had sunk to the ground, broken-winded and dying. Ah Shu had wept unashamedly as he begged the beast's forgiveness, then severed the big vein in its neck to give it a quick death.

Staggering along the road, Ah Shu still wept to think of it. The roan stallion had been a great animal, the best he had ever owned. But even his enormous strength could not survive the pace of an eight-day journey squeezed into five. Ah Shu had never intended to ride the poor animal the entire way. His plan had been to lead a spare mount and to purchase another horse as the need arose, all so that a steady gallop could be maintained.

But with the bloodbath that began the day of Ch'iu Shih-liang's death, Ah Shu's plan had gone awry. The gods, or perhaps the old Chief Eunuch's ghost, had certainly been protecting him, but still he had barely escaped Ch'ang-an with his life, much less with the sturdy horse that had carried him so bravely.

A few drops of rain hissed down, then several more. Soon they were pelting Ah Shu's filthy face, mingling with the dust and sweat to form muddy rivulets down his cheeks. He opened his mouth, letting the drops splash onto his tongue as he passed the quiet village and continued down the road to the monastery. He was thankful for the rain, which was rapidly becoming a heavy downpour. Not only would it cool him, it might also keep away bandits.

Even as that thought crossed his mind, he saw two figures step out of the trees just ahead and stand facing him. *Bandits!* Frantically he fumbled for the dagger at his waist, realizing as he did that he should flee rather than fight. He could not risk the letter he carried falling into the wrong hands.

Before he could move, the taller of the two shapes called out in a loud, ringing voice, "Who comes to the Temple of the Jade Waterfall after darkness and in such weather as this?"

Ah Shu paused. Fingers curled tensely around the hilt of his dagger, he made his voice as deep and strong as he could. "I am a traveler seeking shelter for the night. Who is it that asks?"

Looming up in the rain-swept darkness, the tall man walked toward him. "I live in the temple," he said. "I am called Red Tiger."

Ah Shu felt his knees buckle. "Red Tiger?" He barely realized he had cried the name out loud. "The gods be praised!" He stumbled forward.

Chapter 19

Now idle clouds are images in pools, and
those days remote and hazy.
All things are altered, the stars shifted, many
autumns meted out.

—Wang Po

Matteo hated to feel unsettled. He had been swimming
along the shores of the Middle Kingdom's southern coast
for hours, plowing furiously through the choppy waters of
what the merfolk called the Jade Sea, hoping a solution to
his dilemma would present itself. It hadn't. Instead, the
teeth of his quandary had grown sharper, and he more
edgy.

Uncertainty had not always affected him this way. In
his youth he had enjoyed the heartpounding sensation of
being unable to predict what was going to happen next. It
had been exhilarating, driving him to seek out adventures
that would stimulate that excitement. Then he had joined
the Amazons and learned the awful lessons of war and

killing. He had suffered the birth of the black monster—
the beast that still lived within him, although now it only
slumbered.

In recent centuries, Matteo had learned to guard
against the monster's awakening by avoiding anything that
hinted at adventure, by keeping to known and familiar rou-
tines. Therein lay peace, and he had gained a great appreciation for that peace. The role of Historian among Terrans
provided him the exact refuge he needed.

As a Historian, all he had to do was observe, remaining untouched by the events he witnessed. Maintaining a
scholarly interest in Terrans and their doings was the only
thing necessary to do his job, and Matteo had become
quite good at his job.

But now his precious and coveted reserve was being
ripped apart. It angered him, especially since the one responsible for it was his own sister!

If Matteo had possessed a tail like the mermen of
Terran legends, it would have struck the water with a resounding slap as he upended himself in a furious dive. He
undulated through the depths for some time, yet instead
of heading out to open sea as he knew he should, he continued to pace the shoreline. Why he lingered was a mystery. Rhea was gone, *again*, and he knew where his duty
lay.

When she had appeared seven days earlier, gliding toward him through the wind-whipped swells of a late-
afternoon tide, his heart had turned over at the grief on her
face. He had been waiting for some days, held by the feeling that she would come. Eagerly he had pushed through
the waves to meet her.

"So," he had said, his tone harsher than he'd intended.
"What did that fool Terran do to hurt you?" When she

didn't answer, he added, "Probably no more than behave like all the rest of his kind. That alone would be sufficient."

Without a word she dived beneath the waves, and suddenly worried, he followed her. *Let us not discuss it,* she said to him telepathically when he caught up to her. *I have been long away from Mother Ocean and I need Her healing. Leave me in peace.*

Matteo had never heard his ebullient sister speak like that, with such heaviness and pain. It shook him, and oddly respectful, he swam after her, following in silence as she descended to the deepest waters of the Jade Sea.

For some time they swam through the depths, taking no particular course. Rhea continued to lead, and when she finally chose a direction, Matteo was immensely relieved that it was away from the land and out to sea. He swam up beside her, and she smiled wanly at him through the gloom.

This is good, she said. *Truly, there is no feeling like the touch of salt water against your skin, and the push and tug of Mother Ocean's currents. I swam often in the rivers and streams of land, but they were nothing compared to this.*

How well I know it, he agreed. *Why do you think I pressed you so hard to come back? This is where you belong, sister. Not on the land, trailing after some Terran, trying to protect him from his own bloody nature. I am glad you have come to your senses at last.*

Her silver eyes burned at him through the dimness, then she turned away and swam on.

She had not come to her senses. Within a few days Matteo realized that all too clearly. Rather than continuing on toward the limitless reaches of the sea, she went only far enough to put the Middle Kingdom's coast well behind her. Then, despite all of his entreaties and arguments, she flatly refused to go any farther.

"Abandon this preoccupation," he shouted in his frustration on their fourth day together. "Or by the Great White's Tooth, I *will* go to the Elders and tell them everything!"

They had just finished hunting for their afternoon meal and were resting in a pocket of water where the Jade Sea was calm. After their long stay upon the land, neither could get enough of food caught and eaten in the natural way. They gorged themselves upon tender prawns, scallops, and cuttlefish, devoured large quantities of oysters and the shell-less mollusks known as sea cucumbers, delighted in gathering up long tasty runners of sea grass to eat along with handfuls of slender, succulent little squid.

But though Rhea's appetite had been as hearty as her brother's, she had grown less interested in food as the days passed. Now she looked at Matteo with that set expression he was beginning to dread. He spoke before she could.

"Rhea, you told me that the red-haired Terran's relations cast you out. They thought you a sorceress or a spirit, didn't they? Gabbling incantations and making signs of protection against you like the superstitious idiots they are. And you deserved it! What else did you expect?"

"You forget," she said steadily. "Red Tiger did not cast me out. I came away on my own."

He rolled his eyes. "The only sensible thing you've done yet. And the next sensible thing will be not to go back."

"Matteo." Her voice was quiet and sad. "When I left the monastery, I had it in mind to do just that. I had brought such pain to Red Tiger and his mother. Perhaps the dream-walk had been wrong, I thought, or perhaps I had misunderstood. So I came back to the sea, answering the craving in my blood for the waters of Mother Ocean. Here, with the wind in my face and no sign of land anywhere, I will be whole, I told myself. But I was wrong."

"You were not wrong." Matteo scowled at her. "The sea *is* the only place where any of us are whole."

"For me that is no longer true. Without Red Tiger, a part of me is missing, and not even Mother Ocean can replace it. It would be better for us both if that were different, but it is not."

He could still see her as she had looked that day, wet black hair blowing in the fresh breeze, the strong sunlight bouncing off the tossing waves to reflect in her eyes. How haunted those eyes had been, how they had pleaded with him to understand.

He had not. What she spoke of was insane, unnatural, completely beyond his comprehension, yet all his attempts to make her see reason failed.

In the drab twilight of their seventh day together, she suddenly faced land. "He is calling to me," she muttered. "More loudly than ever before."

"Preposterous!" Matteo exploded. "You have been touched in the head by Terran lunacy until you are as demented as they!"

Before he could move, her arms, wet and smooth, twined around his neck. She hugged him with all her strength, whispered, "Forgive me," then was gone, swimming back to the Middle Kingdom as he shouted furiously after her.

Now it was morning again and Matteo was still there. Something held him. But what?

Gliding to the surface, he thrust his head through the roof of the sea. Dawn was breaking, a stormy dawn. Lightning flickered over the mountains to the north, and rain and wind lashed at the waves of the Jade Sea until they pitched and galloped like maddened Terran horses.

Matteo barely noticed the heaving turmoil around him. He rode the water easily, gazing at the dark walled bulk that comprised the seaport Yangzhou.

The city sat directly upon the coast, an important center of trade because of the variety of sea traffic that stopped there. However, on a dawn like this, no boats dared to brave the angry seas.

Beyond the city walls Matteo could see the glimmer of the broad river Terrans called the Long and the road that wound its way from the city along the coast. Suddenly he raised himself higher. A man and a horse had just left the city by the south gate. Heads bent against the wind and rain, they slogged their way along the road.

His gaze fastened on the mounted figure, Matteo swam toward the land. The man's brawny shape aroused a strong suspicion in him. As he drew closer, he saw he was right.

The solitary horseman was his erstwhile companion, Strong Man.

Matteo frowned. He and the Terran had parted upon reaching Yangzhou, and during the short time they had traveled together, he had learned a great deal about Strong Man.

Despite his ignominious defeat, Strong Man had waxed gregarious on the trek to Yangzhou. When he had talked about his reasons for traveling to the south, the skin on Matteo's neck had prickled, a sure sign that here was something of portent.

"I have journeyed here on an important task for a certain person." Strong Man's tone had been distinctly boastful. "A most wealthy and influential person. I am the only one who can do what he wishes done."

"And what," Matteo had asked, keeping his own tone mild and uninterested, "does he wish you to do?"

Strong Man had laid a thick finger alongside his nose and winked. "I should probably not say anything more, but to be frank, Matteo, I do not like this man. Actually, I like you far more. But he is paying me. Indeed, when this task is completed, I will have enough taels of silver to live comfortably the rest of my days. And because I like you and do not like him, I will also tell you this. When my job is done, someone will no longer be among the living."

Recalling that conversation, Matteo's frown deepened as he watched Strong Man ride past. The route he was taking would lead him to the Temple of the Jade Waterfall, where Rhea said Red Tiger lived. The place she had gone back to.

"Why should I care?" Matteo muttered aloud. "Rhea can take care of herself. And as for these Terrans, they are forever murdering each other. Such matters are no longer my business."

Still he watched Strong Man as he rode farther south. Rhea would have reached the temple and the Terran she was so obsessed with by now. Matteo sighed and slapped the rocking water with a heavy palm.

"Go south," the emaciated monk by the Dragon Pool had said to him. "Your destiny lies there."

Perhaps he had better follow Strong Man.

Ah Shu gulped his third bowl of *t'e* and leaned back, sighing heavily. Across from him, the tall foreigner with hair the color of flame and eyes as green as jade sat in a graceful lotus position, the thin parchment letter spread out upon his knees. The arresting face with its high cheekbones and strong, prominent jaw was impassive. It had been so since the man first entered the guest chamber that Ah Shu, exhausted and semiconscious, had been brought to the night before.

Rested now, although he could have slept much longer, Ah Shu felt greatly refreshed by the gruel and *t'e* the foreigner had brought him. But with his physical needs seen to, the eunuch found himself fidgeting, held in the grip of a feverish impatience as he waited for a response to the message he had risked his life to deliver.

To his increasing frustration, Red Tiger said nothing. Save for an occasional but unrevealing glance at his guest, the foreigner's gaze remained fixed on the letter.

Finally Ah Shu could stand it no longer. Sitting forward, he cleared his throat. When that produced no reaction, he coughed. "The Chief Eunuch," he said, "was most adamant that that letter reach you as soon as possible."

Zhao looked up. "Was he still alive when you departed the capital?"

"No." Ah Shu lowered his head, suddenly unable to speak. This time when he cleared his throat, it was unfeigned. "Ch'iu Shih-liang entered the Terrace of Night soon after imparting the scroll to me."

"I am sorry." Zhao, too, lowered his head. "He was a great man, as well as a brave and wise one." His voice hardened. "The one he named as his murderer has one more evil deed to answer for."

The foreigner's tone prodded Ah Shu's grief and anger, emotions he had held in check during his arduous journey. "Yes," he said bitterly. "And not only was his death hard and filled with excruciating pain, but the funeral rites, all the proper ceremonies due a man of his station, were forbidden!"

Zhao's head came up, his eyes piercing. "By whom?"

"I am not sure, Youposai. I fled the Imperial City in great haste, you see, for the murder of the Chief Eunuch was only the beginning. On the day of his death, every member of his household was beheaded."

Ah Shu paused, grimacing. "And as if that were not abomination enough, all of Ch'iu Shih-liang's wealth, down to the very last copper cash, was looted, carted off to the imperial treasury like spoils taken from rebel barbarians. It was terrible, Youposai Red Tiger, terrible. But even that was not the end. Palace soldiers were then sent to seize the old man's friends and close supporters and their entire households as well, all to receive the same fate. I myself barely escaped with my life."

The door to the chamber opened, and a foreign woman entered. After bowing courteously to Ah Shu, she crossed the room and dropped with fluid grace to sit beside Red Tiger.

She was tall for a woman, Ah Shu noticed, even for a barbarian. She was also extremely beautiful.

He rarely paid attention to such things. This woman, however, was worthy of notice, and not only because of her stately height, and the striking combination of rich ebony hair and pale gray eyes. She had seated herself next to Red Tiger with casual ease, as if she belonged there. It made the eunuch stare at her thoughtfully, and with some dismay.

He had heard rumors of Li Shan-po's obsession with a black-haired foreign woman, a woman he could not find. Could this woman be she?

"Youposai Red Tiger," he said carefully. "I—I thought we might continue our discussion alone." He gave the woman a smile that was meant to be both placating and humorous. "After all, it is not in the nature of women to be discreet, is it? It would be unfair to ask this lovely creature to behave with circumspection and secrecy, when such qualities are so unnatural to her sex."

He continued smiling, but observed with some discomfort that the woman did not smile back. Instead, she looked at him with eyes that bore an amazing resemblance to ice on a frozen river. Nervously he returned his gaze to Red Tiger.

"This woman is called Rhea," he said. "I assure you that she is most circumspect. And since she is the subject of a good part of Ch'iu Shih-liang's scroll, she has as much right to be a part of this discussion as anyone."

"But . . ." Ah Shu stopped. The foreigner's tone was impeccably polite, but his eyes, while not as cold as the woman's, held an expression that made the eunuch think better of further argument. He shrugged, then muttered, "It is your business, I suppose. If you want—"

Red Tiger cut him off. "Have you read this letter, Eunuch Ah Shu? Are you aware of what it says?"

Ah Shu drew himself up. "I have not read the scroll, Youposai." His tone was solemn and affronted. "I carried it here with its bindings undisturbed, wrapped as tightly as when Ch'iu Shih-liang—honored be his memory—gave it into my hands."

"I was not questioning your honor, Eunuch Ah Shu," Zhao said gently, "but trying to discover how much of this grave situation you know about."

Mollified, the eunuch nodded. "I believe I know most of it, Youposai. Ch'iu Shih-liang spoke to me at length that night, both of what was in his mind, as well as his reasons for writing the letter."

"Eunuch Ah Shu," Rhea asked, "how did Ch'iu Shih-liang die?"

Ah Shu turned to her. She spoke with a slight and strange accent, but she had a lovely, almost mesmerizing voice. It reminded him of flute music played low and soft. He was beginning to see why Li Shan-po wanted her so badly.

"Have you heard of the Ku worm, Lady?" Ah Shu tried without success to repress a shudder as he asked this.

Rhea shook her head and gave Zhao a curious glance. He explained. "There is a certain worm that can be used for bewitching people. It is called Ku, and in conjunction with the proper incantations and rites of magic, it can be a devastating tool against one's enemies.

"And no one," he went on grimly, "knows its uses better than Li Shan-po. He used it to kill the Chief Eunuch."

"Yes." Ah Shu poured the last of the *t'e* into his bowl. The delicate liquid had grown cool, but he gulped it without noticing. "I know that in this scroll Ch'iu Shih-liang described the Son of Heaven's madness, how he had the Dowager Empress interred before the appropriate forty-nine days of prayer were completed, that he did not observe mourning, because he thinks she is still with him. And now, there is this ill-conceived foolishness called the Terrace of the Immortals."

"Yes." Zhao's gaze dropped to the letter across his lap. "Among other equally dire developments."

Ah Shu drew a deep breath. "Even more has happened that Ch'iu Shih-liang could not tell you of, because it took place after he passed into the Underworld.

"Imperial decrees have gone out," he continued in a low voice, as if fearful of being overheard "that give authority for every Buddhist monastery and temple to be looted. Of course, that is not the word the edicts use, but it will be the result nonetheless. Just as Ch'iu Shih-liang's wealth was stolen, so will the riches of the temples be taken and carried off to enrich the imperial coffers."

Zhao's eyes widened, shock flowing across his face, disturbing his imperturbable calm for the first time since he'd entered the room. "This is sacrilege," he said in disbelief. "Even the Emperor would not dare . . ."

"He has dared. With Li Shan-po bewitching him, he has dared. For *that* one will dare anything."

Zhao stared out the guest chamber's one small window. His face was set in stern lines and his eyes were ablaze with emotions Ah Shu could easily guess at. Beside him the woman called Rhea watched him with a look of deep concern.

He forced himself to sit patiently, waiting for the *jushi* to speak. When the room remained wrapped in silence, Ah Shu leaned forward.

"Youposai Red Tiger," he began. "The edicts concerning Buddhism are only the beginning. The Chief Eunuch died knowing that Li Shan-po wants more, much, much more, than the suppression of a foreign religion. You were Ch'iu Shih-liang's only hope. He told me you are the one man capable of bringing about Li Shan-po's downfall before it is too late. He believed this very strongly. Now that I have met you, I see he was right."

Zhao's stern features was lightened by a slight smile. "Do you?"

"Yes," Ah Shu replied stoutly. "So now, Youposai Red Tiger, might I ask what you intend to do with the knowledge Ch'iu Shih-liang has given you?"

The smile vanished, and Zhao turned to look at Ah Shu. His expression was so cold, Ah Shu felt his very blood chill.

"I have long sought retribution from Li Shan-po for certain things he has done," Zhao said softly. "Now I see what form this retribution must take." He was silent for the space of a heartbeat, holding Ah Shu's gaze with frightening eyes. "Li Shan-po must die. It is the only way. And it seems that the fates have elected me to be the instrument of his death."

Chapter 20

In former times too were clouds and rain—
In present times as well are clouds and rain.
Hence when wild depravity abounds
Men meet in dreams the woman of Shaman
Mountain.
Up to now even a paragon—an enlightened
monarch—
Might heed such weird goblin talk;
But nowadays the clouds above those peaks
Yield freely only freedom from care.

—Su Cheng,
*The Divine Woman: Dragon Ladies
and Rain Maidens in T'ang Literature*

The Terrace of the Immortals was finished.

It had been erected in an astonishingly short time, and more than one man, driven to exhaustion by heat, thirst, and overwork, had died in the building of it.

To Emperor Wu-tsung, such deaths carried no more

weight than if someone had told him a few rabbit-horses had broken down while transporting goods to Ch'ang-an. The soldiers who had constructed the terrace were beasts of burden, nothing more. In any case, Wu-tsung's madness had grown beyond the point of worrying about soldiers.

The day the terrace was completed, the oldest of the previous Emperor's concubines approached the Son of Heaven while he was walking with his royal entourage through the imperial gardens. In a voice somewhat querulous but remarkably steady for a woman of her age, the Dowager Empress gently reproached Wu-Tsung.

"Royal One," she said. "Forgive a foolish old woman for daring to speak to a ruler so wise as yourself, but do you not think your honored father would be disturbed by the excesses that have been occurring of late?"

She got no further.

Without a word, Wu-tsung turned to one of the Imperial Guards, motioned brusquely for the man's bow and arrows, and shot the hapless Dowager Empress dead. Then he continued on his walk, conversing cheerfully with what many believed to be his mother's ghost, not sparing so much as a glance for the pathetic corpse left sprawled behind him on the path.

As the afternoon shadows lengthened Chen Yü hurried off to Li Shan-po's estate to bear him word of this latest atrocity. He found—not entirely to his surprise—that the Spider had been present at the slaying.

"This is a terrible thing, Master," the eunuch said. "An act that was most unprincipled!"

Li Shan-po did not reply. Reclining on his favorite chaise, he studied his distressed minion with cold and thoughtful eyes.

Since his appointment to the post of Chief Eunuch, Chen Yü had exhibited flashes of independence that indicated he might be allowing the importance of his new role to go to his head. He also might be forgetting who had put him there.

"And that is not all," Chen Yü continued, oblivious to his master's scrutiny. "Yesterday the Son of Heaven went to that infernal terrace and for no reason whatsoever drew a bow and shot one of the general supervisors. It is the third general supervisor he has killed since the building of that cursed thing began! Where will it end, my lord? And when?"

Li Shan-po answered him at last. "That is not for you to concern yourself with, Eunuch." His voice was soft, but there was a crackle in it that stung Chen Yü with the accuracy of a whiplash. "It will end where and when I say it shall end. And not before."

Chen Yü's reaction was immediate. "Of course, Master, of course. I did not mean to question you, truly I did not—"

"Good. For if you ever did, I would be forced to remind you who made your ascendancy to the glorious heights of Chief Eunuch possible. Need I say that such a reminder, while amusing for me, would be most unpleasant for you?"

Chen Yü's face had taken on the grayish cast of dirty snow. "No, Master."

The quiver in his voice made Li Shan-po smile.

The next day, however, as pale gold light illuminated the vast city, a more somber Li Shan-po left his mansion and set off for the ceremony that Wu-tsung had commanded would be held atop the finished Terrace of the Immortals.

Always vain of his appearance, Li Shan-po was on this morning positively resplendent. His long gown of red damask flowed gracefully about his ankles. Patterned with a bold design of medallions worked in gold thread, the gown had been ordered especially for this occasion.

The rich heavy material was too hot for the season—already, sweat dampened the back of his neck—but he had no choice except to wear it. Wu-tsung had given detailed instructions as to how his favored adviser, whom he planned to honor with immortality on this glorious day, should be garbed. So Li Shan-po stomped along under the steadily brightening sky, feeling his own dour mood build with the heat of another torpid day.

Wu-tsung's instability was an ever-increasing menace. Li Shan-po's fears that he might not be immune to the Son of Heaven's unbalanced rages had already been realized. Twice his quick wit and skilled tongue had been all that saved him from becoming the target of a royal arrow or the executioner's sword. The fact that Wu-tsung forgot both of those incidents almost as soon as they occurred did not reassure Li Shan-po. If anything, it worried him more.

Yet it was too early to do away with this caricature of a ruler. Removing the Empress and Ch'iu Shih-liang had been a simple matter. What was more, the troublesome behavior that had led to their removal paled to the insignificance of flea bites on an elephant, when compared to the actions of the Son of Heaven.

Li Shan-po sighed. There was nothing to be done about it—not at the present time anyway. Mad as Wu-tsung was, the court still regarded him as the legitimate Son of Heaven, and the groundwork to change that view was far from complete. Morosely he considered this unpleasant truth as he strode past cordons of Imperial Guards, making his way toward the Terrace of the Immortals.

One hundred and fifty ells high, just as Wu-tsung had specified, the terrace soared into the brassy sky. Stairs, hastily lined in precious yellow jade, led to the summit—a flat area wide enough to hold a building of several stories. On top of this apex reposed a tower, draped in brilliantly colored curtains and boasting five elaborately carved peaks.

All about the four sides of the terrace, boulders were piled. They were to give the terrace the look of having sprung from nature itself, and surprisingly, the idea had succeeded.

With artful skill, the boulders had been arranged to create mountain cliffs and small grottoes adorned with pools. Even rocky paths had not been forgotten. In an unexpected touch, a number of fragrant green pines had been planted around the terrace, along with a virtual legion of flowering arbor plants and rare trees.

The Terrace of the Immortals was magnificent. Wu-tsung's obsession—the result of a deluded and erratic mind—had actually resulted in a structure that was truly impressive. Seen from afar, the Terrace of the Immortals rose higher than anything around it, looming up like a solitary mountain peak, not a man-made building at all.

There was an air of mystery about it, too, enough so that even a sane man—much less an unbalanced one—could almost believe that if he ascended those jade stairs, he would indeed achieve immortality.

A great many people had already gathered around the edifice. Murmuring among themselves, they stood at a respectful distance from the gorgeously attired Emperor, who was striking proud poses in front of the jade staircase.

Li Shan-po saw an apprehensive Chen Yü standing on the outskirts of the crowd, and he scowled. Clearly he had miscalculated in his choice of Chen Yü. Weak-stomached and almost always wringing his hands over something or other, the eunuch was rapidly becoming unreliable.

Glumly Li Shan-po turned his attention to the others who made up the throng. Scores of officials and aristocrats had been summoned to watch the Emperor climb to eternal life. Prominent among them, indeed almost outnumbering the bureaucrats and the highborn, were the Taoist priests.

Few of them appeared happy. That was hardly surprising. They had more to lose than anyone if the events planned for this day went badly.

"There you are, Li Shan-po." The Son of Heaven's tone was peremptory. "We have been waiting for you. We were beginning to grow quite wrathful."

Li Shan-po made his obeisance. "Forgive me, Divine One. I was under the impression that the ceremony was to take place at the propitious Hour of the Dragon, in which case, I am early. If my extreme stupidity led me to misunderstand your royal wishes, I most humbly apologize and beg for your pardon and mercy."

Wu-tsung cocked his head as though listening to someone. "Yes, yes, you are right," he muttered, and all those watching knew it was not Li Shan-po to whom the Emperor spoke.

The Son of Heaven returned his gaze to Li Shan-po and said cheerfully, "Honored Mother reminds us that the Hour of the Dragon was indeed the time she considered most favorable. Therefore, you are forgiven." He smiled, and Li Shan-po commanded himself to smile back.

Wu-tsung's mind was deteriorating steadily. Li Shan-po saw him nearly every day, and each time he did, he believed more flesh had wasted away from the royal bones.

The eyes in that skeletal face had descended into hollows so deep, they resembled caverns. The expression they contained was chilling, so empty and haunted that sometimes even Li Shan-po had trouble meeting them.

Li Shan-po knew, from bribed servants and imperial-household eunuchs, that the Emperor often refused to eat. He rarely slept, either, insisting on staying awake almost the entire night while he held lengthy conversations with what was undoubtedly the invisible presence of his mother.

Perhaps, Li Shan-po thought hopefully, Wu-tsung would pass into the Terrace of the Night all by himself, without any assistance. That would be a blessing indeed—provided it happened at the proper time.

The Emperor flung out an arm. "Look you!" he cried. "Eighty-one Taoist priests have we assembled on this auspicious day, nine for each of the Nine Heavens. Since the beginning of the last moon, they have been making sacrifices for each of the twelve hours of the day, so that the maximum amount of spiritual aid will be summoned to assist us in this noble endeavor."

He turned his head, beaming at the yellow-robed priests gathered around him—a great number of whom looked as though they could barely stay on their feet. The priests had been commanded to make these constant sacrifices in an open courtyard, and exposed both to burning sun and drenching rain, many of them had fallen ill.

Wu-tsung paid no heed to the tottering posture of his religious advisers. The royal head cocked again, although this time the Emperor listened for an earthly sound—the drumbeat announcing the Hour of the Dragon.

Within moments it came, a distant boom carried on the still hot air. Whirling around, Wu-tsung let out an exultant laugh.

Beckoning Li Shan-po forward, he shouted, "Come and stand behind your Emperor, my trusted adviser. Prepare to follow us into immortality! Let the procession form. Musicians, begin the songs we have composed for this great occasion. It is time!"

Hastily Li Shan-po took his place, keeping his face impassive. From the corner of his eye, he could see that others were not as successful. With the exception of the deluded Emperor, every man bore the same expression: a look sick with dread at what was to come.

The melody of flute, drum, lute, and cymbals that followed the procession up the jade stairs was discordant. Some of the musicians were clearly indignant, unable to contain their embarrassment at what they were being forced to play.

Fortunately for them, Wu-tsung was happily ignorant of their discomfort. Clapping his hands in time to rhythms only he could hear, the Son of Heaven marched up the stairs with long, purposeful strides, mumbling to himself.

Despite the terrace's height, at the pace the Emperor set, it did not take long for the procession to reach the top. Many of those who followed the Emperor, particularly the feverish and ill priests, were panting by the time they stepped onto the wide platform. Not Wu-Tsung, though. Malnourished and weak though he was, his obsessions lent him a force and energy that only the truly mad possess.

Li Shan-po stared at the Emperor, contempt washing through him. How little this emaciated figure, his magnificent headdress perched askew on his disheveled head, resembled a Son of Heaven. And how much more so did he, Li Shan-po! In time, he assured himself, that headdress would sit upon his own head, and he would be founding his own dynasty.

From the ground below, the jangled playing of the musicians was borne upward. They had been instructed to perform until told to stop. Several flutists and court singers had also received the honor of accompanying the procession up the stairs, so that music could be provided on the platform itself during the ceremony.

The ceremony.

Li Shan-po stifled a grunt. Wu-tsung had never explained how he planned to achieve immortality and return his mother to life, and no one, not even Li Shan-po, had dared to ask.

He probably believed, Li Shan-po thought in disgust, that all he had to do was spread his arms and wait to be engulfed in incandescent light, as though he were one of the true Immortals.

He was shocked to find out he was right.

Wu-tsung made an imperious gesture toward the musicians who had grouped themselves at the edge of the platform. "Perform the song we wrote for this moment," he shouted.

Instantly a chorus of flute notes and singing washed over the group, as discordant as the music still coming from below. Several winced at this massacre of talent, but Wu-tsung smiled with delight.

Spreading his arms so that the billowing sleeves of his robe hung down like great triangular wings, the Emperor glanced over his shoulder. His black gaze searched for and found Li Shan-po.

"Make haste, Li Shan-po, make haste," he ordered. "You must step up here and stand beside us."

Feeling like an utter fool, Li Shan-po stepped forward to join his ruler, keenly aware of all those watching. Wu-tsung frowned at him.

"With your arms held out like so." The Son of Heaven jerked his own to demonstrate. Swallowing a curse, Li Shan-po followed suit.

In silence, sweating in the summer heat, surrounded by

the dissonant clash of instruments and voices, the two men stood motionless, arms raised straight out.

Strong as Li Shan-po's arms were, they soon ached, then burned from being held so rigidly. He risked a glance at Wu-tsung.

His eyes glazed, the Emperor stood with arms straight and stiff as boards, seemingly unaffected by the awkward pose. The minutes stretched on and still they stood, while the flutes trilled, the singers chanted, and the drums and cymbals beat out a steady rhythm from below.

The discomfort in Li Shan-po's arms was nearly unbearable, when, with terrible suddenness, Wu-tsung shrieked wildly.

It was a horrific sound. Filled with agony and seething with rage and frustration, it froze the blood of every soul present.

"Where is the light?" Spittle exploded from the Emperor's lips, some of it flying into Li Shan-po's face. *"Where is the light!"*

No one spoke. The flute players and the singers faltered and fell silent. On the ground their companions continued to play, although the notes that drifted upward were increasingly hesitant, as the musicians sensed that something was wrong.

Wu-tsung spun around. The gaze he turned on his terrified subjects was totally devoid of reason, flaming with fury and bewilderment.

"We were first to be suffused with the incandescent light of the Immortals," he screamed. "And then Honored Mother was to take the shape of the Queen of the Western Heaven and appear on this platform with us. Why has it not happened? *Why? Why? Why?*"

Raising clenched fists, Wu-tsung beat at his forehead until the headdress of his royal office toppled to the platform's floor. Several men gasped at the sight, but not one dared step forward to retrieve the head covering and re-adorn the Son of Heaven.

Unaware of his head's bareness, Wu-tsung continued pounding at his temples, his screaming now a wordless howl. Then, with an abruptness that was even more fear-some than his shrieking had been, he fell silent.

Shaking in every limb, sweat dampening his glorious robes in great dark splotches, the Emperor pointed a trem-bling finger at the Taoist priests.

"This is *your* fault," he screeched hoarsely. "Yours and no others! We believed in you, trusted that the Taoist path is the one true path to immortality, and this is how you re-pay us!"

He paused, panting for breath, and into his insane eyes came a new glitter, so frightening that many of the priests stepped backward. "Perhaps," Wu-tsung said in a voice thick with menace, "a certain number of Taoist deaths are required. Starting with you priests, who prattle on and on about the way to immortality."

The threat sank into Li Shan-po as though a spear had been cast into his belly. He had been standing beside Wu-tsung during the Emperor's frenzied tantrum, temporarily forgotten. That, however, could change if the mad Em-peror started massacring all the Taoists up on this accursed terrace. The Son of Heaven might not recognize much in his deteriorating state, but one thing he *would* remember: Li Shan-po was, above all, loyal to Taoism. He had better act, and swiftly.

"Divine One." Gambling that a soft tone would pene-trate the Emperor's madness more effectively than a strug-gle to compete with him by screaming, the Spider lowered his voice to a whisper. It worked.

"Eh?" Wu-tsung swung around, staggering a little as

he sought to focus on the one who had spoken. "Ah, it is you, Li Shan-po." The hoarse tone was distinctly hostile. "You, too, said we would attain immortality. Indeed, I *honored* you with this great gift. But you also lied. You also—"

"No." Li Shan-po snapped the word out with authority, allowing his voice to become loud. It was the sheerest audacity to interrupt a Son of Heaven while speaking, but this Son of Heaven was a complete lunatic. Extreme measures were necessary, if he was to come down from this platform alive.

"I did not lie to you, Majesty," he said firmly, even angrily, then dared to go a little further. "You malign me to say that I have. You insult my honor as a noble, as your loyal servant, and as a man."

The Spider paused. Sweat was pouring down his back in rivers, causing his gown to stick to his flesh as though it had been glued there. He ignored the temptation to reach behind him and pull the sopping cloth free, standing very straight instead, his gaze fixed upon Wu-tsung.

To his immense relief, his bold manner seemed to confuse the Emperor. However, Wu-tsung's next words made it clear he was still dangerously belligerent.

"Well, if you didn't lie, then why are we not bathed in the light of the Immortals at this very moment?"

Li Shan-po drew a deep breath. "Because," he replied with an attitude of indignation, "you have not allowed me to explain what is needed to complete the ceremony."

A rustle of astonished murmurs ran through the crowd, and the Spider risked glancing around with an expression of studied triumph.

"Early this morning," he said calmly, "I used my arts to speak with Lao-Tzu, the Supreme himself. That noble Immortal appeared to me, and he revealed that certain things must be done if what you seek on this terrace is to be attained. Without these steps, the power of the terrace will not work. I was awaiting the proper moment to tell you."

Wu-tsung swayed forward. "What steps?" he cried. An expression of eagerness blended with suspicion flowed over his gaunt features. Tugging at his hair, he peered doubtfully at Li Shan-po. "Mother said nothing to us of any further steps. Are you certain it was Lao-Tzu, the Supreme, who told you this?"

"I am certain." Li Shan-po summoned up a serene smile. "And though your mother was—is—a worthy and wise woman, perhaps Lao-Tzu did not tell her of this. She is a woman, after all, and Lao-Tzu, the Supreme, is one of the Immortals."

The collective indrawn gasp from the others told the Spider he had gone too far. He had consigned himself to the Western Heaven. The realization brought mingled disbelief and horror. The mad fool would take what he had said as an offense against the old woman and order his head rolled into the dust.

As if to confirm this, Wu-tsung's eyes narrowed in an ominous glare. But suddenly, in one of those odd moments of pliability that sometimes visited him, the Emperor's face cleared, and he nodded in agreement.

"Yes, that is true," he said. "Lao-Tzu would not speak with a mere female, even though she is Honored Mother." He ruminated on this a few moments longer. "Well, then," he finally demanded, "what needs to be done?"

Li Shan-po's breath left him in a soft exhalation. In gratitude he offered up a prayer of thanks to the kindly fates that had just smiled upon him.

"If Your Majesty will recall," he began, "Lao-Tzu, the Supreme, was born here in the Middle Kingdom, as a proper Immortal should be. He roamed our Flowery Land and spontaneously and naturally attained immortality after concocting and drinking a certain elixir.

"What you must have, Divine One, is the same elixir. Today's failure is not the fault of Taoism. It is only through the Taoist path that you will ascend to the heights of eternal life, for only Taoists can prepare the elixir, which, drunk upon this terrace, shall grant you immortality."

"Then bring us this elixir." Wu-tsung's pliable mood evaporated with the speed of water dropped into a heated wok. He spun on the priests, who had been standing in frozen silence throughout this exchange. "Do you hear the command of your Emperor? Bring it!"

"Divine One." Li Shan-po kept his voice soft and even. "They cannot. It must be concocted first, with ingredients obtained from far places, and from persons who might not wish to give you such ingredients."

"Who?" Wu-tsung asked, swinging back toward Li Shan-po. "Who would presume to withhold from their Son of Heaven *anything* he might desire?"

"Why, Buddhist monks would, of course." Li Shan-po lowered his head to hide a smile. His fears of dying had all but gone, and expansively he said, "We all know they seduce the common people away from Confucian values and encourage them in practices unproductive to the welfare of the empire. How could one expect that if they possess knowledge like this, they would not withhold it for their own ends?

"Especially"—he placed his next words with delicate care—"the monks of a certain monastery, who have several of these ingredients hoarded away."

"I see." Wu-tsung was breathing in heavy spurts, his hands flitting like spasmodic insects, from savage tugs at his hair to fierce twistings of his robe. "And which of these barbarian monasteries dares to defy us?"

Li Shan-po assumed a regretful expression. This weaving of a strand he had had to devise so quickly was going even better than he had hoped. And it made perfect and beautiful sense to proceed in this direction. Wu-tsung's madness this day had provided an opportunity that was surely a gift from the gods.

"Answer us, Li Shan-po!"

"Yes, Majesty." He met the Emperor's gaze. "I hesitated out of grief—grief at distressing you. For the monastery we are speaking of is called the Temple of the Jade Waterfall. It is the place from which the Zhuhu *jushi*, who *supposedly* healed your honored mother, came."

Smothering the treacherous smile that kept trying to spring to his lips, he waited for the fireworks he was certain would now result. Wu-tsung surprised him, though.

The Emperor's face was mottled with rage, and the spasmodic movements of his hands continued, but his voice was astonishingly steady as he said, "This monastery is in the south, is it not?"

When Li Shan-po nodded, he continued, still in that oddly composed tone. "We will send soldiers, many more soldiers, to swell the numbers of those already there. They will destroy the Temple of the Jade Waterfall, tear it apart stone by stone, to find what we want."

Wu-tsung fell silent. Slowly, with awkward, jerky steps, he paced the platform, staring closely at all who had accompanied him. His subjects stared back, looking for all the world like a pack of terrified monkeys held captive by the gaze of a snake.

At length, Wu-tsung singled out a particular official, a eunuch named Yang Ch'in-i. Li Shan-po knew the man slightly. Despite his position as one of the lower Commanders of the Left Army of Inspired Strategy, he was a mild sort, widely regarded as someone who tried very hard to keep out of trouble.

Swaying back and forth, the Emperor glared at this unfortunate man. A thread of saliva dribbled from his lips, and he absently wiped it away. Then he raised an unsteady hand. Pointing at the trembling commander, he said flatly, "You are against us. I can see it in your eyes."

Yang Ch'in-i shrank back. "No, Divine One," he quavered. "I would never—"

"You *lie*!" Waving his hand, Wu-tsung shrieked the two words. "Do you take us for a fool? Everyone knows that you eunuchs are sympathetic to Buddhism. You hate the imperial edicts we have handed down, and you hate this Terrace of the Immortals!"

"That is not true, Great Ruler! I am your humble servant in all things! Please, plea—"

"Honored Mother warned us," the Emperor raved on. "Honored Mother is always correct about these—What? What is that?" Falling silent, Wu-tsung gazed intently into the emptiness beside him, nodding several times. "Yes, yes, we quite agree." Once more he spoke in that flat, expressionless tone. "It shall be done."

He turned back to the terrorized eunuch. "The Terrace of the Immortals needs the blood of a heretic to bring good luck to the task of creating an elixir of immortality. You shall provide that blood."

Yang Ch'in-i collapsed to his knees. "No, Majesty, no!"

"You." Pointing randomly, Wu-tsung selected one of the singers. "Push this eunuch over the edge of the terrace. Now."

A terrible quiet descended on the closely packed platform, broken only by the breathless pleadings of Yang

Ch'in-i. The singer, a slender man of perhaps nineteen or twenty harvests, gulped audibly. "Divine One," he mumbled, eyes fastened upon his feet. "I—I—"

"We have told you to push him," Wu-tsung interrupted dangerously. "Why do you not obey?"

The singer gulped again. "The commander is an important official of the land," he managed at last. "I dare not push him down."

The Emperor's eyes widened in furious disbelief. Before he could react, the oldest of the Taoist priests intervened. "Son of Heaven," he called, and though his voice was respectful, it contained an unmistakable rebuke. "I have listened long enough, and now I must speak. Although we priests are grateful for your devotion to Taoism, you must understand, Majesty, that to take life is not a part of the Tao. Spilling the blood of this innocent man will not bring good luck to the elixir of immortality. It is a wrong act, and an unprincipled one. Lao-Tzu, the Supreme, would be saddened by it."

"Are we surrounded by defiance?" Wu-tsung spun around in a circle, his eyes wild with fury. "Will no one push the eunuch down as we command?"

Li Shan-po stepped forward.

During his life, he had brought death to many, but he had never killed a man himself. It had always been done by his arts or his hired minions. Now he found himself drawn to the idea of standing behind the doomed man and placing his hands on the warm back—wet with fear and the stink of impending death—of shoving inexorably at that living flesh until it toppled helplessly out into space.

"Majesty," he said, "I will do it."

Wu-tsung beamed at him. "Ah, Li Shan-po, my trusted friend. We can always rely upon you. As for them . . ." He gestured at the singer and the elderly priest. "On descending from the terrace, see to it that the singer is given twenty strokes of the cane, and the priest, one hundred."

The young singer blanched and the Taoist monks cried out in dismay, though their aged companion remained utterly serene.

Twenty cane strokes was a dire punishment, enough to maim or cripple if the cane was wielded with sufficient strength. One hundred blows was a death sentence to anyone, much less a frail old man.

Intent on his own murderous deed, Li Shan-po paid little heed to the outcry. He backed the eunuch to the edge of the platform, paused in anticipation, then shoved. The sensation was exactly as he had imagined. Lost in the odd pleasure of it, he scarcely heard the hapless wail of Yang Ch'in-i as he plummeted one hundred and fifty ells through the air to the jagged rocks below.

Chapter 21

Once I sought the City of White Jade in
heaven.
The five palaces and twelve lofty towers,
Where gods of felicity stroked me on the
forehead,
And I bound my hair and received the
everlasting life.
Woe to me, I turned to the pleasures of the
world,
Pondering deep on peace and war . . .

—Li Po,
Taoist Tales

"My good friend." The Taoist priest set down his *t'e* bowl
and regarded Master Wu with barely concealed alarm. "In
the name of all that is sacred to both of us, I beg you to
do as I ask."

Master Wu smiled sadly. "Zi Laineng, if I were to
come to the Temple of the Three Forces and tell you to re-

move your sacred statues and scrolls and hide them, along with yourself, in my monastery, would you do it?"

Zi Laineng shrugged in irritation. "Perhaps yes, perhaps no. Since I am not in that position, the answer is of little significance."

An agonized expression suddenly twisted the kind features of the Taoist priest. "What *is* of importance is that I cannot watch these terrible events unfold and do nothing. I had hoped this madness would confine itself to the north, that here in the remote south we would be safe. I was wrong. The malignancy spreads like a wildfire sweeping through the wooden buildings of Yangzhou, and it comes quickly. With each passing hour, the danger to you grows."

"I am aware of it," Master Wu said gravely. "Word has reached me that temples and monasteries between here and the eastern capital are being looted at the rate of several a day." He lowered his head and sighed. "Even the sacred White Horse Monastery has not been spared."

"The one near Loyang?" Zi Laineng was stunned. "Didn't your fighting arts begin at the White Horse Monastery?"

"It is the birthplace of Shaolin, the very center of our discipline. Many—"A hint of pain cracked the serenity of the master's voice. "Many of its monks died in defending it against the soldiers. But they were greatly, greatly outnumbered."

"The same fate awaits the Temple of the Jade Waterfall," Zi Laineng pointed out. "Will you sit upon your prayer mat and wait for it to come?"

"If Buddha wills," came the quiet answer, and Zi Laineng sighed.

"These unprincipled acts are an obscene perversion of the Tao," the priest said. "My brothers and sisters who seek the path to transformation through the ways of Taoism are appalled. Only the greedy priests in the western capital have gone along with the Son of Heaven's mad edicts, and now many of them are distressed over what is happening. I have heard this myself from a Taoist nun who recently fled Ch'ang-an under ... disturbing circumstances. Her story is yet another example of how greatly out of balance the harmony in this land is."

Zi Laineng rose from his place. "If you would permit me, I would like to bring this nun in to speak with you, Master Wu. She has some news which she wishes to give you personally."

Master Wu nodded, and the priest went to usher in the nun. She was a self-possessed young woman, slender and pretty, with gentle eyes that seemed far older than the length of her harvests. She proffered the aged Buddhist a deep and reverential bow, and when she straightened, Master Wu saw tears were glistening in her eyes.

"Seat yourself, my child," he said kindly. "What is it you wish to tell me?"

The young woman sank gracefully to the floor. "Master," she began in a soft voice, "I am a nun in one of the convents near Ch'ang-an. Or was, until I was unlucky enough to be discovered by the Son of Heaven on one of the wandering walks he takes so often these days."

She held herself very straight. "I am a devout Taoist, Master Wu, who seeks enlightenment through the renouncing of worldly pleasures. But after seeing me at my prayers, the Emperor bestowed one thousand bolts of silk upon me as a gift. I gave them to the nunnery, of course. Then, on the advice of the abbess, I came here, to seek refuge among my Taoist brethren in the south. The Son of Heaven is quite without reason, and the abbess believed he would force me to his bed, despite my vow of chastity."

"I grieve for your sad experience, my child," Master Wu said. "But although you were forced to leave your nunnery, you averted a disaster. For that you must give thanks."

"I do, Master," the nun replied. "But it is I who grieve. I grieve for the madness of the poor Son of Heaven, for the dreadful events falling upon the enlightened religion of Buddhism, and most of all for you, and the news I must bring."

Master Wu looked at her calmly. "A burden shared is a burden lifted. Tell me this news."

The young woman's hands clenched in her lap. "On the day I left Ch'ang-an," she whispered, "the Buddhist places of worship were being looted. Soldiers carried away everything of value. Even the massive bronze temple bells were not spared. They were taken, I heard one soldier say, to be melted down and used for cash."

Her eyes filled with fresh sorrow. "Weeping and pleading, those nuns and monks who had managed to escape being forcibly defrocked fought to protect their holy treasures. All in vain. But it was in a place called the Temple of the Peaceful Mind that I saw the worst. . . ."

Master Wu straightened on his *k'ang*. "I have a close brother monk who is abbot there. He is of small yet rotund stature and is called Hui Jing. Did you see him?"

The nun could not meet his eyes. "I saw him."

Master Wu watched the woman with growing concern. "Did he seem safe and well?"

The nun swallowed. "He has entered the Western Heaven, Master." She swallowed again. "I saw him killed."

There was a long pause.

"I see," Master Wu finally said in a strangely peaceful tone.

"He was a very brave man, Master." Now that she had begun, the young woman was gripped by a desire to tell the rest of the story. "When the soldiers started taking the sacred objects from his temple, your brother monk did not stand idly by. He tried to protect a jade statue of Buddha by covering it with his own body.

"The soldiers jeered and made sport of him when he did this. Then the officer in charge stepped up and stabbed him with a spear. Several times. It—it seemed very deliberate, Master Wu. Almost as if it had been planned, for they killed no other monks in the temple. Only Hui Jing. I am so very, very sorry."

Master Wu smiled sadly. "Do not be sorry, child. Earthly life is only an illusion. Hui Jing has ascended on to the wheel of life, to be reborn on a higher plane. He was an enlightened soul and may have already passed into Nirvana. You must rejoice, not sorrow for him."

"I sorrow for us all," the young woman said, "for the evil that has befallen the land. I sorrow most that this evil is being committed in the name of Taoism."

"It is time for us to take our leave," Zi Laineng said. "The hour of meditations approaches, and Master Wu wishes to be alone."

With an ease that belied his age, the elderly monk rose to his feet. "Thank you for coming, Daughter," he said to the woman. "Please walk home safely."

Tears still sparkling in her eyes, the young nun nodded. Rising to her feet, she again bowed deeply to the Buddhist before gliding from the room. When the door had closed behind her, Zi Laineng rose also.

"I will argue with you no further," he said. "But please remember my plea to you, as well as my offer of sanctuary. Remember, too, old friend, that I am an adept. It may be that I can help you in ways not of the body."

Master Wu smiled. "So you would cause me to disappear when the imperial soldiers come? Can you cause the entire Temple of the Jade Waterfall and all within its walls to vanish as well?"

Zi Laineng smiled back. "That I do not know. I have never attempted anything so formidable. For your sake, I would be willing to try, even though I think it would be far better if you simply came and hid at the Temple of the Three Forces instead."

"Brother Zi—"

"I know, I know." The Taoist sighed. "My thoughts are with you, Master Wu. I will go to my temple and pray that you come to your senses. And if you fail to do so—well, then I shall pray for your safety."

Master Wu laid a gentle hand upon Zi's shoulder, and the two men walked to the door. In the doorway Zi paused.

"There is little time, my friend," he murmured. "Very little time."

In a grove of peach trees outside the monastery, Matteo had just spoken the same words to Rhea.

"I do not know for certain what this Terran called Strong Man intends," he continued. "But whatever it is, it will most assuredly be violent. He has it in mind to take another's life."

The merman's mouth twisted in distaste. "What is more, he expects to be richly compensated for his deed. Unfortunately, I do not know whom he plans to kill."

"I do," Rhea said. "I am very certain I do."

Her brother shrugged. "I did not leave the sea out of concern for some Terran. There is great unrest in this land; I feel the vibrations of it in my very gill slits. To stay here while these mad creatures sort things out among themselves is foolish. There will be killing, probably a great deal of it. I have seen my share of that, Rhea, and I do not wish to see more. So I've come to ask you once again to leave with me."

She looked at him silently, and Matteo clenched his teeth. "I will even," he gritted out, "promise to say nothing to the Elders of this muddle you have gotten yourself into, if only you come with me. It is a great concession I make here, Sister. I hope you appreciate that."

"Oh, Matteo." She gripped his arm. "I do appreciate it. And I thank you for it. But how can I do as you wish? The one this Terran seeks to harm is Red Tiger."

Beneath her hand, her brother's muscles tensed. He shook his head. "You have no proof of that! If I, who was with the man, have no idea, how can you?"

"I know," she said with quiet stubbornness. "I wish I were wrong in this, but I am not. The Terran and I are bound together. My dream-walk predicted it."

"Pah." Matteo could scarcely contain his frustration. "You persist in talking this utter foolishness. Nowhere, in all the seas and all the eons of our people, have the visions of any dream-walk for any merman or woman ever held—"

"Don't you see, Matteo?" she interrupted. "That may be the whole point! Perhaps these visions came to me for a reason. To show that merfolk and landfolk can bide together in ways beyond the royal mating. After all, there was once a time when our kind was much closer to those of the land."

"It was long ago," Matteo snapped. "Beyond the memories of even the departed mothers and fathers of our most venerable ones. And things have changed greatly since then.

"You know as well as I that in the days you speak of, women ruled the world of land. Life was sensible and tranquil, until men wrested power from the Mother and tore apart the Ancient Harmonies."

Rhea started to speak, but Matteo plunged on. "Terran men do not know how to live in peace with one another, let alone with women. They are so fearful women will one day regain their lost power, they have done little but devise ways to keep the Mother from Her ancient place, and women along with Her. The world of land is a hopeless tangle now, rife with bloodshed and hatred and fear. It is not worth bothering with, except from the perspective of a Historian."

"You did not always feel that way." In the heat of the moment, Rhea said what in other circumstances she might not have. "You went to the land yourself to fight in one of their wars. And it is not true that Terran men are the only violent ones, for you fought alongside women, who I have heard were as vicious and bloodthirsty in battle as any man."

"That was also long ago." Her brother's voice was tight, and as cold as a northern sea. "And the Amazons had no choice but to become terrible warriors. Men could not bear to see any woman, much less a whole tribe of them, living free and beyond their control. They still can't."

"Yet you became involved because you felt you had to. Now I must do the same."

"My getting caught up in the affairs of landfolk was a mistake, the gravest I ever made! Why can't you see that you're about to swim into the same dangerous waters I did?"

Abruptly Matteo caught himself. "Someone is coming," he said with irritation. "A Terran."

Rhea nodded. "I know." She had sensed Red Tiger's approach before Matteo had. "It is Red Tiger. I told him I would be here."

"Ah." Matteo turned and stared at the approaching man with grim interest. "The personification of your dream-walk himself."

Rhea winced at the cynical tone. "Be courteous to him, Brother. He has had as little to do with appearing in my visions as I had with summoning him there."

Matteo did not reply. In silence the two merfolk watched the tall red-haired man stride rapidly through the trees. As he neared, they could see he was tense and filled with urgency.

"Something has happened," Rhea murmured. "Could the one named Strong Man have found him?"

Zhao loped up to them and halted. He looked from Rhea to the man at her side with a question in his eyes. Coldly Matteo returned his stare, feeling both a curiosity about this Terran male who so commanded his sister's attention, and anger that he had.

Seeing the threat in her brother's expression, Rhea said quickly, "Red Tiger, this is my brother Matteo. He has come to speak with me about something of importance."

Despite his obvious worry, Zhao stared at Matteo with astonishment and fascination. Rhea could easily picture his thoughts: here was one of her mysterious kin, the brother he had heard of but never seen. Zhao must be burning with curiosity about him. It was a measure of his preoccupation that rather than indulging his interest, he only bowed politely to Matteo before switching his gaze back to Rhea.

"Forgive me for interrupting," he said, "but for your own safety, you must return to the temple with me at once. Your honored brother will be welcome as well, if he wishes to come. We must go now, though, without delay."

Matteo made a contemptuous sound at this offer of Terran protection, and Rhea demanded, "Why? What has happened?"

"The soldiers are coming to us at last," Zhao said, his voice low and heavy. "A great number of them, we hear. Many more than have been sent to other temples and monasteries. There is a serious portent in the air. We all sense it.

"Master Wu has called everyone who has anything to do with the monastery; monks, nuns, peasants, servants, guests, even slaves, all together so that he may address us. I suspect he wishes to release us of our obligation to stay at the temple."

"And you?" Matteo broke in. "Will you leave if your Master Wu says you can?"

The glance Matteo gave Rhea made the meaning of his question clear: if Zhao removed himself from danger's path, it would no longer be necessary for Rhea to stay at his side with such determination.

Zhao's answer promptly dashed any such hope. "I will act in accordance with my honor," he said. "And that means staying where I am needed, using my strength and training to protect from harm those who are too weak and helpless to protect themselves."

Matteo sighed. "How very noble."

Rhea threw her brother an angry glare. "Yes, it is. Red Tiger is a man unlike the ones you have had experience with, Matteo."

"Perhaps," the merman said, shrugging. "At any rate, it does not matter. I require no help in defending myself from a rabble of landfolk soldiers. And neither does my sister."

Zhao gave him a brief, thoughtful glance. Clearly he was puzzled by Matteo's hostility, and concerned. However, this was not the time to investigate. "As you wish," he murmured. The look in his eyes said he hated to relinquish Rhea to anyone, even her brother, yet he added, "After all, as Rhea's male kin, you certainly have the right to choose how best to protect her."

"Sea and Sky!" Rhea burst out, and Matteo looked at her with sardonic amusement.

"Our people are not like yours, Man of the Land," Matteo said. "Being born a male does not give me rights over women, even my own sister. Yet I will be frank. Nothing would please me more than if Rhea were to bid farewell to you forever and come with me this very moment. But"—disapproval crept into his voice—"she is an adult. Therefore, she is free to do as she pleases."

"And what I please," Rhea snapped, "is to return to the Temple of the Jade Waterfall, with or without you, Matteo."

Zhao glanced from her to her brother, but all he said was, "Then we should make haste. The others were already assembling when I went to look for you, and we must not be late. There is much to be done before the soldiers arrive."

As they turned toward the temple, Rhea paused and gave Matteo a long look. "If you change your mind, Brother . . ."

His face was expressionless. "Do not worry about me. Worry about yourself and the consequences of what you are doing instead." Without waiting for a reply, he stalked off through the grove.

Frowning thoughtfully, Zhao watched the broad back recede among the trees. Rhea put a hand on his arm. "Shouldn't we go?" she asked.

"Yes."

They set off in the opposite direction, although Zhao's

pensive expression remained. "Rhea," he said carefully, "does your brother know we have lain together? Is that why he is so angry?"

"No." She gave him what she hoped was a reassuring smile. "It is not that."

"Well, it is clear he does not like me."

"It's not exactly that either. He just doesn't like what you represent."

"What I represent? I am a man, like any other in the Middle Kingdom."

"That," she said with a sigh, "is the problem."

The main courtyard of the monastery was as massed with people as Zhao had predicted it would be. Overflowing as it was, though, there was an eerie lack of noise, of even low-voiced conversation. Those whose destinies were bound, either through work or spirituality, to the Temple of the Jade Waterfall stood silently in the muggy warmth, awaiting the confirmation of their worst fears.

Master Wu did not dissuade them.

The old man's face, as he walked out of the prayer hall and ascended the steps of a hastily erected platform, was unperturbed, even peaceful. But to Rhea, who stood with Zhao at the edge of the crowd, the ancient Terran seemed to have aged overnight. In the harsh afternoon light, he looked every day of his unusually many seasons.

"My children," he began in a voice that carried over the heads of all who listened. "I will not ease you with honeyed words, or inflame you with searing ones. I will only say that the time has come for each of you to make a choice. Imperial soldiers will soon arrive at the Temple of the Jade Waterfall. I do not need to tell you what will happen when they do."

He paused, and he seemed to look with compassion and sadness into the face of each person there.

"I release all of you from either vows or obligations," he said formally. "The slaves among you are hereby freed. We will provide you with food, clothing, and cash, but I advise that you journey far away from here, lest the soldiers seize and reenslave you for the imperial court, as they have been doing elsewhere. Those peasants who live in the village outside the monastery walls, look to your belongings and your families and keep them safe. Those who live on temple lands or within these walls, take what you can carry, hide the rest, and flee.

"As for my honored brothers and sisters ordained in the service of great Buddha . . ." Master Wu paused again. "You must each act according to your own heart. Those who stay to face the soldiers will be welcome. Those who leave will go with my blessing and will be judged no less worthy than those who do not."

"Master," a lone voice called out. "What will you do?"

Master Wu smiled. "I, too, have looked into my heart, and it has told me my destiny. I shall return now to the prayer hall. There I will supplicate Buddha to watch over us, and offer my blessings to all who wish them. I shall stay within these walls until whatever is to pass has passed. This is all I have to say."

Not a murmur could be heard as Master Wu slowly and with great dignity descended from the platform and walked back into the hall. Only after he had disappeared into the inner shadows did a clatter of voices break out.

Fear began to surface. It had been held back, but now it swept through the courtyard, pushed by bursts of wild conversation and frightened weeping. The sweat-thick odor of it clogged Rhea's nostrils as the panicked Terrans milled about, then began rushing from the courtyard.

Everywhere the gray and yellow robes of monks and nuns immediately became evident. Quickly and quietly they moved through the crowd, soothing and comforting, using their calm presence to maintain order.

Zhao shook his head. "I must tell my mother of this, Rhea. I forbade her to leave her bed and come to the courtyard to hear Master Wu."

Into Rhea's mind came a vivid image of Zipporah's face as she shrank away from what she could not understand. "I will wait for you here," she said. "Seeing me would probably distress her all over again."

"No." Zhao's jaw set. "I will not leave you standing outside as though you were a servant. You will come with me. I insist."

"Red Tiger!"

An older monk was pushing his way toward them, beckoning impatiently. "Master Wu wants to speak with you. Amitabha, Brother, I have been seeking you since before we all assembled in the courtyard!" Having delivered the message, he hurried off through the throng without waiting for a reply.

Zhao looked at Rhea. "Now you may come with me to Master Wu instead, for I still will not leave you alone."

"Red Tiger." She eyed him thoughtfully. "I believe you think that if you leave me alone, I may not be here when you get back. I told you I would stay, didn't I?"

"Yes, you did. But I wish you to come with me anyway. Humor me, Lady."

They wound their way across the rapidly emptying courtyard and with some difficulty maneuvered themselves inside the already crowded hall. After the heat and noise outside, the prayer hall seemed like a sanctuary indeed. It was shadowy and cool, softly lighted by dozens of flickering lamps. People who had been weeping and wailing in the courtyard were quiet in here, almost calm, as they murmured prayers and awaited their turn to pass before Master Wu and receive his blessing.

Zhao stepped up to one of the monks assigned to the hall. After speaking with him a moment, he gestured to Rhea and ushered her forward. Gently, assisted by the monk, they pushed through the scores of waiting supplicants and entered a small chamber off the main room.

Inside Master Wu sat cross-legged upon a prayer mat spread out on a small platform. Standing beside him, pale but steady, was Zipporah Tamudj.

Chapter 22

True words are not fine-sounding;
Fine-sounding words are not true.
The good man does not prove by argument;
And he who proves by argument is not good.
True wisdom is different from much learning;
Much learning means little wisdom.
The Sage has no need to hoard;
When his last scrap has been used up on
behalf of others,
Lo, his stock is even greater than before!
For Heaven's way is to sharpen without
cutting,
And the Sage's way is to act without striving.

—*Tao Te Ching*, Arthur Waley Translation

"Mother." Zhao quickly crossed the chamber to Zipporah.
"What are you doing out of bed? I told you—"

"I am well aware of what you told me. Kindly remember that I am your mother, not some silly child who can be ordered about."

At the sharp words, Rhea bit back a grin. Zipporah Tamudj was indeed feeling better.

"I am quite recovered," the older woman continued. "It was foolish of me to behave as I did toward this . . . young woman. I have spoken at length with Master Wu about my fears, and he has been of great help. I hope, Lady Rhea, that you will accept my apologies."

Zipporah looked directly at Rhea as she said this, and the latter could see traces of nervousness and uncertainty lingering in the woman's eyes. Wondering what Master Wu, who had never spoken a word to her, might have said to bring about such a change, Rhea bowed.

"No apologies are necessary, Lady Tamudj. I am pleased you have been reassured that I mean no harm to you or yours." She glanced speculatively at Master Wu's imperturbable face.

Zhao was apparently mulling over the same thing. "I also am pleased," he said. "But may I inquire what the two of you talked of?"

"You may not," his mother replied pleasantly. "In any case, it is not important. What matters now is that I am up and around again, and that Master Wu wishes me to undertake a journey. I disagreed with him at first, but I have come to see that he is right in this, as he is in so much else."

"A journey?" Zhao asked sharply. "What do you mean? Master, why have you advised her to do this? You know she has not been well."

"She is well enough, my son," said the monk. "And she may become less than well if she stays here. I can no longer guarantee her sanctuary, for I do not know what will happen when the soldiers come. It may be that, since she is not a Buddhist, they will pay her no heed, yet it is not worth the risk. I do not forget the name of Li Shan-po, or what brought the two of you to our temple gates so many harvests ago."

Zhao's voice was harsh. "Neither do I, Master. You believe as I do, don't you, that Li Shan-po is behind the soldiers coming here in such great numbers?"

Master Wu nodded. "I have thought he is behind much of what is happening in our Flowery Land, for until recently, Brother Hui Jing kept me well informed of events in the capital."

"Until recently?" Zhao repeated. He and Rhea looked at each other. "Has the Abbot Hui Jing become caught up in this?"

"Few of the faithful have not been caught up in it, my son. These edicts mean to spare none of us. But Hui Jing—honored be his memory—is no longer concerned with earthly matters. He has ascended to a higher plane."

"You mean he is dead." Rhea could not keep the bitterness from her tone. She had been genuinely fond of the kindly little abbot who had given them refuge in his temple.

"Who was responsible?" In the golden lamplight, Zhao's features seemed carved from stone. "Soldiers? Or assassins sent by the Spider?"

"In these evil times," Master Wu said softly, "it seems that they are one and the same. Li Shan-po sits very high in the Son of Heaven's favor."

In a sudden rage, Zhao slammed his fist against the wall. "I grow very weary," he said in a fearsome voice, "of seeing innocent people suffer and die at this man's hands, only to be told that the murderer sits 'very high' in the Emperor's favor. By all that is sacred, *I* shall bring him down from his high place and see to it that he never rises again!"

"Red Tiger!" Master Wu's voice whipped out with sudden strength, echoing in the small antechamber. "Remember your teachings. Is this how you exhibit the control and discipline of Shaolin?"

Zhao bent his head. "I apologize, Master." From beneath the fringe of his lowered eyelashes, though, Rhea could see a flaming fury that belied his respectful tone. "I allowed myself to be carried away by emotion. It will not happen again."

"My Son," Master Wu said more kindly, "this is difficult for you, I know. But in such ways are you tested. You must remain calm and ever mindful of your obligations, for difficult days lie ahead. Your main obligation now is to your honored mother. She has agreed to rejoin the Zhuhu community in Yangzhou, where I believe she will be safer than here. You, Red Tiger, must take her there without delay."

Zhao looked from the serene face of his teacher to the quietly determined one of his mother.

"Mother," he said, both amazed and concerned at her decision, "I will certainly take you to Yangzhou. But since the night we fled that city, you have always refused to go back. Now you say you will return to the Zhuhu. Are you sure this is what you want?"

Zipporah gazed at her son, her heart heavy with an old grief. Standing close to Zhao was the spirit woman. Despite her apology, Zipporah still had difficulty thinking of Rhea as a mortal female. Still, the sight of that straight, silent figure sent her thoughts spinning back into the past.

As enigmatic and baffling as Rhea was, she had about her a self-possession and fearless pride that Zipporah recognized. She, too, had once possessed a wealth of dignity and self-respect. The distant memory of the glow in her husband's eyes when she expressed an opinion on some difficult subject rose within her, searing her like fire.

That was long ago, she said to herself. Long, long ago. She pushed away those old emotions that were struggling to awaken, jarred painfully back to life by Rhea.

"I am sure," she said to Zhao. "Shame kept me hidden here for all these harvests. I had been so debased, so dirtied by what Li Shan-po did to me, I could not bear to face my people."

"Lady," Rhea said, unable to stop herself. "How can you believe that what happened to you was your fault? You are not to blame, any more than your poor family was for their own deaths."

"But I am," Zipporah said without doubt. "These things are always the fault of the woman. Unwitting though it may have been on my part, I still attracted the eye of an evil man. . . ."

She stopped for a moment to gather herself. "For that I shall always carry the burden of guilt," she added softly. "And I grieve for the life it has brought my son as a result."

She looked at Zhao again. "In calmer times, I would have been content to live out the rest of my days here, but that is not to be. Two days ago, Master Wu sent word to the chief rabbi of the Yangzhou Zhuhu. This morning he received an answer. The rabbi says there has been enough suffering, and that our return to Yangzhou is awaited. Once I have cleansed myself in the ritual bath, your boyhood friend, Dasheng Tian, has said I will be most welcome in his household. He hopes you will come also."

A note of pleading entered her voice. "I have prayed, my son, that one day you would return to a rightful place among your true people. Here at last is an opportunity for you to do so."

Now Rhea understood why Zipporah had made an effort to put aside her terror and distrust. She believed that if Zhao went back to his own kind, he would leave Rhea and her disturbing influence. And would he?

She looked at the man next to her. Zhao's features had grown impassive once more, no longer revealing the turmoil she still felt emanating from him. But when he spoke, the rage was there, vibrating beneath his measured reply. "Forgive me, Mother. That is something I cannot do."

"But you can!" Zipporah turned desperately to Master Wu. "Master Wu has released everyone in the temple from their commitment. You are not a monk—you have taken no vows."

"Perhaps not," Zhao said, "but I am bound nonetheless. It is not the people of my birth who took me in, fed and cared for me, and taught me their secret arts. It was these monks, and Master Wu in particular. I will not, I cannot desert them now, not when they have need of me.

"I will take you to Yangzhou, Mother, and I will rejoice at seeing you reunited with the Zhuhu there. But please do not ask me to stay. To do so would mock all that I hold honorable."

Zipporah crossed the room to him and stared up into his face. "So you would mock your birthright instead, and the wishes of the one parent you have left. A son's filial duty is more important than all else! Is that not so, Master Wu?"

"Filial duty to one's mother and father is indeed important," the master said. "But a son whose father has entered the Terrace of Night becomes head of his clan once he grows to manhood. At that point, his mother gives him her obedience, not the reverse.

"Your son will take you to a place of safety, which is right. But beyond that, he must look into his own heart to decide what is best for himself, and you must respect his decisions."

Rhea agreed with none of it. She was certain Zipporah did not either. Despite her ridiculous notions about guilt, the Zhuhu woman possessed a strong will and was unafraid to speak her mind. Expectantly Rhea watched her, waiting for Zipporah to protest the old man's nonsense about obedience.

To her astonishment, Zipporah merely nodded her head. "Very well," she said unhappily. "I shall go to my chamber and finish gathering my belongings. Then I must say my farewells."

Slowly she turned to leave the antechamber. Zhao leapt forward to take her elbow. He glanced back at Rhea, signaling her with his eyes to join them. She started to follow, but Master Wu stopped her.

"Perhaps you could remain a moment," he said softly.

Startled, Rhea turned. Zhao, too, paused, looking back over his shoulder.

"See to your mother," Master Wu told him. "This young woman and I must speak. She will rejoin you presently."

Zhao nodded. "I will wait for you," he said meaningfully to Rhea. "In the courtyard." Bowing to Master Wu, he accompanied his mother out of the room.

There was absolute silence after the door had closed behind them. Yet if Master Wu intended for his quiet to make Rhea feel ill at ease, he failed. She stood calmly before his dais, returning his thoughtful gaze and waiting for him to speak. Finally he did.

"It is clear," he said, "that you possess power. I see it in your eyes and the manner in which you behave. I hope you will accompany Red Tiger and Zipporah Tamudj on the journey to Yangzhou. They will be safer with your protection."

"You ask for my protection?" She smiled. "An unnatural creature such as myself?"

He smiled back. "I have seen many strange things during this brief dream we call life. Few, if any of them, have ever been unnatural. It is only a question of understanding that everything in life has its place and is therefore sacred."

Rhea gazed at the old man with respect. "True enough, Master Wu. But how do you know I will be able to safeguard Red Tiger and Zipporah? Red Tiger is well able to care both for himself and his mother. He is smart and cautious, and above all, well trained. His only fault, if he has one, is his terrible hatred for Li Shan-po, and his fierce desire for revenge."

Master Wu nodded. "That is what I hope you can protect him from. Such uncontrolled feelings may drive him into committing foolish and dangerous deeds, deeds he will regret later, if he is alive to regret them. I hope you can prevent that."

"Why? Aren't you afraid of me as Zipporah was?"

He did not answer, and she went on dryly, "You told Red Tiger that I could be a wicked spirit sent to devour his soul or drink his blood or some other such nonsense. What has changed your mind?"

"I never believed it." Completely unruffled, Master Wu smiled at her. "I only speculated upon it. However, I have meditated long on your appearance and what it portends, both for Red Tiger and the Temple of the Jade Waterfall. I have walked on other planes during those meditations, and what my inner eyes have seen has convinced me that the future of my temple lies with Red Tiger, and with you. How I am not exactly sure, but you must see to it that he does not fall prey to his obsession with revenge. That much I know."

Rhea, Zhao, and Zipporah were ready to leave within the hour. Although it was a short journey to Yangzhou, they would have to start right away and maintain a steady pace in order to arrive there before dark.

Master Wu had provided them with a team of good horses and a covered cart, its interior thickly padded with rugs and cushions. He had also pressed upon Zhao several well-filled bundles, each containing cash and other items that would insure his mother lived out the rest of her days in comfort.

And so, with Zipporah ensconced in the back of the cart tearfully waving good-bye to Master Wu and the others who had gathered to see them off, they rattled out of the courtyard.

They were not the only ones.

Many had taken Master Wu's suggestion to look into their hearts and had decided it was time to leave. The courtyard and the lands around the temple resounded with their going. Scores of newly freed slaves jostled nervously against departing ex-servants and worried peasants, all of them filing through the temple gates in a steady stream of shouting humanity, braying pack animals, and loaded-down wheelbarrows and carts.

Only the temple monks and the nuns from the nearby convent were immune to the hysteria. They moved through the bedlam without pause, offering aid and gentle farewells to those who were departing, while they themselves prepared to stay, faithful to their vows, content to await impassively whatever was to come.

Seated beside Zhao in the front of the cart, Rhea gazed at these calm faces. "By the Mother," she murmured, "how brave they seem. What will happen to them when the soldiers come?"

"They will fight if need be," Zhao said. "As will I."

"Red Tiger! Youposai Red Tiger!"

Mounted upon a gray mare, one arm waving wildly above his head, the eunuch Ah Shu cantered toward them. Zhao returned the wave, but kept his horses moving along at a steady trot.

Ah Shu reined his mount into step with the cart and glared at Zhao. "I have been searching all over for you and now I find you leaving! Fleeing along with slaves and peasants!"

"Calm yourself," Zhao said evenly. "I am taking my mother to Yangzhou where she will be safe. Then I will return."

"To where? This temple, or to Ch'ang-an, where your duty lies?"

"I do not believe," Rhea said in a polite voice, "that Red Tiger needs to be reminded of his duty."

The eunuch glowered at her for an instant, then switched his gaze back to Zhao. "The Temple of the Jade Waterfall is doomed. I sorrow for it, but you have other matters to deal with. Li Shan-po must be stopped. Have you forgotten your vow to kill him?"

Zhao's hands tightened on the reins. "No," he said softly, "I have not. Keep your voice down, Ah Shu. I will not have my mother disturbed."

"Well?" the eunuch demanded, though in a more subdued tone.

"Li Shan-po will die," Zhao promised, "but in a time of *my* choosing, not his."

Momentarily silenced, Ah Shu continued to trot his mare alongside the cart. "There will surely be fighting when the soldiers come to your temple," he said at last. "What if you are killed?"

"I am doing what is right," Zhao said. "And because I am, I do not believe I will die. Not until my tasks have been discharged."

Rhea twisted around on the narrow seat to stare at him. There was a fatality in his voice that she had never heard before. It shocked her, even frightened her. Did he believe his destiny so interwoven with Li Shan-po's that they would both have to die to achieve a divine reckoning?

Somberly Ah Shu said, "I see I cannot change your mind. I can only pray that your feelings in this are correct. Ch'iu Shih-liang believed to his dying breath that only you could challenge the vast wickedness of this man. If you die, Youposai, there will be no help for any of us."

He looked up at the sky, then back at them. "I also must take my leave. Your Master Wu insists that all guests find lodgings elsewhere. This fine mare"—he patted his mount's neck—"was a gift from the temple. They are fine men, the monks of your temple."

"They are indeed," said Zhao. "That is why I will not desert them." He steadied the horses over a rut in the road, then looked at Ah Shu. "I worry for your safety as well. Where will you now go?"

The eunuch shrugged. "Back to Ch'ang-an, to await your arrival."

"Ch'ang-an?" Rhea echoed. "Is that wise? Won't Li Shan-po try to kill you?"

"He will if he knows I am there, Lady." Ah Shu gave her a rakish grin. "I shall do my best to see that he does not. Ch'ang-an is my home. I have friends there who will protect me, no matter what the danger." He looked at

Zhao. "Yet I shall not rest easy until I see your face in the capital, Youposai Red Tiger."

He reached into his tunic and pulled out a tiny scroll of paper. "Please take this. I have written down the names of several teahouses, shops, and stalls in the East and West Markets. The proprietors at each may be trusted. Go there and ask for news of me. They will see to it that I am reached. Once you have memorized the names, Youposai, destroy the paper, lest an evil wind allows it to fall into the wrong hands."

Zhao took the scroll and tucked it into his robe. "I will do as you ask," he said gravely. "In this, as well as in the matter of Li Shan-po. Do not believe otherwise."

Ah Shu studied him. "Very well. I shall try to be patient. But until Li Shan-po is screaming with agony in the Ten Courts of Hell, my thoughts will not know harmony." Bending forward in the saddle, he bowed to Zhao, then to Rhea. "May your journey be safe and pleasant."

Zhao returned the bow. "Yours also, Eunuch Au Shu."

Rhea watched the gray mare and its rider canter off, then glanced into the covered bed of the cart. Obviously tired from the strain of the last days, Zipporah had fallen into a deep sleep, soothed by the motion of the cart.

Rhea turned to Zhao again. "I still think it's foolish for Ah Shu to return to Ch'ang-an. Can he truly be safe there?"

"No." Zhao scowled at the crowded road ahead. "But he must do as he sees fit." Giving her a probing glance, he abruptly changed the subject. "What did Master Wu say to you?"

She thought a moment. "For one who has seen so few years, your Master Wu is rather wise. Of course, I realize he is old for a Terran."

"Yes, yes." Zhao said impatiently. "But what did you talk about?"

"Nothing important. Only that he is concerned for you."

Zhao grunted. "That sounds like him. Ever worrying about others without sparing a thought for himself."

"In that way, the two of you are not so different."

Zhao's brows rose in shock. "Master Wu is an evolved being, my love. I am not worthy of being compared to him in any way."

A stirring in the rear of the cart forestalled Rhea's reply. "I must have dozed off," Zipporah called out sleepily. "Is our travel going well, my son?"

"We are making good time, Mother," Zhao answered in a reassuring voice. "Try to sleep again."

There was an indistinct mumbling as the elderly woman shifted around on the rugs. Presently Rhea's sensitive ears told her Zipporah had once more fallen asleep.

She and Zhao rode on in silence. But no more than a few minutes had passed before Rhea looked around in alarm. Something was nagging at her, a deeply rooted sense that sent tingling messages of unease up and down her spine. In her mind an image formed of dark Terran eyes fixed upon their cart. Eyes that promised harm to those who rode in it.

Behind them the road was massed with other travelers. But as though an invisible thread pointed the way, Rhea's keen gaze swept through the clattering array of pedestrians, animals, and other carts to pick out a lone horseman.

Even at this distance, she could see that he was powerfully built. His own gaze fastened on their cart, he trotted his horse steadily along in the crowd, taking care that he neither drew abreast of them nor fell too far behind. When he saw that Rhea was staring at him, he did not alter his course. He merely stared back at her, an odd speculation in his small eyes.

"What is it?" Mindful of the sleeping Zipporah, Zhao spoke in a whisper. "What are you looking at?"

"A man," she answered in the same quiet tone. "He's following us, and for no good purpose, I think."

Zhao glanced over his shoulder. "Many are following us. What makes you believe this man is a danger?"

"It is enough to tell you that he is."

Zhao frowned at her, and she elaborated. "Matteo told me about him. They encountered each other on the road to Yangzhou. He boasted to my brother that he'd been sent here by a rich and noble master in Ch'ang-an to kill a certain man. Beyond a doubt, the master he spoke of was Li Shan-po."

"Ah." Zhao's voice remained soft, yet once more Rhea felt the rage that consumed him. "We must continue on to the city in all haste," he went on. "I do not think he will try anything in daylight upon this busy road, but we dare not take any chances. We must not allow him the opportunity to find us alone until my mother is safe in Yangzhou."

"I forbid it!"

Zipporah's voice rang out from the rear of the cart. Startled, both Zhao and Rhea twisted around to gape at her. She had awoken without either of them realizing it, and the same question arose in both their minds: how much had she heard?

She had heard a great deal. Awakening from a restless doze, Zipporah had lain in silence, listening to the spirit woman warn her son of yet another evil sent by Li Shan-po. And as she'd listened, something had broken loose in this woman grown old before her time.

Anger, long buried beneath layers of guilt and shame, rose in Zipporah like a living thing.

It started in her belly and spread with a fierce heat into her chest, and then her head. Not since that terrible night so many years ago had she experienced such fury. On that night she had quickly submerged it, knowing women should not feel such violence, much less give vent to it. Now, with death threatening once again, that knowledge gave way to something far deeper.

"I will bear no more," she said, and her voice was one that Zhao had never heard from her before. "We will *not* rush away from this man like frightened monkeys fleeing a snake. I am an old woman. I am ready to die, and I have run enough. If this assassin is truly sent by Li Shan-po, then I will look him in the eye and tell him to take a message back to that wicked piece of crawling filth he calls master—Zipporah Tamudj is no longer afraid!"

"No, Mother!" Zhao said. "I cannot allow it. You don't understand the danger."

"*I* do not understand?" She drew herself up as much as the low ceiling of the cart would permit. "I who have lost everything but you to this man? You heed me now. I will go to Yangzhou and stay there without you because it is your wish. But in this matter, you will do as I wish."

Her eyes blazed out from the shadowy interior as though lit by torches. "Turn off the road, Zhao, and let this creature of Li Shan-po face me. In the name of your father and your uncle and all the rest of our family, I demand this. It is my right!"

There was a throbbing moment of silence, then with an abrupt motion, Zhao pulled up the horses.

"Very well," he said. "I will do as you ask. But may this man's gods have mercy on him if he seeks to harm you, for I will not."

Chapter 23

When an archer is shooting for nothing
He has all his skill.
If he shoots for a brass buckle
He is already nervous.
If he shoots for a prize of gold
He goes blind
Or sees two targets—
He is out of his mind!
His skill has not changed.
But the prize divides him.
He cares.
He thinks more of winning
Than of shooting—
And the need to win
Drains him of power.

—*The Way of Chuang Tzu,*
Thomas Merton Translation

Zhao pulled the horses to the side of the road. As the traffic swirled past them, he and Rhea leapt from the cart. Together, with Zipporah sitting inside, they led the team far through the trees until they came to a small clearing.

The noise and commotion of travel was muted, giving way to the music of birds, the wind rustling through leaves, and the bubbling of a nearby spring. To Rhea the sudden peace was a great relief. "We're a good distance from the road," she said, glancing back the way they had come. "Perhaps he's decided not to follow."

"He will follow," Zhao said without doubt. "If he is sent by Li Shan-po, he will follow."

Even as he spoke, Rhea heard hoofbeats. She sighed. "Unfortunately, you're right." She pointed at the trees. "Through there."

Zhao nodded. Drawn up to his full height, he stood still as a rock beside the cart, waiting. It was not long. Within a few minutes the team of horses lifted their heads from cropping the grass and nickered. A moment later the horseman rode into the clearing.

Seeing the waiting man and woman, he frowned in wary puzzlement. Slowly, with his gaze fastened upon them, he swung a brawny leg over the withers of his horse and slid to the ground.

"I am called Strong Man," he said. "You"—he stabbed a blunt finger at Zhao—"are the one known as Red Tiger. We have business together, you and I."

"No, young man," a firm voice said. "The business you have is with me."

Zipporah pushed aside the curtain covering the opening of the cart. Zhao reached up and lifted her to the ground.

Strong Man's puzzled frown deepened. "Who in the name of the Yellow Emperor are *you*?"

Zhao tensed at the discourtesy, but Zipporah lightly touched him on the arm. Holding herself very straight, she stared at the stranger. "I am Zipporah," she said with dignity, "widow of An Tamudj—blessed be his memory—he who was murdered by a noble named Li Shan-po, because I would not forsake my marriage vows and climb happily into his bed like a singing girl in the cheapest of wine shops."

Strong Man gaped at her. "Li Shan-po . . . ?"

"Raped me," she said bluntly. "Twelve harvests ago. Not content with that, he also sought to destroy our clan. Until recently he thought he had succeeded. But then he discovered my son and I had escaped his evil. Have you been sent by him to remedy that situation?"

"Just a moment here." Flustered, Strong Man shifted his weight. His gaze flicked from Zipporah's set face, to Zhao's, to Rhea's. "Nothing was ever said to me about anyone's mother. I'm supposed to kill the *jushi* and bring the black-haired woman with gray eyes back to Li Shan-po. And that is all I'm to do. Nothing was said about mothers—nothing!"

"That *jushi*," Zipporah told him coldly, "is my son. And if you have come to do him harm, then you will have to inflict the same harm upon me."

"Aha." Striving to recover himself, Strong Man forced a laugh. "So this Red Tiger I've heard so much about—the foreigner who is trained in the arts of Shaolin—has brought his mother along to hide behind her skirts!"

The comment was clearly intended to goad Zhao, but he would not be goaded. Standing beside him, Rhea could feel his anger pulsing beneath the surface, though there was no sign of it in his smooth face and calm eyes. His chilling control was far more ominous than Strong Man's overt threats and boastful manner.

"Not to seek violence," he said quietly, "does not mean one is incapable of reacting to it. Particularly when a man's loved ones are standing in its path."

"Hmmph. The only violence here is aimed at you, my foreign friend. Harming women sticks in my gullet, and anyway, I'm not being paid for it. That wasn't in any bargain I made with Li Shan-po."

"Indeed?" Zhao said coolly. "Well, if part of your task is to bring this woman beside me back to Li Shan-po, then you will do her terrible harm. What if she does not go willingly? Will you bind and gag her to prevent her escape? And once you have delivered her to Li Shan-po, then the true harm will begin. What do you think he will do with her, drink *t'e* and study the poetry of Li Po?"

"That is not for me to say," Strong Man snapped. He looked away from those piercing green eyes and spat into the grass.

Although he had no intention of admitting it, he found the thought of pimping for Li Shan-po increasingly repugnant. Of course, now that he had seen the black-haired woman, he could well understand why the noble wanted her. Women could be easily had, though, so that an obsession with any single one—even one who looked like this—was ridiculous. However, that was beside the point. An enormous amount of cash would fall into his hands upon the female's safe delivery, and that was all that mattered.

Still, this entire affair was making him more uncomfortable. After much lurking about and impatient waiting, he'd believed the gods had finally decided to smile on him. He had scarcely believed his luck as he'd watched the *jushi* and the woman leave the safety of the temple, just waiting for him to avail himself of the jeweled opportunity they had presented him!

Who would have thought that inside their covered cart was yet another woman, this fierce mother with the blazing eyes? Now she would have to be dealt with, and he hadn't the least idea of how to go about it. He hated the unforeseen. Even as he brooded upon what he should do, Zipporah spoke.

"You are wrong, one who calls himself Strong Man. It *is* for you to say what Li Shan-po will do. You have made a choice to serve evil, but you can unmake that choice. Will you serve a man who tore a defenseless woman from her husband and dishonored her? A man who is too cowardly to do his own killing and sends others to do it for him? Why should you harm us? You have no quarrel with us, nor we with you. Get upon your horse and ride away. Leave us in peace."

She paused, then in a rising voice cried, "Go instead to Li Shan-po and tell him to come to me himself—if he dares! Tell him I would welcome standing before him, so that I may spit in his wicked face!"

Strong Man found that he could no longer meet that fierce gaze. "Amitabha, woman," he said with unconscious admiration. "You are truly a fire-eater. I wish I could do as you suggest. But I cannot."

Sighing, he stared at the ground. "I'm a poor man, Lady Tamudj. I have always been a poor man. Soon the harvests will pass and take the power of my limbs with them. My muscles will stiffen and grow weak, and I will no longer be able to make a living performing feats of strength. I must provide for that time, Lady. Surely you can understand that."

Raising his eyes to Zhao, he added, "Let me say, Jushi, that I bear no grudge against you. I've never had anything against the men whose lives I've taken. But this is a question of survival. When I bring back the woman, along with proof that you've gone into the Underworld, Li Shan-po will give me as much cash as three strong mules can carry.

"Personally, I have no use for Li Shan-po. Yet"—an odd note, almost of pleading, came into his voice—"I cannot allow such an opportunity to pass. I will allow you, Lady Tamudj, to take your cart and leave. Your son, though, must stay, and the woman, too, so that I can do as I was instructed. You see my position, don't you?"

No one answered, and Strong Man looked from mother to son with hopeful eyes.

"You do see, don't you?" he asked again. "It's all I can offer. I can't think of anything else!"

Zipporah stared at him with contempt. "I will not seek out safety while my only son faces danger. But if cash is so precious to you that you would murder a woman's child before her eyes, then I will give you all I have."

"No, Mother," Zhao said. "You will not."

Strong Man turned away from Zipporah and glowered at him. They all stood in unmoving silence until Rhea spoke.

"I think it would be wise for you to leave," she said. "It is foolhardy to speak of killing people when you are outnumbered. Perhaps you do not know Red Tiger's abilities. You most certainly do not know mine."

"By the Celestial Dragon's balls." Strong Man gave her a glance of astonishment tinged with contempt. "She talks! Well, you may as well go back to keeping your mouth shut, Woman, for you are making no sense. What can you, a mere puny female, do against *me*, the strongest man in all of Ch'ang-an? And if you want to speak of abilities, let us see if your Red Tiger can equal this!"

Swinging about, he stomped to the edge of the clearing. Growing in the sunlight were a number of tall saplings. Selecting one that was about the height of two men, Strong Man gripped it in his powerful hands, gave two mighty yanks punctuated by loud yells, and tore it roots and all from the ground.

"There!" He swaggered triumphantly back with the uprooted tree held over his head and threw it at Zhao's feet. "Can you do that?"

"I don't know," Zhao said blandly, "the need to uproot a tree has never arisen. I've never been attacked by one."

Rhea swallowed a chuckle. The uncomprehending expression on Strong Man's face almost made her feel sorry for him. It was obvious that the art of subtlety was not one of his strong points.

"Very well," he growled, obviously sensing an insult in Zhao's words. "I was going to give you time to bid farewell to your mother before sending her on her way. I was even going to see to it that your passage into the Terrace of Night was as painless as possible. But now I've lost patience. It is time to get this over with. The sooner I get back to Ch'ang-an, the sooner I can begin my life of ease."

Zhao shrugged. "As you wish. But you would do well to listen to Rhea and leave while you are still able."

"While *I* am still able?" Strong Man let out an incredulous laugh. "We shall see about that."

As he started forward, Zipporah cried out something in the tongue of her people. For an instant Strong Man's steps faltered. Guilt swept through him. Then, as if an invisible hand had placed it there, a vivid picture popped into his mind of mules laden with so much cash and other riches, they could scarcely be seen beneath their loads.

That sparkling image pushed his remorse aside, and he started toward Red Tiger. "Prepare to go to your gods, foreign Jushi," he muttered.

Utterly impassive, Zhao watched him come. "Remember," he said softly. "I did not seek this fight."

"It does not matter if you did or not," Strong Man replied, and hurled himself at him with the speed of a charging bull.

He fully expected the slighter man to try to jump out of the way, but Zhao did not. Instead, he stood calmly, waiting. Confusion penetrated Strong Man's battle lust. Did the foreigner want to die?

He let out a triumphant roar as his hands reached for his quarry's throat . . . and watched the *jushi* leap into the air, aiming his feet straight at Strong Man's chest.

It was too late to avoid the kick. Strong Man was too close and too slow. The blow struck him like a kick from an enraged stallion, sending him flying across the clearing.

Even as he hit the ground, Zhao, a blur of leaping motion, was already there. Desperately Strong Man struggled to his feet, only to take a punch to the temple that sent him reeling. It could have killed him, but Zhao was not yet trying to kill him.

With powerful hands, he lifted the dazed assassin into the air. Long fingers wound around Strong Man's throat while Zhao's other hand drew back in what his choking adversary recognized as the dreaded iron fist—a fist that could smash the wall of his chest into bloody splinters.

Zhao's face was no longer calm. It held a fury so intense, Strong Man knew there was no hope for him. The *jushi*'s eyes flared with a hatred that scorched through him like fire incinerating rice paper.

Gathering his strength, struggling to breathe, Strong Man made one last effort to save his life. Savagely he brought both hands up in a double-fisted blow at Zhao's head while he sought to knee him in the groin.

Zhao's reaction was instantaneous. Before his blows could find their targets, that terrible fist shot forward.

Agony exploded through Strong Man's chest, agony such as he had never felt in his entire life.

Then heavy blackness descended, blotting out the pain and everything else.

Consciousness returned slowly, and with it the pain. At first Strong Man did not believe he was alive. After the look he had seen in the foreigner's eyes, he couldn't be. But as the moments passed and he lay on the ground retching and groaning, he became convinced that he had not entered the Terrace of Night. He was too wretchedly miserable to be anything but alive.

It was a long time before he could finally crawl to his knees, and even longer before he could stand and take stock of his surroundings. He was alone in the clearing. The cart, the *jushi*, and the two women were gone—yet they had left his horse!

Stumbling and falling and cursing, Strong Man made his way to the nearby spring. Reaching it, he let his wobbly legs collapse and sat down heavily on the grassy bank.

The water was cool and as soft as a caress on his battered body. Gratefully he splashed it over his aching head. As his mind slowly cleared, one thought stood out with clarity in his befuddled brain.

The *jushi* had not killed him.

Strong Man found that incomprehensible, and highly embarrassing. He who had never been defeated in combat, had twice now been vanquished in fair fighting. While there was at least some honor in being bested by a supernatural being such as Matteo, in this latest battle he had been defeated by a mere man, and a barbarian at that!

It was too much to be borne. But what a fighter that red-haired foreigner was! Strong Man had never seen anything to equal it.

"I could like such a man as that," he muttered aloud. "Whereas I do *not* like Li Shan-po, and never will. Of course, one does not need to like a man to carry out his will, but I have had nothing but shame and misfortune since I began this accursed task. By the Celestial Dragon's balls, perhaps there is an omen in all this."

Ponderously the heavy wheels of Strong Man's thought processes began to turn. When they had finished, he climbed to his feet and mounted his horse.

He had to hold the gelding to a walk at first, but as his strength returned, he urged the animal into a fast trot. Ignoring the curses and shaking fists of travelers who had to scurry out of his way, he was soon cantering along the road to Yangzhou. He knew he must hurry. He had no idea of how long he had lain senseless, but from the position of the sun, it must have been quite some time.

There were many covered carts on the road, and when he finally caught sight of the one he sought, the gates of Yangzhou were already looming in the distance.

"Youposai Red Tiger!" he bellowed, and kicked his horse into a full gallop. "Hold a moment. Hold!"

To his immense relief, the cart slowed and pulled off to the side of the road. As Strong Man rode up to it, he saw Zipporah Tamudj glaring at him from within, while on the driver's bench, Rhea and Zhao sat looking at him, their faces wary and closed.

Tongue-tied, Strong Man gaped at Zhao a moment. Then, for lack of anything better to say, he blurted out, "You spared my life, Youposai."

"Yes," Zhao said coldly. "Aren't you satisfied with that, or do you want to fight again to see if I will forsake my discipline and send you to the Underworld?"

"*I* thought," Zipporah added, "that he made a great mistake in not killing you. I was very angry when he decided to let you live. I still am."

Strong Man nodded vigorously, then winced at the pain that shot through him. "I certainly deserved to be killed," he agreed. "But when I woke up alive, it gave me some time to think. I'm not a very good thinker," he said to Zhao. "However, I've decided that your honored mother is right, and I have been serving the wrong man. So none of you have anything to fear from me any longer."

Zhao's eyebrows lifted, and Rhea said smoothly, "That is very kind of you."

"I may not be a thinker," Strong Man went on, "but that doesn't mean I'm stupid. I can recognize omens when I see them. No one needs to drop *me* on the head more than a few times to make me see what's plain as rice in a pot."

There was a small silence. Rhea glanced at Zhao and Zipporah, and when it seemed that neither of them was going to speak, she asked in a polite voice, "And after being dropped on your head, what have you learned?"

"Ha," Strong Man said. "It is clear that there is a curse upon this task Li Shan-po has sent me on. I suspect there may even be a curse upon him as well. I want no part of it any longer, or of him. His position is illustrious now, but who knows how long it will last?"

Rubbing his bruised chest, he added ruefully, "This is a bad business, a bad business. I have already been beaten in battle twice since I came south, and that should be enough of a warning for any sensible man. If Li Shan-po wants you dead, Youposai Red Tiger, he will have to see to it himself. And as for this young woman here, let the Spider scratch his own itches, I say! I am a strong man, not some wheedling stinky-stinky eunuch who deals in concubines!"

"I see." Zhao exchanged glances with Rhea. "I am pleased by your change of heart, Strong Man. Thank you for telling us of it." He picked up the horses' reins. "But now I must get my mother to Yangzhou, then return to the Temple of the Jade Waterfall."

"Uh, yes." Strong Man cleared his throat. "Well, you see . . ." He was mumbling, and when Zhao gave him an impatient look, he coughed again, then continued in an awkward rush. "That is what I wanted to speak with you about. I—I think the bad luck is still on my head and will stay there unless I can make amends for the evil I tried to work upon you. So I would like to go from Li Shan-po's service into yours, Youposai Red Tiger."

"Mine?" Zhao's eyes widened in astonishment. "I have no service for you to go into, Strong Man. What could you possibly do?"

"I could guard your honored mother," the other said eagerly. "As long as Li Shan-po is alive and now knows that *she* is alive, she may need a bodyguard. Who better to watch over her than someone who was once in his service? Or I could go back with you to your temple. Soldiers are coming there, as many soldiers as there are fleas on a dog.

Even though you priests are trained in Shaolin, it will still be a hard fight."

He grinned wryly. "Another pair of strong arms won't do any harm. I may not be able to best *you*, Red Tiger, but there hasn't been a soldier born who can stand against me."

"You would fight in defense of the temple?" Zhao asked. "Why?"

Strong Man shrugged. "Why not? I used to be a soldier myself, and believe me, when soldiers are sent into a battle, they know nothing about the causes for it, nor do they care. Fighting is fighting. And anyway, if I could serve Li Shan-po, I can certainly kill a few soldiers in defense of your temple."

Zhao shook his head. "Such reasons are not the right ones, but . . ." His expression turned thoughtful. "You could be of some help in guarding my mother. If you are sincere."

"I am, Honored Jushi, I am."

Zipporah let out an indignant exclamation in Hebrew. "Zhao Tamudj!" she snapped. "Have you gone mad? I need no one to watch over me. And even if I did, it would not be this—this uncouth person who tried to kill you! What can you be thinking of?"

"I am thinking," Zhao said, "that you do need someone to protect you. Bringing you to Yangzhou seemed far safer than letting you stay at the temple, but that was before we knew Li Shan-po had sent out an assassin. To have that assassin turn around and protect you is something even Li Shan-po would not expect."

He gave Strong Man a sharp glance. "The only drawback is that we don't know if he can be trusted."

"Indeed, we do not," Zipporah declared. "Nor can we find out."

"Yes, we can," Rhea said.

They all looked at her, and she explained. "I have a way of divining whether he is speaking truthfully."

Strong Man grew apprehensive. Leaning down from the saddle, he asked Zhao in a loud whisper, "Is she a spirit woman?"

"Not exactly," Zhao said. He nodded to Rhea. "Go ahead, my lady. Use your powers."

Under Strong Man's worried gaze and Zipporah's irritated and skeptical one, Rhea leapt easily to the ground. She made a peremptory gesture to Strong Man. "Get off your horse and come here."

He hesitated, and she beckoned again. "Sea and Sky, man, hurry up! I'm not going to turn you into a strand of seaweed!"

Strong Man flushed. Dismounting, he stood before her and flushed even more when he realized she was taller than he. Her eyes, the eerie color of a pale moon, shone down into his. Deeper and deeper they shone, until in great astonishment and fear, he felt his thoughts drain away.

Much as he wanted to struggle against that horrifying blankness, he could do nothing. Every part of him had become as heavy as trees rooted into the ground, and all he could do was stand motionless, staring into those silvery, magical eyes.

Abruptly, with such suddenness that he actually stumbled, she released him.

Rhea turned to Zhao and Zipporah. "Strange as it seems," she said, "he is being utterly truthful. I think we should let him come."

Zipporah's expression was no longer skeptical. She was staring at Rhea with as much fright as Strong Man was feeling. Wordlessly she nodded. Zhao only smiled at Rhea and held out a hand to help her back into the cart.

"Well then," he said briskly. "Shall we continue on our way?"

Chapter 24

After gazing fixedly upon expressions and
substance
The mind returns with a spiritual image,
As when seeking the outlines of waves,
As when painting the glory of spring.
The changing shapes of windswept clouds,
The energies of flowers and plants,
The rolling breakers of ocean,
The crags and cliffs of mountains,
All these are like the mighty Tao,
Skillfully woven into earthly surroundings . . .
To obtain likeness without form,
Is not that to possess the man?

—*Taoist Tales*

Rhea had forgotten about the noise and the stench of
Terran cities. Though considerably smaller than Ch'ang-an,
the port of Yangzhou nevertheless bristled with activity.

Zhao skillfully guided the horses through the steady

stream of traffic around the city gates, the traffic jam of donkey- and mule-drawn carts and shouting tradesmen, and on into the city.

Once they had passed through the massive South Tower gates, Zipporah refused to remain in the cart's cushioned interior. Despite Zhao's objections, she sat between him and Rhea on the hard driver's bench. Although she carefully avoided meeting the latter's eyes, she had no qualms about casting glowering looks at Strong Man, who now rode beside them. She alternated those glares with sad and pensive gazes about the city of her birth.

"Mother?" Zhao asked gently. "Is it difficult?"

She sighed. "No, it's ... strange more than it's difficult." She stared at a passing caravan led by Arab merchants, their white turbans brilliant against their dark skin. "How little things have changed in all this time. It seems as though I never left these streets. I could almost expect to see your father. . . ." Her voice broke.

"Yes," Zhao said. "I know. I have felt that way when I've come here."

Zipporah gave him a surprised look. "You never said."

"How could I, when you refused even to speak the name of this city? I feared that if I did, it would worsen your terrible memories and add to your pain."

"That," Zipporah said, "would be impossible."

The cart clattered on through the hubbub, heading toward the southern part of the city known as the Foreigners' District. Here traders from other lands resided with their families, some of them in homes as sumptuous as those of any wealthy Han merchant.

Rhea studied the busy streets with interest. This was the place of Zhao's birth, the city where his true people lived, yet it was hard to believe he had ever been part of this bustling scene.

None of the men riding or walking along the streets, or conducting business in front of their shops and stalls, resembled him in the least. Most were no taller than any other Terran man native to the Middle Kingdom, and despite Zhao's claim that his red hair and green eyes often cropped up among his people, she saw few signs of it. Almost without exception, the Zhuhu—men and women alike—were olive-skinned, with black hair and even blacker eyes.

As it did in Ch'ang-an, the great Pien Canal—pride of the Middle Kingdom—flowed directly through Yangzhou carrying its heavy burden of water traffic. Bordering the quays were flowering trees, plum, peach, pear, and apricot, all of them still in bloom. Their fragrance, however, even to Rhea's keen senses, could scarcely be detected.

A convoy of boats carrying the city's garbage floated along the water, bound for the country. Rhea wrinkled her nose, and from the corner of her eye saw Zipporah and Zhao do the same. Despite their relative cleanliness, the streets gave off an all-pervasive odor of human excrement and rotting garbage.

As night fell over the city, multicolored lamps were lighted in the entrances and covered courtyards of the city's many restaurants, teahouses, and taverns. The music of professional singing girls drifted out into the streets to mingle with men's laughter and the sounds of their dining and drinking.

Zhao had grown accustomed to the serenity of the Temple of the Jade Waterfall, and this city in which he had spent the first fifteen years of his life was like another world, vivid but disconcerting. Still, his hands handled the reins with a will of their own, directing the horses with unerring accuracy along the twisting alleys where he had run and played as a boy, as though he had left these crowded and noisy streets only yesterday.

As they rode farther into the Foreigner's District, it grew quieter. The shops that took up the ground floor of the poorer residences were already closed. Those upon the streets were mostly men, dressed in the flowing robes and blue or white hats of the *se mu ren*, wearing preoccupied expressions as they hurried home after concluding last-minute business in other parts of the city.

In front of a large house that stood in a lane lined with similarly prosperous-looking homes, Zhao halted the horses. His thoughts bleak, he stared down the street, its narrow length shadowy in the gathering dusk.

He felt his mother tense as she gazed in the same direction, and he knew exactly what was going through her mind. Farther along, toward the Jin River, lay the house that had belonged to the Tamudj family. Zhao had often wondered what he would do if he ever came back to this lane. Now that the moment had come, he knew the answer without question.

He would not, could not, go look at the house where he had been born. It was his no longer. Strangers lived there now.

Reining up beside the cart, Strong Man looked around. His craggy face brightened with surprised pleasure as he dismounted.

"Is *this* where we're going to live?" he asked with delight. "I had no idea your kin were so wealthy. You see? I throw in my lot with you and my luck turns already!"

Zipporah bristled. "Curb your tongue, impertinent cockroach. If you live here at all, it will be in the stables."

Zhao jumped from the cart, then turned to assist his mother as Rhea leapt down with her usual grace. Zhao sent the gatekeeper to fetch Dasheng Tian, then the four waited in silence for him to appear.

Zhao listened as the families who lived in the nearby homes laughed and talked in their courtyards. Every so often, raucous voices and laughter burst from a wine house or restaurant. In front of the house at the far end of the lane, a watchdog came out. Seeing the people standing in the distance, it barked furiously until the gatekeeper at that house shouted at it to be quiet.

At last slippered feet whispered on the tiles of the courtyard, and Dasheng Tian hurried out into the street. Garbed in the long robe and blue hat of the Zhuhu, he was about Zhao's age, taller than average, and possessed the dark skin and eyes of his people. His smile radiated warmth and welcome.

"Shalom, shalom," he cried. "Peace be upon you. May Shang Tian be thanked for bringing you back to us!"

Clasping his hands to his chest, he bowed deeply to Zipporah. "Lady Zipporah, you shall have an honored place in my household to the end of your days. And as for you, beloved friend of my youth." He turned to Zhao and joyfully embraced him. "How I have prayed for this day, to see you back amid your own. Ah, this is indeed an auspicious day!"

Bubbling with enthusiasm, he released Zhao and took a step backward, beaming at him. "I shall teach you the honored trade of your father—blessed be his memory. Though no man was a better silk trader than An Tamudj, I haven't done too badly for myself. My own father— blessed be his memory—taught me much before he went to Shang Tian. I shall pass on to you what I have learned, and soon you will—"

"He is not staying," Zipporah said.

Dasheng Tian cocked his head as though he had not

heard her correctly. "Not staying?" His joyous smile dissolved into a look of bewilderment. "But it has all been arranged. Rabbi Zhong sent word to the head monk at the temple, and he agreed that you should come here. . . ." For the first time Dasheng noticed Rhea and Strong Man, and his eyes widened. "Zhao, who is this? May the Lord be praised, are you betrothed?"

"No," Rhea, Zhao, and Zipporah said in unison, and Dasheng's expression grew even more uncomprehending.

"I do not understand," he said. "What goes on here?"

"Old friend," Zhao said gently, "you are a good-hearted and honorable man. I will never forget your kindness to us, but only my mother and her . . . uh, servant will be staying with you. I must return to the Temple of the Jade Waterfall before the soldiers come."

"Ah, yes, the soldiers." Dasheng sighed. "The Flowery Land is without a doubt in the grip of utter madness." His face was suddenly stark in the dancing lantern light. "There is a rumor going through Yangzhou," he murmured, "only I fear it may be more than that. I have friends in high places and they have repeated it to me as well. They say"—he lowered his voice to a whisper—"that every province in the Middle Kingdom must present to the court the hearts and livers of eight youths and eight maidens, each of them fifteen years old."

There was a moment of absolute quiet, then Zipporah said firmly, "I do not belive it. This is still a civilized land. Such a thing could not possibly be true. And even if it were, what conceivable purpose could there be for such barbarity?"

Dasheng shuddered with revulsion and horror. "The Emperor has become possessed by a desire to achieve immortality. He is seeking an elixir that will grant him eternal life, and apparently the hearts and livers of those poor innocents are one of the ingredients. I cannot say for certain that it is true, Lady Tamudj. After all, we are far removed from the capital and things often get distorted in the telling. But it's a horrible thought. How could the Son of Heaven imagine something so awful?"

"I'll wager he didn't."

At the sound of the gruff voice, everyone turned. It was the first time Strong Man had spoken. Ill at ease, he looked away, clearly wishing he hadn't.

"What are you talking about?" Dasheng asked. "No one else but the Son of Heaven has the power to issue such pronouncements. And what would you, a servant, know about it anyway?"

"More than you think, Zhuhu. And I am *not* a serv—" As if a hand had suddenly pulled his head around, Strong Man's gaze was drawn to Zhao's. A flush mounted into his face, and lowering his eyes, he muttered, "I meant no disrespect. But I come from the capital, you see, so . . . I know things."

Raising his eyes, he looked at Zhao again. "And I still say it wasn't the Son of Heaven who thought up the idea of cutting out the hearts and livers of boys and girls. It was my old master. You know as well as I that he has knowledge of the Dark Arts. And he boasted to me, Youposai Red Tiger, of his increasing influence over the Emperor. If it's true, then it's my old master who is behind it, I tell you."

"And who," Dasheng asked, "is your former master?"

Zhao answered for him. "Li Shan-po."

Dasheng stared. "Shang Tian have mercy on us," he whispered, and made the sign for protection against the evil eye.

·　　·　　·

It was well after dark that night when the soldiers under the command of Grand General Wang finally halted to make camp. In a steady drizzle, the men set to work, their faces grim, their silence broken only by muttered cursing. The encampment was erected with little joy, the tents thrown up, pickets set out, and cooking fires kindled with few smiles and even less laughter.

These soldiers of the imperial court were weary, not so much in body as in spirit, tired of the devastation they wreaked every day, jaded by the grief they left behind. A pall lay over the detachment and the long row of treasure-laden wagons that accompanied it, a pall that grew heavier with each temple that was looted and left to burn.

General Wang was no happier than his soldiers, though his discontent stemmed from a different source. With the arrival of more troops several days earlier, the company had grown too large to be accommodated at villages. This meant an end to Wang's comfortable quarters, and the beginning of trying to sleep in a mosquito-infested tent.

His mood was not helped by the presence of the new detachment's commander, a hard-faced professional soldier named General Chu. Powerfully built and obviously seasoned by many difficult campaigns, he was able to spend hours on horseback with infuriating ease, and was completely impervious to fatigue, exertion, or any of the other discomforts that so plagued General Wang.

General Chu was said to be a eunuch—a great surprise to Wang. He had always looked upon eunuchs with indulgent contempt, viewing them as physically weak creatures, even more subject to their emotions than women. He'd heard of eunuchs becoming soldiers, but until now he had never quite believed it. Truth be told, Wang was utterly intimidated by his new cohort.

The two generals were supposed to be equal in rank,

but General Chu's superior abilities had been evident from the moment he arrived. Self-contained and competent, his authority was a direct contrast to Wang's floundering leadership, and the soldiers responded to it. Wang felt edged out, superfluous. It galled him, yet there was little he could do about it.

Perspiring heavily despite the drizzle, he sprawled upon the mats that had been laid before the entrance to his tent, futilely waiting for a cool breeze to waft over him. With glum indifference, he noted that General Chu and several of his officers were standing by the picket lines where the horses were tethered, deep in conversation. It presently ended with the officers bowing and Chu turning to walk toward Wang's tent. Sourly Wang watched him approach.

"A pleasant evening, is it not?" the eunuch greeted him.

Wang glowered. "Pleasant? I suppose if one were a mosquito or a snail, he would find it so. I, however, have more civilized tastes."

General Chu did not reply to this. "An important task lies before us tomorrow," he said. "I thought we might speak of it, General."

The subtle emphasis on the last word made Wang bristle. Did this eunuch dare to make sport of Wang's divinely appointed title, conferred upon him by the Son of Heaven himself? "All my tasks on this mission have been important," he declared with what he fancied was great dignity. "And so they have been since before you arrived, *General*."

"Hmm. Yes. In any case, it is time to speak of precisely why the Son of Heaven dispatched so many soldiers to join you here." An expression of curiosity tinged with contempt crossed Chu's normally impassive features. "Haven't you wondered?"

Wang certainly had, but he would not give this intimidating fellow the satisfaction of knowing it. "The Son of Heaven is all-knowing in his wisdom," he said severely. "A good general does not question, he merely obeys."

"Actually," General Chu said, "strict obedience is a soldier's function. A good general must constantly be using his wits, as well as questioning everything around him, or he does not remain a good general for very long. Surely you agree?"

Wang flushed. "Of course, of course," he snapped. "That is what I meant."

Chu's lips twitched, but he continued in the same mild voice. "Tomorrow we are to visit the Temple of the Jade Waterfall. It is a wealthy monastery, likely containing riches that will take the greater part of the day to tally and load. I was hoping you would be good enough to see to that part of it."

Wang tried to keep his face neutral, but his eyes lighted up with avarice. So far, the only redeeming factor of this accursed exile in the southern frontier had been the discovery that he could secrete small items of value that had somehow not found their way onto the treasure lists.

He had amassed quite a store for himself in this way. With the arrival of these unwanted reinforcements, he had resigned himself to halting his attractive sideline, for General Chu's eyes seemed dismayingly sharp. But now the foolish eunuch was giving him a chance to continue!

"Yes, I will see to it," he said. "I was planning on it, in fact. It is important work, requiring the supervision of a skilled and competent overseer. Indeed, General Chu, I was wondering if you and your men might not find yourselves somewhat in the way tomorrow. We've been at this a while, you see, and have become quite proficient at it. We really don't need your help."

"Oh, you might," General Chu said blandly. "Have you not heard? The Temple of the Jade Waterfall is Shaolin."

Wang blanched. "N-no." He realized he was stammering and strove to match the aplomb in Chu's voice. "I had not heard. Are you certain of this?"

"Oh, yes. Even with your . . . uh, wise leadership, the taking of such a monastery will be difficult. I can handle the resistance that will surely arise, while you take a few of your men and see to the clerical end of the business."

By all Under Heaven! Wang thought. He barely repressed a shudder as all the stories he had ever heard about the inhuman prowess of Shaolin monks bubbled into his mind. He might actually have had to face such men tomorrow if not for the timely arrival of this eunuch!

"I would welcome a good fight," he said, "but your suggestion is well-taken. Since that is no doubt why you and these reinforcements were sent to join me, I would not wish to deprive you of your duty."

Chu smiled but remained silent. Suddenly uncomfortable, Wang looked at him. "That is why you were sent here, isn't it?"

"Yes," Chu said. "Among other things."

"Oh." Still sprawled on the mats, Wang gave another long glance up at the stolid, rather daunting general. His face did not reveal one shred of his inner thoughts, but something in his voice and manner warned Wang not to question him too closely.

Chu, however, was not ready to let the matter rest. "These other reasons, General Wang, do not concern you, although I wanted to bring the subject up so you will know not to interfere."

Now the warning was no longer a warning, but a clear threat. "You do not need to tell me anything," Wang began hastily. "I—"

Chu continued as though he hadn't heard. "This temple is of special interest to the Dragon Throne. Certain items are hidden there which the Son of Heaven wants. It is my task to recover those items. As for you, General Wang, you would be wise to disregard whatever you may see tomorrow. Unless, of course, you prefer peddling turnips to retaining this comfortable and recently acquired station in life."

Wang's mouth fell open. He knew! But how could he? Who had told him?

"Close your mouth," Chu said pleasantly. "Like you, I have friends in high places, with one difference. No one handed me my success on a porcelain plate. I worked for it, using strength, wits, and whatever opportunities came my way. Whereas you, *General*, are no more a soldier than that pretty little concubine you just purchased for yourself. Although," he added with a malicious smile, "with all those baubles you've been hiding away, you should be able to afford one or two even prettier ones. If you get back to Ch'ang-an, that is."

Wang gaped in horror, then tried to speak. Only a weak gargling sound came out of his mouth, and General Chu looked down at him with unconcealed scorn.

"Calm yourself. As long as you stay out of my path, General, you and I should get along fine. Just remember: stick to your scavenging and do not interfere. Whatever happens."

With neither a bow nor a backward glance, he turned on his heel and strode off in the direction of his own tent.

Watching him go, Wang shuddered violently. What a cold-eyed demon that eunuch general was! Well, the creature didn't have to worry. He, Wang, would be only too happy to stay uninvolved in the hellish events planned for the next day.

Still, a niggling thought scurried around in the back of his mind. What was to happen tomorrow that was so horrible? He promptly shoved the treacherous speculation away. Whatever it was, it did not concern him, and he had better keep it that way.

General Chu entered his tent and pulled the door flap down behind him. Inside, it was surprisingly comfortable. Cushions had been spread around to soften the hard ground, and numerous lamps were already lit, giving the spacious interior a mellow, welcoming glow.

Opening a small leather-bound chest, Chu took out a jewel-backed mirror and held it up to his face. For several moments, he studied his reflection; then he smiled, a slow and satisfied smile.

"A superior disguise," Li Shan-po murmured. "That fat fool does not suspect a thing. Which means my surprise at the Temple of the Jade Waterfall will be a surprise indeed."

The smile became a grin, and he chuckled softly. "I do enjoy a well-turned surprise. What a shame that Master Wu will not. And neither will the Zhuhu whelp and his mother."

Chapter 25

What hill lacks clouds at dawn?
These clouds too are bleak and faded.
What hill lacks evening rain?
This rain too is a gray expanse....
Now boldly embossed, the twelve peaks
Are cast forever as a weird and ghostly home.

—Yu Fen,
*Divine Woman: Dragon Ladies
and Rain Maidens in T'ang Literature*

Despite the inner urging that told him to leave for the Temple of the Jade Waterfall right away, Zhao reluctantly agreed to spend the night at the house of Dasheng Tian. It was not his friend's entreaties that convinced him, but Rhea. She had not used words, but directed his gaze to Zipporah. One look into her eyes had dried his objections in his throat.

Dasheng was elated. "You are right to spend the night," he said to Zhao. "The prefect himself is one of my best customers. Just this morning he came into my shop and we had *t'e* together. He says there are indeed soldiers marching toward the temple, but they are several days away at least. If you still insist on returning, you will have plenty of time to get there before the soldiers do."

Over the meal that followed, though, it soon became evident that Dasheng hoped to dissuade Zhao from doing just that. "You must come with me to the synagogue tomorrow," he said after he had finished reciting the ritual benedictions for food and wine. "There are many who will be happy to see you, despite those *jushi* robes you insist upon wearing."

Zhao looked down at the main course—tender young chicken cooked in honey—a large helping of which steamed fragrantly upon his plate. This and the other dishes on the table were the foods of his youth, spread out in lavish profusion before him. Seeing them made the world tip dizzily, as though he would look up to see his own family gathered around the long table, all of them healthy and whole.

The huge appetite of his youth was gone, however. He did not eat meat anymore, and the Zhuhu prepared many dishes in honey, and he no longer cared for such rich, sweet foods.

Yet the chicken and all the other delicacies that loaded down the table had been prepared especially in their honor. Zipporah was already eating with delighted pleasure, and Zhao would not offend Dasheng's hospitality by not doing the same. He took a few bites of rice delicately flavored with saffron.

"The Lady Rhea and I must leave tomorrow," he reminded Dasheng.

Dasheng glanced from Zhao to Rhea. He was obviously puzzled and uneasy about her presence, though he did not question it. "I still think you should come with me. Perhaps being among your own again will change your mind about leaving us so soon."

"Husband," broke in Dasheng's wife, a pretty woman named Yaffa. "It may be that our guest has no prayer shawl or phylacteries with him. Given the destruction visited upon his poor family, it would not surprise me if they had been lost or taken from him. But we can supply you with new ones," she said gently to Zhao. "It would be a mitzvah to let us do so."

Zipporah smiled at the younger woman. "You are a good Zhuhu daughter, Lady Yaffa. How I wish . . ."

Her gaze drifted across the table to Rhea, and she did not finish her sentence. She did not need to. Rhea saw the tears glistening in the older woman's eyes, and she repressed a sigh.

Zipporah's thoughts were as plain as sea foam upon the waves. The Lady Yaffa, with her gentle dark eyes and gleaming black hair coiled neatly around her head, was no doubt exactly the kind of wife Zipporah had always envisioned for her son.

"Thank you, Lady Yaffa," Zhao said. "But my tallith was the only thing I managed to keep. I took it with me on the night we fled Yangzhou."

"I should think so," Dasheng said. "A Zhuhu should never be without his prayer shawl and phylacteries. Zhao, it is your duty to go to synagogue."

"I know my duty, Dasheng," Zhao said. "You do not need—"

"Zhao," Zipporah interrupted as her son's voice began to rise. "It has been a long and tiring day, and I would like to go to bed, to feel the peace of resting among my—our people after all these years. But I will ask one thing of you, son. Please go with Dasheng tomorrow. The prayers begin early. You can go at first light and still leave for the temple in plenty of time. Since the soldiers will not arrive there for several days, where is the harm?"

Zhao nodded to Zipporah. "Of course I will go, Mother," he said. "Actually, I would like to, and if it pleases you, so much the better."

A pang went through him at the joy in his mother's eyes. "It is little enough that I have done to please you of late," he added. Involuntarily his gaze slid to Rhea.

Zipporah's gaze followed her son's, and her joy faded. "Yes," she said. "That is true."

When the grayish-black of false dawn lighted the mighty ocean waves that danced near Yangzhou, Rhea slipped into Zhao's bedchamber. She was not surprised to find him awake. Standing at the window, clad only in his loose pants, he had already turned to face the door as though he had sensed her presence outside.

"You should not be here," he said, but the warmth and gladness in his tone belied the words. "Someone will see."

"No, they won't. I can move more quietly than even your Shaolin monks when I wish to."

"Yes," he said huskily, his eyes suddenly devouring her. "I believe you can, at that."

Though he smiled, she saw the weariness on his face, as though he hadn't slept. "You should try to get some rest, Red Tiger," she said, concerned. "Difficult days lie ahead. Who knows when you will get the chance again."

"Difficult days, indeed." He turned back to the window. "Have you seen the moon, Rhea? Look."

She gazed past him at the silver and black sky. High above the restless ocean, the Moon Goddess flowed through her dark domain, encircled by a pale halo of ghostly white.

"A white rainbow," Zhao muttered. "I have been watching it since moonrise. Many believe it is really a dragon, a rainbow dragon."

"But do you believe that? I know a ring around the moon is not often seen, but my people say that when one appears, it is merely a trick of wind and light, nothing more."

"No." Zhao's voice was quietly emphatic. "It is more than that, Rhea. A white rainbow is a portent, and an evil one. There is an omen associated with its appearance: 'Blood shall flow beneath it.' Whenever such an apparition has occurred in the Middle Kingdom, dire consequences have always followed."

Coincidence, Rhea wanted to say, but with the images of her own forebodings so vivid, it seemed hypocritical to make light of Zhao's. As if he had read her mind, he said, "The sight worries me, Rhea, as much as the warnings you saw in your dream-walk."

"Then look at it no longer." She took his hand. "Go to bed and rest instead. That will do you more good than standing here brooding over things you can do nothing about until morning."

"True enough,' he said, and gave her a slow smile. "Perhaps you should stay a while to see that I do."

She smiled back. "Perhaps I should," she said, and added judiciously, "Just to see that you rest, of course."

"Of course."

He cupped her shoulders in his hands, then swung her up in his arms. "We can rest together," he said, his mouth against the silk of her hair. "Afterward."

Later, as they lay wrapped in each other's arms upon his bed, Rhea murmured, "When you go to practice the rituals with your friend this morning, I will go to practice my own."

"Your own?" He lifted his head off the pillow and looked down at her. "I don't understand."

"I'm going back to the sea."

His eyes darkened, his arms tightening around her until a woman of the land would have winced. "Have the people in this house been discourteous to you?" he demanded, low-voiced and protective. "Or is it my mother? Has she said something to offend you?"

"No, Red Tiger. Nothing like that."

He did not believe her. "You must pay no heed to what she says, love. All of this has been very difficult for her." He smiled, trying to lighten his own bleak mood and hers. "The Zhuhu do not believe in fox spirits and ghosts and gods and goddesses. Accepting your presence goes against all she has ever been taught about the world."

"I know that. But neither your mother nor anyone else has upset me. I will come back, dearling, but I must visit my own world again, if only for a little time. . . ."

She looked away, toward the open window where the sound of the sea was borne to her on the last breezes of the night. "To be so near the sea," she whispered, "and not go there. I cannot stay away from you, but neither can I bear to hear Her song and not answer it."

"I understand," Zhao murmured. He stroked a hand down her smooth, naked back. "You do not need to explain, dearest. Only come back. Once this is over, once all the bonds laid upon me have been served, you and I must . . ."

His voice trailed off and he lay in silence, his large hand continuing to caress her back. She did not press him to go on, for what could he say? What could either of them say? The difference between their worlds was so great, any future was impossible. He could not join her in the sea, yet neither could she leave it. Not for good. Not even for him.

Before the Hour of the Dog had begun, Zhao and Dasheng started for the synagogue. A few minutes after they left, Rhea slipped out of the house and headed down to the sea. She needed no one to show her the way through the jumble of narrow winding streets. The sea called to her so that she went forward unerringly, scarcely aware of anything else.

Her strides flowing and swift, she passed the opening stalls and shops, the owners who rolled down their awnings as they shouted greetings to one another and passersby. Soon the foreign district was left behind and the harbor lay before her. She paused on the quay, her mouth puckering in disgust.

The waters of the Mother were dirtied, polluted by the careless landfolk. Dead fish floated among the refuse that had been thrown from the docks or from the countless sailing vessels that littered the water.

Still grimacing in distaste, Rhea picked her way through the chaos of the docks, seeking a spot where the waters were not too dirty and where she could slip into them unobserved. She had to go far down the beach, but ah, the pleasure she felt when she finally entered the waves.

Far down the shore and then out to sea she swam, joying in the freedom and the speed, released from the encumbrances of landfolk garments, released from the encumbrances that becoming involved in their lives had brought.

Finally she surfaced and looked around. Yangzhou was no longer in sight, lost in the wave-tossed distance and the hazy mists of early morning. But from behind the trees that lined the gentle rise beyond the shoreline, innumerable curls of smoke drifted up into the air—long, orderly swirls that could only come from cooking fires. Many fires.

The soldiers.

Tense and worried, Rhea raced back toward the beach. She swam along the land, her sharp eyes straining for a glimpse of what lay behind those screening trees. At last, she saw them.

It was an enormous encampment, far bigger than anything she had expected. And it was on the move. Even as she watched, the armed soldiers, some mounted and others on foot, were forming ranks and departing under the shouted orders of their commanders. Departing in the direction of the Temple of the Jade Waterfall.

"By the Mother," she whispered. "Dasheng Tian's friend was wrong. They are not several days away, but only hours."

She dived beneath the waves, hurling herself back toward Yangzhou. Even as she sped along, she knew she would be too late. Too late to find Red Tiger and warn him. Too late for them to reach the temple before that giant company of soldiers did.

Matteo. She spoke the name in her mind, sending it desperately across the ocean. *If you are out there, hear me and answer.*

There was no reply, which did not surprise her. Her brother had been very angry when he left.

Join me in stopping this tragedy, she pleaded nonetheless. *I love the Terran. For good or ill, I love him. Please help me to protect him and those at his temple.*

Still, the sea within her mind remained silent. She sent out one last call. *I do not ask you to do this for the land-folk, but for me, your only sister.*

There was no time for more, though likely it wouldn't

have done any good. The change in the currents told Rhea she was nearing the city, and within moments she surfaced at the spot where she had left her clothes.

She had not been gone long, no more than two or three hours, but Dasheng Tian's household was fully awake when she returned.

"Where is Red Tiger?" she demanded of the first person she saw, a servant on her way to the dining hall, laden with platters of food to break the family's nightly fast.

Unnerved, the serving woman gaped at Rhea, whose hair tumbled in wet tendrils down her back.

Zipporah appeared in the doorway of the dining hall. "Zhao is where he should be," she said coolly, "at the synagogue with Dasheng, although their devotions are probably finished by now. They should be returning any moment." She scrutinized Rhea. "What do you want with him?"

Rhea spun around without answering. Out in the street once more, she slithered through the throngs of pedestrians and carts, following the route she had seen the two men take earlier. At last she saw them, and with no heed for ceremony, raced up to them and grasped Zhao by the arms.

"We must leave and right now," she said. "The soldiers have arrived. They are on their way to the temple."

Dasheng was gaping at her as the servant had, but Zhao neither questioned nor argued. He broke into a run, and with Rhea effortlessly matching his pace, they soon left Dasheng behind them.

"It would be wise if we brought Strong Man with us after all," Rhea said when they reached the Tian house. "I think your mother will be safe enough without him for a few days, and though you did not care for his reasons in offering to fight the soldiers, I believe you will be glad of him when the time comes."

Zhao glanced at her sharply. "You did not say that before. Why do you feel he is needed now?"

She met his gaze. "Because I have seen the number of soldiers they are sending against your temple."

Strong Man was as eager to leave as Rhea was for him to come. "Your honored mother does not like me," he complained to Zhao, "and I fear she never will. By the jade stem of the Thunder God, she should have been a man, for she certainly has the manner of one."

Zhao was silent. He, Rhea, and their new ally were riding through the streets, headed for the city gates. Dasheng had offered them three of his horses, and driven by his urgency, Zhao had gladly accepted.

He was as grateful for Dasheng's kindness as he was grieved by his hasty farewell to his mother. There had been no time for reassurances and words of love and respect, only for a brief embrace and a whispered, "Do not worry about me. I will come back."

Zipporah had surprised him. Taking his face in her hands, she had stared at him for a long moment, then said in a steady voice, "Do as the teachings of our people tell us, my son. A man must stand with integrity against all that is wrong in this world. Stand with integrity, Zhao. Do what is right. And please, please come back to me."

As they forced their horses through the swarm at the gates, Zhao could still see his mother's face, the deep lines of despair etched into it, her eyes brimming with sorrow and fear as she watched him ride out of the courtyard.

It was a clear day, and they rode the horses hard through the morning hours, pausing only to rest them in the ever-increasing heat, then pushing on again as soon as they dared. There was little talk, even between Zhao and Rhea. Of what use could words be now?

Zhao's urgency heightened with the heat, building into a desperate sense of dread that ate at him with every li covered by the horses' pounding hooves. In rhythmic cadence with the beat of galloping feet, a refrain pounded in his brain: *It is too late. It is too late.*

Long before the lathered horses reached the monastery lands, the first plumes of smoke rose in the distance. Long and thick and black, they spiraled up against the pale blue sky, fouling the day with malevolence and death, like the wings of the evil dragons Zhao had spoken of the night before.

The burning of the temple had begun.

Chapter 26

Those who actively initiate will be defeated;
Those who hold fast to anything will lose it.
Therefore, the Sage is never defeated because
he is passive;
and never loses because he is detached.

—*Tao Te Ching*

All that morning the monks had battled desperately to stave off the torching of their holy place. Against overwhelming odds they had acquitted themselves valiantly, with a courage and a skill beyond anything their foes had ever seen.

But now the outer buildings of the monastery were on fire. It could only be a matter of time before the temple itself would be in flames.

Shortly after sunrise, the first soldiers had appeared on the horizon. Master Wu called into the main courtyard every person who had chosen to remain. Silent in their determination, serene in having made a decision that would likely cost them their lives, they gathered.

Many had stayed. But five hundred priests and novices, one hundred and fifty nuns from the neighboring Buddhist convent, and the one hundred or so peasants who were too stubborn to flee with their fellows could never hope to counter the vast force that rode up to the temple walls.

The detachments of soldiers, each with its own brightly colored standard snapping in the hot, sticky breeze, progressed ominously up the road, extending for li after li like an enormous winding snake. Thousands upon thousands of them glittered under the early sun, and Master Wu smiled upon seeing them, as if at some joke.

General Chu, with Grand General Wang bouncing along a few paces behind, was at the head of the mighty army. Reining in his prancing stallion at the gates, he bellowed without preamble,

"You in this temple. The Son of Heaven—magnificent be his name—has judged all within these gates to be enemies of the empire. You have willfully hidden from the imperial court secrets of immortality, substances that could have brought the Dowager Empress back to life and permitted the Emperor himself to transcend to one of the Immortals.

"Now your treasonous blood must stain the ground in recompense. Only when it does will your sins be erased. Surrender yourselves and your ill-gotten goods to the Emperor's will. Then prepare to die!"

Master Wu responded to this challenge in a voice that was strong yet gentle, even amused. "If we are to die regardless of whether we submit or resist you," he called, "then what is the advantage to either, my son?"

The question enraged General Chu. "You are very clever at twisting your words to make it sound as though you possess great wisdom, Old Man," he snarled back. "But I am not one of your malleable priests or gullible peasants. By your very existence you offend the Confucian order of what is natural in the world. And within your temple you harbor riches that are an offense to the Dragon Throne. Your defiance will only make the fate you suffer all the harder."

"We defy no one," came the quiet answer. "And yet, how greatly you must fear malleable priests and gullible peasants to have brought such a great force against us. Do we terrify you so much?"

General Chu's response was immediate. "Storm these walls!" he roared.

The fighting was savage, for the defenders would not bend their necks tamely for the executioner's sword. In the wide courtyard where Rhea had watched Zhao and his fellow disciples practice their sparring techniques, skilled priests and young novices alike fought for real, using every bit of skill they possessed to defend their sacred place from the invaders.

Uncaring, the sun shone down, gleaming brilliantly on the shaved heads and yellow robes of the Shaolin monks, and on the glowing blood that spilled from their mortal wounds. One by one, the defenders, with their magnificent swirling kicks, their graceful arching punches, and their incredible speed, fell before countless slashing swords and spears.

Grand General Wang, who had managed to keep himself well out of the paths of conflict, was astounded, sickened, and terrified by the sight of this, the first battle he had ever seen. Though hopelessly outnumbered, the Shaolin priests refused to surrender themselves and their monastery, and they fought with demonic skill.

If he hadn't watched so many die, Wang would have

sworn they were not human at all. Yet they could be killed. It took almost a score of armed soldiers to kill just one Shaolin monk, but with such a vast inequality in numbers, it scarcely mattered.

Wang was appalled. He had never held anything or anyone more precious than his own self, and he now witnessed acts of heroism and valor that took him outside of that absorption with himself—and shamed him.

It also made him wonder if a divine retribution, some punishment so ghastly the mortal mind could not even imagine it, would be visited upon all those who were committing such wickedness. If that were so, then any vengeance would include him, wouldn't it?

Tears streaked down his plump cheeks as, attended by a protective cordon of subordinate officers, he stumbled along the outermost edges of the raging conflict.

Everywhere his blurred gaze fell, a new scene of bravery smote him with still more blood and death. What added boundless horror to the already terrible day were the nuns. Trained also in Shaolin, each one of these females, with her orange robe and shaven head, was more than a match for any two or three soldiers. But there were far more than two or three to contend against.

Right in front of Wang's eyes a skirmish involving a monk and a nun was rushing toward its inevitable end. Surrounded and outnumbered, the two fought with a determination and skill that were well-nigh incredible.

The nun had armed herself with double swords, and sunlight danced off the metal as she twirled the weapons in movements too swift for Wang's untrained eye to follow. Her face unbelievably calm, she slashed at the soldiers that ringed her on every side. Screams and curses joined the wild battle cries as man after man toppled, a victim to those murderously wielded swords.

But the nun herself was not unscathed. One by one, wounds appeared, staining her orange robe a bright wet scarlet. Yet she fought on, seeking to clear a path to the monk who was perilously close to being felled by soldiers.

To his horror, Wang saw the monk was not a monk after all. He was a boy, barely into the first blush of manhood. Even as this fact registered, the skirmish was over.

With savage yells, more soldiers dashed up, and in moments the heads of both nun and monk rolled into the crimsoned dust. The twitching bodies followed with the awkwardness of slaughtered chickens.

Wang rubbed desperately at his face. "Women and boys," he wept. "Women and boys. What have we done? I would rather peddle turnips again than gaze on this a moment longer!"

Behind him the officers looked at one another and rolled their eyes. The group passed on, unaware of the three figures that suddenly loomed out of the dust and smoke, appearing in this tiny space where, for the moment, the fighting had ceased.

Zhao's gaze fastened with horror and fury upon the fallen youth. "I knew him," he cried hoarsely. "I gave him his first training in fist art!"

Rhea grasped his hands. "Yes," she said, and there was comfort in her low voice. "But there is nothing to be done for him now."

His face alight with joy, Strong Man ran over to the piled bodies of soldiers and snatched up several swords. "They certainly cut themselves a respectable swath before they went to the Underworld," he shouted. "And you two had better do the same unless you want to join them there. At last, a fight that is worthy of me!"

Rhea looked from the obscene headless bodies of the

boy and the woman, to the tumbled heap of foes they had taken with them in their death, then back to Strong Man.

He would not survive this day. She knew it with utter certainty. The cloudy emanations that foretold his death hovered around him already, darkening the brightness of the day.

Not all merfolk possessed this ability to see. Even those who did could not call it up at will. The knowledge appeared when it wished to, and this was the first time it had happened to Rhea. Staring at the grim message contained in those shadows, she wished it had not.

Abruptly she turned away. "I am sorry," she murmured, unable to gaze any longer at that face in which life, so unsuspecting and joyful, still ran with such strength.

Zhao glanced at her questioningly. Before he could speak, voices rang out. "Over there! Look, three more of them!"

A dozen soldiers were rushing toward them, and as they charged, one yelled, "If the *jushi* has red hair, General Chu wants him taken alive. The woman too. Alive, men, alive!"

On hearing this inexplicable command in the thick of such madness, Rhea and Zhao looked askance at each other. But there was no time for anything more.

With an exultant shout, Strong Man leapt into the fray. A sword gripped in each hand, he set to work happily, hewing away at the limbs and heads of his foes as though he were chopping wood. Beside him Rhea and Zhao fought also.

It was over quickly. The last of the soldiers fell, toppled by a kick to the chest from Zhao. Roaring triumphantly, Strong Man raced over to finish him.

"Wait!" Zhao shouted.

Strong Man brought himself up short, his sword quivering above the gasping soldier's neck. "Why?" he demanded irritably. "He needs to die."

"Not yet he doesn't." Zhao knelt by the fallen man. The gaze he fastened on the soldier was alive with menace. "Why does your general want me taken alive?"

The dazed soldier gathered his courage. "Foreign piece of dung," he spat. "Why should I say?"

Before the last word had left his mouth, Zhao's hands leapt out. Clutching the soldier's tunic, he jerked him off the ground as though the man were weightless. "Because," he hissed, "I have asked you."

In the grip of that terrible strength, the soldier's courage fled him. "I don't know. All I know is that the orders were given. The general must be commanded to bring you back to the capital."

"Where is this general now?"

"How should I know? I've been too busy fighting." He choked as the hands cut off his breath.

When Zhao eased his grip, a bluish tinge shaded the man's cheeks. "Where is Master Wu, the head of this temple?"

"How should I— Wait, wait, I'll tell you. General Chu deployed a great force to capture him as soon as our battering rams knocked down the temple walls. He was taken inside, to the rooms below ground, I think. That's all I know. I swear it upon my family's ancestors."

Yells went up as yet another group of soldiers saw them. In an instant Zhao had released the soldier and was on his feet. As he did, Strong Man's sword descended with a heavy *thunk*, severing the man's head from his neck.

"There," he grunted. "One less to worry about." Snatching up his other sword from the bloody dust, he hurled himself toward this new horde of enemies, his exuberant battle cry ringing out with every stride.

Zhao clutched Rhea by the arms. "I must find Master Wu," he said, and for the first time since she had known him, she heard fear, stark and urgent, in his voice. "Seek out a safe place for yourself until this is over. Then I promise I shall find you."

"No, Red Tiger, I will not leave you!"

"Please." The soldiers were nearly upon them, their shouts louder as they met the fury of Strong Man's swords. "I beg you to do this, Rhea. Help Strong Man against these others and then seek safety. I'll find you. I promise."

The swirling chaos of the battle engulfed them, and Rhea was forced to swing away from Zhao to confront the thrusting spears of several soldiers. When she had a moment to turn back, Zhao was nearly gone from her line of vision.

But as his long, powerful legs carried him swiftly away, it seemed to Rhea that her lover was running through a dark cloud. Not as black as the shadows she had seen hovering around Strong Man, but dark enough to chill her blood.

It cannot be, she told herself. *It is only the dust and smoke of battle. Surely it is only that.* Yet a fearsome dread enveloped her, a dread she could do nothing about. For just as swiftly as Zhao disappeared, so did more of the foolish, bloodthirsty Terrans rush forward to lose their lives at her hands.

It was cool in the underground storerooms of the monastery, dark and cool. It was easy to imagine no battle was being fought outside, for the dank and weeping stone of the thick walls muffled sound with the effectiveness of a tomb.

In one of these rooms, the darkness had been relieved by half a dozen torches placed in niches. Six soldiers stood at attention, faces hard and expressionless, eyes fixed upon their general. Five of them held thick bamboo staffs. The sixth held an iron poker, the end of which was immersed in the glowing coals of a large brazier.

The eyes of the general were fastened upon another—an old man, whose naked body hung by a rope knotted around his wrists, suspended from the wooden beam that spanned the center of the chamber's ceiling. The general gestured carelessly to the soldier next to the brazier.

"Again."

The man drew the poker from the heat and stepped forward. The end of the long iron bar burned a fiery red-orange. Halting below the beam, he eyed his victim with professional concentration, then thrust the red-hot metal against the naked belly. He held it there for a long moment, and the smell of sizzling flesh filled the close air. Then he lifted it, selected a new spot—the inside of the thigh—and laid the poker there.

Absolute silence reigned while this was being done. The helpless man made no sound, as the ghastly procedure was repeated again and yet again. Instead, he looked down at those who surrounded him with an expression of profound sorrow.

The soldier used the heated iron five more times, then the General called out, "Enough." The smell of burned flesh was foul and thick in the dank room, as he beckoned to the men holding the staffs.

Without hesitation they went to work, savagely slashing the supple bamboo against the already bleeding body of the dangling man. Sweat poured down their faces, as heavy as the blood that poured from their victim, when the general finally ordered them to halt.

He gazed with open irritation at the tortured man. "I will ask you once more, Priest Wu," he said. "Where is the Zhuhu woman, her son, and the black-haired female from Ch'ang-an?"

Master Wu regarded him steadily. Despite the agony he must have been suffering, there was no weakness in his vibrant voice. "And I will tell you again. They are not here."

"That they are not here is obvious, you fool!" Li Shan-po regretted the explosion instantly. How frustrating that this imperturbable old monk could cause *him* to lose control!

"I have always heard that telling falsehoods is against the tenets of Buddhism," he said more calmly. "What a fine representative of your faith you are, lying and deceiving to protect those who are not even Han. But then I suppose one can expect no better, since this religion of yours is foreign."

"I have told no falsehoods," Master Wu said. "But it is interesting to hear you speak of deceit, General Chu. Or should I refer to you by your true name—Li Shan-po?"

The man holding the hot poker dropped it, and it struck the paving stones with a ringing clang. His companions scarcely reacted. As one man, their heads had swiveled toward the general, and they gaped at him in disbelief. Even in the army, the Spider's reputation was unknown. That he might actually be there in the guise of a general . . .

"The torture has unhinged his mind," Li Shan-po said. "I will deal with him alone. Leave the staffs and the poker and wait for me outside. I will call when I have need of you."

The soldiers hesitated, glancing uneasily at each other. "Now!" Li Shan-po barked in his best military manner.

Their doubts vanishing, the men scurried from the chamber.

"So you know," Li Shan-po said when they had gone. "My disguise was an excellent one, old man. No one else had any inkling. How did you, who have never seen my face, recognize me?"

"I see with more than earthly eyes, my son. And that is why I see the twistedness within you, the warping and twining of all that is not good. The dark powers are strong in you, but they do not have to remain so. It is not too late for you to find your way back to the paths of righteous men."

Li Shan-po smiled. Picking up a staff, he swiftly dealt Master Wu several swishing blows across his chest and back. The master accepted the strokes in silence. His tranquillity so angered Li Shan-po, he struck the monk another bone-cracking blow.

Master Wu took this one, too, in silence, though the staff had caught him across the cheek, opening a deep gash. He gazed with sadness at the man before him.

"I pity you, my son," he said, his voice still strong. "He who will not learn lessons from the accumulated wisdom of others is doomed to learn those lessons in ways not always of his choosing."

"There is nothing I need learn from you, Old Man," Li Shan-po replied coldly. He threw down the staff and bent to retrieve the poker. "It is I who will teach you. You will learn to appreciate the true extent of my power. You will learn to regret the night you so unwisely decided to hide the woman and boy from me, and your foolish refusal to tell me where they are now. And after you have learned all of that, I may permit you to die."

In the corridor outside the storeroom, the six soldiers

waited impatiently, listening to the sounds of fighting that still raged over the temple grounds.

"Do you think he could really be the noble Li Shan-po?" one whispered, staring uneasily at the closed door.

The most senior of the soldiers, a grizzled campaigner, grunted. "Who knows? I'd never heard of a General Chu before this, but a man cannot be expected to know every general that comes along, especially at the rate favorites get appointed these days."

"The priest is probably out of his head," another man muttered, "just as the general said. Why would a nobleman want to disguise himself as a eunuch and come to this land of perishing heat and mosquitoes?" He chuckled coarsely. "We could always hide in the bushes and watch him the next time he takes a piss to see if he's a full man."

He laughed again, and as he did, a tall figure swooped out of the shadows and with the chilling, unmistakable crunch of broken cartilage, snapped his neck.

The soldier's chuckle dissolved into a hideous gurgling noise. Like a pile of dirty clothes, he slumped to the floor before the astonished eyes of his companions.

The dark figure was still moving. His hands shot out in a blur of clawing motion, connecting viciously with the jaws of two more soldiers, smashing them upward. Necks broken, they too collapsed.

The grizzled veteran yanked out his sword as his two remaining companions dropped, felled by swift kicks that smashed their breastbones. He swung his sword at the attacker's head, but the man danced away. As the soldier tried frantically to aim another blow, he swept back in, broke the man's wrist, wrenched the weapon from him, and struck off his head.

The entire encounter had taken only seconds. Not spar-

ing a glance at the crumpled bodies, Zhao eased open the
heavy door. His heart was pounding, not from exertion,
but from trepidation at what he might find inside. Yet the
reality that met his eyes was far worse than any imagining.

Lit by flickering torches, a naked man hung from a
ceiling beam. A large brazier glowed beneath him, and in
it rested an iron poker. Evidence of the use that poker had
been put to gaped with raw horror all over the man's body.

A second man stood before the swinging figure, holding a thick wooden staff soaked in blood. The man was
laughing, a thick chortle of amusement that was even more
ghastly than the stench of charred flesh.

Zhao took in the horrific scene with one glance. His
breath stopped in his throat as he stared at that laughing
figure.

The orange torchlight illuminated his face. His eyes
glittered with the dark brightness of spilled blood, and in
a voice that was strangely seductive, almost sexual, he
murmured, "You are not learning your lessons very well,
Master Wu. I see you require more teaching."

His features had been cleverly altered, yet Zhao knew
of only one man to whom that cruel, silky voice could belong.

The staff whistled through the air, but its sharp whine
was drowned out by another sound: an inhuman roar that
swelled through the chamber, reverberating like the howl
of some great beast enraged beyond reason.

Li Shan-po spun around to see Zhao flying across the
room in one gigantic leap, his face nearly unrecognizable
in its fury. The Spider barely had time to swing the staff
up in defense before Zhao was upon him.

He deflected the staff with a rock-hard palm that
landed with such power, it smashed the weapon in half.

Then he attacked, maddened, his every thought focused solely on killing, on seeking Li Shan-po's blood.

But Li Shan-po was not like the intimidated soldiers who had fallen before Zhao's skill. His eyes gleaming in feverish delight, he closed eagerly, arms and legs snapping out blows and kicks with savage speed.

Zhao batted the attack aside, blocking each strike with such grim dexterity, his motions seemed instinctive. Not only age, but skill was on his side. As relentless as a tiger, he bore in for the kill.

With all his arrogant pride in the fighting skills he had developed with teachers paid to let him win, Li Shan-po was no match for a man who had studied Shaolin with religious devotion. A man who was now driven past reason and would use every fragment of that art with only one purpose. Li Shan-po understood that, and understood as well that if he wished to live, he would have to use powers beyond the physical.

Appearing abnormally huge in the flickering light, the Zhuhu's hand, clenched into the deadly iron fist, hurtled at his throat. Accompanied by a violent yell, it was clearly a death blow—coming so fast that no untrained man could block it. If that blow landed . . .

Zhao's fist tore through empty air. Where the hated face of his enemy had been, there was now only space. He wheeled around, his eyes stabbing the shadows, his body crouched low in a cat stance, ready to spring at the slightest movement.

But there was no sign of Li Shan-po.

"He is gone, my son."

Master Wu's serene voice penetrated the red mists in Zhao's brain as nothing else could, driving away all thought of Li Shan-po's inexplicable disappearance. "My master," he cried, and ran to him.

Though he tried to be gentle, he knew it hurt Master Wu terribly to be untied and lowered to the floor. But the old man gave no indication of pain. He did not moan or even gasp as Zhao laid him down.

After fetching the priestly robes that had been thrown carelessly into a corner, Zhao covered the mutilated body with the long outer robe and began to tear the inner one into strips for bandages.

Master Wu touched him lightly on the wrist. "Do not trouble yourself," he said. "Soon I will ascend the wheel of life, along with so many others who have gone before me this day. It is an honor to leave one's earthly life in such brave and virtuous company."

"No, my master." Zhao's voice trembled. "You will recover. I will get you to a safe place."

"Come now, Red Tiger. We both know that is not true. I go quickly. Now listen."

For the first time, a spasm crossed the old man's face. He quickly hid it, but Zhao saw it nonetheless. A sorrow so intense it was like madness, welled up in him. Was he to lose this dear, good man to that evil one as well?

"Listen," Master Wu repeated. "Pay heed to me, my son. Li Shan-po is an adept. Although he is devoted to the Dark Arts of Taoism, he is still an adept and possesses knowledge of the Disappearing Art. That is what he did here. He removed himself by magic means because he knew you would tear him limb from limb if he did not."

Master Wu's voice was weakening, the light in his eyes growing dim. "You must go after him, Red Tiger. I have looked into his soul, and what I saw told me that there is only one way to deal with him. Sometimes it is necessary for a person to die before he learns anything, and that is most certainly true for Li Shan-po."

Master Wu paused and drew a shuddering breath. His

eyes started to close as his bloody hand dropped from Zhao's wrist.

"Master," Zhao pleaded. "Speak no more. Save your strength, I beg you."

The master's eyes opened. Their light was almost extinguished by approaching death, but his voice was clear again. "Find him, Red Tiger. And when you do, use One Finger Kung, the last of the secret skills I have taught you. Yet I wish you to control yourself in this, my son. Do what must be done without hate. Do not behave in madness as you just did. Control your heart, obey the principles of life. To do so does not mean that others are stronger."

He smiled. "Farewell, my beloved student. Ah, how bright is the wheel of life. How beautifully it glows as it beckons to me. . . ."

The voice faded into silence, and the light in the wise old eyes went out.

For a long time Zhao stayed motionless, cradling in his arms the body that had housed the spirit of his beloved teacher. Then with utmost gentleness he lowered the body to the stone floor. He gazed down at the sightless eyes, and unbidden the ancient words of the kaddish, the Zhuhu prayer for the dead, flowed from his lips.

Chapter 27

Men cannot for a thousand days on end
enjoy the Good,
Just as the flower cannot bloom a hundred
days.

—Tseng-kuang,
Kung Fu: History, Philosophy and Technique

Stumbling, Zhao emerged into the hot sunlight.

Scattered throughout the temple grounds, battles were
still being waged to their certain conclusions. Stunned, his
mind hazy with grief and rage, Zhao scarcely saw them.
Only one thought stood out with any clarity: to find Li
Shan-po and destroy him.

When the first arrow struck him, he felt little pain.

The arrow pierced his chest with lethal speed, punctur-
ing deep before hitting his ribs. It was quickly followed by
three more, each of them lodging around the same spot.

Now he felt the pain, searing and blinding. Through a
bloody mist he sensed rather than saw the soldiers charg-

ing at him. He struck at the first ones who reached him, his fists lashing out viciously and killing almost instantly.

The strength that poured through him was entirely unconscious. Without thought or volition his body reacted to the attack, and five more soldiers died before the arrows inevitably weakened him. He wavered as the power seeped from his disciplined muscles.

So he will win after all.

The thought floated into Zhao's brain, and with it a desperate instinct for survival. Temporarily it banished the weakness, driving him to kill several more soldiers before he faltered again.

The red mist before his eyes was edged in darkness, deep shadows spread rapidly until he could no longer see. Slowly he toppled to an earth already stained red from his wounds. He never saw the battle-axes aimed at him, nor heard the soldiers' victorious yells as the glittering blades flashed down toward his head.

Savagely Rhea struck the axes out of the soldiers hands. Catching one of them in midair, she swung it with a vicious fury reminiscent of the birth-people of Thalassa, queen of the merfolk. It connected solidly, removing the men's heads so easily, it seemed she had done nothing more difficult than slice through paper.

Nonplussed, the other soldiers drew back. They had been fighting and killing nuns all morning, yet there was something deeply unsettling about this particular female. Her head was not shaven, nor did she wear the robes of a nun. And her eyes were so strange. Who was she?

Rhea gave them little time to think about it. Lunging forward, she loosed an ululating shriek that shivered through every man present. That unholy sound stampeded them as much as the viciously wielded axe, which struck down three more soldiers before the remainder fled.

They did not need to fear pursuit. As soon as she saw their retreat, Rhea forgot them. Her heart pounding, she knelt at Zhao's side and saw again the shadows gathering swiftly around him. Gripped by a terrible sense of futility, she desperately tried to staunch the bleeding.

"By the Mother . . ." Her voice was ragged and shaking. "Please, Red Tiger, do not die."

Briefly his eyes opened. Their emerald brightness was dulled beneath a grayish film. He tried to smile. "My own fault," he gasped. "I should have been paying more attention—"

He coughed, and a globule of blood bubbled over his lips.

"Shhh." She stroked the damp hair back from his forehead. "Do not speak, my love."

"I must. I love you, Rhea. I want you to know that before I pass from this life."

"Be quiet. You are not going to die. You'll recover from these wounds and live."

Another droplet of blood swelled and burst from the corner of his mouth. A faint smile touched his bloody lips, then his eyes closed.

"No," she whispered. "You cannot die. The dreamwalk did not foretell it. It did not!"

"And yet," a familiar voice said, "that does not mean it cannot happen."

Rhea jerked around. Matteo stood a short distance away, regarding her gravely.

Li Shan-po brought himself back into the earthly world not far from the monastery. No one saw him appear, for he took care to return within the screening cover of several large trees. He also made sure his disguise was once more intact before he stepped out from behind the wide trunks and waved a summoning arm at the first officer he saw.

Cantering his lathered horse over, the officer saluted. "These priests are accursedly stubborn, General Chu," he reported. "And even more accursedly, they are the most skilled fighters I have seen. But once the men saw that Shaolin monks can indeed be killed, they got over their fears. We shall soon have them in hand."

Li Shan-po nodded briskly. "Good. See to it that General Wang has enough soldiers to load the treasure wagons. I myself will finish the task of assembling the special items these traitor priests hid for their own ends.

"As for you, see that the youths and maidens who still live are gathered together. Pick out the most attractive ones and shackle them. I will select the fifteen that will go to Ch'ang-an. Make certain, of course, that the girls are virgins."

The officer grinned. "Yes, General. What shall be done with the ones who are not untouched?"

Li Shan-po shrugged. "What do I care? Kill them."

The officer saluted and started to turn his horse in the direction of the temple, but Li Shan-po gestured him back.

"By the way," he said in an offhand tone. "In the storerooms of the temple, the head abbot of this place probably lies dead. Thereabouts can be found a tall foreign *jushi* with red hair and green eyes. I want him killed. Painfully. He is trained in Shaolin, and thus will be— somewhat formidable. Make sure enough men attack him so that the end of his inferior life is beyond question. Then bring what is left of him to me."

The officer saluted again. "It shall be done as you wish, My Lord General."

As the man rode off, Li Shan-po abruptly became aware that eyes were upon him. He felt their keenness so sharply, knives seemed to be stabbing his flesh. Frowning, he looked around. At first he saw no one. Then a woman, tall and lithe, stepped from the trees.

His mouth fell open. Appalled at himself, he quickly closed it. What was *she* doing here? Zhao Tamudj must have been mad to have let this beautiful creature out of his sight!

"I see," Rhea said conversationally, "that you possess some knowledge of the magic arts. An interesting ability, to appear and disappear at will. Do you use it often?"

Li Shan-po stared at her, as disconcerted by her witnessing his reappearance in the grove as by her casual attitude about it. With an effort he recovered himself.

"So, we meet at last. No doubt my face is unknown to you, Lady, but I have sought yours for an exceedingly long while."

He narrowed his eyes. "However, you have sorely disappointed me. If the men I sent to find you had succeeded in bringing you to me untouched, I would have garbed you in the most costly silks and jewels to be had anywhere in this world. In my household you would have shone like the moon itself, more glorious than all the other concubines I have ever possessed."

Insolently his gaze traveled up and down her tall, elegant body. By the Sacred Dragon, despite her defilement by the Zhuhu, he *still* wanted her! "But you threw the favored life I could have offered you away, and all because you preferred to give yourself to a worthless foreigner. You made a poor choice, indeed."

"Did I?" The silvery eyes that so fascinated Li Shan-po regarded him dispassionately. "Concubine is simply another word for possession, and my people do not keep each other as possessions. We give ourselves freely, whenever and to whomever we wish."

"A most curious practice," he said, "and quite impractical where women are concerned. Females need a strong male hand to master and guide them. You, Lady, are no exception to that."

She laughed outright, a response which both angered and excited the Spider. What dark pleasure would await the man who succeeded in breaking the proud spirit of this strange creature!

"Oh, but I am an exception," she replied. "Far more than you know."

"Nonsense. All women are the same, regardless of how they may look or behave."

"Are they? It appears you know very little about the women of your land."

He stiffened. "I am unaccustomed," he said in a soft, deadly voice, "to being addressed with such a lack of respect. Only a woman foolish enough to believe she is capable of thinking for herself would make the mistake of showing impertinence to a man, after having witnessed the obvious power he possesses."

"And only a man foolish enough to think women have no sense would fail to realize that this woman may have powers of her own."

The lightly spoken words gave Li Shan-po pause. Recollections flashed into his mind of strange rumors that the Goddess Nü Kua had appeared to some of his spies, and that she looked exactly like this woman standing before him.

"Tell me your name," he commanded abruptly.

She raised a delicate black eyebrow. "I am called Rhea. Which you should well know, man who calls himself Li Shan-po."

She *was* the goddess! How else could she penetrate his pretense?

"It seems my disguise has failed me once again," he said. "Twice before this day my true identity has been revealed. The first of those who recognized me is no doubt in the Underworld by now. The second will join him there shortly. Which leaves you."

"What makes you think," she asked in a mocking tone, "that you will be able to do anything with me? And why are you so surprised that I know who you are? You certainly prattled on long enough about all the people you had searching for me. Did you think I did not know?"

For once Li Shan-po was silenced. Unable to think of an appropriate response, and feeling shockingly foolish because of it, he glared at her.

She gave him an enigmatic smile in return. "I also know that you seek one named Zhao Tamudj. You need seek him no longer. Just as you have destroyed his temple, so have your soldiers destroyed him."

Li Shan-po regarded her with suspicion. "He is killed, then?"

She nodded, her face solemn.

"How?" he demanded. "And why should I believe you?"

"Because as you noted yourself, I am a goddess. As to how, I saw with my own eyes. A great number of your soldiers attacked and killed him when he left the lower chambers of the temple."

"Ah. If that is so, then it is welcome news you bring me. However, a man must witness the destruction of his enemies for himself, so that there is no doubt."

"Look into my eyes then, Lord Li Shan-po, and see there the fulfillment of your desires."

Her compelling voice drew him forward, as did her eyes. Gazing into their gray depths, he witnessed a scene so vivid, he could have been watching it in person.

Zhao Tamudj stood wavering before the entrance to the monastery storerooms, arrows pierced deep into his flesh. As soldiers swarmed around him, he fell. Blood rippled out to stain the ground as the last man of the Tamudj clan shuddered his way into the final stillness of death.

The scene faded, and Li Shan-po was staring once more into eyes that were only eyes. "Magic," he muttered. "Magic of the purest sort. You are powerful, Lady. More powerful than I had thought."

"Yes," she said. "You would be wise to remember that, although I doubt you will. Farewell, man who calls himself the Spider."

"Wait!" He called out the word with sharp authority. "I am not through with you yet!"

She turned to look at him, and for the first time in his life Li Shan-po could not meet a woman's gaze.

"But I am through with you," she said. "Do not trouble yourself, though. You will see me again."

She walked slowly away, her carriage as erect and dignified as an Empress born of the royal house.

Li Shan-po stared after her, consumed with sensations that rocked him with lust and awe. It was a powerful combination, and his jade stem bulged sharply against his belly in response.

"Where?" he called, scarcely realizing he had spoken. "Where will I see you?"

She threw him a glance over one shoulder. "In Ch'ang-an," she said, and disappeared among the trees.

Chapter 28

A gale ruffles the stream
And trees in the forest crack;
My thoughts are bitter as death,
For she whom I asked will not come.
A hundred years slip by like water,
Riches and rank are but cold ashes,
Tao is daily passing away,
To whom shall we turn for salvation?

—*Taoist Tales*

It fell to Li Shan-po in the guise of General Chu to arrange for the disposition of the riches of the Temple of the Jade Waterfall. Grand General Wang was of no more use when the fighting was over than he had been when the battle was at its height.

Throughout the courtyard and the temple grounds, the dead lay where they had fallen. Already they were beginning to bloat in the heat, giving off odors that had afflicted the grand general with a violent attack of nausea. Hanging over the edge of a wagon, he moaned piteously, heedless of the disgusted gazes thrown at him by the soldiers who hurried past, bent under the weight of temple booty.

Though Li Shan-po was eager to start back to the capital, the wealth of this beautiful temple was not to be left behind. It was up to the tired soldiers to load onto wagons all the painted scrolls and brilliantly hued tapestries, rare books and heavy rolls of fine silk, patterned carpets and precious statues of jade.

Exhausted though the men were, an aura of excitement hung in the air, born of violence and bloodshed and victory, and they reacted to it. With black eagerness they stripped the monastery of virtually everything it possessed.

Anything that had even the slightest value and could be carried was taken to the wagons. The rest was chopped to pieces and left to await the fires that would be set when the looting was finished. The outer buildings that had housed livestock and extra stores of food were already smoldering wreckage, the grain and animals within them loaded onto the wagons or herded into bleating groups to be driven along with the army.

Last to be taken were the great prayer bells. These were magnificent creations, crafted of solid bronze or copper, and many of them very old. In a final act of desecration, the largest of them were broken up and carried to the wagons in pieces.

Li Shan-po watched the destruction of these giant bells with pleasure. They were the ultimate symbol of the temple—its very heart—and now they were rubble. He smiled. Yes, it had been an immensely satisfying day.

Outside the temple compound, burials were being arranged for the many soldiers who had died. Li Shan-po ordered that the priests and nuns, however, were not to be buried, but to be left where they were. As he gave this order, he realized that word of Zhao Tamudj's death had not yet been brought to him. What if, despite the goddess's vision, the Zhuhu had somehow managed to live?

"Assemble any of the monks and nuns who still live," he told an officer. "I wish to look upon them before they are dispatched."

The process of separating the wounded soldiers from the dead had already begun. Two harried army physicians moved among the long rows of wounded, their sweat-drenched faces conveying an air of frustration that verged on the hopeless. They and their stores of medicines and bandages were completely unequal to the task of caring for so many casualties. Few, if any, of the seriously wounded would make it back to Ch'ang-an, for the scores of wagons that accompanied the army were for the transporting of riches, not of helpless men.

Still, they were the lucky ones. A sword across the throat awaited any temple defenders who still lived but were too badly injured to hide from the soldiers.

Dark thunderheads were gathering over a wind-ruffled sea when the last of the temple's wealth was loaded onto the wagons, and soldiers finished collecting the traitor wounded.

His face expressionless, General Chu walked along the lines of injured and dying prisoners. Those that could stand gazed steadily at him as he passed.

Unlike the wounded soldiers, these doomed priests and nuns bore their wounds in silence, awaiting death with an impassive dignity that caused more than one soldier to mutter uneasily that slaying them in this fashion was wrong.

The captives' stoicism did not affect General Chu at all. He paced through the bleeding and tragic ranks searching for only one face. He did not find it.

Satisfied that the Zhuhu was not there, he was just turning away when he suddenly swung back. At the end of the last row was a familiar-looking man, who wavered from side to side as he endeavored to stay upright.

Frowning, Chu walked toward him. The man was wounded in several places—bad wounds that were seeping blood all over his torn tunic and trousers. He gave the general only a brief glance. Weak from loss of blood, he was more concerned with keeping on his feet than in trading stares with the leader of his captors.

General Chu halted directly in front of him. The man continued to sway, his gaze focusing on the general's face with boldness and no hint of fear, but no sign of comprehension either.

Chu gestured at one of the officers. "Leave this one here for now. Remove the others and send them to the Terrace of Night."

At the sound of his voice, the wounded man's demeanor changed. Consternation and amazement flooded over his face; he opened his mouth, but no words came out. Instead, he stared at Li Shan-po with bulging eyes, as the soldiers herded the rest of the prisoners away.

"Well met, Strong Man," the Spider said dryly. "I never bothered to disguise my voice since none of these lower-class military men would recognize the voice of the noble Li Shan-po."

"What are you doing here?" Strong Man croaked.

Li Shan-po continued on as if he hadn't spoken. "I understand now why I received no further communications from you. I thought it was simply due to the disorder of these exhilarating times. But then I discover you here, fighting on the side of my enemies. How has this happened?"

Strong Man was silent.

"Answer me!" Li Shan-po ordered, his voice a whip-lash.

"What does it matter? You're going to kill me, aren't you?" With an effort Strong Man forced his body to stay still and tried to draw himself erect. "But since it makes no difference, I suppose I can tell you this much: I'm a man who pays attention to omens. It was a bad business, the task you sent me on. The omens convinced me of that."

"Omens!" Li Shan-po laughed derisively. "What omens?"

"I'll not take on the bad luck of killing a man's mother before his very eyes, especially if he fights like the demons of the Underworld and goes about in the company of a spirit woman who can read the thoughts in a man's mind. I didn't think such things would matter, but they do."

Li Shan-po snatched at what remained of the wounded man's blood-drenched tunic. "You saw the Zhuhu's mother? Where? Tell me."

"On the road into Yangzhou. But she is with her own people now." The realization of what he had just said penetrated Strong Man's pain-dulled brain. "She's only a woman and of no importance," he added hastily. "There's no need to harm her. You won't, will you?"

Li Shan-po smiled, though his eyes remained frigid. "Why should you care? As you said, such things do not matter."

His cold gaze fixed upon Strong Man, he muttered something under his breath.

Strong Man gasped harshly, his hands rising to his throat. Straining for breath, he stared at Li Shan-po in horror.

The flow of blood from his wounds suddenly increased, darkening his torn clothing in great splotchy patches. Within seconds the bleeding had spread, and Strong Man's face turned purple.

He sank to the ground. Helpless, he stared up at Li Shan-po through rapidly glazing eyes. "Ma-gic," he wheezed.

Li Shan-po was still smiling. "Only the smallest bit. You would have entered the Terrace of Night very soon anyway. I have merely helped you along."

Strong Man was no longer capable of hearing. When the last rattling wheeze had whispered out of his lungs, Li Shan-po gave the corpse a gentle shove with his foot.

"It seems," he said mildly, "your omens were right, after all."

"It is done," Rhea said to Zhao when he awakened for the second time. "He believes you dead. And I left him haunted by my promise that I would come to him in Ch'ang-an." An ironic smile curved her lips. "He thinks me a goddess."

"As well he should."

To Rhea's great relief, Zhao's voice, though tired, was much stronger. Almost like his old self, she thought, though that was not so, and never would be again.

Just as the Temple of the Jade Waterfall would never again be the same.

Inexorably her gaze was drawn to the wide swath of sky above the trees. Iron-gray clouds were roiling in from the south, mingling with even more ominous clouds that were the result of man. The main hall of the monastery and the rest of its buildings were on fire, creating a vast funeral pyre that sent its ashes relentlessly upward.

Rhea grieved for the destruction of it, and for all those

who had died with such futile courage. At least the rainstorm would soften the scarred earth, wash away the charred smoke, and drown the flames. The blackened ground would run red with blood, and the bodies of the dead would be cleansed. The rain would bring peace.

She looked back at Zhao. His eyes had drifted closed once again, and she watched the smooth rise and fall of his broad chest with joy.

He would need several more hours of rest before he could travel, but that would be all. The gaping holes left by the arrows she and Matteo had pulled out were closing, the torn flesh mending with an ease that was due to his natural vitality as well as the healing spell.

It had not been that way when she and Matteo had first brought him there. As they'd laid him down in this quiet grove, Zhao's face had been gray, his breathing labored and shallow as his life rushed away on a current of steadily flowing blood. If Matteo had not found them when he had . . .

Rhea shivered and pushed the thought from her mind. He had. Her brother had listened to the desperate call she had sent out over the waves, and he had come. Now Zhao lay at peace, because her recalcitrant brother had inexplicably decided to help her.

Matteo had paid a price for that help, and so had she. They were both exhausted, drained by the difficult and demanding process that had saved Zhao's life but had strained their physical and mental powers to the fullest. What they had done had been a gamble. No one knew if the ancient healing spell for a Terran was reality or myth, but they'd had no other choice.

Positioning themselves on either side of Zhao's unconscious body, they had laid one hand against his neck and the other upon his chest. Matteo, who knew the words, chanted the incantation and Rhea repeated it, then they lowered themselves into a deep concentration, calling up every shred of inner strength they possessed.

Precious minutes passed, and Rhea feared the spell was only legend after all. Then the power, vast and all-encompassing, started to flow. It spun out of them, surging from the whirling intensity of their minds into their bodies, then freeing itself through their hands and into Zhao's body.

The terrible bleeding slowed. His labored breathing grew easier and stronger, losing that shallow rattle that preceded death. As the spell continued, Zhao moaned, as though in some deep unconscious part of himself he sensed the momentous changes occurring within his body.

The spell began to wane. Zhao's bleeding had stopped, and he lay unmoving, his breaths deep and regular, his face relaxed and free of pain. The two merfolk lifted their hands, and where their fingers had pressed against each side of Zhao's neck, two even gill lines showed.

"He recovers quickly," Matteo said from behind her, bringing Rhea out of her thoughts. "For a Terran he is very strong."

"Yes." She gave Matteo a long look as he sank down beside her. "Thanks to you."

"Thanks to us," he corrected her. "Without the combined powers of at least two of our people, I'm certain the spell never would have worked. But that's no longer important. He heals, and so you must tell him, Rhea. Now."

"I know." Her face troubled, she glanced at Zhao. "The Terran army has departed at last?"

Matteo nodded. "The darkness forced them to give up searching for Red Tiger. I watched as they took the road north." He grimaced with disgust. "They would not even allow their wounded to ride in the wagons. Their corpses will leave a rotting path all the way to Ch'ang-an."

Rhea's gaze was still on Zhao. "How will he react?" she whispered, more to herself than her brother. "What will he say when he finds that he is different now?"

"If he has any sense, he will be pleased." Matteo's voice was tart. "Who wouldn't prefer a merman's existence to the short and brutish lives Terrans lead? At any rate, it does not matter. It was either that or death."

Unconvinced, Rhea shook her head. "I'm sure there are many Terrans who would feel that way, Matteo, but I do not think Red Tiger is one of them. He has his own abilities that place him far above other men of this land. And he will not be inclined to leave the land with Li Shan-po alive and riding back to Ch'ang-an in triumph, Master Wu's blood still wet upon his hands. Have you forgotten what he was like when he awoke after the healing?"

"No, I haven't. He is possessed by his desire for revenge, and you are assisting him in that desire. You should know better than to go along with this plan he has concocted."

"Should I?" Her voice was hard. "Before I searched for Li Shan-po, I went to the chamber where Red Tiger told me Master Wu lay. I saw what was done to that poor old man. Even though he was a Terran, he was filled with wisdom and goodness. If you had seen him, I don't think you would question Red Tiger's desire for revenge, or my wish to see that he gets it."

"I have seen that and worse," Matteo began sharply, then stopped.

"I do understand," he went on in a softer tone. "Far more than you can ever know. But as I have told you so many times, these are landfolk matters. Let landfolk deal with them. When I went so eagerly to war with the Amazons, I did not understand that. But I learned, Rhea. Oh, how well I learned, when I brought death over and over again to the Terran farmers—little men trying to protect their pathetic little fields and their ragged little families. Men no more able to stand against me in battle than a newly hatched seabird."

They sat in silence for several minutes. The wind had gained strength, rustling through the trees and bringing with it wood cinders and ashes that stung the eyes. Far off in the distance a rumble of thunder sounded, the first herald of the approaching storm.

In just such a storm, Rhea thought, she had embarked on the dream-walk that had so changed her. And now when Red Tiger awoke, he, too, would be different. What would he do, changed forever as he was?

Reading the thoughts in her mind, Matteo muttered, "You will still have to tell him he is changed. And who knows? The healing spell may ease his desire for revenge."

She shook her head. "Red Tiger will no more forget his vengeance than I will lose my gills. But you, Matteo, what will you do now?"

He smiled, the first truly spontaneous smile she could remember seeing on her brother's face since her childhood. "I will go home, of course. With the darkness gone from my soul at last, thanks to you."

"Me?" She stared in surprise. "After all your chastising of me, you now give me your thanks?"

"I do, indeed. For the first time in a very long while, I feel whole. I don't understand it, but helping you save the life of this Terran has banished the blackness that has weighed upon my soul since my days with the Amazons."

His smile faded, and he gazed off through the smoky dusk, staring at some distant spot only he could see.

"Perhaps," he mused, "helping Red Tiger was a form of recompense for all the other lives I took when I was so young and foolish. The Terran priest in the mountains told me to come here, that the answers I sought awaited me in the south. How interesting that he should have seen so much."

He brought his gaze back to her. "When this is over, you will have to return to the sea, and he will have to come with you. I will go to the Elders and try to explain all that has happened here. Although," he finished in a glum tone, "it will not be easy. Let us hope that by the time you arrive, they will be less unhappy."

Concern mixed with guilt stabbed at Rhea. To say that the Elders would not be happy was sheer understatement. Without prior consent or ritual she and Matteo had taken it upon themselves to join a man of the land to the people of the sea. And though Matteo had been a part of it, the entire situation was truly her responsibility.

"Wait to go back to the deep waters for a time," she said. "These events are my doing. You should not have to face the Elders alone."

He shook his head. "No, I am ready to go." He smiled ruefully. "Perhaps it runs in our clan, this ability to anger the Elders. Ah, well, they sent me to the land to heal, and so I have. But somehow I do not think this is what they had in mind."

He rose to his feet. Rhea did also, and he embraced her. It was a long, hard hug, filled with love and concern. At last he stepped back.

"Guard yourself and him, Little Sister. And return to your people soon."

She touched his cheek. "I will."

. . .

Some time later Zhao awoke again. The first sensation he was aware of was water dripping onto his chest. Then he heard the swift drum of raindrops on leaves. He was lying under a tree, it was night, and Rhea was beside him.

All of this registered in the same instant. The two other times he'd awakened had been different. His mind had been burningly clear on those occasions, branded with visions: Master Wu's mutilated body dangling from the wooden beam; the eyes of Li Shan-po, glittering like those of a feral beast; and the arrows, striking deep into his flesh.

There had also been pain. Ah, how he remembered the pain, biting deep into his guts with every breath, clawing out rivers of blood that drained him steadily of life. Now the pain was gone, vanished with such completeness he might never have been wounded at all.

Cautiously he pushed himself up into a sitting position. He passed a hand over his naked chest, expecting to feel jagged wounds. But his exploring fingers found only small scabs, and he met Rhea's eyes in amazement and perplexity. It did not yet occur to him to wonder how he could see her so clearly on a night when there was no moon and no stars.

"I was mortally wounded," he said in a low voice. "No man could have taken arrows such as I took and lived. Tell me, Rhea, what has happened here?"

Her eyes were warm as heated silver in the rainy darkness. "Some of it may please you," she said. "And some may not."

Chapter 29

More than 4,600 monasteries are being destroyed throughout the empire; more than 260,000 monks and nuns are being returned to lay life and being subjected to the double tax [the chief land tax of the time]; more than 40,000 temples and shrines are being destroyed; several tens of millions of *ch'ing* [about fifteen acres] of fertile lands and fine fields are being confiscated; 150,000 slaves are being taken over to become payers of the double tax. Among the monks and nuns are both natives and foreigners.

Alas that this was not done before! It appears to have waited for Us to do. How could it be called untimely that We have at last wiped them out?

—Imperial edict issued
in the eighth moon of A.D. 845,
Ennin's Travels in T'ang China

Zhao was quiet for a very long time after Rhea had finished—so long that she grew worried.

"You must understand," she said. "We had no choice. If we had not acted as we did, you would now be dead. You do understand that, don't you, Red Tiger?"

"Yes." His voice was distant and oddly calm, as though the things she had been explaining applied to someone else. "You are saying I have become as you are."

She sat back and looked at him. He was too accepting, too tolerant, when he should have been speechless with disbelief—even outrage. His mind was shielding him from the truth, she realized.

"Is that not so?" he asked when she did not answer.

"In many ways, yes. But not completely."

"How am I different, then?"

She hesitated. "We who are born of the sea are not confined to it. We may visit the land whenever we desire, staying indefinitely without any physical harm. For you, however, that is not true."

The remoteness left his eyes, though his voice was still steady. "Why?"

"There is a price for giving you back your life," she said. "If I could have made you whole and paid that price in your stead, I would have. But since I could not, it is you who must pay. By leaving the land. You must now make your home in the sea."

"And if I choose not to?"

"Then you will suffer extreme pain in both body and mind until you see that you must."

He did not reply, and she regarded him gravely. "This is not something you have a choice about, Red Tiger. To change a Terran as you have been changed is no small thing. The healing spell Matteo and I worked upon you causes the one who is healed to change quickly."

She smiled wryly. "To be truthful, we had no idea if it would work. Even the oldest among us has no memory of it being used."

Staring at her intently, he did not smile back. Rhea felt the heaviness of his new destiny as though it had landed upon her own head.

"I am sorry," she said, her voice as soft as the pattering rain. "I could not let you die, Red Tiger. *I could not.* And not only because a part of me would have died with you." She sighed. "Master Wu asked me to use my powers to protect you, and I promised him I would. I only wish I could have used those powers to protect him as well."

Still he sat silent under the great dripping canopy that the trees spread over their heads. His expression was stern, but after a minute it softened.

"Do not blame yourself for failing to save Master Wu," he said. "What happened to him was his fate, just as it was my fate to see what happened so that I might avenge it. But as for the rest . . ."

Unable to remain motionless any longer, Zhao stood up. Gingerly he tested his legs. They were stiff but steady, and he paced restlessly beneath the rain-drenched leaves. Abruptly he swung around.

"I can credit none of this!" he burst out. "I know I was dying and that you and your brother saved me. But in the name of all that is holy, what have you saved me for? What have you done to me?"

Her eyes were unwavering. "I have given you the opportunity to go on living. A far different way of living, but life nonetheless. Is that not better than being dead?"

"It depends," he said tightly, "on whether this new life allows me to avenge the wrongs done me and mine."

So there it was, Rhea thought. The spell had done nothing to banish his obsession with Li Shan-po. But then, she hadn't really believed it would. Suddenly she felt achingly weary, and she shook her head. "You astonish me. After all that has happened, all that I have told you, you still think only of Li Shan-po. I don't think you understand what has taken place here."

He knelt beside her. The expression in his eyes was as warm and gentle as the hand he laid upon hers. "Thank you," he said simply. "You are right. I don't understand. I don't even know if I believe. But I am here, and I have you and your brother to thank for it."

She gazed out at the rain-soaked clearing. "My love, you may not be so grateful when you finally do understand. But whether you are happy or unhappy about it, you will have to come to my world. There is no other place for you now."

"You haven't told me," he said, a note of challenge entering his voice, "what would happen if I did not."

She met his gaze once more. "To begin with, fever. It will rage increasingly hot within you the longer the inevitable is delayed. Then terrible pains will tear throughout your whole body. Finally, you will feel as though a fire is consuming your vitals. And those are only the physical symptoms. The voice of Mother Ocean will awaken in your soul, and when it does, you will find no peace anywhere on the land."

He stared at her in horror. "Do you mean you've been suffering such things during all the moons you have spent in the Middle Kingdom?"

"Not the physical symptoms. But the voice of the sea, yes. That is in all of us from the moment we are born."

Zhao was silent for a long time as he thought about this. "I feel none of those things," he said at last. "Indeed, all I can think about is putting my hands around Li Shan-po's throat. And I feel strong enough to run the entire way to Ch'ang-an to do it. Why hasn't this voice awakened in me yet?"

"I have no idea," she said honestly. "This is as new to me as it is to you. Perhaps your desire for vengeance is so powerful, it is able to overcome even that. However . . ." She paused, gazing at him uneasily. "It is said in the legends that a Terran so changed *must* come to the sea or . . ."

"Yes?" he prompted when she did not finish.

"He will die."

Lightning flashed over the trees and skittered through the wind-tossed grass in the clearing. On its heels came a crack of thunder that gradually lowered to a growl as it went rumbling away to the east.

When the night had quieted to only the sound of rain again, Zhao stood up. Pacing to the edge of the trees' shelter, he halted with his back to Rhea. "I don't want to believe this," he said. "I *cannot*. But if what you say is true . . ." He turned to face her. "Will I ever be able to leave the sea and return to the land?"

She slowly stood up. "I don't know. The Elders might, but I do not."

"I see." He walked over to her. "It's a chance I will have to take then. I must go to Ch'ang-an. I must finish with Li Shan-po.

"Rhea." He took her hands in his. "You have helped me so much already. Will you continue to help me, to see this terrible thing through to its end? Without you my plan cannot succeed."

She looked into his face, so vibrant and filled with life and strength once more. His preoccupation with Li Shan-po was so great, he might not accept the significance of what she had told him until the Terran noble had been dealt with once and for all.

If he lives that long.

Instantly Rhea pushed the thought out of her mind. He will, she told herself. And if it began to look as though he were in any danger, she would find a way to get him to the sea.

"I will show you a path to Ch'ang-an," she said, "that will enable us to arrive there well before Li Shan-po and his army. Now that you have changed, you will be able to take it."

Interest sparked in his eyes. "Magic?"

She smiled. "Not at all. We will travel as the merfolk do. By water."

Leaving a trail of dead behind to mark its path, the army traveled north, through a country bleak with devastation and beset by omens of worse to come.

Famine was spreading its skeletal arms to embrace what had been, a few moons earlier, a land rich with life. For the locusts had come.

Word of the approaching plague was brought to Li Shan-po by peasants fleeing ancestral villages now laid to waste. Already, the gaunt farmers said, the demon creatures had passed through the swampy delta region, where they had stripped the land of every speck of grain and shoot of rice.

Steadily, like a perverse insect emulation of the imperial army, the grasshopper hordes were working their way north, following the route of their human counterparts and ravaging fields, gardens, and orchards.

On the fifth day of its journey north, the giant army found itself in the center of this scourge. From the rear of the train a great cry went up as the southern sky darkened so swiftly, a night not of this world seemed to be approaching.

As the bright day grew even blacker, they heard the clicking. It filled the air, drowning out the shouts of men and the frightened neighing of horses, as, with whirring wings, millions upon millions of locusts flew toward them. Within moments they had engulfed the army.

Horses and humans alike screamed in terror, their cries choked off as hundreds of insects flooded into their mouths. In that blackness of swirling, buzzing confusion, horses and oxen fell kicking, landing upon a ground so thick with insects, it was like a living carpet of noise and prickling movement. Men stamped and beat at themselves in a frenzy as locusts wriggled down their clothes and invaded every orifice large enough to crawl into.

Then, as suddenly as it had come, the horde was past. It flew on toward the north, in search of anything that could be eaten.

It left devastation behind.

Dozens of wagons had been overturned, their cargo scattered all over the road. The jade statues and the images of gold, silver, and bronze had held no interest for the locusts, but the sacks of rice, millet, and grain were quite another story.

Nearly all of the food was gone, even the sacks themselves. The hungry cicadas also had attacked the rich tapestries and the bolts of fine silk damask, so that many of those would now be useless for presentation at court.

The locusts had wreaked havoc on two-legged and four-legged life as well. Several score of horses and oxen had suffocated from inadvertently swallowing the creatures, and the same fate had met a number of men.

This desolate scene met Li Shan-po's eyes as he crawled to his feet and mounted his trembling stallion. In a matter of minutes, the locusts had not only wreaked havoc on the imperial train, but had turned the entire countryside as far as the eye could see into a desert.

Days of travel still lay ahead, before this ponderous army would reach the great bend of the Ho River, which heralded Ch'ang-an. And now they would be hard days, with little food for the men and the animals.

Staring at the ravaged fields, Li Shan-po scowled. "I should have known," he muttered. "A blackbird circled overhead three times this morning. No doubt it was the ghost of that accursed Wu, telling me to expect this."

He gathered up the reins and swung his horse around as Grand General Wang staggered up. The pudgy general was on foot, his lathered mount stumbling along after him. Li Shan-po heard the man's terrified babbling well before he reached him.

"Pestilence, pestilence!" Wang wailed. "This was sent by all Under Heaven in retribution. Thus are we repaid for what we have done. Doomed, doomed. All of us are doomed!"

As the grand general came up beside him, Li Shan-po raised his riding whip and struck Wang across the face.

The grand general's wails ended in an abrupt shriek. Pressing a hand to his bleeding cheek, he stared at his co-commander while tears of pain and terror leaked from his eyes.

"Be silent," Li Shan-po said coldly. "You keen like an old woman, and you are as quick to weep as a virgin being raped by soldiers.

"Pull yourself back up on that poor horse that has the misfortune of carrying you and try to make some use of yourself. We must continue on with all speed to the capital.

"We will take whatever food we require from towns and farms along the way. There are bound to be some who escaped the locusts. And we will step up the pace of travel. This is not the time for a leisurely jaunt."

"But the men," Wang protested. "They are exhausted. Many are wounded, and we lack the horses to carry all of them. How will they keep up?"

"Any who cannot will be left behind. Including you." He fixed his expressionless gaze on the round sweating face below him. "Do I make myself clear?"

Wang looked away. "Yes," he mumbled. "Very clear."

In mindless determination, the locusts ate their way over the land, moved by some mysterious impulse to march north. The towns and villages they passed over were ground down so completely that in the creatures' wake not a blade of grass was left standing.

From the southern coast to the Ho River region, the grasshoppers cut a swath of destruction whose legacy would be famine. Even upon the great waterways of the Middle Kingdom, the wails of the peasants could be heard. Word of the disaster spread rapidly among the boats and barges struggling to make one more trip before the rivers and canals grew too swollen with rain. Thus Rhea and Zhao saw for themselves what was sweeping over the land.

They had begun their journey north on the very night Zhao had awoken to his new life. Silently they had gone down to the Pien Canal. There, as Zhao watched attentively, Rhea took off her clothes and stuffed them into an odd shiny bag she then belted around her slender waist. She contemplated him for a long moment, then asked, "Do you know how to swim?"

"Of course," he said. "I learned as a boy."

She nodded. "You learned how the landfolk swim—

clumsy, slow, and inefficient. Terrans fight the water, but our people accept Her, become one with Her. We move deep below the surface, blending into the waters. Come with me now and you will see."

The rain had finally stopped. In the washed-out glow of a wan half-moon, Rhea's naked body glimmered an eerie white. She slid into the wide, dark canal and turned, and like a silver wraith beckoned to him.

A chord tolled deep within Zhao's soul, a new note, startling in its intensity, calling forth a powerful and answering need. It sang to him of deep waters, rushing currents, and the voice of the sea—the voice Rhea had told him he would hear. It spoke so loudly, it drowned out all else.

Yet he hesitated on the edge of the bank, instinctively fighting these inexplicable and unfamiliar urges, held back from this new world by the ties that bound him to the old one. "I don't . . . ," he said softly. "I don't know how."

"But you do." Rhea's voice was warm, intimate. "The knowledge is in you without your being aware of it. You have only to join me, and your body will do the rest. Come, my love, come to where you belong."

With the odd sense that he was dreaming, Zhao walked down the sloping bank. As he did, a picture came into his mind, the last thing he had seen on leaving the grove. His *jushi* robes, lying in a heap on the wet grass, torn and discarded—as abandoned and covered with blood as the monastery they had once symbolized. Gone, gone, all of it gone. His thoughts reeling, he stepped into the water.

He had expected the canal to be cool. Instead, the water felt comfortable as it eddied around him, so soothing and familiar it seemed he had just immersed himself in a warm bath.

Rhea was waiting for him, her hands stretched out to

his. He took them, and suddenly he was beyond the shallows, guided out into the murmurous waters by Rhea, by the currents, and by something deep within himself. Without realizing it, he let go of her hands. His body acted independently of his mind, responding to the water as though it were the most natural thing in the world.

Before he fully grasped what was happening, he was diving beneath the surface. The small finger-length slits on either side of his neck opened. Rhea had told him they were gills, but he had not truly believed her. Now the reality was undeniable. The water rushed through the slits, jarring awake every nerve in his body. The sensation was not painful, only different—stunningly, impossibly different.

At the astonishing feel of those breathing gills, he looked around for Rhea. Incredibly, he could *see* her, as clearly as if they were standing in broad daylight rather than floating below murky waters on a nearly moonless night. She was smiling at him, her expression patient and gentle. As he stared back, she curved her body with wonderful, supple grace and shot away through the depths.

He followed her. He didn't think about it, he simply moved. He was swimming, but in Rhea's way—undulating through the water with an ease and strength beyond anything he had ever known. Even the most secret and miraculous arts of Gungfu could not compare to this astonishing power. Drunk with the freedom of it, he pushed himself until he caught up to the sleek form that shimmered ahead of him like a lovely beacon.

Side by side they swam, perfectly matched, linked in a rhythm that was like making love. Zhao exulted in it. Suddenly a new knowledge burst upon him, and looking into Rhea's eyes, he saw the same joyous awareness gleaming there. He was like her now! When the last of his debts had been paid and Li Shan-po was destroyed, they would be together. He would not have to say good-bye to her.

One joyful thing had been born in the midst of all this madness and grief and death. Their love.

Swimming strongly, Rhea and Zhao passed rapidly through the Pien Canal. She continued to teach him, showing him how to find food, read the currents, tell the weather, and most of all, understand the new abilities he had been gifted with.

They entered the Huai River on the next phase of their trip north, and it was along this twisting waterway that they encountered the locusts.

Although his gills were developing rapidly, Zhao still needed to spend brief periods of time breathing air, so that his newly developed abilities would not be strained.

Shortly after they had slipped past the busy city of Suchow, they surfaced for that reason and beheld an astonishing sight. The day was no longer day, but a preternaturally dark night, and the air itself seemed alive with the sound of clicking.

To Rhea, who had never seen such a phenomenon, the vision held a hideous fascination. Fortunately for both herself and Zhao, the cicada horde, though so enormous it blocked out the sun, was far in the distance. Nevertheless, it was unnerving to see the vast swarm of insects swirl over the land in great greenish-brown clouds. Zhao, who had been utterly preoccupied with the changes in his body from the moment they had entered the Pien Canal, was now jolted from that preoccupation.

"May both the Supreme Being and Buddha watch over us," he muttered as he watched the horde buzz away to the north.

"What are they?" Rhea asked.

"Locusts, or as some call them, cicadas. Their coming

will cause great distress. If this plague is bad enough, people will begin to eat each other."

"Eat each other? Why?"

He gave her a surprised glance. "Because of the famine. These locusts will destroy everything in their path—rice, grain, vegetables—and the people will starve. I have seen it before, when I was a boy. Cities like Yangzhou and Hangzhou were overrun with husbands selling wives and parents selling children, all for a few copper cash or a sack of rice. And many, especially the children, were not sold as slaves or concubines. They were purchased by eating houses that specialized in preparing 'two-legged mutton.' "

At Rhea's questioning expression, he added, "Human flesh."

She stared in horror at him, but he seemed not to notice. "There is nothing we can do about it," he said. "We must go on to Ch'ang-an and pray that the coming famine will spare at least some of these unfortunate people."

"Is that all you're going to say?" she exclaimed in frustration and disbelief. "Perhaps we could stop at some of the villages along the way and—"

"And what? Wherever the locusts have passed, there will be nothing left. Unless you have food to offer, no one will be interested in anything you have to say."

So they continued on, pausing periodically to walk upon the land. Wherever they were, they witnessed not only the devastation wrought by nature, but a deeper destruction of the soul—one that had been wrought by man.

Across the length and breadth of the Middle Kingdom, the imperial edicts had done their work. The great and ancient religion of Buddhism had indeed fallen on evil days.

Although the havoc was shocking enough in the remote south, in the north the damage was horrendous.

As they drew nearer to Ch'ang-an, they learned that in

the capital alone, some three hundred Buddhist institutions had been destroyed. And that was not all. As Wu-tsung embraced Taoism with the fervor of both an increasing fanaticism and a progressive insanity, the "regulation" of the foreign religion turned to outright extermination.

Along the Huai River, and later, along the great Ho, Rhea and Zhao saw endless shuffling lines of monks and nuns being sent back to their places of origin, their shaven heads wrapped in cloth, their faces blank with stunned grief.

Everywhere, piles of bronze and iron Buddhas, bells, gongs, even copper eating utensils, cauldrons and pans, were heaped together, waiting to be smashed. And when the sky was not darkened by clouds of locusts, it was hazed by the smoke from countless fires.

At first Zhao and Rhea thought these fires had been lit by farmers in a frantic attempt to keep away the marauding insects. They did not learn the truth until they were only a day away from the capital. A defrocked monk, marching slowly toward his home village, told them.

"It has been ordered that the clothing of all the monks and nuns of the land shall be collected and burned," he said in a thick voice that strove to be impassive.

"Why?" Zhao asked, his eyes wide with shock.

The ex-monk mumbled a prayer beneath his breath. "It is said that the Emperor fears officials sympathetic to Buddhism have hidden monks and nuns in their private homes, enabling them to escape the defrocking and to wear their robes in secret. Therefore, all robes must be confiscated and burned, and anyone found wearing robes shall be sentenced to death."

Rhea and Zhao looked at each other before staring again at the man in dismayed silence. Two tears trickled down his cheeks, then he cried out,

"Have you not heard? Even in the most remote provinces, they are peeling the very gold off the statues of sacred Buddha and measuring its weight. Once there was no limit to the gold, bronze, and iron images of this Flowery Land. Now they have all been destroyed—turned into trash. Aiiie! Where will this wickedness end?"

He shambled on, his anguished moans rising on the smoky air.

Zhao and Rhea stood for several minutes without speaking. The pain of this lone monk seemed worse than all the desecrated monasteries, heaps of religious statues, and long lines of defrocked clergy they'd seen.

At last Zhao turned to Rhea. "If it is this bad in the countryside," he said quietly, "what will it be like in Ch'ang-an?"

Rhea had no answer.

Chapter 30

The monks and nuns of China are naturally
poor. Throughout the land they have all
been returned to lay life, and, now that
they have been secularized, they lack clothes
to wear and food to eat. Their hardships
are extreme, and they cannot assuage their
cold or hunger, so they enter the cantons
and villages to steal the property of others,
and their transgressions are very numerous.
Those whom the prefectures and subprefectures
are arresting are all monks returned to lay life.
Because of this, the check on monks who have
been regulated and have already returned to
lay life is still more severe.

—*Ennin's Travels in T'ang China*

The Emperor Wu-tsung was not well.

The physical decline that had begun with the Dowager
Empress's death had continued. Already sporadic, the Son

of Heaven's taking of nourishment and rest had become virtually nonexistent as his habits grew ever-more bizarre. For within his fevered mind, a mania had been born.

From the moment Li Shan-po had spoken of an elixir that would grant eternal life, Wu-tsung's thirst for immortality had centered itself on one thing: that potion.

It was ever in his thoughts, a shining but elusive prize, and its elusiveness sent him further down the road of madness.

Vaguely he remembered sending Li Shan-po south, to the Temple of the Jade Waterfall. The noble had said certain ingredients for the potion were hidden there by the treacherous monks. Now and then he also recalled that his trusted adviser had told him he wished to keep his true identity a secret.

That mattered little to Wu-tsung. Occasionally he babbled of it to the Taoist priests who surrounded him almost constantly, but they also paid scant attention. They had more pressing concerns.

With the passage of each day, dealing with this too sincere and fanatical imperial convert had become more difficult for the Taoists. Wu-tsung spent morning, afternoon, and night in consultation with his priests. Some were pleased and eager to be summoned to the divine presence, but most others viewed the Son of Heaven and his tenuous hold on reality with increasing alarm.

The Taoists' anxiety was not eased by the reason for their being called to court. They were to concoct various drinks, the ingredients of which were given to the Emperor by his mother. One of these drinks, the Emperor was convinced, would grant him immortality. None of them did.

It was a bleak and gloomy Ch'ang-an that greeted Zhao and Rhea as they passed through the city gates. Rhea was dressed in her tunic and pants of gray satin, and Zhao wore the loose black garments of a peasant. They went immediately to one of the teahouses Ah Shu had told them about, and the eunuch joined them there less than an hour later. Glum and dejected, he told them what had been happening in the city.

"In the teahouses and market stalls men talk either of the locust plague sweeping the countryside, or of the outbreak of fires here in the city. Seven have occurred in the Imperial Palace alone, and only last night one started in the Eastern Market. It caused terrible losses in goods and lives before it was put out."

Although they were alone in the cluttered alleyway behind the teahouse, Ah Shu looked around carefully before continuing in a low voice.

"It is being said that these fires are sent by Heaven," he whispered, "because of earlier imperial edicts that demanded the burning of all Buddhist scriptures in the palace. Between you and me, Youposai Red Tiger, I believe it. Things in Ch'ang-an are growing more perilous every day.

"As is the Emperor's madness," he added in a dire tone. "Even the Taoists are becoming upset, for between that absurd Terrace of the Immortals and his insane passion to attain eternal life, they are being made to look like fools."

"Terrace of the Immortals?" Zhao asked, frowning. "What is that?"

Ah Shu sighed. "More evidence of Wu-tsung's madness."

Briefly he described the terrace and the stories that had already sprung up around it. "It was Li Shan-po himself who pushed my friend off the platform that day," he finished angrily. "And what is more, those who saw the deed said that it looked as if he enjoyed it!"

"No doubt he did."

Zhao's voice was so cold, so filled with hatred, that Ah Shu stared at him, suddenly fearful of what this man might be capable of. After a moment, he went on. "Whatever else Li Shan-po is, he is still the favored adviser of the Emperor. And the Emperor cannot live much longer. He is so obsessed with finding an elixir of immortality that he is ordering wholesale beatings of the merchants in the medicine stalls, along with pouring all manner of strange things down his royal throat. One of those brews is bound to send him into the Terrace of Night, and when that happens, Li Shan-po will be ideally placed to do whatever he desires."

Suddenly unable to meet Rhea's and Zhao's eyes, the eunuch turned away. Facing the dirty wall, he said in a muffled voice, "It grieves me to say this, Youposai Red Tiger, but I fear we have lost. Dark forces have taken over the Flowery Land, and the Spider is too strong to fight. You and the Lady Rhea must leave Ch'ang-an. Save yourselves while you still can."

"No," Zhao said. "We will not."

Ah Shu spun around. "You must! Even if you managed to get inside Li Shan-po's estate and kill him, it would make no difference. He has convinced our poor deluded Emperor that he alone can find the needed ingredients to make him immortal. If you slay the Spider, it will likely elevate his status and give even more power to the ideas he has placed in Wu-tsung's head."

"That," said Zhao calmly, "is why Li Shan-po must first be discredited."

"A fine idea," Ah Shu said dryly. "But how is it to be accomplished?"

Zhao and Rhea exchanged a long look, then Zhao smiled at the skeptical eunuch. "The Goddess Nü Kua is going to pay a visit to the Imperial Palace. And you, Ah Shu, can be of great help in seeing that she, and I, get inside."

Three days after Rhea and Zhao reached Ch'ang-an, the imperial army arrived at the capital city's gates. Streets were closed to traffic to allow the army to march through to the Imperial City. At the army's head rode Li Shan-po, and beside him was Chen Yü, in his official capacity as Commissioner of the Streets of the Left and Commander of the Armies of Inspired Strategy. He had ridden out from the Imperial City to accompany his master and this triumphant train of booty back to court.

The remainder of the army's journey to Ch'ang-an had been arduous and filled with hardship, due to the locust depredations and the subsequent difficulties in obtaining adequate food for both men and animals.

But thanks be to the gods, Li Shan-po thought, all that was over now. Garbed once more as himself, he rode along before his bewildered officers, astride a fresh mount that pranced and curvetted beneath him as the treasure caravan wound its slow way past crowds of staring citizens.

"Since you left the capital, my lord," Chen Yü said in a voice pitched low so that only Li Shan-po could hear, "Wu-tsung has twice ascended the Terrace of the Immortals, only to come down from it the same as before. And despite how terrified everyone at court is by the Son of Heaven's unbalanced state, this terrace has become a laughingstock. It as well as the Taoists he loves so dearly."

Seeing that he had Li Shan-po's attention, Chen Yü warmed to his topic. "The last time he mounted it, he commanded myself and Chang, the other Commander of the Armies of Inspired Strategy, to go with him. Chang was—uh—somewhat less credulous, shall we say? When we reached the platform, he spoke to the Taoists outside the Emperor's hearing, saying, 'Today we have come to the Terrace of the Immortals. We wonder if you, my lords, will seek to become Immortals?'

"The priests were exceedingly unhappy at this disrespect, but what could they say? They could only lower their heads and remain silent."

Chen Yü let out a chuckle of cynical amusement, not noticing how Li Shan-po glared at him.

Chen Yü's behavior was no longer spineless, the nobleman thought. The eunuch's bearing and demeanor smacked of an irritating independence. Clearly his suspicion that Chen Yü's new status might go to his head had been accurate.

Garbed richly in robes of silk damask, and proudly carrying the seals of his office, the young eunuch held himself ramrod straight, mounted upon a fine piebald stallion that Li Shan-po suspected was newly purchased. And this emasculated creature, who was supposed to be the servant of his will, dared to ride side by side with him, as though he were Li Shan-po's equal!

"I see nothing here to chortle about," he said softly. "But perhaps I have been away from Ch'ang-an too long. Once again it seems I must remind certain foolish ones of whom they serve, and who is responsible for their auspicious rise in the world. It is becoming wearisome to have to keep doing so."

He waited for Chen Yü to pour forth protestations of loyalty in a voice quivering with fear. To his amazement, the eunuch remained silent.

Li Shan-po was astounded. First there was Strong Man's outrageous betrayal, and now this bobtailed dog was giving himself the airs of a man! Scarcely able to believe that one of his weakest creatures was daring to show such defiance, Li Shan-po tightened his hands on the reins. Irritated by the pressure on its mouth, the restless stallion snorted and tried to rear.

He absently controlled the angry movement as Chen Yü finally spoke.

"You do not need to remind me of my obligations, Lord," he said, his jaw clenched. "However, although it was through your power and influence that I gained this honorable office, I am proud to say that I have become proficient and comfortable with its great responsibilities."

"Have you. And has this newfound importance of yours been such heady stuff that you have taken leave of your senses?"

"Why no, Master, I have not."

"I think you have, else you would not forget that I, who put you in your lofty place, can just as easily hurl you from it."

Chen Yü lowered his eyes. "I have not forgotten," he said humbly. "Nor shall I."

But to Li Shan-po's ears, resentment tinged that submissive tone. He glanced sharply at the eunuch and saw anger burning in Chen Yü's eyes, belying his meek assurances. He would have to join Strong Man in the Terrace of Night before he became too dangerous, the Spider thought.

He smiled coldly. "I am pleased we understand each other once more, Eunuch Chen Yü."

As the procession approached the Imperial City, the huge gates swung ponderously open. In honor of the train's arrival, soldiers from the Imperial Guard and the Right and Left Armies of the Inspired Strategy had been assembled all along the inner grounds. Drawn up in orderly rows, they stood at attention, as behind them the officials of the Imperial City and the entire court, even down to the servants and slaves, shifted and milled about, eyes staring and voices muted.

Li Shan-po frowned. "Why do they seem so subdued?"

"They are afraid," Chen Yü said. "And I do not mind telling you, Lord, so am I. Wu-tsung's madness grows worse and worse, and with it comes acts of violence that terrify even the most cynical members of court. I think they may frighten even you."

"I doubt it," Li Shan-po said coolly. "However, we shall soon see. Here is the place to dismount and await his arrival."

They had not long to wait. Within a few minutes the familiar drums announced the royal entourage and everyone fell forward in obeisance.

Permission was given to rise, and Li Shan-po started when he saw the Son of Heaven.

Tottering between his attendants, Wu-tsung gazed about the assemblage with eyes that were like black holes sunk deep in the cavern of his emaciated face. To look into those eyes was to look into the howling face of madness. His skin was stretched so tightly over his skull, he reminded the Spider of a living corpse more than a man—much less the divine Son of Heaven. He even smelled like a corpse, imbued with a rotting sickly sweet odor of decay that wafted from him despite his magnificent robes.

The time fast approaches for him to take the road to the Underworld. Li Shan-po swallowed a smile, patiently waiting while the Emperor's glassy gaze meandered around the motionless court, then focused at last on his face.

"We are happy to see that you have returned to us, our trusted adviser," Wu-tsung mumbled. "We remember now that we sent you south. Have you brought us the secret substances?"

Li Shan-po bowed deeply. "Your Majesty, I have indeed."

The Emperor nodded absently, his attention already wandering. "Good, good. At least one man around us knows his duty and is capable of performing it." His voice suddenly rose. "For truly, we are surrounded by incompetents and fools!"

Whirling, he thrust out a shaking arm and pointed a bony finger at the assembled Taoist priests. "Twice more have we mounted the Terrace of the Immortals, but neither we nor a single one of you has ascended to immortality. What does this mean?"

Wu-tsung's voice had risen to the familiar ragged shriek that all had come to dread. No one dared speak, though, for who could tell what terrible fate would befall anyone so foolish as to direct that insane wrath toward himself?

Stepping forward, Li Shan-po spoke smoothly into the trembling quiet. "Divine One, permit your humble adviser to make the observation that as long as Buddhism exists, your way to immortality will be blocked."

The Emperor struggled to concentrate on Li Shan-po's words. "But—but we have destroyed Buddhism. Have we not?"

"Not completely, Great One. Vestiges of it persist, like weeds that immediately grow back when one does not cut out all their roots."

"Hmmm." Wu-tsung shook his head and, muttering to himself, walked away. Increasing his pace, he broke into an awkward run, the long sleeves of his robe trailing behind him like the wings of some demented bird. Soon he disappeared from view, lost within a grove of plum trees.

Several minutes passed while everyone stood motionless, not even daring to exchange glances. Then the Emperor reappeared at the edge of the grove. He strode briskly back to his court, seeming calmer and more rational.

"We have been thinking," he announced. "The pit from which the soldiers took the earth to build the Terrace of the Immortals is very deep. We know that it makes the people afraid and uneasy. We therefore wish for it to be filled up. And here is how it shall be done.

"On a day designated as one for sacrifices to be made to the terrace, you should falsely say that a maigre feast is being held to pay reverence to the terrace. Then do we command you to go out and gather up all the former monks and nuns of Ch'ang-an, as well as those who have gone into the surrounding countryside. Bring them to the great empty pit. There the Left Army of Inspired Strategy shall be waiting for them. . . ."

Wu-tsung paused. Wrapping his arms around his wasted body, he hugged himself in excitement. "And they shall cut off their heads and fill the pit with them!"

The silence before was nothing compared to what descended now, a quiet so absolute, so utterly still, it seemed as though every man and woman there had suddenly died.

Only Li Shan-po reacted. An expression of shocked surprise crossed his face, then was replaced by a small, thin smile. "Divine Majesty," he called out with hearty approval. "How wise are the thoughts of the Son of Heaven."

"No," a woman's voice said clearly. "They are not wise at all."

"Whaaat—?" Wu-tsung's bloodshot eyes bulged at this incredible impertinence.

Throughout the throng of spectators, heads turned and mouths fell open. What mad, witless woman had decided to end her life by speaking so?

But Li Shan-po did not wonder. He had recognized that firm, strangely accented voice instantly. His eyes were almost as wide as the Emperor's as he spun around.

Tall and impossibly beautiful, she was standing beyond the last row of servants and slaves.

The Goddess Nü Kua.

Chapter 31

In youth I went to study Tao
at its living fountain-head.
And then lay tipsy half the day
upon a gilded bed.
"What oaf is this," the Master cried,
"content with human lot?"
And bade me to the world get back
and call myself a Sot.
But wherefore seek immortal life
by means of wondrous pills?
Noise is not in the market-place,
nor quiet on the hills.
The secret of perpetual youth
is already known to me:
Accept with philosophic calm
Whatever fate may be.

—Ma Tzu-jan,
Taoist Tales

"Seize that creature!" Wu-tsung screamed in a high, shrill voice. "She has dared to insult the Son of Heaven!"

Instantly two soldiers ran toward the woman. She watched them come with detachment. As they reached out to grab her arms, she shoved both men away with a force that sent them tumbling head over heels.

A gasp went up from the crowd of spectators. His voice ascending to even higher registers of hysteria, the Emperor shrieked, "We said take her! What manner of soldiers protect us who cannot subdue a mere woman?"

Before the fallen ones could get to their feet, four more men charged the lone woman. She batted them off as if they were flies, using her fists and legs with a speed that even the keenest eyes could not follow.

Superstitious fear now gripped many, especially the soldiers. However, several of the bravest started forward to challenge her again, but Li Shan-po intervened.

"Cease," he shouted, then hastily added to Wu-tsung, "She is a goddess, Divine One. Seeking to restrain her with earthly means will only prove futile."

Nü Kua laughed, a clear silvery sound on the hot air. "Heed him, men of the Middle Kingdom. In this one thing he is right, though not in much else."

"A goddess?" The Son of Heaven lowered his arms and stared at Li Shan-po, blinking rapidly. "Which one?"

"The Goddess Nü Kua." Li Shan-po did not look at Wu-tsung as he spoke. His gaze remained fixed with rage and longing on that tall, regal figure. "She who rules the mighty Ho River and all of its streams."

Wu-tsung turned and regarded her with a narrowed, wary gaze. "Why have you left your watery kingdom to come here among mortal men?" he demanded in a suspicious, though more rational, tone.

"To warn you, Emperor of this Land."

"Warn us! Of what?"

"Do not listen to this man who praises the slaying of countless innocent beings. Such an act is unworthy of a great ruler. And it is illogical as well."

"Illogical?" Insane rage surfaced once more in Wu-tsung's voice. "What care we for logic? We are the Son of Heaven. We define the very word!"

"In that case," Nü Kua said calmly, "you must surely see the wisdom in allowing the monks and nuns to live. Their heads will do your land a great deal more good on their shoulders than dumped into an empty pit."

"Majesty," Li Shan-po growled, "do not listen—"

Wu-tsung overrode him. "How?" he snapped. "How will it do more good?"

"The nuns and monks are basically ordinary people of your empire. If they are returned to lay life and each makes his own living, it will benefit the land, which will in turn enrich your treasury. There is no need to drive Buddhists into extinction. It will benefit no one. Least of all you or your rule."

Every person there gazed surreptitiously at the Son of Heaven, wondering how he would react to hearing the truth spoken so plainly.

The Emperor did not react at all. Shifting from foot to richly slippered foot, he stood in silence, wearing a pensive expression that contrasted oddly with his disheveled and unbalanced appearance.

At last Chao Kuei-chen, the head priest of the Taoists, gathered his courage. "Whether this creature is a goddess or no, Majesty," he said in a tentative voice. "there is much merit in what she says."

Li Shan-po cast the priest a look that should have struck the latter dead on the spot. Steadfastly the Taoist ignored it as Wu-tsung nodded.

"We agree." The Emperor scowled at Li Shan-po. "Why did *you* not say so?"

Before the nobleman could reply, he looked back at Nü Kua. "If you were mortal," he said in a conversational tone, "we would order you executed for how you have addressed us here. However, it is quite clear you are indeed the Goddess Nü Kua." He let out a braying laugh. "For no woman born of earthly means could possess the sense to speak as you have. Except for our Divine Mother, of course. She, too, is a goddess." He gazed reflectively at Nü Kua. "Perhaps you know her?"

"No, Emperor." Her voice was oddly gentle. "I do not."

"Ah. Well, I suppose we should not be surprised. She is a far more powerful goddess than you."

"Perhaps." Nü Kua's voice lost its gentleness and took on a cold sternness. "But she was once a mortal woman, a woman whose days in this world were tragically ended with the aid of poison. Beware of the one who gave her that poison, Emperor of the Middle Kingdom. Beware of the one you think is trustworthy, but who is not. He is evil. You preserve him in a place of honor while killing those around you who are good."

Li Shan-po stiffened, his lips drawing back in an unconscious snarl. Fortunately no one noticed. Their attention lay with Wu-tsung, whose reasonable good humor had vanished like a breath of wind. Breathing hard, his eyes narrowed, the Emperor spoke in a sneering, dangerous whine.

"You speak in riddles, goddess or woman or whatever you may be. Why should we believe anything you say?"

She shrugged. "It does not matter to me if you do or don't. It is not my life that is at stake. Darkness hovers about you, man who calls himself Son of Heaven, darkness and the ending of life. *Your* life. Mark well my warning. The one you place your trust in with such willingness is not deserving of it. He has directed you into doing deeds that have already brought great ill upon this country. Famine and ruination will visit great numbers of your people because of it."

"The locusts." A murmuring ran through the crowd. "She must mean the locusts."

"And now," the goddess continued, "the one who has seduced you down that dark path means to bring even greater ruin. To you."

Swinging gracefully around, Nü Kua began to walk away, heading for a thick stand of pine trees at the far end of the park.

"Wait," the Emperor shouted after her. "Who is this man you speak of? Tell us. We command it!"

She turned to look at him. Her eyes seemed to catch the sun and reflect it back so that her gaze glittered like polished mirrors. "Who is the one you call your most trusted adviser?"

Li Shan-po pushed forward. His face was thunderous. "How dare you accuse me? *Me*, the noble and pure-blooded Lord Li Shan-po!"

Nü Kua's beautiful face remained serene. "I accuse no one. I speak only what is true and ordained by the fates. Take care in your search for immortality, Emperor Wu-tsung. You may find it, but not in the way you think."

She resumed her graceful walk toward the trees, and not one person, not even Li Shan-po, attempted to stop her.

From his hiding place in the trees, Zhao watched Rhea approach. Her clear voice had carried easily to his ears, and his love for this amazing woman welled up inside him, surging through his veins with such force, he could scarcely contain himself from rushing out of his hiding place and taking her in his arms.

But running through him also was hatred for his enemy, as unbridled and powerful as the love he felt for Rhea. Seeing Li Shan-po again, watching him strut and posture with that inborn arrogance, sent urges pounding thick and blood-red behind his eyes. Ah, to go out there and . . .

Not yet, he ordered himself. *Not yet.*

Rhea slipped into the trees. Swooping forward, he caught her in his arms and kissed her hard on the mouth.

"You were magnificent," he whispered exultantly. "Magnificent!"

She smiled. "It was not very difficult. These Terrans are superstitious and gullible creatures."

He kissed her again, then released her. "That part about the dark clouds surrounding the Emperor was truly inspired. However did you think of it?"

She gave him a long look. "I did not have to think of it," she said quietly. "It is true."

"Outrage!" Gripped by a venomous rage, Li Shan-po paced the length of the audience room adjoining his bedchamber. "Outrage, outrage. The *bitch*! Goddess or human, she is a sly foreign bitch."

He was alone in the luxuriously appointed hall. Outside in the corridor, Chen Yü had been waiting for some time to be admitted. Despite his fury, the Spider's wits had not deserted him completely. With the eunuch's new unreliability, Li Shan-po would not let Chen Yü see him until he was once more in control. So he paced, aflame with frustration, fists clenched at his sides.

The silver-eyed foreign woman. Nü Kua. Goddess or

woman or whatever she may be, he was possessed by her. And she had betrayed him.

"Why?" he muttered aloud. "Why would she grant my desires by showing me Zhao Tamudj's death, then turn on me before the Emperor? What manner of game is she playing?" In growing anger he slammed a fist down atop a cherrywood table. "Does she seek to amuse herself at my expense?"

The last glow of this long day was fading when he finally strode to the door. Summoned inside by a brusque gesture, Chen Yü looked around apprehensively, as though he expected to find the chamber in disarray, with every breakable object lying in shards upon the gleaming tile floor.

"What do you gape at?" Li Shan-po asked in disgust. "Do you think I was in here having a tantrum like a jealous woman?"

"No, of course not, my lord." The eunuch's words were correct, but the Spider bristled as he heard the subtle lack of deference. "However, I certainly thought you would be very angry. And very nervous. The Goddess Nü Kua has openly accused you of heinous deeds. And she *is* a goddess."

"I am neither angry nor nervous. Goddess she may be, but I have powers of my own. Dark powers. She will be sorry to have made me an enemy."

Seeing the sudden unease in the eunuch's eyes, Li Shan-po pressed his advantage. "Have you ever known anyone who became my enemy not to end up regretting it?"

"I have not," Chen Yü said softly. "But then, you have never pitted yourself against a deity before. And Nü Kua is a powerful and ancient deity. Perhaps . . ."

"Perhaps what? Speak up, Eunuch. Stop cowering in the corner like a whipped cur!"

"I am not cowering, Lord. But I do think we should wait several moons, perhaps even a full harvest, before we proceed any further. If Wu-tsung were to meet with ill fortune now, there are many who would recall the warnings the goddess gave this day."

"Ah." Li Shan-po smiled a chilling, mirthless smile. "So now the servant advises the master. You have acquired much wisdom during my absence. So much that you seem confident in placing your wisdom above mine."

"No, my lord. I would never presume so far. It is just that I think—"

"Do not think! And allow me to advise *you*, Eunuch: you are my inferior. I am not interested in your thoughts. I did not accept you into my service to think, but to obey. We will proceed as planned."

Chen Yü lowered his gaze. "Very well, Master. Might your servant inquire, though, what you will do if suspicions are indeed cast in your direction?"

"You may not," Li Shan-po told him crisply. "Yet I will tell you this: I am prepared for that eventuality. Now leave me, for I wish to rest."

He smiled at the lacquered door after Chen Yü had closed it behind him. "Yes, my newly arrogant Commissioner for the Streets of the Left, I am indeed prepared. And you, Chen Yü, shall be my sacrifice."

That night, as usual, Wu-tsung could not sleep. But this time there was a different reason for his wakefulness. The Chief Eunuch of the Bedchamber, who had sent a messenger to Li Shan-po asking that the noble attend the Son of Heaven immediately, explained when Li Shan-po arrived.

"The Emperor," said the official in the drained tone of one who has had little opportunity for sleep in a great many days, "is convinced that the appearance of the Goddess Nü Kua was an omen."

"So?" Li Shan-po, too, was tired. After the rigors of the journey and the long, exhausting day, he had enjoyed relaxing in a hot bath and then being serviced by two of his concubines. He had not appreciated being jerked from his pleasant slumber by a summons to what promised to be a wearisome and even dangerous night spent listening to the ravings of a royal madman. "It probably was an omen. Is that what he wants, to talk about the appearance of that creature?"

The eunuch shrugged. "Who knows, my lord? His wishes change with each moment. But when he sent for you, his desire was for yet another of those potions he believes will grant him eternal life."

The eunuch opened the doors to the royal bedchamber, and Li Shan-po strode inside.

Lit by dozens of lamps, the huge chamber was deserted. He waited until the doors had closed behind him before he spoke into the emptiness. "Majesty, I am here as you commanded."

"Finally!" The Emperor emerged from the outer balcony, his robes untied and falling haphazardly, so that they dragged on the floor. "We would have had you beheaded for your tardiness, Li Shan-po, but Mother warned us not to. She reminded us that you went to the south to obtain items which are most important."

Li Shan-po bowed. "Yes, Divine One. And as I have said, I was successful."

"Well, then." Wu-tsung glowered at him impatiently. "What do you stand there for?"

Confused, Li Shan-po met that bloodshot stare. "Majesty?"

"Get them, fool! Get them! We wish to drink the elixir now. This very night. Otherwise, it will not work."

Even with his planning, this was too soon. It had to be three or four days from now, after he had sacrificed the captives brought back from the south and cast the spells over their hearts and livers! He maneuvered for a delay. "But Divine One, surely tomorrow or even the day after that would be sufficient time—"

"No. It must be tonight. Do you not see, Li Shan-po? Nü Kua's coming was a portent. By the Dragon Throne we sit upon, only a blind man could not see it! She was bringing a message, telling us that our quest for immortality shall tonight be finished. The powers are very great this night." Wu-tsung looked around the chamber, his widened eyes glittering with a deranged light. "Do you not feel them?"

It was useless, Li Shan-po thought. There was no way to reason with a madman, especially a divine one. "Yes," he said resignedly. "I feel them, Majesty."

"Good. Go then. Use your arts to concoct the potion and bring it to us here." He pointed a dirty finger at Li Shan-po. "But see to it that it is done before first light. We warn you, Li Shan-po. Before first light."

Li Shan-po bowed and backed toward the doors. His mind was already racing over the twists and turns created by this new development. With his hand on one of the twin gold doorknobs, he paused.

"Divine One," he said with care, "I will have to work swiftly to accomplish this task. Once the elixir is concocted, it shall be carried to you immediately. But it must be brought by someone other than myself, for incantations and prayers of great mystic power and magic will need to be said from the moment the potion is completed until the moment it has passed your lips. Those prayers and incantations will succeed only if they are recited by a master of my arts, in utter seclusion. Otherwise this elixir will fail, as all the others have."

Holding his breath, he awaited Wu-tsung's response. The Emperor's eyes were still filled with that demented glitter as he spun around. Stopping, he cocked his head. "Yes, yes. We quite agree. But see to it that the person you send is utterly trustworthy."

Li Shan-po bowed again. "Of course, Majesty."

During that murky time when the Hour of the Tiger was ending and the Hour of the Hare beginning, the Chief Eunuch of the Bedchamber entered the royal chamber.

The eunuch was in an excellent mood. The Son of Heaven had been quiet for the latter part of the night, affording the servants who attended him a much-needed chance for sleep. Feeling more rested than he had in days, the official called out cheerfully, "Your humble eunuch announces the new day, Son of Heaven."

There was no answer from the figure huddled upon the huge bed couch. Looking closer, the eunuch saw that several of the ornate bed hangings that caparisoned the royal bed had been pulled down. Thrown around in disarray, they half-covered the recumbent Emperor. A queasy sensation pulsed in the pit of the eunuch's belly, and cautiously he inched closer.

"Divine One?" It was a question now. "Divine One? It—it is time to arise."

From that still form there was neither sound nor movement. His heart pounding erratically, the Chief Eunuch reached out to touch the divine shoulder. It was rigid. Too rigid. The edge of one of the bed hangings was draped over the Emperor's face, and trembling, the official pulled it away.

Wu-tsung's face was bright purple. His tongue protruded grotesquely from one corner of the mouth, and greenish spittle had dried on his cheeks and neck. The bulging eyes stared up at the chief Eunuch with an expression of unhappy surprise.

Dropping the cloth as though it were on fire, the eunuch whirled and ran for the door. As he hurled himself down the corridor, he heard someone screaming.

I must order that fool to be silent, he thought angrily. Then he realized it was he who was screaming.

Before the drums had finished sounding the Hour of the Hare, the news had traveled the length and breadth of the Imperial City and was spreading out into the capital itself.

From their hiding place within the thick stand of pine trees, Rhea and Zhao watched the commotion as the court disintegrated into pandemonium. They had spent the night in each other's arms and had been jerked out of their light doze by the first wail splitting the peace of the still-slumbering grounds.

Instantly awake, they sat up. The wail was followed by others. Within moments the entire compound reverberated with them, and countless shadowy figures rushed aimlessly back and forth.

Rhea gave Zhao an inquiring look, and he nodded grimly.

"It is done," he said. "Wu-tsung is dead. I did not think Li Shan-po would act with such haste. This seems unwisely played, especially for one of his cunning."

"Perhaps he did not believe Nü Kua discredited him so much after all."

"Perhaps." Zhao rested his chin on a clenched fist, watching thoughtfully as a cordon of Imperial Guards ran past in the direction of the main palace. "But it still is very strange."

"The Emperor was terribly ill in spirit," Rhea mused. "That illness was driving him toward his own death. It may be that he drank another of those noxious potions, and this time it killed him."

"Look, Rhea." Zhao sat forward tensely. "Here come more soldiers. And they are bringing someone with them."

From the direction of the central office buildings a squadron of the Imperial Guard was approaching. Following along behind them surged a crowd of people, their numbers swelling, their fury palpable.

It was impossible to make out individuals in that swirling, raging mob of cursing mouths and wildly shaking fists. In the midst of the soldiers, though, Rhea's and Zhao's keen eyes picked out a solitary figure being hauled forward by his arms. He staggered along, his face twisted with terror, his cries and protests unheeded in the uproar that surrounded him.

As the throng drew nearer, Rhea and Zhao could make out words. "Murderer!" "Assassin!" "Killer of the Son of Heaven!" "He must pay for his awful crime!" The words were repeated with monotonous yet hysterical regularity, and the more the people screamed them, the more agitated they became.

Rhea nudged Zhao as the melee moved past the grove of trees. "It is not Li Shan-po they have," she whispered.

Zhao's gaze was still on the pathetic figure. "I see that."

"Well? Do you know who he is?"

"Yes. He is one of Li Shan-po's creatures, a eunuch named Chen Yü."

"Ah." Rhea regarded the stumbling, terrified prisoner with a mixture of pity and contempt. "Do you think he murdered your poor mad Emperor?"

The noisy procession was passing on into the distance, and Zhao stared after it, his eyes hard. "Maybe yes, maybe no. But I do know this. Even if Chen Yü performed the act, it was Li Shan-po who was behind it."

"What will happen now?"

"A new Son of Heaven will be chosen from among Wu-tsung's clan. And then those responsible for the murder of the old Son of Heaven will be punished. We must make certain that the one who truly deserves that punishment receives it."

With hasty pomp and ceremony, a successor ascended the Dragon Throne that very day.

It was not Li Shan-po.

The overthrowing of a dynasty was a difficult and tricky business. Li Shan-po had known that. Yet with the Mandate from Heaven on his side, a mad Emperor on the throne, and the Middle Kingdom in chaos, what better time could there be to attempt it? True, he had wanted several more days to work his Dark Arts—just in case Heaven needed help. But even without that, everything *should* have gone in his favor.

It was traditional for Emperors to select their own successors. If they did not, it fell to the highest ministers and nobles of the land to choose a new Son of Heaven from whatever dynastic clan was currently in power. Wu-tsung had named no successor. Even better for Li Shan-po's plans, the ministers and nobles were weak, so weak he held them all in contempt. It should have been easy to take advantage of the rampant confusion left in the wake of Wu-tsung's death by manipulating the frightened group into naming him to the Dragon Throne.

However, those high officials and nobles who had dithered and trembled all through Wu-tsung's madness, suddenly and inexplicably acted like *men*. They came together with a speed that caught Li Shan-po totally by surprise, naming a member of the divine dynasty to the Dragon Throne while he, gloating over the Mandate from Heaven now well within his grasp, celebrated his success by taking a new concubine to his bed and whipping her until her blood ran.

It was as though something supernatural had motivated the officials into behaving with such strength and purpose. Could Chen Yü have been right after all? Li Shan-po wondered. Had the appearance of the accursed Nü Kua brought this calamity about? The thought made his skin crawl.

The new Son of Heaven was Hsüan-tsung. He was an uncle of Wu-tsung's, and a more levelheaded or well-respected man could not be found at court. He possessed all of the traits his royal nephew had been so sadly lacking.

The coronation was held immediately, and in a stunning blow, Li Shan-po's participation was politely but firmly refused. He was not even allowed to attend as an observer. These were astounding and pointed insults, ones that would never have been dared a day earlier. They indicated a dire shift in Li Shan-po's importance.

Of course, such falls in fortune were to be expected when one ruler died and another took his place. Li Shan-po had witnessed the wholesale killings of once-favored officials when Wu-tsung began his reign. But it was *he* who should be sitting on the throne ordering killings, rather than worrying about such a fate befalling him!

Like a house constructed of rice kernels, everything was tumbling apart. Fuming as well as baffled, he stood in a corridor of the main palace, waiting to be admitted into the ceremonial audience chamber that had once belonged to Wu-tsung. He, a Han noble of pure blood, a high-ranking lord, the all-important favored adviser of a Son of Heaven, waiting humbly in the hall like the lowest of servants!

By the time the polished doors finally swung open and a stiff-faced eunuch bowed him inside, Li Shan-po was in a killing mood. He took a long look at the eunuch's face, marking the features well. The bobtailed dog's attitude was blatantly insolent. Silently the Spider promised him that he would pay for that insolence, writhing in the grip of a spell that twisted his bowels into a thousand knots. . . .

"Come forward, Lord Li Shan-po. Let me see you."

The voice of Hsüan-tsung, the new Son of Heaven, was calm and measured, a startling contrast to the shrill shriekings of Wu-tsung.

Hastily Li Shan-po started to fall forward in a kowtow, but with a touch of impatience the Emperor beckoned at him. "Never mind about that. Come here."

Hsüan-tsung was known in court circles as a scholar. Easygoing and with little taste for formalities, he was almost an ascetic in his devotion for the classics. The light in his dark eyes was both shrewd and dispassionate, also in contrast to the man who had preceded him.

As he stood before this pleasant-faced Son of Heaven, Li Shan-po brought all his senses to bear, seeking to pierce that serene facade and glimpse what really lay behind it. But all he felt emanating from the man was that annoying serenity, mingled with a genuine grief.

"Although my nephew was greatly troubled and out of harmony within himself," Hsüan-tsung said, "I am saddened by his untimely passing into the halls of the Ancestors."

Li Shan-po inclined his head. "I, too, Majesty," he murmured in a tone of deepest sorrow. "My heart aches at his loss."

"Does it?" There was a distinct note of skepticism in the calm voice, and Li Shan-po glanced up sharply. Hsüan-tsung was regarding him speculatively. "The court physicians have told me Wu-tsung died of a ruined constitution, brought about by the last of the elixirs he hoped would grant him immortality."

Li Shan-po assumed a dismayed expression. "Are you saying the drink was—poisoned, Divine One?"

A brief twinge of disgust crossed the Emperor's face. "You would know that better than I, Lord Li Shan-po. Was it?"

There was a beat of profound silence, then Li Shan-po drew himself up to his full height. "Son of Heaven or not, you could not possibly think that I, one of the highest nobles of the land, would commit such a crime!"

"Ah, but I can, My Lord. And so can others."

"Who?" Li Shan-po's blood was pounding in his head. Disconcertingly vivid, the haunting and beautiful face of the goddess-woman Nü Kua appeared in his mind. The look in her eyes was mocking.

He raised his voice. "Who dares to accuse me? The eunuch Chen Yü the soldiers arrested this morning? That spineless dog! It was I who recommended him to his high post after old Ch'iu Shih-liang's entrance into the Terrace of Night. Never did I dream that *this* is how he would repay me!"

"If it was just the eunuch," Hsüan-tsung said mildly, "I would be tempted to agree. However, it is not."

He gestured at a soldier who was standing beside a side door, and instantly the man pulled it open. Speechless, Li Shan-po stared at the two who walked into the chamber. The silver-eyed goddess-woman and behind her, tall and powerful, Zhao Tamudj.

Chapter 32

Wu-tsung's uncle almost immediately set about undoing his nephew's work. . . . In the fifth moon of 846 there was a great amnesty . . . accompanied by an Imperial edict that each prefecture of the land was to build two monasteries and that the regional commanderies were permitted to build three, and each monastery was to have fifty monks. The monks over fifty years of age who had been returned to lay life last year were allowed to take Buddhist orders as of old, and on those who had reached eighty years were bestowed five strings of cash by the state.

—*Ennin's Travels in T'ang China*

For the first time in Li Shan-po's life, stark terror swept over him. Numbed by its intensity, scarcely aware of what he was doing, he took several stumbling steps backward.

Pointing a trembling finger at the silent and towering figure of the red-haired Zhuhu, he cried out in a voice hoarse with fear, "I caused you to be sent into the Terrace of Night. How did you come back among the living?"

Zhao favored him with a small, menacing smile. "Through her." He nodded at the woman next to him. "She possesses powers that are far greater than yours, Evil One."

Li Shan-po fought for control. Inexorably, as though a hand had pulled it there, his gaze flew to the still face of the goddess-woman. "But you showed me a vision of his destruction. You told me to look into your eyes and see the fulfillment of my desires. That is what you said!"

"The scene I revealed to you was true," she replied calmly. "What I did not show you was what happened afterward. But then, you did not ask."

A blinding fury blazed through Li Shan-po, and its heat banished momentarily his superstitious dread. "Witch," he spat. "False lying creature. You appeared on my behalf, and now you betray me. Lying malevolent spirit!"

She smiled. "I did not lie to you, Lord Li Shan-po. I said you would see me again in Ch'ang-an. Am I not here?"

"She did not appear on your behalf, *Spider*." Although he spoke quietly, there was a note of triumph in Zhao's voice that sent prickles of warning up and down Li Shan-po's spine. "She appeared on mine, to throw you off my track so that she could heal me. And it worked. Your days of plotting wickedness have ended. The time has come for you to suffer as you have made so many others suffer. It is just."

"No!" Li Shan-po was trembling, not with fear, but with rage. "You fools. You do not know the extent of my powers. But you shall find out. By the Dark Arts, you shall find out!"

"Cease!"

Hsüan-tsung's voice echoed commandingly in the huge audience chamber, recalling Li Shan-po back to himself and his situation. The Emperor was staring down at him from the dais. His pleasant features were stern, his wise eyes very cold.

"I have heard enough," he said. "I do not care for you, Lord Li Shan-po. I never have. I know this mad persecution of Buddhists is in large part due to you, yet I did not want to believe that even your ambitions could extend as far as the Dragon Throne itself. Now, however, I do."

Raising a hand, he glanced toward the stiff-faced eunuch, who all this time had been standing at his post by the main doors. A smile broke out over the official's face. He quickly hid it and pushed open the great doors.

Armed and in full ceremonial dress, ten soldiers of the Imperial Guard marched into the room. Halting, they stared straight ahead, awaiting the Son of Heaven's command.

Indicating Li Shan-po, he gave it.

"Arrest this man for murder and treason against the empire. Confine him in the imperial prison. He shall be executed before the populace of Ch'ang-an tomorrow at the Hour of the Dragon."

The soldiers closed in around Li Shan-po. All but a few avoided his eyes, and their thoughts were clear. Despite his fall into dishonor, the Spider's powers were well-known, and even these elite members of the Guard were loath to challenge those powers.

Several reached out cautiously to take the prisoner's arms, but in a fury Li Shan-po shrugged them off. "Do not *dare* to touch me," he warned them. His flaming eyes sought out Zhao. "This is not over, Zhuhu dog. *It is not over.*"

Surrounded by guards, yet managing to hold on to his arrogance, the noble turned and strode from the hall.

Alone in the audience chamber with Zhao and Rhea, Hsüan-tsung shook his head. "From now until the moment of his destruction," he said, "I will order that he be guarded well. There is no doubt he possesses mastery in the Dark Arts of Taoism."

Zhao bowed. "That is most wise, Majesty."

"Yes." The new Son of Heaven's face was grim. "Rest assured that he shall not escape payment for his evil deeds."

Sighing, the Emperor shifted upon the royal dais, as though still uncomfortable with his new station. "And now, I must thank you once again, you and Her Holiness the Goddess Nü Kua. First you appeared to those responsible for passing on the Mandate from Heaven, and then you came to me, to reveal the truth of my nephew's fate. It was remarkably done, remarkably done."

He looked at them sadly. "But no more remarkable than the terrible events that have ravaged this land for these last moons. Now, with my nephew as an Ancestor and the evil of Li Shan-po checked and punished, the yin and yang of the Middle Kingdom can be restored.

"However." Hsüan-tsung's compassionate gaze rested on Zhao's face. "I deeply regret, Zhao Tamudj, that it was too late to save your family, or your temple and its Master Wu. I can only promise that retribution awaits the one responsible."

"Thank you, Majesty." Zhao's voice was quiet and fiercely contained. "I, too, wish things could have been different, but such are the destinies meted out to us. All we can do is accept them and live with honor."

Hsüan-tsung nodded approvingly. "Your teachings have made you extremely wise for a young man. But then, the suffering in one's life often has that effect"—he studied Zhao's set face shrewdly—"if temper does not counter wisdom."

Before Zhao could answer, he rose in a rustle of silk and brocade, and bowed deeply to Rhea.

"Lady," he said, "I shall cause shrines to be built in your name up and down every river in the Flowery Land, and from this time forth I shall order a festival held every harvest in this moon solely to honor you.

"And as for you, my son." He turned back to Zhao. "I am hoping you will become a part of my court. There are few enough here whose courage and intelligence matches yours. Much needs to be done to rectify the deeds of my poor nephew, and it would be helpful if you were here to assist me."

"The Son of Heaven does me honor with his praise," Zhao said, bowing. "But permit me to say that you are a wise and good man. I do not think you will need my help. And forgive me, Divine One, but Ch'ang-an holds painful memories for me. If I am ever to be free of those memories, I must leave."

Hsüan-tsung nodded. "I understand. I will—"

"Gone, gone! He is gone!"

The great doors flew open with a loud crash, and the eunuch who had been gloating over Li Shan-po's arrest practically fell into the chamber. Hard on his heels stumbled two of the soldiers who had led the prisoner away. The faces of all three men were drained of color. Drenched in perspiration, they were trembling so violently, they could scarcely stand.

"Majesty . . ." The eunuch's eyes were wild as he knelt before the dais. "Majesty . . ." He gasped for breath, gazing mutely at Hsüan-tsung, as though the Emperor could somehow pluck the words he could not utter from his terrified brain.

In one stride, Zhao was beside the eunuch. His expression was fierce, but his voice was low and kind as he raised the official by the elbows. "Calm yourself, honored sir, and tell us what has happened."

The eunuch drew a deep, shuddering breath. "It was magic." He gulped audibly. "I was not afraid of him. But the magic he performed . . . It—it was beyond imagining!"

Hsüan-tsung stepped down off the dais. "What magic?" he demanded tersely. "Speak!"

The eunuch's terrified gaze went from Zhao to the Emperor. "He disappeared, Divine One. Like a puff of smoke. Right out of the hands of the soldiers. The guards ran screaming in all directions, and only these two possessed the courage to stay."

Hsüan-tsung made an angry sound deep in his throat. "Son of Heaven, I may be, but I am also a fool. I should have known he would not allow himself to be chained in a prison cell."

"It is not your fault, Ruler of this Land."

Rhea's soft voice drew the others' eyes to her. She was still standing beside the dais, watching neither Emperor nor eunuch, but Zhao. When their eyes met, she shook her head and glided toward him.

"She is right, Majesty," Zhao said. "Li Shan-po is an adept, able to appear and disappear at will. He has done it before. But he must be worried indeed to try this now, rather than waiting until darkness."

His eyes, as he looked at Rhea, were terrible, filled with hatred and determination and a strange exultation. He was *glad*, she suddenly realized, that the Spider had escaped. Seeing that understanding on her face, he added, "He is mine now."

"But he is gone!" the eunuch cried. "Vanished! Who can know where he might be?"

"His servant Chen Yü will know," Zhao said.

Chen Yü could not stop trembling. It was stifling in the cell, the air fetid and rank with the odor of feces and vomit, and his thoughts skittered about as erratically as the rats that infested the massive prison.

He was so wrought up in terror that when the first thud sounded outside the door, he paid little attention. When the second one came, he stiffened and sat bolt upright on the rough wooden bench.

Those noises . . . They sounded like a man's body falling heavily to the floor. The guards . . . They were all that stood between him and . . .

The door creaked open, and unable to help himself, Chen Yü cried out.

"It is well that you should cry out," a voice said coldly. "For you know, do you not, why I have come?"

Outlined in an orange glow from wall torches, Li Shan-po walked into the cell.

Chen Yü gaped at him. "The guards," he said foolishly. "The guards . . ."

"Have entered the Terrace of Night. As you will, Chen Yü. You know too much, and events have taken an unforeseen turn."

An almost wondering expression crossed the Spider's face, and seemingly unaware of the eunuch, he mused to himself, "For the first time in my life, I, the noble Li Shan-po, am . . . afraid!"

He shook his shoulders as if to throw off the sensation.

"However, I must return to the matter at hand. You, my ill-fated servant, have become an impediment."

"I've *become* an impediment?" The peculiar courage that sometimes visits those who face death with no hope of redemption came now to Chen Yü.

"Obviously I was an impediment already, else you would not have arranged for me to deliver the poison to Wu-tsung. Amitabha, but I am the greatest of fools to have given myself into your service, all on the false promise of learning your precious secrets!"

"I would never have taught them to you," Li Shan-po said bluntly. "And now I have merely betrayed you before you had the opportunity to do the same to me."

Chen Yü's brief spurt of desperate courage ran from his veins like freshly spilled blood. Tumbling from the bench, he knelt on the filthy floor.

"Spare me," he pleaded brokenly. "I beg you, Master. Use your powers to release me from these chains and take me with you. Please, Master, use your powers!"

Li Shan-po smiled, and in the flickering light of the torches, that smile was a thing of malevolence. "Why, of course I shall use them, Chen Yü, since you ask it of me."

When they reached Chen Yü's cell, Zhao thought the eunuch was dead. The guard who had led him and Rhea along the dark winding corridors had not entered the dank little room with them. His concern was with the two murdered guards who lay outside.

"We were not in time." Zhao's voice was harsh with barely controlled frustration. "He was here before us."

"Yes, but he did not succeed." Rhea knelt beside the still figure. "There is life in the man yet, though very little of it."

Gently she lifted Chen Yü's head, touched his temples, and murmured some words in the tongue of the merfolk.

His eyelashes fluttered, then with a vast effort, the eunuch opened his eyes. In them was the far-off indifference of approaching death, but as he focused on Rhea and Zhao, the vagueness left them, replaced by a gleam of malicious triumph.

"Hurry." Chen Yü's whisper was the merest thread of sound. "He has just left. He heard you coming and fled. He said I would die before you found me, but . . ." The eunuch's pain-wrenched features twisted into a horrible travesty of a smile. "I vowed to live until you came, to tell you that he is afraid of you, Zhao Tamudj."

"If you know where he went, you must tell us," Zhao said. "To perform an act of integrity now may mitigate some of the evil deeds you must atone for."

"I know." The light in the eunuch's eyes was fading rapidly, and blood dribbled from a corner of his mouth as he gasped, "That is why I have held on to life. He is still in the imperial prison, or close by it."

"How can you be so certain?" Rhea asked quickly. "We cannot waste time in useless searching. Li Shan-po must be found before he uses his arts to disappear again."

The ghastly smile reappeared on Chen Yü's face. "Ah, but he cannot. He cannot use the Disappearing Art again so soon. He must wait and gather his strength. He is still close, but beware. The rest of his powers are intact. Go. Go quickl—"

The last word ended on a hideous rattle as more blood welled up into his throat. One of Chen Yü's hands clawed the air, then it fell limp. His eyes, still open, gazed sightlessly into the space above Zhao's head.

Without speaking, Rhea and Zhao rushed from the cell and ran down the dim corridor. It was ironic, Rhea thought. Here they were racing through this dark and sinister place, exactly as they had on that other night when Zhao had been imprisoned.

So much had happened since that dreadful night. By the Mother, Rhea prayed fervently, she hoped this was the end.

Zhao slowed his strides. In the shifting light of the torches, his eyes glittered with the greenish intensity of a hunting cat.

"I see him." His voice rang out in savage eagerness. "I see him in my mind! Is this more of the powers of your kind?"

"It is more of the powers of *our* kind," she corrected him. "Only I do not see him as you do, because my need is not so strong. Where is he?"

"This way."

They found him quickly, for Li Shan-po could run neither as far nor as fast as these two, who sought him with such relentless determination. They found him as he was trying to scuttle out of sight in one of the larger empty cells.

Panting and out of breath, he wheeled to face them. His face was a twisted mask, filled with such evil and such fear, it looked scarcely human. His body, too, seemed bloated, its squat and powerful stockiness emphasized by the way he crouched, his chest heaving to drag in air.

"So you have discovered me." There was an oddly sibilant note in Li Shan-po's voice, as though he'd taken on not only the name and appearance of a spider, but the sound it might make if it could speak. "The fates have an ironic sense of humor to bring us together in the prison where I expected to see you meet your destruction."

"I find it most fitting," said Red Tiger. "For it was in a prison such as this that my father—blessed be his memory—met his death."

His voice was a startling contrast to the other man's. Quiet and pensive, it lacked the barely leashed fury that had possessed him just moments ago, and Rhea glanced at him in surprise. What had happened to the hatred Red Tiger bore for this wicked Terran?

Li Shan-po stepped away from the wall. "Yes, I suppose you would find it fitting. You and this"—his hating eyes lit upon Rhea—"divine whore who left her watery home to give you her aid. It is only because of *her* that you defeated my plans for you, Zhuhu whelp. Otherwise, I would have triumphed."

"You are wrong. In the Emperor's chamber you boasted that we do not know the extent of your powers. It is a fool who praises his own abilities while ignoring those of his opponent. You do not know what I am capable of, Li Shan-po."

"Then show me!" Li Shan-po flung wide his arms. "Use these Shaolin abilities of yours. Blast me, pummel me, beat me into the dust. Take my life! That is what you want, isn't it?"

There was a quivering silence, then Red Tiger said, "No, it is not."

"Red Tiger!" Rhea spun around to stare at him. "After all that he has done, how can you spare him?"

Red Tiger's face gleamed in the shifting torchlight, his features unyielding as stone. "I do not intend that he should be spared."

"Then do what must be done," she said in exasperation, "and let us put this world and the mad people in it behind us!"

"Yes," Li Shan-po said, his tone silken. "Go ahead, Zhuhu. Unless you are too much of a coward to face me, after all."

Red Tiger's gaze had not left the bloated, malignant

face of the man before him. He shook his head. "No," he said again, and touched Rhea's hand.

"For twelve harvests, I have yearned for this day, imagined over and over the happiness I would feel when I watched the life fade from your eyes, Li Shan-po. The pleasure I would experience as I listened to you shriek in agony from the kicks and blows I inflicted upon you."

He paused, and the Spider stared at him. An expression of baffled fury mottled his features, and he seemed to hold his breath as he awaited Red Tiger's next words.

"But that moment has come at last," Red Tiger finally said, "and I see now that it is not enough. It would be easy to kill you, Li Shan-po, too easy, so I will not. With his dying breath, Master Wu said, 'Do what must be done without hate.' He warned me not to act in madness, for that is *your* way, Li Shan-po. It will not be mine. Your retribution awaits you, Evil One, but it will be at the hands of the imperial executioners before the people of Ch'ang-an."

"Oh?" The Spider tried to laugh, but it came out as a strangled croak. "And who is to see to it that I show up for my appointment with the headman's ax?"

"I pity you," Red Tiger said, as though he had not heard him. "The retribution you will face once your twisted soul has left this earthly world will be even more terrible than any harm you have worked during this life."

For a moment the two men stared at each other, then Li Shan-po laughed, a real laugh this time. "Fool!" he roared. He thrust a finger at Red Tiger. "Your deluded nobility gives me the opportunity to escape as I did before. Only this time you will not find me until I am ready to find you."

"You are the fool," Red Tiger answered in that same unmoved tone. "Did you think we would wait for you to gather your strength? Your judgment will take place now, not at tomorrow's dawn. The new Emperor will most certainly agree to it, and we"—he nodded at Rhea—"will take you to the execution ground ourselves."

"Will you?" Li Shan'po's eyes went opaque. Hands moving in swirling motions, he began to mutter under his breath.

Rhea could almost see the coiling shapes of the evil he was sending at her and Red Tiger, and before her lover could move, she was in front of him.

Gazing coldly at Li Shan-po, she said in a penetrating voice, "How silly you are, man of the land. Do you think your pitiful little spells will work against *me*? The powers of my people were already ancient on the day your backward ancestors first realized magic exists in the world."

Red Tiger stepped out from behind her. Side by side they stood in silence, staring at Li Shan-po, waiting, daring him to do his worst. Minutes passed, and before those icy silver eyes and blazing green ones, Li Shan-po faltered. The fear the dying Chen Yü had spoken of could be seen in his face—and he knew it.

Without warning he turned and ran, hurling himself into the empty cell. Pulling the heavy door after him, he paused in the entrance. "In the few moments it takes you to find guards to unlock this door, I will have had all the time I need." Grinning, he spat out, "Farewell, noble idiot."

The door clanked shut with a resounding crash.

Rhea looked at Red Tiger. His face was frozen, his eyes wide with rage. Then the rage vanished, and the eyes turned eerily calm.

He took a step toward the door. It was massive, made of wood and stone and barred heavily at the top.

"Red Tiger . . ."

"Master Wu told me what to do." His voice was slow and thick, as though he had forgotten how to speak. "I see now that he was right."

He took another long stride forward. He drew in a deep breath, exhaled it with a deep *whoosh*ing sound, then raised his right hand and pointed his forefinger at the door.

Rhea heard a crackling, a sort of sizzle that flowed into the air. She not only felt but saw an incredible surging power flowing from Red Tiger. It built steadily, until he was immersed in it, the lines of his body blurred by the hissing, leaping cloak of this uncanny force he had called up. He stood motionless, in implacable silence, his finger pointed at the door.

From inside the cell, a shriek slashed the air. Agonized, filled with the most unbearable pain Rhea had ever heard, it pierced the thick stone walls as if they were made of paper.

Red Tiger lowered his hand. He did not look at her, but in the weak light, she saw that his face was drained of color. Slowly he walked toward the door and reached up, closing his hands around the bars. He gave a powerful jerk. Complaining heavily, the door shuddered. She went to help him, and together, the tendons in their arms bulging out in ridges, they both yanked again. The door creaked open.

Inside the cell, clutching his chest and moaning, Li Shan-po lay upon the filth-strewn floor. As they entered, he gazed up with a look of such hatred, it seemed he had struck them.

"Your plan was flawed," Red Tiger said quietly. "Do you think wood and stone could keep me from you? You have brought this upon yourself."

Li Shan-po bared his teeth in a grimace that might have been a smile. "One Finger Kung," he rasped. "Who would have thought you ... would possess the ability to send such a massive surge of yin energy, it ... would penetrate iron and ... destroy my very vitals? I did not ... think your Master Wu would have given ... a foreigner the knowledge."

"Another mistake on your part. Master Wu foresaw that one day it would be necessary for me to use such a terrible weapon."

"I underestimated him. And you." The contorted smile on the dying face was vicious. "But still, I defeated you. I made you give way ... to hatred. In destroying me, you ... lost your sanctimonious nobility. You ... are no better than I."

Red Tiger went down on one knee. "Look into my eyes, Li Shan-po. To inflict pain or death out of malicious retaliation is revenge. But to inflict punishment on behalf of others is a just retribution. Look and you will see that I have learned the difference between the two."

The smile left Li Shan-po's face. He stared up at the man above him, his own eyes reflecting a wealth of bewilderment and fury and fear. He tried to speak, but pain clutched his chest. When the spasm was over, he lay still, his eyes glazing, emptied of all expression save one. Fear.

Red Tiger rose slowly, and Rhea went to him. For a long time they stood beside the body, neither of them speaking. In the distance they heard guards calling to each other as they searched for the escaped prisoner.

Rhea laid a hand on Red Tiger's arm. "We can stay and tell them what passed here, or we can go. What do you wish to do?"

He turned to her, and she saw on his face weariness, and a grief and a wisdom beyond his Terran years. Despite the terrible sorrow, there was also a peace that had never been there before.

"Let us leave this place," he said. "Now."

The heaviest rains of summer had finally hit, drenching the land and flooding the rivers and canals in torrential downpours that lasted for hours. Occasionally sunlight struggled to break through the clouds, only to die a quick death beneath the fierce onset of a new storm.

Rhea and Red Tiger left Ch'ang-an, slipping unnoticed into the Wei River. Without the need to speak, they turned to the south. Along angry rivers rushing with their extra burden of rain they swam, leaving the land of Red Tiger's birth, the land to which he no longer belonged, heading steadily toward the sea.

During the few days it took them to reach the coast Red Tiger felt wonder, a sparkling pleasure in both Rhea and this new life she had brought him to. Rhea rejoiced to see it. All obligations were fulfilled, all debts were paid, and now he was free. And they were together. The knowledge rang in her heart like the song of the sea.

The swollen Pien Canal brought them to Yangzhou, and from there to the ocean, limitless, primeval, and calling to them under a gray-streaked sky. During a brief spell of clearing, with the sun fighting valiantly to lighten the heavy clouds, Rhea and Red Tiger found their way to a deserted beach.

"Do you recognize this place?" she asked him.

He looked down the strand and then up at the cliffs, gloomy and forbidding as the sun lost its battle with the clouds. His face came alive with memories. "This is where I found you that day, when you lay unconscious on the sand!"

"Yes."

He walked toward the sea until the first waves curled around his feet. "I stood here just like this," he said, "and watched you swim away. Even when I could no longer see you, I stayed, staring out to sea, hoping that if I waited long enough you would come back." He turned to look at her. "I yearned for you already. How I yearned."

She smiled. "But we are together now, dearling. This time when I leave, it will not be alone."

"My Love." He held out his arms to her, and she pressed herself against his broad, naked chest.

"You are troubled," she said softly. "Is it your mother?"

He sighed. "I wish she could have accepted this—accepted me. But I think I always knew she would not."

Rhea held him silently. She had not gone with him to see Zipporah, but the look on Red Tiger's face when he returned had been enough to tell her what happened. She grieved for him, but she was not surprised. And painful as it had been, the last of the threads that bound him to his old world was broken. The voice of Mother Ocean was pounding through her. She ached to enter Her depths and, with Red Tiger by her side, leave the land far behind. She leaned back in his arms so she could see his face.

Entranced, he was gazing out over the rippling iron-blue waves. "I hear it." His voice was quietly exultant. "I hear the sea. She is calling to me." His eyes found Rhea's. "Let us go to Her, my love. Let us go."

Epilogue

Yangzhou ... two harvests later ...

Zipporah Tamudj was happy in the house of Dasheng Tian. With the parents of both Dasheng and his wife dead, she had become a mother to them, as well as a grandmother to their children. She was treated with honor by the Zhuhu people of Yangzhou, and with love by the family that had taken her in.

But in the dark hours of the night, the dreams still came. She would awaken from them with tears on her face and the sound of the sea in her ears. She would lie under her silken coverlets in the spacious chamber her adoptive family insisted she occupy, listening to the distant music of waves beyond the sleeping city and remembering.

Zhao was believed dead, though among Zhuhu and Han people alike, he was a hero, avenging the honor of family and temple by destroying the great evil that was Li Shan-po.

Hsüan-tsung had erected shrines in Zhao's honor, declaring that he was responsible for far more than just the restoring of his family honor. And indeed, with Li Shan-po's death, the locust plague had suddenly disappeared. Famine had still been inevitable, but it was not nearly so terrible as it could have been.

Countless legends had sprung up about Zhao and the Goddess Nü Kua. It was said that she had left her watery realms to help this mortal she had seen bathing in the river one day and fallen in love with. But her price for aiding Zhao had been that he return with her to the kingdom of waters, and in doing so, he had drowned. His body had never been found, people whispered, because the jealous goddess kept it in her jeweled palace, where she could look at it whenever she wished.

Only Zipporah knew the truth, although when she awoke weeping in the night, she felt as if Zhao were indeed dead.

"Do not grieve for me," he had said to her on that long-ago night when he had returned from Ch'ang-an and sought her out in secret. "I will always be your son. But in so many ways, I am no longer the same."

He had begged her to let him come back to visit her, but distraught with fear and anger, she had backed away from him. "Demon!" she had cried. "Unclean thing! You are no longer my son. Go! Return to the demoness who has made you like her!"

Throwing up her hands in the sign against the evil eye, she had averted her gaze. When she had dared look again, Zhao was gone. But the pain she had seen on his face in the moment before she had turned away haunted her still.

Then one night Zipporah awoke, and there were no tears.

Sitting up in bed, she looked at the small dog that lay comfortably beside her. Dasheng's children had given the animal to her as a New Year's gift. It had been her constant companion ever since.

"I am an old woman," she said to the dog. "And with each passing day, I grow older still. I have lost so much. Am I to lose my only son, as well?"

The dog thumped its fluffy tail, and absently she stroked the silken head. "What if I went down to the sea? Do you think he would forgive what I said to him and come to me just once?"

The dog licked her hand. "Yes," she said. "I think I must try too."

In the pale light of dawn, Zipporah Tamudj, still strong and vigorous, left the walled city of Yangzhou to walk beside the sea. Boats were plying into the always-busy harbor, but they were far away. Standing on the flat sand just above the waterline, she gazed out at an infinity of tossing waves, sparkling white and turquoise beneath the morning sky. Then she saw them.

Their beauty as they leapt and swam caught her unawares. It was a beauty not of this world, not human, and yet too joyous to be evil. It tore at Zipporah's soul, bringing tears to her eyes, not of grief, but of a singing joy.

They swam to her. His eyes glowing with love and happiness, Red Tiger rose out of the water and held out his hands.

"Mother," he said. "Mother."

Beside him, Rhea smiled.

Across a Wine-Dark Sea

By Jessica Bryan

author of

Dawn on a Jade Sea

"A grand effort for a new writer — thoroughly absorbing, combining good story-telling talents with an unusual twist to legends which does not violate their integrity. I'd recommend ACROSS A WINE DARK SEA to anyone who wants a yarn that's enough out of the ordinary to leave the reader unable to guess what comes next!"
   -- Anne McCaffrey, author of
   DRAGONRIDERS OF PERN

"For those lovers of the unusual, Jessica Bryan has come up with a fantasy/adventure/romance that is a real winner. . . . Bryan has deftly combines unusual elements of fantasy and romantic historical adventure into a spectacular first book. Keep your eyes on this new talent!"
   -- <u>Romantic Times</u>

"Ms. Bryan is a super storyteller. She combines Greek mythology, fantasy, ancient history, and romance into an engrossing, entertaining story. I couldn't put it down until it was finished. Different, exciting, excellent content."   — <u>Rendezvous</u>